The Effin

from Jim

by **Ron Accrington**

(the greatest football manager in relegation history !!!)

Ron Accrington!!

Published by Luvbutton Press, Cambridge, England
a division of Luvbutton Ltd

www.luvbutton.co.uk

ISBN 978-0-9557635-1-9

1st imprint November 2009

Copyright © Jonathan Mountfort 2009
writing as "Ron Accrington"

The right of Jonathan Mountfort to be identified as the author of this work has been asserted by him in accordance with the Copyrights, Designs and Patents Act 1988.

All rights reserved.

Typeset by Luvbutton Press
Printed and bound in Great Britain by
Think Ink of Ipswich, Suffolk

Cover illustrations: John (Bucket) Routledge

For everyone who still loves the
Football Association Challenge Cup –
the oldest cup competition in the world

and for Mr Christopher Dugdale,
who can't stand football,
but whose surname I borrowed

For those readers who only want to see what happens in the football matches, these are the pages you should look at:

2 – 8, 24 – 28, 45 – 88, 221 – 241, 320 – 343

For those readers who want to avoid the football and only read about the sex and politics, do the opposite.

For those readers who like a story, read all of it !

Ron Accrington

The Effing A Cup

by Ron Accrington (the greatest football manager in relegation history !!!)

Introduction

Hello – I'm Ron Accrington – manager of a few football clubs (well quite a few actually) in a lifetime of bling, booze and blatant honesty with the fans. I was inspired to write this story by events during the 1999-2000 season in English football when a certain famous club declined to take part in the FA Cup because they were coerced by the Football Association, UEFA and the England 2006 World Cup Failed-Bid Committee to take part in the inaugural FIFA World Club Championship in Brazil. However, beyond that single fact, this story bears no similarity to, and is not based upon, any real events in history. Any resemblance between any character in this story and any real person, alive or dead, is entirely accidental, other than "the Don" Revie and the Leeds team of the 1970s, and Bobby and Jackie Charlton, who are all mentioned in the nicest possible way. Oh, and Gary on the telly.

The Hetherington Sidney FC teamsheet

1 Piccalilli

2 Splutter   5 Dorksy   6 Tubsy   3 Gherkin

4 Stainsy   7 Nobsy   8 Korma

10 Freddy Bell   11 Billy Bell

9 Shagsy

The Effing A Cup

by Ron Accrington (the greatest football manager in relegation history !!!)

Saturday, 4 in the afternoon – the last game of last season, 1-nil down – only a win will keep us up ……

"Dorksy !! … Dorksy !! … To me !! … Cross it !! … CROSS IT !!"

Sean's run was timed to perfection. He was ten yards outside the box and hurtling towards the back post, the defenders around him all facing their own goal, panicking at his pace and poise. Sean heard the pounding of feet on the right wing and the dull thud of Dorksy's boot connecting with leather ……

…… then watched in disbelief as the ball swerved behind the goal and smacked the sports photographer from the *Daily Smut* in the head.

Sean grabbed the netting in the back of the goal and tried to wrench it off its mounting.

"What the *fuck* was that Dorksy? … You DORK !! You complete fucking DORK !!"

"Sorry Shagsy … It sliced off the outside o' me boot – I couldn 'elp it !!"

"You're a NOB !!"

"No I aint ! … Nobsy's a NOB…"

"He's a NOB cos e's called Nobsy – you're a proper *NOB* all by yourself… You could give lessons on how to *be* a NOB."

"He's right you know…!" One of the opposition players decided to join in the conversation.

Sean felt his blood pressure shoot up.

"*What* did you say?"

"I said yer right – yer mate *is* a NOB."

Sean grabbed his opponent's collar in both hands and dragged him face to face, nose to nose with his own

"Listen pal. *I* can call him a NOB cos *I* am one of his team-mates!... But *you* can't. And that's CAN'T with a U – got it? C U next tuesday!!! Charlie-uniform-november-tango!!!"

"You're gonna be relegated son. An that's just what you fuckin' deserve!!!"

"Oh no we're not mate – cos I'm gonna score two fuckin' goals!!"

"Dream on pal!!!"

In the heat of their argument, neither player heard the referee's frantic whistling, nor took any notice when he tried to separate them. They never even noticed when nineteen other players surrounded their little huddle, turning it into a giant rugby scrum. The crowd all cheered and bayed for blood. Ron Accrington, up in the stand, commentating on the match, was having an organism, while the referee was now buried in the pack. The sound from his whistle dipped a little, faded, then petered out altogether as the air was squeezed from his lungs and he had no puff left to blow with. The sweat from Sean's and the defender's face mingled and dripped into their soaking shirts as they were crushed further into their embrace at the centre of the mêlée.

"What's the referee doing? Where's 'e gone? He's going to have to book a few here!! Come on ref!! Get your act together!! This is just chaos!! He's got to take control!!" Ron Accrington, screeched into his microphone, leaping up and down and waving his arms.

Meanwhile, the photographer was stretchered off the field and into the awaiting St John's Ambulance.

The referee, buried beneath the heap of shouting jostling players, felt that he had to do something or his disciplinary reputation would be tarnished. Unfortunately, he'd lost his whistle in the fracas which was continuing unabated above his head, but he caught a glimpse of something silver sticking out of a pair of Hetherington shorts and made a lunge for it.

"Waaaaaaahhhhh! Let go – that's me piercing!!!" screeched Billy Bell, one of the well-famous Bell wingers (well, famous in Hetherington anyway).

"Oops sorry mate," stuttered the referee. "You aint seen ma whistle 'ave yer?"

"No I aint – and don't think yer blowin' that fucker either, ya tart. You can keep yer 'ands off it! And yer gob!"

Ron Accrington: *"It's a riot!! The referee's got to do something!!"*

Referee: "Where's me fuckin' whistle? I know it's around here somewhere…"

Ron Accrington: *"Something's got to happen – I think the police will have to get involved!! Ah yes – I can see a couple of the local constabulary warming up on the touchline now!!"*

Referee: "I wonder if it's been 'anded-in to lost property… Oh no – there it is – I can just see it sticking out 'o them shorts…"

Ron Accrington: *"I can't even hear 'im whistling!! What is the ref up to? UEFA are going to have something to say about this!!"*

Peeeeeeeeeeeeeeeeeeeeeeeeeeeeeeepppppppppppppp!!!!!!

Ron Accrington: *"Oh he's found his whistle at last – thank fuck for that!!…… Oh fuck! Sorry everyone – didn't meant to say fuck on the radio. For all you kids out there listening – please don't listen to that last comment and don't whatever you do say fuck in front of your mum, or I'll lose me job… Again…"*

Splutter who was jammed up against Stainsy while enjoying himself whacking one of the opposing players round the ear'ole suddenly felt a cold shrill blast of air up his pants.

Peeeeeeeeeeeeeeeeeeeeeeeeeeeeeeepppppppppppppp!!!!!!

"Aaaaaaaaah!!! – shum fucker'sh got their 'andsh up me sshorts and'sh blowin' on me nutsh!!!!!!" he spluttered.

Stainsy was unsympathetic. "Shut the fuck up Splutter – yer slobberin' all down me neck!"

Peeeeeeeeeeeeeeeeeeeeeeeeeeeeeeepppppppppppppp!!!!!!

Peeeeeeeeeeeeeeeeeeeeeeeeeeeeeeepppppppppppppp!!!!!!

"Aaaaaaaaaaaaaaaaaaaaaaaashshshshshshshshshshshshshshshshsh ……!!!"

"Splutter – quiet-up will ya? – I'm fuckin' drownin'!!!"

Peeeeeeeeeeeeeeeeeeeeeeeeeeeeeeepppppppppppppp!!!!!!

"Heeeeeeeeeeeeelpshshshshshshshsh……"

“Splutter!!! I’m gonna ram my arm down your throat if you don’t fuckin’ shut up, you big wet drippin’ tart!!!”

Peeeeeeeeeeeeeeeeeeeeeeeeeeeeeeepppppppppppppp!!!!!!

“Oh pleashhhhe pleashhhhe heeeeeeeeeeeeelpshshshshshshshsh...... it ticklesshh!”

WHACK...

The players were getting bored with fighting and arguing. Normally the scrap had been split up by now, but this one had been going on for ages and they were knackered.

“Where’s t’referee?” Tubsy stood his immense body up to its greatest height and, looking over the heads of all those around him, tried to find the mystery whistler. The players around continued battering him with fists and headbuts, but their tired efforts had no effect on his gigantic frame. “I can ’ear ’im, but I can’t see t’fucker!... ’ERE – YOU LOT – QUIET DOWN YA DICK-’EADS!!!... We got t’find ref so’s ’e can dish out t’yellow cards!!!”

Gradually the noise subsided. As it did so, the sound of plaintive whistling hung on the warm Spring air. “Heeelpsh!” mumbled Splutter. “Pheeeep,” went the ref’s whistle.

“Fook!” said Korma. “Ref’s got ’is arm up Splutter’s shorts!”

“Aye! An’ e’s still blowin’ ’is whistle... That’s dedication t’job all right!” observed Tubsy.

“Let’s ’ope e’s lost ’is notebook ’n pencil,” Shagsy announced cheerily. “Otherwise, I reckon I’m off!”

The referee, realising that the darkness all around him had given way to daylight, stopped blowing his whistle and gingerly removed his arm from Splutter’s shorts.

The players stood in a ring, all around, looking down at him where he lay on the ground.

“Right you lot. You’ve ’ad yer fun.” He looked up at the subdued faces, awaiting their bollockings. “I ought to send you all off... but that might spoil the game... On the other ’and – the way you’ve bin playing – it might not...”

The players looked at each other, not knowing whether to laugh, until the silence was broken by Nobsy.

"Nice one ref… that were funny…"

"Thank you Nobsy. I'm glad one of you noticed… I now intend to calmly get up off the ground as if nothing's 'appened and carry on with the game."

"Nice one ref…"

"An don't you fuckers give me any more grief… OR ELSE!!!"

He lifted himself up then offered his hand to a forlorn figure lying in a heap on the ground, caressing his nuts and a sore lip. "Come on Splutter – time to get on with the game old son…"

"Thanksh…"

*   *   *

"Korma !! … Korma !! … To me !! … Cross it !! … CROSS IT !!"

Sean's run was timed to perfection. He was ten yards outside the box and hurtling towards the back post, the defenders around him all facing their own goal, panicking at his pace and poise. Sean heard the pounding of feet on the left wing and the dull thud of Korma's boot connecting with leather ……

…… then watched in disbelief as the ball swerved behind the goal and smacked a St John's Ambulanceman in the head.

Sean grabbed the netting in the back of the goal and tried to wrench it off its mounting.

"What the *fuck* was that Korma? … You CURRY !! You complete fucking CURRY !!"

"Sorry Shagsy … It sliced off the outside o' me boot – I couldn 'elp it !!"

"You're a BELL-END !!"

"No I aint ! … Billy Bell's a BELL-END …"

"He's a BELL-END cos e's called Billy Bell – you're just a proper *BELL-END* all by yourself… You could show a nun what a BELL-END looks like, just by standin' there!"

One of the opposition players ran up to Sean and stuck his face in his. "I'm stayin' outta this one…"

Sean grabbed his ears, rubbed noses together, then let go and ran off back up his own end of the pitch.

Meanwhile, the St John's Ambulanceman was stretchered off the field to await the return of the St John's Ambulance which was taking the photographer to hospital.

*   *   *

"Splutter !! ... Splutter !! ... To me !! ... Cross it !! ... CROSS IT !! ... Oh fuck it he can't understand... CROSH IT, Splutter, CROSH IT !!"

Sean's run was timed to perfection. He was ten yards outside the box and hurtling towards the back post, the defenders around him all facing their own goal, panicking at his pace and poise. Sean heard the pounding of feet on the right wing and the dull thud of Splutter's boot connecting with leather ......

then – PING – straight off his forehead and into the back of the net!!!!!

Sean grabbed the netting in the back of the goal and tried to wrench it off its mounting while waving and screaming at the roaring supporters, then leapt out of the goal with his arms raised.

"Yessssssssshhhhhhhhhh" spluttered Splutter, kissing Sean and jet-washing him with saliva at the same time. "We've Shcored...!!!... One-all!!!... One-shfuckin'-all!!!..."

*   *   *

"Stainsy !! ... Stainsy !! ... To me !! ... Cross it !! ... CROSS IT !!"

Sean's run was timed to perfection. He was ten yards outside the box and hurtling towards the back post, the defenders around him all facing their own goal, panicking at his pace and poise. Sean heard the pounding of feet on the right wing and the dull thud of Stainsy's boot connecting with leather ......

...... then – PING – straight off his forehead ......

...... then watched in disbelief as the ball smashed against the crossbar and flew back past him, just out of reach over his left shoulder.

Sean spun around to look where it had gone, just in time to see that luckily the referee had been following-up right behind him. Unable to take evasive action due to the lightning speed of the rebound, the ball slapped against the ref's chest, and into the far corner of the net, just beyond the despairing dive of the opposition goalkeeper.

The linesman flagged for offside, but that was because he was a tit.

"It came off the referee's left tit, you tit !" bellowed Sean at the linesman while Sean also gave the ref a big hug for scoring such a magnificent goal.

The poor referee shrugged, blew his whistle and pointed to the centre circle. The other team surrounded him and demanded an explanation, while the Hetherington team all piled in a heap on top one each other and shouted with delight.

Ron Accrington roared into his microphone: *"I've never seen anything like it!!! Is that the goal that will save Hetherington Sidney from relegation? Scored by the referee in the 90th minute! Well would you believe it…… What an amazing turnaround…… At one-nil down they looked dead and buried, heading for the 4th division or whatever it's called nowadays. But now fate has intervened in the most exceptional way... And it was a good goal too, chested in with a deft touch into the far corner – the goalie had no chance!!!"*

Sean grabbed the referee and lifted him off his feet while waving and screaming at the roaring supporters, then kissed him all over his face. "Whatta goal ref!!!" he congratulated him as if he were a centre-forward. "Did you ever play for Jam United by any chance?"

The referee, who had turned bright purple with embarrassment, looked at his watch, saw that the 90 minutes were up, blew his whistle twice then did a runner for the tunnel. He wondered how much he could get for selling his story to *The Fun* or the *Daily Smut* or the *Daily Filler*. He might be able to retire…

"Yesssssssssshhhhhhhhhhh" spluttered Splutter, kissing Sean and jet-washing him once again with fresh spittle. "We've Shcored…!!!… shTwo-one!!!… shTwo-fuckin'-one!!!... We're shfuckin' shtayin' UPPPPPsh……"

Six months later – 9 o'clock on a Monday morning in late November

"Look at this photo, Mr Dovehawk."

On the panelled boardroom wall of Hetherington Sidney FC, a little football club in the north of England, the club Secretary pointed to a sepia faded old print installed in a distinguished frame which was, Dovehawk thought, possibly over-elaborate for the crumpled ageing picture within.

"First time we won the cup – what a team! I don't suppose you've seen this photo before, this being your first time int' boardroom."

"No I haven't. It's very good of you to show me round Mr Smoggrate."

"Aye, and it aint got nothin' to do with the fact that you're goin' to be our new MP at the upcoming by-election, I can assure you on that point."

"I never considered that a possibility."

Dovehawk grinned at Smoggrate, then gazed at the figures in the picture, the seated men at the front with their arms crossed, a ball by the captain's feet, just like any other team photo except for one thing – a skinny dog at the left of the picture, the team's right, its lead looped over the baggy shorts worn by the player sitting at that end of the front row.

"Now, look at this." Smoggrate launched into speech, his enthusiasm hissing from every pore as if he'd sat his gigantic bottom on the spout of a boiling kettle. "Oaks in goal – he were like a tree-trunk – rooted to the spot but so wide there weren't no way past him into net. Dibbsey and Needham full backs – mean in the tackle; aye, Scabby were the best tackler inside the area what's ever been seen. You know why they called him Scabby, Mr Dovehawk?" His eyes were glinting as he awaited the politician's reply.

"Did he have a skin complaint? Or, if he was Needham, perhaps it was something to do with having scabs on his knees, maybe?"

"Great one, Mr Dovehawk, magic! But no. Listen – you'll like this." Smoggrate paused dramatically, the tendrilous hairs in his nostrils rippling in time with his excited huffs before he spoke...... "He were called Scabby cos he weren't never a striker!"...... And Smoggrate cranked himself up like an old bus with its starting handle before chugging with laughter as the stubborn engine burst into life. "You get it? Scab? Striker? Scabs don't go on strike?... See, I told you you'd like it – now don't spill your scotch – we aint much left in the bank after installing the under-pitch heating. Costs five 'undred a day to run when it's switched on, you know; but worth every penny if it means we can play all through January and February, specially third round of the F A Cup, eh Mr Dovehawk?

"Now where was I. Mortimer centre half – he could run. Well he could in 1933. Pity cup final were almost twenty year later. But his positioning made up for it. Ball used to be attracted to him like a magnet – he were always there, underneath it, laying a precision header off to Dogett on the left or Squeaker on the right. Squeaker'd get t' by-line and then *eee* – tiny little squeak he'd make just before he put the cross in. That little squeak wouldn't hardly make a sound 'cept to Trumpet in the box – he's the only one what 'eard it – so he didn't even have to look up – just side foot it into net."

"Trumpet was the centre-forward then?"

"Aye – course he was – centre-forward all t' bloody time – never made a tackle in his life – in fact he never left the penalty area only to change ends at half-time. Heh, Mr Dovehawk – know why he were called Trumpet?..... No? 'Ave a guess, go on."

"Because he had ears like trumpets so's he could hear when Squeaker crossed the ball?"

"Aye well that's what you'd think wouldn't you, obvious! But no. It were like this: he couldn't bloody see, right. Not a bloody thing. So 'alf the time when he'd gone for 'eader he 'it bloody thing wi' 'is nose, which went bright red and stuck out like a bloody great brass trumpet. Eh it were a laugh."

"So what about Dogett?"

"Dogett? That were 'is real name. He kept a whippet – it pissed up the Chairman's wife's leg when she were shopping on Ecclesby market. He said it were good luck and team'd win come Saturday. She said it were bad luck cos they were a new pair o' shoes what she was wearin' and she'd get her 'usband to dock Dogett half a week's wages to pay for 'em. The whippet were the club mascot – you can see Dogett and the dog on the end of the front row int' photo."

“Yes, I was going to ask you about the dog.”

“The team are still called *The Whippets*. ‘Up the Whippets’ they all shout on Saturday and smart arse opposing fans try and say something clever in reply like ‘Shag the Whippets you whippet-shagging whippet shaggers!’ It’s amazing the wit of your average football supporter.”

“I look forward to hearing a chorus of ‘Up the Whippets’ for myself.”

“Aye, me too. If they’re singing ‘Up the Whippets’ it means they’re not shouting ‘Sack the Board!’. We ’ad to get a police escort out the ground at the end of the ’96-’97 season. Relegated. First time in bottom division, what used to be called Division 4, in club’s history. But we got Ron Accrington as manager in close season, sponsorship from Twigley’s Homes to pay his wages and some good free transfers of ex-Faroe-Isles international players and we bounced straight back up.”

“Is he still manager?”

“No – he’s had six clubs since then – gets around a bit. Big fat cheque off each one that sacks him an’ another to sign on at the next. Grand life. Lovely bloke.”

Smoggrate was chuckling to himself at the memories of good times in the bar with Ron Accrington when there was a gentle, almost timid, knock at the door. The two men turned round to look while Smoggrate called, “Come in......” The door slowly opened and a young girl’s head appeared in the opening, a dainty and finely crafted head, delicate, almost fragile looking.

“Ah, Miss Twogood,” twittered Smoggrate in his most irritatingly unctuous voice as the frail little figure appeared at the entrance to the boardroom. “Meet Mr Dovehawk, our next MP. Mr Dovehawk, this is Angela, our lass – she runs the place really, don’t you Angela – and only left school last year.”

Dovehawk ran his eyes up and down her slim body which was now framed in the doorway. He walked towards her, holding out his hand for her to shake, expecting the girl to come into the room and do likewise. But instead she just shuffled on the spot, her toes barely encroaching on the deep green carpet.

"Sorry, Mr Dove'awk, I'll 'ave to shake yer 'and 'ere int' doorway." She looked at Smoggrate. "See, women aren't allowed int' boardroom."

Dovehawk went to her and grasped her hand warmly, the tiny little cold fingers snugly sinking in the folds of flesh of his ample palm.

"Very pleased to meet, you," he gushed. "Eh, you're a cold little thing aren't you – you need some good meals inside you."

Angela smiled nervously. "I'm on a diet."

"Ridiculous. You girls are all on diets from the age of twelve. You'll all die of annie-wrecks-yer. You come round my 'ouse and you'll get proper fed up."

She laughed, then swallowed abruptly in case Dovehawk was offended.

"What did I say?" Dovehawk laughed too. "See, even us politicians get our words messed up sometimes – usually costs us a week in the newspapers though, especially when we do it in public."

"What is it then, Angela?" Smoggrate enquired.

"It's Mr D ont' phone, Mr Smoggrate – he wants to check that you've filled in the form to enter us in the cup for next year."

"Of course I 'ave! Every year he asks me that. One 'undred and twenty year we've been int' cup – does he think I'm going to forget one?"

"I don't know. Shall I ask him?" Angela smiled brightly.

"No, you'd better not upset 'im. Thank you Angela."

She smiled again, turned round and closed the door behind her. Her perfume fluttered into Dovehawk's nose as the wash of air from her leaving instantly freshened the musty atmosphere in the room.

"You see," began Smoggrate earnestly, "These people put a few bob into a club, take a controlling interest, 51% of the shares and all that, and they think they own the place." He shook his head. "They don't really understand what they're buying. The history that comes with a club places responsibilities on the new proprietor which are often lost in a haze of balance sheets. But I'm afraid we need these people – the TV money doesn't spread far down this end of the league. The Chairman, Jack Dugdale – Mr D – he an' meself 'ave a good workin' relationship most of the time. Then again, he'd o' got rid of me by now if we didn't – more than ten year he's been took over!"

"When I'm your MP, I shall try and raise the issue of smaller clubs with the Sports Minister. After all, they are the lifeblood of the game."

"That they are, Mr Dovehawk, that they are. It's refreshing to hear you talk this way."

"And I really believe it too; not just a politician's words to get elected...... But..." Dovehawk lowered his voice and continued, "...If you could get some editorial in the local paper on my support for the club, it'd do no harm. And it wouldn't be set against my allowable election expenses."

"I see no problem with that, Mr Dovehawk, no problem at all."

Smoggrate thought he had been sufficiently amenable to the prospective MP to get on his good side, but he could tell from the look in Dovehawk's eyes that free publicity wasn't the only thing on the politician's mind. He also didn't know that with Dovehawk, there *was* no good side.

"Of course..." Dovehawk fixed Smoggrate with a look that could skewer an uncooperative kebab, "...It will be difficult for me, a modern politician, a representative of New Labour, to be associated with some of the... how shall I put it... more traditional and, some might say, outmoded customs which you have at an old football club like this."

Smoggrate's heart skipped a beat. "Meaning?" he said, not really wishing to know the answer.

"Well, take the business of young Miss Twogood, fidgeting at the threshold there like the carpet was bloody electric or something."

Smoggrate felt some relief. "The *no women in the boardroom* rule comes up for voting on *this* year, as it 'appens Mr Dovehawk."

"Aye?" Dovehawk looked unappeased. "And that'll be because you want a Lottery grant for the new stand I assume Mr Smoggrate. It's one of the conditions for receiving the cash, is it not?"

"Well, yes. That is true. But it gets voted on every twenty five years in any case. This year is twenty four years from the last time, so the vote has been brought forward one year. We didn't need to call an

Extraordinary General Meeting to do it – the articles state that the vote can be held up to eighteen months early at the club Secretary's discretion."

Dovehawk turned and began to walk slowly away from Smoggrate, taking his time, looking interestedly at each picture on the wall, talking softly as he moved between them, mumbling, so Smoggrate had to strain to hear. "A club like this has to make progress...... Nothing stays the same – even if it wants to...... Change or die – that's nature...... The supporters don't stay the same, so how can a club?......" After his last remark, Dovehawk found himself facing a large photograph on the wall at the end of the room. From high above his head, it cast the gaze of the individuals embosomed within its walnut frame down the full length of the boardroom table, dwarfing the pictures scattered around the other walls depicting the various teams through the years. Dovehawk was not long studying the large picture before turning around and staring at Smoggrate, making him feel uncomfortable, like he had felt when he was about to be told off at school, all those years ago.

"Are these the current members of the Board?", Dovehawk bellowed, pointing upwards without releasing the tremulous Smoggrate from his gaze, like a bunny caught in the headlights.

"Aye, they are. Would you like me to run through them?"

"Please do."

Smoggrate shuffled up to Dovehawk's side, not feeling so confident any more, but also not yet angry enough to be rude to the man – after all, they would very likely need his help and there was no point in jeopardising the relationship.

"In the centre is Mr D, the Chairman. He's standing next to, and supporting I think if you look carefully, Lord Opiumden. We managed to get him for ten thousand a year, just so's we could put 'is name at the top of the headed notepaper. That one with the bald head and the pony-tail is Frank Dugdale, one of the Chairman's sons, and the one on t'other side, also holding up the noble Lord, is his other son Fred. At the right there is the previous Chairman, Mr Rodderick. He was Chairman for thirty seven years before he finally sold out to Mr D after the disastrous '89-'90 season."

"Did you get relegated that year as well?"

"No, the bloody stand burnt down and Mr Rodderick 'adn't bothered paying the insurance premium. O' course, he blamed me, but we didn't 'ave no money to pay it and I told 'im about it at least twenty times. It were lucky we didn't end up in court – but fortunately no one were 'urt.

"Right, where were we. 'Im on the left is Councillor Balderson. Because the Council give us a grant every year, one of them is co-opted onto the Board to oversee that the money is properly spent. I'll tell you – any money that comes in this club gets right an' properly spent soon as cheque drops ont' mat – it don't even hit bank account hard enough to figure ont' statement sometimes.

"One at right with flash suit an' nose like glossy beak on a puffin – he's the lad we brought in last year to deal with media – Mark Slinger 'is name – drives a bloody Porsche. You gotta 'ave 'em now, you know, these media consultants. Got us a deal with a local garage last year, so now all team 'ave to drive around in Skodas. Notice he's still got 'is bloody Porsche though."

When he'd finished perusing the members of the Board of Directors in the picture, Dovehawk turned to Smoggrate once again. "All right if I sit down?" he asked, pulling the big padded chair where the Chairman sits from under the table."

"Aye – Mr D won't be in today." Smoggrate paused. "I hope."

"You sit too, Mr Smoggrate."

"Call me Stan," Mr Dovehawk.

"Right, Stan – you can call me Stan too."

"Right – Stan it is."

"Stan," said Dovehawk, "I know this is going to be hard for you and the club. But we have to keep abreast of the times. At the end of the day, when all's said an' done, an' the ball's in the back o' the net, the Board of this club don't stack up to much, do they, in the public's eyes."

"Well... It..."

"No, let me finish," Dovehawk cut off the stammering Smoggrate. "Answer me this. How many of your supporters are lasses – olduns and younguns alike – how many?"

"Quite a few now, I suppose. We 'ave the girls' team playing 'ere most Sundays, and them and their mums and dads come an' support the first team on Saturdays – we give special ticket prices and a family enclosure."

"You see!" Dovehawk smacked the desk with his hand triumphantly. "You see – you've got a family enclosure – so you're getting there, making a difference."

"Aye – we do our best, as I said, er... Stan."

"That's very good. But, you see, I still have a problem." And his voice became grave once more. "I can only give this club my 110% wholehearted support if the public can see that the people who run it are representative of their community. So – I'll get straight to the point – you need a woman on the Board of Directors."

"Oh, I see. Well, I'll put it to the Chairman. Mrs D'll probably be able to do it if it don't clash with her hair appointments and charity work."

Dovehawk huffed exasperatedly.

"I'm afraid the Board is already a little overloaded with Dugdales! We need a real woman – someone who supports the club."

"Mrs D does support the club – and she often accompanies the Mayor and other dignitaries to games."

"But that's the point, the whole bloody point – we can't have someone who just uses the club as a place to be seen with the right people. Politics today means we have to be honest – well, appear honest at least – it's what the public have come to expect."

"But..."

"No, let me finish." Dovehawk left Smoggrate floundering once more. "Answer me another one. How many of your supporters are black – you know – Asians and Afro-Caribbeans?"

"We have a big Asian community – but I don't think they come to many games."

"Well exactly. Even more reason then to have a black member on the Board."

"But..."

"I'll be off now – no more discussions till you've thought it over. It's been very nice looking at the lovely photos in you boardroom, Stan. I've enjoyed meself truly today."

And Dovehawk raised himself up to his rather average height and strode for the door, leaving the poor Smoggrate to scuttle after him in an attempt to see him out.

9.30 the same day

The Chairman of Hetherington Sidney FC, who was also the Managing Director of Carefree Caravans, stared out of the window of his office, trying to think of the word he wanted to use in a letter he was attempting to compose to a lady whose caravan's chemical toilet had recently deposited its contents, quite without provocation, all over the slow lane of the M63.

His mind wandered, the sight of the rows of caravans in his yard calming him in a way that only his caravans could. They were in three rows. The first was of brand new caravans. The second was of used caravans just one or two years old, their paintwork almost as fresh and gleaming as those in the first row. The third contained the older caravans, second or third or fourth hand – who could know? – now showing various signs of ageing, but all scrubbed up to look their best, like Chelsea Pensioners at a fête. This row was Jack's favourite, for it represented his successes. These were the caravans which had gone out and about, been around a bit, had done their duty. Each represented one, or possibly several, satisfied customers who had enjoyed them before upgrading to larger and plusher caravans and, by so doing, provided Jack with the means to build up his business. Some of the caravans in the third row had been back to him for resale on a number of occasions, slightly shabbier at each visit, but every time making him a small profit and representing, to their new keeper, a step up the caravan-owning ladder on the way to the ultimate home on wheels.

The weather was not pretty outside the window, but Jack saw beauty in the spears of rain which exploded into puffs of spray on the white plastic roofs of his babies. He drifted off on a mind's journey starting as a raindrop in a cloud, then tumbling, seeing the whole of the landscape spread out below, wondering where he was going to land, the wind blowing him left and right, his resting place looming up: a car park or a grass field maybe...... But no!, the breeze was wrenching him back skywards again, the eddies and currents tossing him until finally he was crashing into the friendly white plastic of the caravan roof where, trickling safely into the gutter, he knew he was home.

Suddenly, with a bit of a jump he was back in his office and couldn't remember what it was that he'd been trying to think of. He took a swig of coffee from the mug on his desk and pondered. "Ah yes," he muttered to himself, looked at his computer screen, checked that he was in the right place, then typed, carefully with a couple of fingers on each hand, the word *unprecedented.* Now he'd have to check the spelling, he thought, but didn't bother because he was not much interested in spelling, so he carried on with his letter, but his mind wandered again, and the letter went all wrong.

Sod it, thought Jack. *I'll go to the football club for an hour, see how the training's going, upset Smoggrate – that'll cheer me up.* He locked the site office behind him and climbed into his lovely old Rover 3500 that he'd had for thirty years, looked in the rear view mirror to check whether or not he had a caravan in tow and started the silky smooth engine.

Quarter to ten

When he arrived at the football ground, Jack went straight to his office and made himself another cup of coffee. While filling the kettle which was on an ornamental plant stand behind his desk, he amused himself by thinking that most football Chairmen wouldn't make their own refreshments, but would get someone else to do it for them. Mr Dugdale was different; the caravanning in his blood meant that the ritual of brewing was the high-point of every day – the thing you first did when you arrived at your destination. He remembered all those times when it seemed the journey was unending, that there was still so far to travel, and you used your imagination to conjure up the smell of tea – and that kept you going. And finally the reality, the first brew-up at the site, that magical moment, the culmination of a day on the road, the achievement, the satisfaction, the relaxation. Could you get any of that from asking your secretary to make the drinks?

He took the first sip just as the door opened and Angela came in carrying a stack of mail.

"Ooops – sorry Mr D – didn't know you were in today – just bringing yer post – all bills as usual – except for this one." And she held up a large envelope. "I didn't open it – it looked important." She placed the other envelopes and their contents in Jack's IN TRAY and handed him the important letter. "It's got ON HER MAJESTY'S SERVICE on it!"

"Thank you Angela." said Jack as he took the letter. "It's probably a tax demand."

"Oh no – I don't think so – I've got a feeling about that letter." As she left the office she declared joyfully "I'll tell Mr Smoggrate yer 'ere."

Aye – that'll make 'is day, thought Jack as he slit open the envelope and withdrew the contents. He stared at it for several seconds, then placed the letter back on the desk in front of him before taking a large slurp of coffee. There was a knock at the door and a cowering Smoggrate nervously asked Jack if he could have a word. Jack looked at the letter, then at Smoggrate and chuckled to himself. *This'll <u>really</u> make 'is day.*

Meanwhile, Angela was in her own office photocopying a batch of letters which were apologising for not paying various bills in the hope that the creditors would be understanding. While the machine whirred to itself in a rhythmic fashion, she wondered if Sean had arrived yet for training. Sean was the rising star of the Hetherington Sidney football team: young, accomplished, cheeky, and a top-notch goalscorer whose value on the transfer market was rising rapidly. He was also Angela's hero; at home, her bedroom walls were papered with his image – signed photos, posters, and of course her treasured replica shirt. She'd applied for her job at the club just to be near him and was so excited when she was offered it, even though there were times when working for Smoggrate was very trying.

Angela knew that the window at the end of the corridor outside her office overlooked the training ground. The photocopier would quite happily continue on its own for some time, she thought, so why not go and see if her beloved centre-forward was there in his track suit?

Because the window was just out of reach even when she was wearing high heels, she grabbed a couple of packs of copier paper to stand on when she got there. She opened her door and looked into the corridor to check that no one would spot her, then, scampering to take up position, placed the two reams of paper on the floor and stepped onto them, her head now at just the right height for a good view. But immediately she was saddened by the view, for there was no one there. She started to climb back down when she heard a horrible noise, a terrible cry of rage from behind her. It was the Chairman's voice and she froze with fear, assuming that she'd been caught. But when she turned around in trepidation, the corridor was empty. With butterflies jumping around beneath her little light blue cardigan, she gathered up her makeshift stool and bolted for the sanctuary of her own office, but had not yet reached the door when another yell rang out so loudly it drowned out the cloppy clatter of her not-very-good-for-running-in shoes on the polished floor. Unable to think of anything except safety, she ran into her office, flung the copier paper on her desk and slammed the door behind her, then sobbed and puffed and panted in her chair while at the same time trying as best she could not to get her mascara runny. The photocopier wheezed its last copy, too, and patiently waited on Angela's next instruction, its fan humming and whirling the hot air around, both she and the machine cooling down together as if their activities had been coordinated.

With her own door shut, Angela could still clearly here the raised voices in Mr Dugdale's room.

"A woman!"

Jack bellowed his indignation so violently that it rattled the panes of glass in his office window and he spat small specks of coffee all down his shirt and onto the letter on his desk telling him he'd at last got his OBE. "I'll not 'ave a woman on my Board – I've never 'ad a woman on the Board of any company of mine. They know sod all about caravans, and even bloody less about football. All 'cause of some MP, who *you* arranged to meet without my permission, just 'cause you're a member of the sodding Labour Party. Well I won't 'ave it – meddling in the affairs of... of.... an institution, that's what a football club is – the rock upon which the 'opes of the local community are elevated at the start of each season then dashed to pieces by Christmas, up and down like the waves on the ocean – in the cup, out o' the cup – promoted, relegated – score 5, let in 6. Bloody woman indeed."

And he proceeded to smoulder while Smoggrate braced himself to tell the Chairman the other half of the story.

“’Ave you done?” the chairman looked up from his papers as if in surprise that Smoggrate was still in his presence.

“Er.. not really.”

“Go on then – it can’t be worse than the last bit – woman on the Board – bah!”

“It’s not necessarily worse – along the same line of thinkin’ – but not worse.”

Dugdale’s eyes bulged as he rammed his glasses back up his nose and sat straight upright in his chair. Smoggrate thought he could see a bead of sweat forming on the Chairman’s brow and wished he’d never asked Dovehawk to look around the club. He’d only done it to be polite. Hadn’t he? Well to be honest with himself he had to admit that the help with grants and sponsorship was really more important, but it was still the right thing to do to invite your MP-elect to survey the crowning glory of his constituency – his local football club. He’d done his duty as club Secretary and didn’t see why he should now be ashamed at having to relay the details of their meeting to his own Chairman, so he decided to come straight out with it.

“He wants a black person on the Board as well.”

Smoggrate saw the words work their way into Mr Dugdale’s head, and then saw his jaw drop open at exactly the same time as a bead of sweat slipped gently off his brow, hurdled the bridge of his glasses, sped down his nose and, as if the great protuberance were a ski-jump, launched into the air and landed smack in between the “h” of Elizabeth and the “R” of R.

Quietly the Chairman enquired, “How black?”

“His exact words were: Asian or Afro-Caribbean,” replied Smoggrate in hushed tones.

“Proper job then – not just well tanned. Right. We’d better get on with it, if you think this MP of ours is so important...... Angela!”

The Chairman called Smoggrate’s assistant and the door from her office opened. “Take this down will you love, then send it to the Gazette for insertion in the ‘Classifieds’. ’Ave you got a pencil?”

“Yes Mr D.” She fluttered the pages of her notepad. “I’m ready.”

The Chairman looked straight ahead and composed: "*Wanted.* That's in capital letters, Angela. *WANTED. One woman and one Asian or Afro-Caribbean person who knows bugger-all about football, to serve on the Board of Hetherington Sidney FC. Signed S Smoggrate, club Secretary.* You can go now Angela."

"Now 'old up! Angela, give me that notepad. You can't put 'bugger all' in the paper!"

"Why not? The Editor does!" The club Chairman waited in expectation for Smoggrate's reply, but it was Angela who next spoke.

"I'd rather you didn't take my notepad Mr Smoggrate – you'll see I don't know 'ow to spell *carabian.*"

"Oh give it 'ere girl." Smoggrate snatched the notepad from her and screwed up his eyes. His nose twitched and his brown teeth drew strings of slaver from his lips as he opened them to speak, then closed them, then opened them again. "You've spelt it *caravan*!"

"Oh yes, so I did. I'm good at *caravan* – I get a lot of practice at *caravan.*"

Smoggrate turned his head to look at the Chairman. "So, 'ow come she knows 'ow to spell *caravan*?"

"How come she knows how to spell *Smoggrate,*" the Chairman quipped triumphantly, "She didn't 'ave no trouble with that, did she?"

"She works for me – she 'as to sign my name. We practised. I wrote it down and Angela copied it. Soon got the 'ang of it, didn't you Angela?"

"Yes Mr Smoggrate."

The Chairman's voice turned more menacing. "And *you*, Smoggrate, you work for *me* – and it's my caravans that pay your wages."

Smoggrate huffed and blustered. "We need to change this advertisement. 'Ere, Angela – 'ave your notepad back and alter it to read as follows: *WANTED. One woman and one Asian or Afro-Caribbean person to serve on the Board of 'Etherington Sidney FC. No knowledge of football required. Signed J Dugdale, club Chairman.* Oh, and we'd better add at the bottom: *This is an equal opportunities position.* All adverts 'ave that on nowadays."

Mr Dugdale looked to the ceiling, buried his head in his hands, then finally emerged, resigned it seemed to whatever was going to happen. "Angela," he said.

"Yes Mr D?"

"I think you'd better put *your* name on the bottom of the advertisement."

"Yes Mr D. And do you want it just in a column with all the others, or in one of those little boxes with a border round it?"

"A little box, please Angela."

"Yes Mr D. Is that all?"

"Yes. Thank you Angela. You are, without doubt, the only sane person in this whole bloody football club."

Angela left the room to go next door to her own office and clicked the door shut behind her.

The Chairman continued, "And, also without doubt, the biggest bloody nutter in this whole football club this morning was that idiot MP!" He glared at Smoggrate. "*It'll be nice to show him round the club*, you said, *Good for the club*, you said. Well, IT ISN'T GOOD AT ALL!"

"You can't blame me."

"I just have."

"Couldn't we just get Mrs D to spend a bit longer on the sun bed, then apply for both posts?"

"You said Dovehawk wouldn't accept another Dugdale."

"Well no he won't. But if she were brown enough, and applied for the job usin' a different name, he might never know."

"Never mind about that, I've got a better idea. Get yourself a notepad, Smoggrate, then take down this letter and fax it to Labour Party 'eadquarters in London......"

10 o'clock on the same Monday morning – team talk for the coming FA Cup match

"Right. Gather round you lot." The Hetherington Sidney manager looked serious. "We need to talk tactics for Saturday. Obviously I don't need to fire you up for the match: second round of the FA Cup – win this one and we're in the hat with the big boys for the first time in seventeen years. What did I say, Nobsy?"

"Eh? Er, seventeen years boss...... same age as the lass I met in the *Late-Tackle Club* last night – right gorgeous she were... She'd of been bein' born when this club were last in't third round!"

"Startling information, Nobsy. You're fined a day's wages!"

"What for? I were listening – honest!"

"I know. But you shouldn't have been in the *Late-Tackle Club*. It's supposed to be for supporters. You lot are supposed to be asleep, dreaming sweet little dreams, so as you can score goals on Saturday."

"But I was workin' behind the bar to 'elp 'em out – they was short-staffed."

"In that case, the money you got from that'll cover your day's wages you'll lose, won't it? Right. Let's get on." The manager turned round to start drawing a diagram of his desired team formation but was immediately thwarted by lack of equipment. "Who's pinched the chalk off the blackboard?"

"Groundsman, gaffer," said Sean, trying to stifle the big grin on his face, casting suspicion on his apparent helpfulness.

"OK. I can't wait for this... What would he want with my chalk, Shagsy?"

"He was re-doin' the penalty-spot, boss!"

"Right, you're fined a day's wages an' all."

"What for?"

"Taking the piss. Right. Where is that bloody chalk?"

He looked at the players, hoping for assistance, while they in turn searched around the places where they were sitting, hoovering their heads from side to side near the floor and banging them on the benches on their way back up from their fruitless efforts. Having scrabbled around on his chair energetically for a while, Korma shouted out, “Here it is, boss! I’m sitting on it. D’you want it?”

The manager thought about it for a second, the lines furrowing across his forehead and curling along the top of his nose giving some indication of his rising level of disgust.

“Christ no! Not after it’s been up *your* arse, Korma!” he said, and instead of taking the two-inch off-white offering which Korma held out for him to grasp, he bent down to retrieve a tiny piece from the floor beneath the blackboard. “I’ll use this pink bit instead.”

“Heh, Boss!”

“What is it, Korma?”

“Why am I the only one in’t team what’s got a foreign nick-name?

“Eh?”

“Korma – it’s a bloody curry!”

“You’re called Korma cos you’re bloody brown – take a look in the mirror.”

“That’s racist! I was born in Shipley! I want an English name.”

“Tripe then. We’ll call you Tripe – that’s a good English name. Now can we get on – we’re supposed to be discussing how to beat Scuntlepool in the second round. Any suggestions?”

There was a long silence before Splutter, the right back, revealed to everyone the revelation he had just experienced during his time deep in thought.

“Lashhhhtt time we shplayed they did ush two nothin’ at their plashe.”

“And your point is, Splutter ...?” asked the manager, fearing the worst.

“It musht be our turn!” said Splutter confidently.

“Oh that’s fuckin’ great then, i’ntit,” said the manager sarcastically. “We don’t need to bother with this blackboard session. We’ll take the rest of the week off, just turn up at their place on Saturday and we’re bound to win anyway cos it’s our turn...!”

There was an immediate and loud grating noise as all the players scraped their chairs backwards and stood up. Tubsy greeted the news with delight: "Great!..... Cheers boss! Can we go 'ome then?"

"Sit down and shut-up."

The manager glared as, grumbling and muttering, they all sat down again; all except Stainsy who hadn't stood up in the first place because he was preoccupied with wiping the back of his head with a brown and yellow snot-covered hanky.

"Boss?"

"Yes, Stainsy?"

"Splutter's made me 'neck all wet again," complained the right-sided midfielder.

"You shouldn't sit in front of 'im, then should you? I've told you before."

"I'm not sittin' in front of 'im! I'm right over to one side – see for yourself. An' I blame you, gaffer!"

"How do you work that out?"

"Last week in trainin' you told 'im he 'ad to improve 'is distribution!"

The players all curled up with laughter.

"Very funny," said the manager.

"Boss?"

"What now Korma?"

"I prefer Korma to Tripe."

"I just called you Korma didn't I? So you should be happy."

"But I'd really like to be called *The Brown Stallion*, or sommat like that."

"We could call you *Brown Sauce* if you like – it goes better."

"With what?"

"With tripe o' course. I thought you said you were born in Shipley? Aint you never eaten tripe? Now for bollocks sake let's get on, or we'll never get out on the trainin' ground. Now I'm gonna show you tossers a video."

"Nice one, boss. Is it the video of our last game, so's you can tell us all how crap we all were?" said Tubsy enthusiastically.

"No. I've decided that, from today, you are going to learn how to play proper football by watching the greatest team what ever God assembled. God bein', in this instance, Don Revie. So here is Leeds v Southampton, 4th of March 1972 – an' if any of you goes to sleep, you go in my little book and you aint playing in the 3rd round if we get through on Saturday – and that's a promise. Now watch this, and try to imagine in your stupid little skulls that you can see the space around you, the next ball with either foot, inside or outside of the boot, the killer pass, just like the team in white. Try to imagine that *you* are the players on the screen; *you* are the team in white.

"Now – here's the team sheet. Shagsy – you're Lorimer, Korma you're Gray, Dorksy you're Hunter, Tubsy you're Charlton, Nobsy you're Bremner, Piccalilli you're Sprake, Splutter you're Madeley, Gherkin you're Reaney, Stainsy you're Giles, Freddy and Billy, you're Jones and Clarke."

Piccalilli
(Sprake)

Splutter (Madeley)	Dorksy (Hunter)	Tubsy (Charlton)	Gherkin (Reaney)

Stainsy (Giles)	Nobsy (Bremner)	Korma (Gray)
Freddy Bell (Jones)	Shagsy (Lorimer)	Billy Bell (Clarke)

The manager pressed the Play button on the DVD, went to the back of the room, switched off the lights and leant on the rear wall behind his lads. His name was Ron Conference and he'd been brought into the club halfway through last season when Hetherington Sidney FC were bottom of the Second Division (which is really the Fourth Division in the old system). He'd done a good job by keeping them up – had to win their last game and they did it – so he'd been given a contract for the new season, but no money for signings. Of course he hadn't expected any – they could barely pay his and the players' wages – and now he had the problem of hanging on to Shagsy, whose fourteen goals so far this season had sent his transfer price rocketing and scouts from the big clubs coming to matches so often they'd doubled the gate takings. And now Shagsy was going out with the Honourable Lady Opiumden he was in all the tabloids; the back pages had him as a future England player, should be in the "B squad" they said, while the front pages had him with Fiona's legs draped about his person, should be in the running for "lucky git of the year" they said. And Ron Conference knew they were right about both and the day was soon coming when the Chairman would call him into his office and tell him that they'd had an offer they just couldn't refuse – five million probably, maybe more. But Ron hoped that he could hang on to the boy just as far as the third round of the cup. And his own future needed a good cup run. Ron wanted to be a top Premier League manager – the only problem was, all the successful ones were foreign – Ron'd have to work on his accent.

Between half nine and half one on the Monday

Dovehawk went to meet the vicar to examine archaeological artefacts just discovered during church renovation. The vicar, Reverend Green (no jokes about candlesticks he requested of Dovehawk when they shook hands) said that some of the objects were fetishes, worshipped by the ancients before Christianity. Dovehawk knew this to be true. He himself worshipped quite a few.

Next he met some children who were on a school trip to a house which the residents had converted into a home for birds that couldn't fly. Dovehawk found it funny that there wasn't an ostrich in sight, and remarked upon the fact. The hosts didn't understand his joke, the children didn't care because they were playing in the mud, and the trainee reporter assigned to following him on his campaign asked Dovehawk how you spell ostrich.

After his visit to a fund raising sponsored marathon-cake-bake at which he was kissed on the cheek by a woman whose bottom lip was so slack it caught itself on his buttonhole and made his red carnation all soggy, he drove to the dingy terraced house that served as the Labour Party HQ during the by-election, the bunting fluttering from the first floor windows. The result of the poll was a certainty, of course, but one still had to put on a show – make sure the locals didn't think you were taking them for granted. Red and white stripy plastic cones in the gutter outside the front door were supposed to reserve his parking place, but someone had left a gleaming new

Skoda there. On its passenger door, neatly signwritten in swirly purple writing, were the words: *Hop in Baby.*

Dovehawk felt the veins in his forehead straining to twice their normal size with every pump of his big old heart. He scrunched his tyres as he stopped his car double-parked against the nasty little foreign pile of scrap, then hammered the horn button down with the palm of his hand and held it there until he saw, with satisfaction, the freshly painted red door of the HQ open and his Party Agent's agitated face appear. On seeing Dovehawk in his car, the agent waved his arms to gesticulate to Dovehawk to stop the noise and he then walked out into the road. Dovehawk released the horn and wound down the window.

"Gerald! What's *that* doing there?" he roared.

"It's all right, Stan, he's just leaving and it's good publicity. It's Sean Shagdit from the football club. We want to get a photograph of him with you before he goes."

"Well tell him to shift his bloody car and *then* he can have the photo."

"No Stan, you don't understand. *He* doesn't need the photo, but *we* do! We need a photo of you with *him*. He's famous, see?"

"We'll both be bloody famous if I have to run his car over. We'll be in all the papers."

"He *is* in all the papers. He's scored fourteen goals already this season and he's going out with Lord Opiumden's granddaughter!"

"That makes fifteen then."

"That's more like it Stan, you're cheering up already, more like your old self. Come on. You go inside and get your photo took, and I'll park your car."

Dovehawk bruised into the constituency office like a bear with backache. Inside was packed with photographers and Dovehawk had to stand on tiptoe and crane his neck to look over them and see the object of their attentions. It was a scrawny kid in his early twenties sporting a line of beard which squiggled down from one ear, took a spiral flourish in the middle of his chin, then snaked up to the other ear. Draped over him was a beautiful brown haired girl who managed somehow to have her knees around his chest even though he was standing.

Dovehawk boomed “Excuse me!” and started to force his way through the crush. On hearing the voice, a couple of acolytes rushed from the sidelines and started parting the assembled paparazzi, but too late, for Dovehawk had already steamed through, finally managing, with a swipe of his arms, to knock over some of his own staff as he emerged from the front row. He beamed at the two youngsters as he approached.

“Sean!” he enthused, and held out his hand for the local hero to shake. Then looking to his partner, “And this is the lovely Honourable Lady Opiumden. Right? Where shall I stand. Here in between you?”

Dovehawk amazingly contorted his body into a knife-shape sufficiently keen to part the two seemingly glued-together youngsters, then stood slightly behind them, his arms around their shoulders. He beamed again while the photographers clicked and whirred their apparatus. “You will tell me if I’ve got gravy down me tie, won’t you Sean?” he whispered in the lad’s ear.

“Aye Mr Dovehawk. But with that tie, you’d not notice.”

“Ha ha – call me Stan. Everyone calls me Stan – except for people who don’t know my name.”

“Stan?” came a different, higher voice.

“Yes, the Honourable Lady Opiumden?”

“You’ve got your hand on my tit.”

“I know I have. It’s true what they say: never trust a politician. Our picture’ll get a better page in the paper. Could even make one of the Nationals. Sean may get an England call up!”

“All that, just from you holding my tit?”

“Aye. Publicity breeds success. I should know. I’ll bet you thought I was doing it for selfish reasons.”

“I’ve never been groped by a politician before. It’s quite exciting.”

“Yes. We work a lot faster than these sports stars. We have to cram much more into a day. No time for lazing around, getting up at midday, two hours jaunt on the training ground, then out clubbing all night. We have policy meetings before breakfast, read all the papers and work out what line we're going to spin to the journos, then meet the party faithful, give encouragement while they go round and do all our dirty work knocking on doors..."

"Lift your head up a bit will you Stan!"

"...meeting all the people that hate the Labour Party, all the people that love the Labour Party, all the people that love the Labour Party but hate *me*, all the people that love me but hate the Prime Minister, all the people who love the Labour Party as long as it doesn't get elected, and all the people who couldn't give a damn..."

"A bit more cleavage please Fiona love!"

"...and that's all before lunch. Then I have to meet the Mayor, visit the football club, the Women's Institute and the Mothers' Union, all before tea time..."

"Come on Fiona – a bit more leg!"

"...and in the evening there's no feet up in front of the telly cuddling the wife and sending out for a pizza. I have to attend public meetings about car parking and dog fouling – did you know they're the two most important things in ordinary people's lives? And I have to be photographed holding a pint in every pub – not so bad I'll admit. And then, before bed, I have to work on next day's speeches and criticise what the opposition have been up to. It's not just a shag in the park you know, trying to become an MP."

"It's a wonder you aren't worn out, Stan."

"Stamina. We're full of stamina us politicians, and an insatiable lust for life. I could still take *you* on, you know."

"Where would you fit me in?"

"Any bloody where you like! None of that rubbish I was just on about is so important I can't cancel it."

"Call for me at two in the morning round Sean's – he'll be so pissed by then he'll never notice I'm gone. And you won't have to cancel anything."

"Good lass."

"Come on Fiona – just a glimpse of your knickers for the front page love."

Whilst Fiona was adjusting her stance to allow a tantalising tease of pure white panties to creep into the photographers' viewfinders, a loud voice swamped the proceedings, drowning out all the clicks of shutters and the shuffle of tripods on the splintery floorboards.

"RIGHT. EVERYONE OUT OF THIS ROOM!" The voice sounded terrifyingly authoritative, and almost female. The photographers spun around to try and see the source of the interjection.

Dovehawk felt his blood pressure rising again. He relinquished his grip on the Honourable breast and thundered off towards the front door from where the voice had come. Before he got through the melee of photographers, his agent, Gerald, scampered out towards him and, taking his arm, dragged him down so he could whisper in his boss's ear.

"Careful, Stan, – she's from central office. She's only Chair of the bloody Women's Committee. Go very careful!"

"I know who it bloody is!" stormed Dovehawk. "Pree Bloody Pincer-Face Puckering, the scrotal-sack-slasher of Labour HQ!"

Gerald appeared terrified. "It's not usual for her to turn up at a by-election, is it Stan?"

"She never goes anywhere unless there are balls to be crushed, Gerald! We're in trouble."

Some photographers moved out of the way and the owner of the voice looked upon the little huddle of policy-decision-making that was Stan and Gerald.

"Did I hear you say *trouble*, Stan?" The voice sounded mellow now.

"I was just saying, I hope it wasn't too much *trouble*, coming all this way just to see us and our little by-election. Here to frighten off a few voters are you?"

"I should have thought you could manage that by yourself. No. I'm here on policy business."

"What a surprise. I don't suppose you go anywhere for any other reason do you?"

"What other reason could there be?"

"You could be up here for a shag for all I know."

"Are you offering, Stan? No – don't answer – you're too old."

Dovehawk's head started to turn purple and Gerald, sensing the explosion to come, grabbed him again and spun him around to face Sean and Fiona. "Your guests are leaving now Stan – say goodbye nicely, won't you."

"Ah yes. It's been lovely Sean.", stumbled Dovehawk. "I hope you score the winner come Saturday. Second round isn't it?"

"Aye Stan. Then we'll be in the draw for the big one – the third round – get one o' them Premier League clubs down 'ere and the papers'll go mad – might get me a juicy transfer."

"Good luck lad. And you too Fiona love. But give him a night off before the game, won't you lass." Stan winked.

"Bye Stan," and she kissed him, taking a little longer than necessary. Then Fiona walked up to Pree, stopped, flung her hair back over her shoulder and announced, "Nice wife, Stanley!" before flouncing out with Sean at her side. The photographers hurried after them leaving the two politicians glaring at each other, each waiting for the other to make the first move. Dovehawk just wished he could bury her under the floorboards and claim asylum in Conservative Central Office. Ms Puckering was relishing a victim.

1:40pm Monday

Dovehawk's office at 29 Cokedealer Street was on the first floor, very small, appearing more so since the desk was made of a large door laid flat across two massive piles of books and magazines as supports. The bunting, displaying itself valiantly in the wind and rain outside at the front of the building, was held in place by being jammed in the bottom of the window behind the desk: one or two of the triangular flag pieces at the end of its string hanging from the middle of the lower sash, draping down to the floor as if trying to climb back indoors to escape the weather. On the wall facing the desk was a nice iron fireplace, probably original, with a fancy pattern cast into an arch around the opening. But it was unlit, and the room was cold, as Dovehawk had complained on many occasions over the last week, and Gerald had installed a mini electric heater to take the chill off. But the fuse had blown yesterday and there was a blackened mark around the plug socket in the dusty skirting board showing where the current had flashed to freedom, and in that same instant had ended its association with keeping Dovehawk warm. On

Dovehawk's desk there was a stack of leaflets, a red plastic tray with URGENT written on it, or rather, scribbled on a white paper sticky label with peeling edges, and a computer on which Dovehawk had lovingly downloaded from the internet a picture of Fiona clad in something which didn't cover her bottom very well. This picture he had chosen to use as his screen-saver or wallpaper or whatever you care to call it.

Unfortunately for Dovehawk, seated behind his desk, under Fiona's posterior gaze, was the primrose-yellow-suited figure of Pree Puckering, her hair neatly raised to the same depth over her entire head with soft brown curls, almost attractive, her bright jacket caressing her mid-to-slender body, her face quite beautiful behind the snarl, her earrings golden, her lipstick red enough to delight a commy's heart and unblemished as if no food had brushed its way between those lips today. Dovehawk himself was seated in the visitor's chair, facing the window and the lady. Of course he had protested that he wished to remain standing. But, without wishing to diminish the value of her fierce expression, it must be stated that her voice was far more terrorsome and he had relented, even calmed himself mentally so as to clarify his thoughts, arrange his arguments in order of persuasion, and reserve some witty lines with which to launch any counter-attack. This was before he found himself mesmerised by those lips, those red lips earlier described, and by the thought he had had about nothing passing between them. And Dovehawk was now in a different universe entirely, his thoughts and gaze, even smell, centered on the imagination of what those lips could do, if only they weren't the delivery system for such a devastating weapon, the most destructive which Pree Puckering possessed, and which she used without discretion or fear of running low on ammunition. Dovehawk was shafted from the start, before she even spoke.

The lips displayed a glimpse of tip of tongue as she started to speak. "Stan..." (Pacifyingly, calming the waters.) "...The women's committee don't like to meddle..." (Blatant lie to rule out hope of a reasoned response succeeding.) "...and we are aware that you're one month into your election campaign..." (It's all been for nothing.) "...But..." (This is the bit where all your hopes and dreams are shattered.) "...it has come to our attention..." (Some bastard grassed you up.) "...that your candidacy for this seat of...." She glanced down at her notes. "...Hetherington South North West..." She glanced again and frowned. "...or something...... did not follow the prescribed selection procedure as laid down in the resolutions of the National Executive meeting held on Tuesday the sixth of September 1994...... in that and insofar as, your candidacy was accepted by the constituency Party without your having to contest it with another candidate, one who would have been drawn from the list compiled by the women's committee for the purposes of positive discrimination: namely to remove fat, middle-class men from the hallowed green benches of the House of Commons and to replace them with working class single mothers, who all happen just by accident to be lawyers. It is therefore the decision of the Women's Committee, taken at an extraordinary general meeting held an hour ago as I was on the train coming here, with myself and the girl on the refreshments trolley sworn-in as proxy for another member who couldn't attend, that a new contest for the candidacy of this seat be held..." (You're shagged mate.) "...Have you anything to say?.." (If you want to waste your breath.)

Dovehawk heard most of what she had just said only through a veil of red imagined heaven, until the final part about a "new contest for the candidacy of the seat being held" awoke him to the danger of what was happening and re-asserted his combativeness. It was futile, but he would fight. And if it came to a scrap with the Women's Committee, at least he could rely on some of the newspapers for support.

"You need a damn good seeing-to," he announced loudly. Dovehawk looked her right in the eyes as he spoke and he felt much better.

"The Women's Committee will take note of your observation. But, as I've already said, you're too old, Stan."

He continued. "I was given this seat because of thirty five years membership of the Party. Because of knocking on doors for my local MP, of sitting in on Union meetings, of being tea-boy, banner holder, rosette pinner, dog stroker, puncture mender when the campaign van went over a nail, pipe lighter, burger fetcher, left wing, right wing, middle wing and now, when it became completely unavoidable, New bloody Labour; and I'll tell you I aint never yet seen a woman who can sit through a nine hour debate in the House of Commons without going for four pit-stops."

"The Women's Committee will take note of your observations.

“But I’ll tell you why I was given this seat – the most important reason, and that’s TRUST.” Dovehawk turned his large palms to the ceiling and held his arms outstretched for Pree to examine. She didn’t flinch at the closeness of his fingernails to her breasts. “*This* is a safe pair of hands.” Dovehawk spoke with finality, the unassailable truth freed from its cage.

“Yes.” Pree spoke without force. “But unfortunately those hands belong to a body wearing a safe pair of *trousers*.”

Dovehawk withdrew his hands and huffed as he stood up. “I don’t know how you got that idea! You must’ve been reading the wrong bloody newspapers.”

Pree shook her head and stowed her notes in her bag, purposely not looking at Dovehawk. She then got out of the chair and, looping the strap of her bag over her shoulder, went to the door.

Dovehawk watched her and, as she turned before leaving, he spoke first. “You didn’t mention the computer.”

“I wasn’t going to bother. Her arse isn’t up to much, Stanley. Mine was tighter in its day.”

Just after 2 in the morning on Tuesday (dead of night)

“Oh Stan, you’ve got a very long tongue! I think in your previous existence you must have been a St Bernard.”

The bed legs were under a lot of strain, since the large pile of heaped-up duvet covering the lovely Honourable Lady Fiona Opiumden’s legs and tummy also, quite remarkably, contained the un-toned barely New Labour figure of Mr Stanley Dovehawk, hoping soon too to be Honourable, just like his hostess, but with his chances threatened by an impending run-off for the Labour candidacy in the by-election against an as yet un-nominated item from a list drawn up on a train by those present at a meeting with a quorum of two, one of which was co-opted from a refreshments trolley.

Stan’s head was full of ideas, but his mouth was unavailable for comment – both things rare in a politician.

“Oh god, Stan. Oh god oh god oh god oh god oh... oooooohhhhhh......”

The Honourable Lady squealed her delight and then watched as the duvet rose from the bed and two corpulent arms extended and twirled around like worms from the seabed searching for food as the tide comes in, until they found her naked shoulders and enveloped her in fatty embrace.

The bedroom in Sean's flat was not very big, so the doorway through which two legs and feet protruded, the body itself outside of the room, the head in the lobby, was not far from the edge of the bed.

"Is he all right down there? enquired Dovehawk, panting from his osculatory exertions, his head over the side of the mattress to examine the body more closely.

"Oh yes. He did unusually well to make it that far – he normally doesn't manage to get off the settee." Fiona tugged at Dovehawk's arm. "Ignore him, Stan," she said as she stroked his lardy shoulder. "Don't you want to give me one?"

"Let me get me bloody breath back first – it's hot under that quilt – I think I've run out of oxygen."

"You'll run out of pussy-patience if you don't start soon."

"Oh go on. Part those lovely legs then."

"Stan?"

"Aye."

"What did that woman want today?"

"You mean the one in the yellow suit?"

"Of course."

"She kindly made the journey all the way from London so that she could sack me! Well, actually to inform me personally that I hadn't gone through the proper selection process to be the Labour Party candidate in the by-election."

"Oh." Fiona sounded genuinely sorry. "So what happens now?"

"I have to stand for selection again – except this time, it's not wholly up to the Party members here. They can make a recommendation, but the National Executive Committee can impose a candidate – accountability doesn't count."

"Why did she arrive here now? The campaign's already been going ages hasn't it?"

"Someone must've dobbed me in! Probably the Secretary or the Chairman of Sean's bloody football club – I upset 'em you see, said they should have someone on the Board who was more representative of the supporters, someone from the ethnic minorities, possibly a woman. Now they're going to get their own back good and proper. You have to admire them – I walked straight into it, like a bollock-level bollard when you're eyeing up a girl on other side of street."

"My grandfather's on the Board – he wouldn't object so long as there were a few gins in it for him. Can't you go a bit faster?"

"Sorry love – the thought of that bollard's made me eyes water."

"You old softy." Fiona mocked him with a glint of love and spite both mixed together in the corner of her eye.

"Old softy!" Dovehawk, in mock outrage, decided to take the comment as a challenge. He knelt up, grasped Fiona's ankles from on the bed behind him and passed them over his head, joining them together in front of him so her legs were straight and vertical, her toes pointing to the ceiling. He rested his nose in the shallow trough between her heels and leant his chest against her calves, using her legs as a spring, like the willow of a longbow, back and forth, joyously exerting himself at their apex. At the precise moment that shrieks and grunts coincided in dissonant harmony, a giant snore ripped from the mouth of Sean's supine figure on the floor. "Christ!" gasped Dovehawk. "He must've bloody come too!"

The crumpled heap of Dovehawk lay gasping on the bed as Fiona skipped over the body of her lover lying in the doorway and into the bathroom. Through the red whistling numbness of high blood pressure, Dovehawk heard the giddy bursting shocks of a thousand tiny water droplets smacking the taught skin of Fiona's body. Soon she was back in the bedroom, a towel briefly around her, then discarded, her hands hauling a pair of black knickers along those long legs whilst at the same time walking across the room to retrieve a tiny little skirt, then a T-shirt falling down her body, her hands reaching high and behind, hooking her long wet hair through the neck-hole, flicking it into the air to splash down her back, her breasts quivering in resonance but briefly until, sitting on the edge of the bed, she leaned forward to fasten some vertiginous shoes to her slender feet.

She looked at the mess on the counterpane.

"When you've had your shower," she enthused delightfully childishly, "We'll go to a party."

Dovehawk was only partially recovered.

"Where's there a party at half past two in the morning?" He hoped that she had not realised the time, and that there wouldn't be one.

"At Tamara's of course...... You know?" She paused to see if he did, but Dovehawk shook his head so she continued, "Squiffy's daughter."

Dovehawk looked blank. He wasn't fully up on the local aristocracy (except for one) – something he would have to rectify should he ever become MP.

Fiona continued. "Squiffy Spankbottom? You've never heard of him? He's got the great big house over at Throginthroat – 127 rooms – and my friend Tamara – that's Tamara Toker-Spankbottom – she's got the Middle Wing – that's the big bit with the front door in it, through which one gains access to the ballroom straight ahead under the balcony joined from either side by the twin staircases – and she has this great party that runs from October right the way through till March to stop her getting too depressed during winter. So come on then!" Fiona threw Dovehawk her towel. Her scent was still on it as it enveloped Dovehawk's head and he drew breath deeply to fill his lungs with her, a glorious life-giving force. "I thought you said you politicians were full of – what was it? – *stamina* and *an insatiable lust for life*, yes?"

Dovehawk hopped off the bed spryly despite his stature. "We are!" he said and slapped Fiona hard on her bum, making a loud crack and a stinging pain on the palm of his hand.

"Oh!" she squeaked as Dovehawk flopped her fluffy aromescent towel across his copious shoulder and clambered over Sean to make his way to the bathroom.

Around 3 in the morning on Tuesday

Dovehawk couldn't believe it. Throginthroat Hall was huge, just as Fiona had described, and the ballroom was truly capacious, but it was the number of people within it and the noise which astounded him. How could so many people be available for partying at 3 in the morning on a weekday?

Fiona gazed around the room, looking for her friend. She soon spotted a young lady a long way away and waved to her before dragging Dovehawk into the crush, the object of their encounter doing likewise until they all met in the middle of the dance-floor. The music was so loud that no one could be heard and introductions were postponed while Fiona and her friend hugged and kissed. Dovehawk couldn't help noticing that Tamara (whom he assumed this person to be) wore something resembling a wide ribbon – a sash perhaps you would call it – which started from beneath her right armpit and crossed the top of her right breast, leaving the bottom of it exposed and hanging by its own weight, the nipple just concealed, then continued diagonally along the same path so that when it reached the left breast it was now beneath it, leaving the top of it exposed and once again concealing, but only just, a perky little nipple which poked through the peacock blue material. The river of cloth then plunged around her ribcage and disappeared behind her back to god knows where. How she maintained its exact trajectory across her chest was a mystery to Dovehawk, as any slight error in alignment would reveal her credentials. He guessed she probably fell out quite often and just hoicked it all back into place. Her bare midriff bore the obligatory belly-button ring with jewel, and to one side, near her waist, a tattoo of what looked in the half-light of the disco like a black penis with a ring through its helmet, but could have been a sea-lion jumping through a hoop. Her skirt was full-length, falling all the way from her hips to her ankles, but the splits up both sides were so long that it was really two pieces of cloth, one in front, one behind, tied together at the waist.

Tamara looked at Dovehawk all the while Fiona talked to her, her right ear next to Fiona's mouth so she could hear above the music. Every now and again she laughed, as friends do when discussing someone out of earshot, all the while continuing her observation of the poor man. Dovehawk hoped that the prognosis on his character dissection would be favourable. Tamara shrilled a final chorus of merriment and came over to Dovehawk, grabbed him around his middle with her arms and hugged him too tight while putting her lips to his left ear.

"So you're a nasty little Labour chappie then darling," she quipped. "I saw you looking at my birthmark. Would you like to kiss it?"

Dovehawk tensed at his mistake in thinking it a tattoo, and thanked the lord that he had not remarked upon it in those terms.

Tamara continued. "It's very lucky, you know – people come from all around to kiss it." She stood back, her arms still around him, and looked him in the eyes.

Dovehawk said nothing – merely lowered himself to his knees, and proffered his lips to her stomach. The halogen light and whirr of the video camera was almost imperceptible amongst the strobe lighting and music, while Dovehawk was engrossed pecking at the darkened skin delineated against Tamara's pure white tummy. She was obviously very proud of it. Dovehawk, having circumnavigated its entire perimeter, withdrew slightly so he could get a better look. It didn't appear so much like a sea-lion from this proximity.

"What do you think?" called Tamara from high above the genuflecting politician.

"It's beautiful." said Dovehawk, his gaze transfixed by the little pulses and ripples which rocked the blemish as she spoke, making it now look, he thought, like a bough fallen from an overhanging tree and floating, bobbing, dabbling on a pale pond of shimmering light.

"What did you think it looked like when you first saw it?"

"Don't worry – she asks everyone," shouted Fiona above the din, squatting down next to Dovehawk. "It's her hobby."

Dovehawk spoke no louder than he had to, so only Fiona could hear. "Tell the truth it looks like a winkie to me. A black man's winkie."

"Yes – most people say that – at least that's what they think. Some are too shy to blurt it out – but Tammy says she can always tell when they're covering up for bashfulness." Fiona raised her head to look at her friend. "Stan's another willy man, Tam," she shouted.

"Oh good!" Tamara beamed her approval as Dovehawk rose to his feet rather sheepishly. "That means we can do our party piece; now where is he?" Tammy looked around the room, her eyes eventually homing in on a group of people at the edge of the dance-floor. “Marlon!” she screamed. She grabbed Dovehawk by the hand and dragged him through the throng, scattering drinks and drinkers alike, her fine body cutting a narrow swathe which the pendulous Dovehawk made wider as he followed, like the fat end of a reluctant wedge. Seeing his attempts to keep up with Tammy’s headlong flight across the room made him look like a dog-owner out for a trot with his too-eager pet.

“Marlon! Marlon darling – come here!” she continued calling as she went, until her quarry noticed her noisy approach. Marlon was black with a lazy smile. *And beautiful*, Dovehawk thought, even though he didn’t fancy men. *Yes, this man was beautiful.*

“There you are darling!” she greeted Marlon. “Meet Stan – he’s another one of the willy brigade. So flop it out for me darling – it must be too hot in there anyway!” Tamara released Stan from her grip, took hold of the waist of Marlon’s trousers with one hand and undid his buttons with the other, concluding with a flick of her wrists so that the garment fell around his ankles. “You finish off dear, or I shall get all overcome!” said Tammy, stepping back so Marlon could carry on the job of exposing himself. He remained smiling as he fed his fingers through the opening in his pants, pulled his wobbly fleshy organ from within its hiding place and flopped it into the outside world. He didn’t let it dangle for long however. In a move which had clearly been rehearsed, he held it out horizontally while Tamara placed herself in a position which presented her birthmark immediately behind it, miraculously the two being at exactly the same height without either having to stoop or adjust their stance.

“There, see Stan?” she shrieked with enthusiasm. “A perfect match!” They held the pose for five seconds whilst Stan verified her assertion. He was amused that no-one else around the little group was much interested, despite Tamara making a deal of noise to advertise the event. *Just another day at the office for these people*, thought Dovehawk. Tamara gave Marlon’s dick an affectionate little squeeze with all her fingers wrapped tight around it. “He won’t dare argue with me now!” she laughed, and demonstrated the predicament in which her friend was placed by effecting a theatrically over-elaborate tug on the knobbly sinew. Marlon winced in feigned discomfort. “Such a pity he’s gay,” bemoaned Tamara as she reinstituted his plaything in its locker. As he bent down to pull up his trousers which were concertinaed around his ankles, Tamara grabbed his head and pressed it hard between her breasts, the ribbon of cloth beneath the left one becoming snagged on Marlon's close-cut hair, releasing her nipple to sniff the smoky sticky fumes that passed for air in the middle of that dance-floor.

Gay? Dovehawk repeated the word silently in his head, and realised that an inspiration had come upon him in a setting that would not normally inspire him.

"Tammy," he called, "Can I ask you something?"

She released Marlon's head and turned to Dovehawk, her left breast lolloping in delight at its freedom; but its escape was short-lived, for in one easy movement she restored the band of brilliant blue into its correct orbit around her body, smoothing the cloth from right to left, from her armpit to her lower ribs with the ease of a painter applying a line of shadow to a canvas. *So that's how it's done* thought Dovehawk.

"Of course – anything darling," She spoke with delight at the prospect of being consulted by someone as worldly-wise as the ebullient Dovehawk.

"This is somewhat delicate, Tammy, and you may find my reasoning hard to fathom, but I need to be gay."

Her eyes dulled over. "Oh not another one – why does this always happen to me? Why didn't you say in the first place, you silly man? Does Fifi know?"

"No......"

"Well I think you'd better explain then, don't you?"

"I mean I'm not...... I'm not actually gay. I realise I've put this all wrong, started in the wrong place; but listen a minute. I was the Labour candidate at the by-election...... *Was*," he reiterated. "But because I wasn't on a list of suitable candidates drawn up by the top brass in the Party, my selection has been questioned and so I face a contest with another prospective candidate – and there'll be no shortage of applicants – this is a safe Labour seat. The candidate they choose will certainly be a woman, and possibly black, so what chance has a white lower middle class middle aged fat bloke got when the day of reckoning is upon us."

"Nasty rotters!" The spark returned to Tamara's eyes.

"Aye. Nasty business all round – and my own fault – because I opened a can of worms at the football club. They'll be sitting back now, enjoying watching me squirm on the end of a hook of my own making. But now...... And this is the good bit what just struck me...... If I could be *gay*, they couldn't de-select me, because that would be *discrimination*!..... Hah, see?"

"Oh, nice one Stan. Now let's just work this out...... How many women have you shagged?"

"I don't bloody know, do I. I don't keep count. Votes is the only thing I count up."

"All right. Let's start with an easier one then. Listen...... How many *men* have you shagged?"

"Me? Shag men? Don't be bloody ridiculous. You can't go around shagging men in my position. Fifty five percent of my support comes from old ladies. My agent's methodical with his canvass returns."

Tamara decided that she liked the cut and thrust of party politics. And the thought of *thrust* made her go a bit gooey.

"So you don't think that being gay, even temporarily, means that you need to shag a few men?"

Dovehawk pondered the problem. "Well, couldn't I get away without that?"

"Without even shagging *one*, you mean? No...... It's absurd...... No one would believe you. Especially all those old women. Have you shagged all of *them*?"

"Of course I haven't. Anyway, this has got nothing to do with them – they're the voters – they mustn't find out that I'm gay...... No, this is for the benefit of the selection panel who will choose the candidate. I can be gay in there, in the interview, behind closed doors. Then afterwards, when I'm out on the hustings, appealing to my natural supporters and winning over the waverers, playing upon every humming, badgering, throbbering, clamouring twist of mood in the crowd, far away from the "sit-on-their-arse-ocrats" of the Party caucus, I'll disavow all aspects of gayness."

The thought of a *throbbering* made Tamara go a little bit gooier.

"How will you convince the... what did you call it?"

"Caucus – it's all the prats that get themselves elected by other prats onto committees that decide the future of various prats within the party, me being at this moment prime prat for dumping myself in all this trouble. I've never made a mistake like this before – I'm almost starting to doubt my own ruthlessness."

"You'll be even more careful in future darling. You'll learn from this. But I still don't see how we can get the selection panel to believe you're gay."

"That's easy – we just need a video – me and your friend Marlon – no need for penetration I hope – have you got a tape?"

"No. I'm strictly DVD darling."

"So was my agent Gerald after his wife joined the Prostitutes Support Group." Dovehawk laughed. "I think she got a bit carried away on her induction course, got too much into the spirit of it – over-indulged."

"No darling. I mean I burn my own."

"Aye, same with Gerald. He won't let his wife near it now."

"DVDs – they're like videos – but posh. Come to my bedroom – you'll see – I'm wired for light and sound."

"Do you scream a lot?"

"Like a Frenchman being sucked off by a porcupine, darling."

"I'd like to hear that."

"You'll be with Marlon. You'll have to save me for another day."

10 on Tuesday morning – team talk for the coming FA Cup match

"Right. Gather round you lot. Why aren't you kitted up, Nobsy?"

"Not just *me* boss! None of us are! Some bastard's nicked our shorts!"

"Oh yes. Sorry lads – that was me!" Ron Conference chuckled as he spoke, watching the angry looks on their faces vanish and turn to grins.

“Bloody ’ell boss,” said Stainsy, “That’s a good one! You’ve never done nothing funny before!”

The whole dressing room erupted into laughter, but Ron became stern. He didn’t understand why they were so amused; he had taken their shorts for a very good training reason. The players looked at him, disbelieving, then exploded with merriment again at the sight of Ron’s sour face.

“Come on you lot,” said Ron, “What’s so funny?”

“Pinchin’ our shorts, boss – that’s funny that is,” joked Dorksy.

“Yeah – an’ you’re fuckin’ borin’ you are. Least we thought you were. But now you’ve pinched our shorts we fuckin’ love you!” Piccalilli came up to Ron and planted a big wet kiss on his lips.

He tried to free himself from the goalkeeper’s strong clinch, and when he finally did Ron gagged and retched to clear his throat; “Christ – no wonder you’re called Piccalilli, lad,” he complained after sampling the foul odours coming from the goalie’s mouth.

“I love you too!” shouted Korma and Ron only had time to utter “God no......” before the amorous Korma’s arms were around him and his feet were lifted off the ground. Korma held his manager in the air, then dropped him into the bath where, all alone, Ron heard the water spray turn on and felt the icy liquid soaking the arse of his track suit.

“OK lads – that’s enough – pull me out.” Ron tried to sound in control as he clambered up the rim of the giant bath, but a row of feet gently shoved him back in again.

“BASTARDS!” he screamed. At that moment the Chairman entered to see what all the noise was about.

“’Urry up an’ get on the trainin’ ground lads,” urged Mr D, not seeing who was in the bath because of all the players standing around the edge of it. “There’s a whole load o’ school kids out there today – apparently Ron told ’em they could watch you lot practise. Where is Ron anyway? And why aren’t you lot kitted up yet? Don’t y’know what t’time is?”

“Gaffer’s nicked our shorts, Mr D.” said Tubsy, so we’re givin’ ’im a bath.”

The players moved aside triumphantly to display their soggy trophy.

Mr Dugdale spoke to the forlorn figure as if his situation was nothing out of the ordinary. “Come on Ron, get these lads outside – or we’ll ’ave to get a bloody juggler to entertain those kids.”

Ron said nothing as Mr D left the room, but lifted himself up enough to sit on the far side of the bath and address his squad. “Right,” he began, the straight faces all around him now reassuring him that he was once again at the top of the pecking order. “I can take a joke lads.” He looked at each player to see if they relaxed. “Despite the fact you think I’m a boring bastard.”

“Oh not any more, boss. Pinchin’ our shorts – that was the best joke you’ve done – we didn’t know you could pull jokes like that! It were fantastic!” complimented Shagsy, and the others all noisily agreed.

“D’you want a towel, boss?” asked Tubsy.

“No. Just pass me that bag over there will you son?” said Ron. He grabbed the bag off Tubsy, unzipped it, and proceeded to dry himself on the pairs of shorts it contained. After using them, he chucked every pair in the bath, one by one, then handed the empty bag back to Tubsy.

“Hang that back on its ’ook, then get outside on the training ground – your audience awaits,” ordered Ron to his players.

“But what about our shorts boss, they’re all wet.” Korma looked at them, and watched them sinking in the bath.

“That’s what I was trying to tell you lads before you put me in the bath: today we’re going to do a special form of training.”

He paused for dramatic effect.

“Today is NO PANTIES DAY. I’ve decided that you lot have trouble scoring goals, and the reason is you’re scared to miss; you’re afraid of looking like tossers. So, today you’re all going to look like tossers anyway cos you’ll be wearing no shorts; in front of Class 11A from Hetherington Community College; instead of worrying about missing the goal, you can worry about showing your tackle to all the schoolgirls who’ve come to watch. Off with your underpants then and lets get out there!”

“No boss! You’ve got to let us keep us underpants on! Think of all them school kids!” said Nobsy.

Ron was unmoved. “Your shirts are long enough to cover you up. Now get ’em off.”

The players looked at each other for help, then they all cheered as Tubsy removed his bright red shrink-fits and held them up in the air.

“If boss thinks we’ll win us the Effin’ A cup with us arses hangin’ out, that’s good enough for me,” he shouted.

Quickly the others all followed his lead, making a heap of assorted underwear on the floor. They then held their arms up, testing to see if anything showed beneath their shirts.

“Bosh”

“Yes, Splutter?”

“When we’ve got no cacksh on, like...... who’sh goin’ int’ wall?”

“Does it matter? You just hold yer ’ands in front o’ yer bollocks, same as normal.”

“Boss.”

“Yes, Dorksy?”

“I feel like Wee Willie Winkie dressed like this, boss!”

“That’s cos you look like Wee Willie Winkie – in more ways than one... Now follow me.”

As the soggy bedraggled Ron led his players onto the pitch, his feet slooshing in his trainers with every step, a shriek filled the air – starting at the entrance to the dressing room and spreading around the training ground touchline like a Mexican wave. Then there was a massive cheer and applause. Shagsy! Shagsy! Shagsy! came the chant from the terraces as 100 crazed schoolgirls strained for a glimpse of their hero...

The players ran onto the field, swinging freely.

In the seven-a-side practice match they played that morning in front of Class 11A, Sean scored 12 goals: 9 at the right end and 3 past his own keeper just for the hell of it. With the wind rushing between his legs, he felt freedom in the box like he’d never known before, like no one could mark him, like he couldn’t miss and the girls in the crowd loved it, went wild and shouted “Show us yer balls Sean!” and he did, with every goal, every twist and turn of his body as he flashed past defenders and headed and flicked and slid. Angela was there too – wishing Sean were hers. She tolerated working for the insufferable Smoggrate just to be near Sean and now, along with 200 (including the boys) fifteen year olds, she'd glimpsed his muddy bollocks.

10 on Tuesday morning – team talk for the coming FA Cup match

"Right. Gather round you lot."

The Scuntlepool manager, Ron Cliché, surveyed his players like a car salesman appraising the lineup on his forecourt, wishing they were slightly lower mileage, slightly brighter in the paintwork, that their exhausts didn't blow, that they didn't smell of fag buts and old sex.

"Football's a game of two halves," he intoned as if delivering a sermon. "Last time we played this Saturday's opposition, we got the ball in the back of the net twice. But you can't take it for granted that'll happen again. Complacency – that's what we must guard against. It's never over till the final whistle. I was sick as a parrot first half – we were rubbish – lucky to go in level at half-time. Second half – different ball game – I was over the moon – game of two halves – fat lady sings – comprendo Wheelspin?"

"Yes boss."

"Players to look out for? Shagsy. Close him down. Don't let him get a sniff of goal. Make sure the only time he gets the ball he's offside. Got that Skidmarks?"

"Yes boss. Heh boss, I don't like being called Skidmarks."

"You shouldn't have shit yourself in the communial bath then, should you."

"But I told you, I didn't – I had a dog turd stuck to me shorts."

"A dog turd – oh listen to this – ho ho ho… And how would a dog turd do that?"

"It's all them old ladies taking their dogs for walks on our pitch. One sliding tackle on Saturday afternoon and you're pooper-scoopered."

"Look – does it matter? I bet they don't talk shit like this in the Hetherington Sidney dressing room. Now – what do I want to be at 5 o'clock on Saturday? All together now......"

"Over the moon, boss!" the whole team shouted out.

"And what do I *not* want to be?......"

"Sick as a parrot, boss!" they bellowed in unison.

"And how are you going to help me achieve that ambition?"

"By getting the ball in the back of the net, boss!" they sang in harmony.

"Music to my ears...... And to help us in that desire, I have a little plan to put them off a bit......" He beamed at each one of his team. "......We're going to nick their shorts."

"Nice one, boss!"

"Soon as their bus turns up I want Wingnut, Backdoor and Rustbucket to nip in their dressing room disguised as tea-ladies, Skidmarks can set off the fire alarm, and those three can nick their shorts while they're evacuating the building. Got it?"

"Yes boss!"

The second Saturday in December – Second Round Day

It was noon and the smell from the hot dog stalls was already hanging heavily in the damp Scuntlepool air as the Hetherington Sidney coach waited its turn in the Christmas shopping traffic. The green and white scarves were out all along the High Street, their owners lying in wait for the visiting team, first jeering as they spotted the coach, then turning around and dropping their trousers, producing the effect of a great Mexican wave of moonies.

"Bloody 'ell," exclaimed Sean, his nose making squdge-prints on the window, "They're all bloody mad 'ere!"

"That they are," said Piccalilli knowingly. "I went out wi' a lass from 'ere once! Scary or what? Took me by the knackers she did and din't let go, just cos I pinched a bit of 'er kebab."

"Should o' pinched 'er betties," offered Tubsy helpfully. "They don't bloody like that!"

Piccalilli looked at Tubsy mockingly. "They don't bloody like you, neither – so 'ow would you know?"

Outside the coach windows, the parade of hairy arses continued to pass by with no diminution in numbers, and the springs sagged down on the left side of the bus as the whole team pressed against the glass to get the best view of the spectacle.

“Look at that one!” said Nobsy, “That’s bloody ’orrible!”

“They’re all bloody ’orrible,” said Sean, “Cos they’re all men. Why don’t the women come out on cup day an’ show us a slop-filled snatch or two?”

“No!” screeched Piccalilli, “You wouldn’t want that! Not Scuntlepool lasses! They’ve got scary arses!”

“Are you a bloody expert or sommat?” enquired Stainsy. “I thought you’d been out wi’ one lass?”

“Aye, that’s right. But while I were buyin’ ’er a drink in’t night-club, I were kidnapped by ’er mates an’ dragged off t’ ladies toilets where they stripped me and sat all over me, pinnin’ me down, six of ’em.”

“Lucky bastard!” said Tubsy thoughtfully and he started to scratch his bollocks.

“An’ I couldn’t escape an’ I were screamin’ an’ the lasses they were laughin’ an’ then some older birds walked in, about thirty year old they were, an’ I thought thank shite I’m gonna be rescued, but they looked at us and they bloody decided to join in an now I ’ad nine of ’em on me an’ I were screamin’ an’ thinkin’ they’re all bloody mad, specially the old ’uns cos one of ’em stuck ’er fingernails right in me tadger – I think she were tryin’ to get it in ’er ’andbag to tek it ’ome wi’ ’er!

“Did you get ’er phone number?” asked Tubsy, scratching faster.

“Shit no – I forgot.”

“So what happened to you pal?” Sean was desperate to know. “How did you escape?”

“I never found out. Another one came in an’ there was only me ’ead left stickin’ out so she sat on that – then t’ lights went out.”

“Oh god!” The over-excited Tubsy ran to the back of the coach and hid behind the big high seat-backs.

Piccalilli continued, “I don’t remember anythin’ else till bouncer chucked me through window an’ I landed on’t gravel. Me bird found me. She thought I’d been beat up and felt sorry for me till I told ’er what 'appened. Then she twisted me knackers again and packed me in...... Do you understand women, Shagsy?"

"Aye, course I do."

"Then where did I go wrong?"

"You told 'er t' bloody truth, that's where you went wrong. Should of kept yer mouth shut. You'll know next time."

"No next time – never with no more Scuntlepool girls – I'll not be tryin' that again."

"They sound like fun to me." said Stainsy.

"Eh Stainsy – you could soon get to find out – look down there!" Sean pointed to the front of the coach next to the entrance where there was a group of girls trying to open the door. A policeman arrived, and Sean thought he would usher them away from the vehicle, but instead he gesticulated to the driver to open the door, and guided the lasses up the step and inside. Ron Conference, seeing what was happening, rushed from his seat to confront the crowd boarding the coach, but he hadn't heard Piccalilli's assessment of the local female behavioural traits and was unprepared: he was immediately flattened by the stampede of shrieking girls charging along the gangway, searching each pair of seats until they found the object of their desires.

"Sean!" they screamed. "Where's Sean! We want Sean!"

The first girl, tall and broad, but not ugly, vaulted into Sean's arms, knocking him back into his seat. Looking into his eyes she mouthed huskily, "Eh up Shagsy. We've come to see you. Yer mean cool you are." And then his lips were gone, smothered in hers, her tongue-stud clattering against his teeth. The other girls cheered and hollered "My turn! My turn! Gerroff 'im y' tart!" and a couple of them piled in on top, one nibbling his ear, the other trying to insert her hand between the girl on his lap and the tops of his thighs.

At the sight of this, Piccalilli shouted, "See! I bloody told you what they're like. You reckoned you could tek 'em on! Now show us 'ow you 'andle women, eh Shagsy!"

The backdrop of moonies in the street subsided as their owners realised something more interesting was happening on the coach. The traffic started to flow and the coach moved off, but the pyramid of male youth which was forming outside the window where the action was taking place shuffled along at the same speed, trying to get a good view.

Ron Conference dragged himself up from the floor and wobbled unsteadily, trying to sound in charge. “Enough’s enough girls. Come on now. Make your way to the front of the bus.” But the scrum, with Sean at its centre, continued like it had a life of its own, like it was a single orgasmic organism, seeking out pleasure wherever it was to be found.

The big girl’s lips relinquished their suction on him for a second and Sean realised he had to think quickly, because he couldn’t run.

“What’s your name?” he asked her, sounding calm.

“Oh Luv, we ’aven’t got time for names. You can call me Puss-Bear if you want.”

“That’s a right nice name,” said Sean, as if he was leaning on the bar in the pub.

“Oh that aint my name luv,” she said with great feeling, “......that’s what I *do*...... Tell me luv, how well do you play football......” she fondled his chest “......when you’re shagged out?”

“We aint allowed t’ get shagged out before a match!” said the flustered centre-forward.

She smiled and slid her head down between his legs, unzipping his trousers as she went.

Tubsy, who was looking on from behind Sean’s seat, grumbled “Bollocks” and sped off to the back of the bus again. One of the girls who couldn’t get near Sean saw Tubsy go and tumbled after him, bundling him over on the back seat and sitting on his chest. Seeing this, the others decided that they’d make do with the rest of the team, and one by one cornered a player in each seat, yanking down their trousers. Sean was groaning the loudest when a whistle blew at the front of the coach; it was the policeman again. As if it were a pre-arranged signal, all the girls stood up clutching a pair of trousers and trotted off the vehicle, laughing and screaming joyfully as they went, showing the garments off to their friends, waving their trophies in the air like flags and receiving a chorus of whoops and whistles from an adoring crowd.

Ron Conference was beside himself. He stood at the top of the steps at the entrance to the bus and screamed at the policeman "Did you see what they did!" But the copper just waved the driver away, the coach door closed in Ron's face, and the vehicle moved off. He turned to face his dumbstruck team, looking pale in their seats, no longer admiring the welcoming Scuntlepool buttocks outside.

"Christ – we've devoted half a page in the programme for the whole season to *The Rancid Rasher*, the only fast food outlet in Hetherington, to get the money for them suits you were wearing. What am I going to tell the Chairman? We're going to look like a right load of trollocks when we get off the coach. What if the press are there?" Ron looked down the rows of faces. "Are you all right Sean?"

Sean wore a smug expression, with no trace of apprehension like the others. "I'm grand cheers boss!" he said, cheerfully. "How are you?"

"How am I? I'm bloody fine I am. I've just got to think of a way to get us off this coach without anyone seeing us, that's all!" He shook his head at what he considered the stupidity of Sean's question.

"Eh, that's easy, boss," said the chilled-out Sean, "We'll just get kitted up on the coach."

Ron blinked, then his eyes popped and he shouted gleefully, "Brilliant! It's a good job one of us can still think straight!" Then he looked suspiciously at his centre-forward. "How come you can still think straight then Shagsy?"

"It's like I told the others, boss. I understand women. And they understand me."

Ron frowned. "Well you're a bloody miracle then, cos you must be the only bloke on the planet what does......" Ron paused for a while, deep in thought, then continued. "Do as he says then, you lot – get your strip on."

The players hurriedly changed while the coach rumbled along on the last leg of its journey to the opposition's football ground, the aptly named *Cunting Lane Stadium*; well, the first part was aptly named; as a "stadium" it had not a lot going for it. At the entrance to the ground a policeman stuck his head through the door of the coach to verify that it was indeed the visiting team's, then dismounted and gave a thumbs up to his mate guarding the gates. Three tea-ladies lurked suspiciously behind the programme-seller's stall.

"It's chuffin' freezin' boss," said Korma as they clambered down from the coach and waded through the puddles in the car-park.

Between the players and the back entrance to the ground there was an expanse of muddy water which was large enough to be called a pond, and to a child would have qualified as a lake. Seagulls circled and dived overhead pretending to be vultures, waiting for the next person to succumb and fall face down in the murky swamp. The largest seagull had a mean black head and was in charge of diving operations. On spotting Korma testing the water at the near bank, he waggled his wings which was the signal for his squawking cohorts to fall silent and form up into a V formation behind him. Korma wasn't too certain about the depth, and was tentatively edging farther out when Tubsy, only wishing to gain the sanctuary of the dressing room on the far side as quickly as possible, plunged across without hesitation, setting up a bow-wave which lapped over the sides of Korma's boots.

"Bastard!" shouted Korma. Tubsy turned his head and jeered at his team-mate, then continued to surge his way to the far bank and the graffiti-covered green door at the back of the shabby stand which proclaimed, in paint-peeled capital letters, that it was "Erected in 1903".

The seagulls, meanwhile, were not interested in Tubsy's torpedo-like progress; perhaps he was too big, or too fast, or making too much of a splash. Or perhaps they didn't like his colour, for when Korma, started to totter nearer the centre of the pool, their eyes gleamed, their head-feathers rippled, their wings folded back close to their bodies, and they fell from the sky like a volley of arrows falling on the hapless French infantry at Agincourt. The rest of the players were now all wading across, either side of Korma, providing plenty of distraction, but the birds did not deviate. Down on Korma they plunged, just missing him before swooping up again ready for another salvo, making him cover is face for protection while screaming, "Gerroffffff!". He didn't worry any more about getting his feet wet, he flipped and flapped through the water while his team-mates howled with taunts and laughter:

"The birds are *all* gaggin' for it round here!"... "'Cept this lot fancy Korma – they must be desperate."... "They must like curry you mean!"

As Korma ran, he dropped his kit bag which landed with a splumcchhhh in the middle of the huge puddle. The birds landed on the bag and proceeded to peck at it with great vigour, now squawking again and squabbling, trying to push each other off the little island they had found. It took them less than twenty seconds to get their beaks behind the zip and push it far enough to get first one head, then two, then many inside the bag, and suddenly the littlest gull emerged with a foil wrapper which he shook as hard as he could until its contents flung in all directions, being snapped up in mid-air by the hungry birds.

Korma, now safe at the door, turned back and wailed, "Me sandwiches!"

The rest of the team were delighted at the crestfallen Korma's predicament. "Go on my son!" they shouted to the gulls as they carried their prizes high into the air to avoid the mugging attentions of their fellows, some succeeding and managing to gulp down what they had stolen, others being harassed into dropping the contents of their beaks. They returned to the puddle below to see if any crumbs remained. The big, black-headed gull, sat on his kit bag island, the King of the Castle, unhurriedly chomping on a large piece of bread, several gulls around him still probing the depths of the hold-all, checking if there was anything for pudding.

Korma, crying, bemoaned the awfulness of the situation to anyone and everyone as they trudged along the grimy passageway to the visitors' changing room.

"Why *my* sandwiches?" grumbled Korma.. "T'ent fair! My mum makes me them; she'll bloody slaughter me when I get 'ome."

"Oh shtop bloody moanin'," said Splutter, sympathetically.

"It's all right for you – you've got your pack-up," Korma carried on, "Mine'll soon be splattered from a great height on all the windscreens int' car park. Why didn't they pinch anyone else's sandwiches, that's what I wanna know? T'ent fair."

"You're just so attractive to birds!" quipped Dorksy. "They can't leave you alone!"

“What did you ’ave in your sandwiches?” asked Sean.

“Only Tuna.”

“TUNA?”... Sean’s face almost split in two before he started to laugh, while the rest of the team began hooting and jumping around on one leg and slapping the walls with their palms and falling to the ground and waggling their legs in the air like schoolkids who’d just caught a glimpse of the teacher’s knickers as she bent over to pick up the chalk.

From the other end of the passageway, the madcap proceedings were being watched by three tea-ladies.

“Bugger it! muttered Wingnut. “They’ve changed already; they must have found out about our plan! How are we gonna nick their shorts?”

Rustbucket hoisted the hem of his cotton-print pinafore and raked his thigh with his fingernails in a most unladylike manner. “I dunno – but I’ve gotta get out o’ these tights soon – they’re makin’ me legs itch like an Alsatian’s bollocks!”

“Yeah – an’ this soddin’ wig – it’s doin’ my ’ead in!” complained Backdoor while slipping his fingers under his toup’ and scratching like fury. “I wonder if Gary on the telly ’as this trouble?”

“Gary on the telly? His is insured for a million quid, you know. Apparently, none o’ the old grannies fancy ’im when he’s not wearin’ it.” said Wingnut helpfully.

Rustbucket thought for a while, then switched thighs and started attacking the other one. “Do *we* fancy ’im then? You know, Gary on the telly?”

“What?” said Backdoor suspiciously.

“Well, us tea-ladies must get the serious hots for Gary on the telly.”

“There’s nought but them buggerin’ tights makin’ you ’ot!” snapped Wingnut. Now come on lads – er – ladies. Let’s get in their dressin’ room an’ see who wants tea.”

He took hold of the tea trolley, its shiny handle stripped of paint and polished by a succession of chubby fingers and snug-fitting wedding rings, and trundled it towards the visitors’ dressing room. As the ensemble bumped along the rough floor, the large brown-stained silver urn rattled on the tin top of the trolley, the cubes of sugar settled in their white china bowl, the upended cups crashed loudly against their saucers while the milk slopped around in its jug leaving creamy halos up the sides, like the scum round the edge of a bath.

Knock knock. Rustbucket tapped on the dressing-room door. "Tea up!" he trilled, giving his best impression of – well he didn't know really – but it was loud and high-pitched and in his opinion scarcely betrayed any sign of its owner having shaved off a beard that morning.

The door opened and Ron stood there looking pleased. "Grand, ladies, grand!" he welcomed the three effusively. "Just what we need after our journey – you wouldn't believe the things that happened to us on the way to the match! Fair buggered we are – oops – sorry ladies – slip of the tongue."

"We've 'eard worse, 'aven't we Nelly?" warbled Rustbucket, now growing into his part."

Both the others began to speak at the same time, not knowing which of them was supposed to be Nelly, then halted abruptly and, with brightly flushed cheeks, they clumsily and noisily started to assemble cups and saucers from the middle tray of the trolley and filled them with the opaque brown liquid which steamed from the limescale coated tap at the base of the urn.

"So what 'appened then luv?" continued Rustbucket, undaunted.

"First we were attacked on the coach by a gang of teenage girls who pinched all our trousers, so we had to change into our kit. Then, while wading through the deep muddy puddle outside the ground here, we were dive-bombed by a load of seagulls and got soaked and muddy – so now we've got nothing to wear."

"Oh, 'ow terrible – you poor lads," simpered Rustbucket. "Now listen 'ere duck," and he whispered in Ron's ear. "You tell your lads to take a nice shower, give us your socks an' shorts, an' we'll 'ave 'em nice 'n washed 'n laundered 'n dry by kick off."

"Would you?" Ron looked like a saved man.

"Aye course we will duck – you just gather 'em up and leave 'em outside dressin' room door."

Ron turned and surveyed his team who were sitting on the benches around the walls, looking sorry for themselves. "Tea's up lads. When you've got your cuppa, I want you to strip off and get in the shower – OK?"

"I'm not strippin' off till *they've* gone." said Piccalilli, pointing at the guardians of the tea trolley. Like I told yer, ya can't trust Scuntlepool women."

"There's no need to worry about that, duck!" trumpeted Rustbucket, his voice getting higher again, and shriller. "We've seen worse, 'aven't we Nelly?"

The other two frantically nodded and carried on filling cups until they were all brimming with the steaming corrosive brew. "'Elp yerselves to sugar, luvs!"

As his players splashed each other in the bath, Ron grabbed their kit in his arms and, without telling them, piled it in a big heap outside the dressing room door.

2pm on Saturday

As Mr Dugdale drove his beloved Rover 3500 along Quagmire Street and turned into Cunting Lane, he noticed something strange fluttering above the Scuntlepool football ground. At first, from a distance, he thought it was one of those giant long flags which you see towed behind aircraft to advertise a takeaway, or a disco, or a timeshare, but as he got closer he could see gaps between the separate elements and so assumed it must be some bunting which had become detached at one end. Then, and even stranger to his mind, he noticed that the bunting was in Hetherington Sydney colours: blue with red stripes! That's a mighty odd thing, he thought, to fly the opponents' regalia on your flagpole. Finally, on drawing near enough for close inspection, Mr D gasped and started counting: one, two, three, four, five......, fourteen. Fourteen pairs of Hetherington Sydney football shorts fluttering from the flagpole in the briskish breeze. What on earth had Ron been doing this time?

Having negotiated the policeman at the entrance gate, he drew smoothly to a halt in the Directors' car park, he turned the key in the driver's door, then walked through the mud, up the stairs and into the Directors' bar. He quickly located the Scuntlepool Chairman and, before his opposite number could offer a pleasantry or a handshake, demanded an explanation of the trouser-wear situation.

"Why've you got my team's shorts up your flagpole, George?"

Chairman George Bun looked genuinely amazed and he took a good slurp of his drink before replying.

"If you've come 'ere t' talk about shorts, Jack, why not 'ave a gin 'n tonic ol' lad?" He held the shimmering liquid up to the light for Jack's inspection, but Jack seemed not to notice.

"There's a row o' washing hoisted up your flagpole that looks very much like our shorts – and I just want to know what's goin' on! And I'm going to find out!" Jack took George's arm and marched him to the window overlooking the ground.

"You'll not see 'owt from 'ere," George informed him, defensively. "The flagpole's on this stand, above our 'eads!"

Jack released his grip on George and huffed.

"Well you just go an' take a look for y'self while I find my manager!" Jack shouted, and headed off out of the room, down the stairs, along the corridors and passageways, following the smell of sweaty boots, nearer and nearer the changing rooms, until he was outside the door with "Away Team" written on it. He gave a cursory knock and walked straight in. The players were sitting around in groups, playing cards and talking, wearing only towels wrapped around their bodies.

"Where's Ron?" Jack demanded.

"Don't know, Mr D." said Tubsy.

"Where's your kit? Don't you know kick-off's in less than an hour? Are those your shorts flying from that bloody flagpole?"

"Gaffer's pinched our shorts again," said Dorksy. "Says it makes us play better."

"What?" Mr D was feeling overcome. "You can't play a bloody cup match wearin' nowt but yer cack-ends! He can't 'ave pinched yer shorts, can he? And how'd 'e get 'em up that flagpole? This don't make no sense at all to me! Where is the bloody man?"

"He's pinched our socks as well, this time," said Korma, looking under the bench where he had changed. "I know they were all muddy, but they were better than nowt."

“Oh no!” groaned Billy (one of the usually very quiet Bell brothers), and he started rummaging in his bag. “You can’t wear footy boots without socks – they’ll chafe.”

“Aye, like an ’Etherington lass givin’ you a frenchy with her tongue piercin’ in,” mused Tubsy dreamily, his hand under his towel.

The door flung open and Ron bustled in. “I’ve got your socks, lads – look – lovely and dry and laundered.” Then he noticed Jack. “Eh up, Chairman. I thought you’d be in the Directors’ Box chatting up the home-brew – it’s gonna be a crackin’ match eh?”

“Ron, Ron!” Jack excitedly tried to gain his attention, but Ron ignored him while he handed out the socks. Mr D trailed after his manager like a boy trying to ask the teacher if he could go to the toilet. “Ron, Ron, listen – what are our shorts doing up the flag-pole? Can you get ’em down?”

“Get ’em down?” Ron paused, then started to guffaw immensely. “Get’em down? – the bloody shorts? – ha ha ha!..... that’s a cracker.”

“Be serious, Ron. Kick off’s in......” Mr D consulted his watch. “Thirty seven minutes now. The lads seem to think you pinched their shorts on purpose.”

“No – I wouldn’t do that on cup day.” Ron defended himself.

Sean interrupted. “Are you sure it aint another one o’ them *no panties days*, boss?..... I like them, I do.”

“Seeing all them moonies down the ’Igh Street, I reckon the ’ole o’ Scuntlepool’s on a *no panties day*. Bloody ’orrible!” said Stainsy who made a spitting noise to show his disgust.

“Christ, did you see all them arses?” said Nobsy, now discussing the matter as if a study of the subject would lead to a greater social knowledge of the towns of the north of England. “Some of ’em ’ad letters painted on their bums, one on each cheek; did you see that, Dorksy?”

“Aye, I did, but they couldn’t even spell the name o’ their own town: (S|) (L|E) (P|O) (O|L) it said!”

“I shaw that!” spluttered Splutter, quite agitated that he should be first to let the others know. “The one on’t left wi jush the esh: ‘(S|)’ on ’er arsh cheeks – she were a *girl* – I shaw ’er when she turned round!..... It all meksh shensh when you think on’t!..... Think o’ the bit o' the name what wash mishin'! D'you get it now? shCUNTlepool !!! Eh that'sh right crackin' that ish !!!"

"Oh god – so it is!" swooned Piccalilli. "Why did you 'ave to say that? I won't be able to concentrate now. The ball'll come towards me an' all I'll 'ave in me mind's eye'll be this 'orrible...... 'airy......"

"*Pussy*," said Sean, concluding the goalkeeper's train of thought.

"For christ sake!" interrupted Mr D, "This place is a mad-'ouse......" and he frowned. "Ron," he said, finally confronting his manager eye to eye. "I want you to get them shorts from off o' that flagpole now, an' I don't want no excuses, an' I don't want no reasons, an' I don't care if it's *no bloody pants day* either!"

Ron looked surprised at the Chairman's abrasive tone. "There's no need to be like that, Mr D – it's not a *no panties day* today!" he said, soothingly, "It's the second round!"

"So why're our shorts flying above the stadium may I ask?"

"It's simply a laundry matter – they got wet in a puddle when we came in – now they're drying."

"Jack pointed to the dressing room door and left Ron in no doubt as he spoke slowly and meaningfully. "Get Them Down!"

"OK boss – I'll just go and find the three tea-ladies – they're the ones that put them up there," and Ron scampered out.

Jack turned to the players. "And you lot. Stop talking bollocks, get your kit on, and clear your minds for the game. Come quarter to five this afternoon, I want us to be in the third round – and that idiot of a manager of yours'll be down the road come Monday morning if we're not!" Jack left the dressing room.

The players looked at each other.

Saturday, two thirty, half an hour to kick off

Ron made several enquiries as to the whereabouts of the three tea-ladies, but none of the replies had been informative beyond telling him his team were shite and about to get a whipping. With just twenty five minutes to kick off, he managed to find the groundsman who said he'd help him out with access to the base of the flagpole, and would also give him a little coaching on its operation.

"Now listen up," he said as they walked across the pitch to the hoisting shed, boos roaring in Ron's direction from the stands which were already almost full, the tinny sound of *We Are the Champions* grinding out of the speakers, as it always does at football grounds on cup days. "When you unsheath the 'alyard from the cleat, you must keep a tight rein," the old groundsman stressed the words, "Or in this wind 'ole bloody lot'll pull through from top, an' rope'll get stuck so fast round bottom pulley it'll look like a lap dancer's gusset."

"Right," said Ron, sensing his instructor was a bit of a flagpole aficionado.

"You'll see from sign on't door that 'oisting shed's an 'ard-'at area – we come under European Law in 'ere y' know."

Ron plonked the bright yellow plastic hard-hat on his head and felt it squash the tops of his ears flat. The two men crawled into the diminutive shack which served as a shelter at the base of the flagpole, but the planks of wood from which it was made were so loosely nailed that it felt just as draughty inside as it did on the pitch.

"Right," pronounced the groundsman. "Ready away with the cleat, then tek one side of 'alyard an' pull to see if flag goes up or down. You look through that 'ole up there." And he pointed to a gap in the apex of the lean-to through which, with a bit of bodily contortion, Ron could just about see the row of shorts flapping sixty feet above them.

Ron uncoiled the doubled string from the metal thing which he assumed must be the cleat, pulled on one side and noted to his satisfaction that the precious washing was descending. Cheers erupted around the ground as he started pulling more vigorously in order to retrieve the prized underwear and return it to its owners. All was going well, when the groundsman shouted in his ear "Not too fast – there's a knot what's comin' down in a sec, an' it shakes flag as it negotiates pulley!" But Ron panicked and pulled even faster. There was some resistance as the knot wedged in the pulley channel, the rope stretched like a spring, then *caboosh* it suddenly freed and the stored energy in the string made the whole lot bounce up and down. "Ahh!" Ron screamed, his eyes gazing through the observation hole for any sign of disaster, even though there was nothing he could do. He was so relieved to see there was no damage, he gave a hearty pull on the string to complete the job. To the accompaniment of even louder cheering from the crowd, he pulled four or five times until he felt resistance again, then took a look and was quite startled to see that the shorts had gone back up to the top of the flagpole. Ron said, “Oh no!” with such feeling that the groundsman looked up at the proceedings through the hole and uttered, with some relish, “You’ve ’ad it now. Y’ must’ve got the strings muddled up an’ pulled t’ wrong one. ’Alf of em’s wrapped round t’pulley at top o’ pole!”

“What do I do?” asked the white-faced Ron, his voice barely a whisper, as if more volume might aggravate the situation.

The groundsman leant over into a very dark corner of the shed, fiddled around on the floor, then produced two nasty looking things like giant sandals with a huge metal spike on each one.

“You’ll ’ave t’ use these!” he announced jovially. “Climbin’ Irons… They clamp on y’ shoes an’ give you amazin’ grip. Post office use ’em for climbin’ telegraph poles.” You’ll be all right wi’ these on.”

Ron looked at the instruments quizzically. “All right where?” he asked, sounding terrified.

“All right oop there o’ course!” and the groundsman pointed his finger to the top of the pole.

“All right bollocks!” shouted Ron. Craning his neck to look up at the pole he tentatively pulled on each string in turn, sorting out which was which. He then lowered away as smoothly as he could, all the way to the ground, dashed outside, gathered up the garments and, heart in mouth, he counted...... One, two, three, four, five, six, seven, eight, nine...... ten.

Ten. Bollocks, he thought. That meant there were four pairs missing. He looked up the white-painted pole and saw its finial pointing to the heavens, but that was all. Ron tried to concentrate: the subs won’t need shorts – they’ll be wearing tracksuit bottoms. That means we only need eleven pairs. But, hang on, Piccalilli can keep his track suit on in goal, so we’ve got enough. Ten pairs – just enough. Ron whooped and ran across the pitch to jeers and chants and laughter, clutching the bundle of cloth in his arms. The groundsman shouted after him “You ’aven’t re-cleated!” but his cries were lost in the wind which was whipping up quite a storm now.

Ron fled to the dressing room – it was now quarter to three – and announced the new garment arrangements to his players, but they were more interested in finding out why he was wearing a hard hat.

In the confusion of trying to get changed in time for the kick off, Sean ended up with Piccalilli's shorts, which would have been OK except that goalkeepers are very large, and Sean was lean and lithe and supple with narrow hips and a cute bum which Angela had a picture of on her bedroom wall. The most valuable player on the pitch that afternoon was in need of a safety pin. But would it affect the outcome of the match?

Four minutes to kick off

Starting in the middle of the stand opposite the tunnel a huge cheer burnt its way around the ground, rushing to the end terraces and back down the other side, each voice exploding in turn as if set off by a fast fizzing fuse, signalling the arrival of the two teams as they ran onto the pitch.

The tinny music reached a new magnitude of distortion as the boy in charge of the sound system turned it louder instead of softer while the announcer read out the teams, so nobody could hear.

The club mascot who headed the home team out onto the field was about six years old and small for his age, his shorts flapping around his knees, his shirt-cuff-covered hands clutching a ball which seemed bigger than him, so he had to peer over it.

A chant of "Come on you Scu-unts" struck up on the terraces, masking the weaker and altogether more feeble cry of "Up the Whippets" which could only be heard during pauses between home supporters' choruses.

The two teams kicked a couple of balls about in their own halves and the tinny music got even more excitable – the speakers rattling on their fastenings as if trying to shake themselves free from their torment. The mascot had his photo taken with the two captains. The referee waited patiently while the seagulls took up their viewing positions on the roof of the stand; the mean one with the black head perched directly above Ron Accrington's commentary box. Sean ran to meet the ball, keeping one hand on the waistband of his shorts.

The referee blew his whistle and beckoned the captains to decide who would call the toss: Dorksy said heads, the coin hit the ground and it was tails. The home captain chose to stay at the same ends, Hetherington Sidney would kick off. The referee blew his whistle again, Shagsy flicked the ball to Freddy Bell who passed back to Splutter and the game was underway. Korma looked up at the roof of the stand nervously, but consoled himself that the feathered members of the audience were more interested in squabbling amongst themselves for the best perch than in who had the ball. Nonetheless, he checked to make sure he had no fish sandwiches in his pockets.

"Team in red and blue-oo, team in red and blue. You're a load of poo-oo, you're a load of poo," cried the unified voices of the home crowd.

"Up the Whippets. Up the Whippets." The small band of Hetherington Sidney supporters held steadfastly to their original game plan, refusing to be swayed by abuse.

"Bollocks!" screeched Ron to Phil his sponge man, and his three substitutes, the five of them being the entire complement of the Hetherington Sidney dugout. "Look at that! Shagsy can't run in them shorts! We're knackered!"

"That we are," agreed Phil, checking the temperature of his bucket with his sponge man's thermometer. *Bloody freezing: just right*, he thought, removing his two numbed fingers from the icy water. "You could bring 'im off and I could stuff some of me sponges in his waistband – magic thing is a sponge you know – can fix anything on a footy player with one o' these." And he lovingly held up the dirty yellow object and gave it a squeeze.

But Ron wasn't looking. He was up on his feet, his hands on his head as a roar filled the stadium while the ball grazed the post and went out. Ron turned back to the bench and shouted, "They almost scored then!" before turning back to the pitch and lambasting the defenders. "Don't give 'em room to shoot!" he ordered to all of them in general before trying to attract the attention of his large centre-back. "Tubsy! Don't get dragged out of bloody position!" But Tubsy didn't hear him so he tried to get the message through via one of the other players who was near at hand. "Here, Stainsy – tell Tubsy not to get dragged over to the touchline – right?"

Piccalilli's goal kick restarted the game. Korma collected it on the left, ran past one defender, cut inside another and centred the ball to

Sean who got four strides towards it before his shorts fell down to his ankles and he fell over.

"Penalty!" screamed the away supporters, even though no one had been near him when he tripped.

"Waahhaaaaaaayyyy!" laughed the Scuntlepool fans.

"Bollocks!" muttered Ron. "He would have scored there for sure!"

"Heh love – we can see why you go out with 'im now!" screamed Dorksy's wife Karen to Fiona as they sat with the other players' wives and girlfriends in the stand.

Angela waved and cheered with her mates, but secretly felt so sorry for Sean, laid in the mud with nothing for protection. Now he'd need a shower before the second half.

Mr Dugdale up in the Directors' box turned a shade of embarrassed vermillion as those around him guffawed heartily and exercised their humour on the hapless Hetherington Sidney Chairman. "There's an 'aberdasher's shop round the corner – why don't you nip out an' buy some elastic, eh Jack?" "Aye – 'ave you got your sewing kit with you, Jack?" "Per'aps 'is centre-forward's shorts are made like that a'purpose to try an' put off the opposition!" "Aye! Or so they're nice an' roomy to smuggle more fags back from Cally on the booze-cruise!" After a minute or so Jack stood up. "Excuse me, gentlemen," he said, and left the box with his peers' jibes following him out of the door. Mr D had decided he needed to see Ron before the half-time cuppa.

The lasses in the crowd had enjoyed Sean's ticklish situation, and now sang their own song dedicated specially to him. As Mr D negotiated the gangway down to the touchline, he could hear nothing except the massed female choir roaring "Shagsy, Shagsy, show us yer bum...... Show us yer bum...... Show us yer bum...... Shagsy, Shagsy, show us yer bum...... And your bollocks too......"

Sean had hastily dragged his shorts back up and tottered around looking most uncomfortable, unable to chase any of the play.

The Chairman invaded Ron's dugout. "What the bloody hell's goin' on on that pitch?" he demanded.

As he spoke the crowd roared and the Scuntlepool players all piled on top of one another, hugging and kissing and tickling each other on the thighs.

Ron didn't know what to say in reply to the question, but seeing his boss's demeanour he knew he must at least try. "Looks like they've scored," he observed in soft tones. "I told Dorksy and Gherkin to mark-up. I'll give 'em a rollocking at half-time."

"One-nil, one-nil, one-nil, one-nil......" jeered the home fans, as Ron's Chairman sat down on the bench in disbelief, his anger now subsumed by anguish. He turned to Ron again and asked, without malice, "What are we goin' to do, Ron? We'll be out o' the cup if Sean keeps fallin' over. What are we goin' to do?"

"UP THE SCUNTS UP THE SCUNTS UP THE SCUNTS," proclaimed the cheering crowd in staccato quick-time, while Ron furrowed his brow and stared hard, right past his Chairman, and saw Ron Cliché in the next dugout embracing his Physio. This annoyed him, but then he became distracted by something golden glinting beneath his Chairman's ample stomach. Ron impertinently pulled aside the front of his boss's jacket to reveal a pair of braces, an article of clothing which had never before appealed to his taste, but at that moment seemed heaven-sent.

Jack looked down at his stomach, then looked at Ron.

"Not my Caravan Club braces," he stammered, but he knew that any excuse he made for keeping them would be futile.

Ron jumped up excitedly. "Get Shagsy to come over to the bench!" he boomed at anyone who happened to be listening. Freddy Bell gave his manager the thumbs up and chased off to where Sean was rooted to a spot ten yards outside the opponents' penalty area, hoping for a pass or rebound that he didn't have to run for.

"Eh up Shagsy. Gaffer wants a word wi' ya," said Freddy.

"If 'e thinks 'e's gonna give me a rollockin' for not scorin' then 'e can bollocks!" said Sean angrily, "An' I'll tell 'im so!" Sean was unimpressed as he jogged to the touchline, holding tightly onto his waistband, the sight of which caused the higher voices in the packed terraces to resume chanting "Shagsy, Shagsy, show us yer bum......" As Sean gesticulated to the linesman to show that he was leaving the field temporarily, Ron was up on his feet proffering the Chairman's braces. The Chairman himself remained seated in the dugout, rearranging his trousers, choosing not to watch the handover of his cherished elasticated suspenders.

"Grand, boss!" Sean beamed at them with glee. "Can you 'elp us get 'em on an' adjusted?" He reached out and took them from Ron, which meant of course that his shorts fell down again. The girls who were all singing now shrieked in ecstasy which gave the away fans the chance to get in a couple of verses of "Up the Whippets! Up the Whippets!" to which the home crowd quickly replied "Get 'em down, Whippet out! Get 'em down, Whippet out!" while Sean scrabbled around his ankles to retrieve Piccalilli's pants. On the pitch, Scuntlepool almost scored again as Sean's antics in front of the dugout provided an unmissable distraction for about half the players on each side, but luckily Piccalilli was watching the ball and tipped it over his bar for a corner. Ron signalled furiously at the referee to show that Sean was ready to come back on the pitch, but Scuntlepool took the kick quickly and Piccalilli had to save another one which was headed down just inside his right post. He clung on with his fingertips, the ball exactly on the centre of the line. Wingnut rushed forward and kicked it into the net from under the goalkeeper's hand and the crowd went wild again, but the referee blew his whistle and pointed to Piccalilli's still outstretched arm to signify the place where a foul had occurred. In an instant the cheers turned to boos as the home fans realised the injustice of the situation. Piccalilli calmly retrieved the ball, placing it on the goal line ready to take the free kick while Sean regained the field, the referee acknowledging his presence. The centre-forward ran to the centre circle, swerving and feinting, testing the holding-up properties of his shorts and their ancillary equipment. The referee blew his whistle; Piccalilli restarted the game – the ball was won in the air by Nobsy who laid it off to Stainsy on the right, gave a first time cross-field pass to Korma on the left who ran down the wing as before and crossed for Shagsy. Sean ran from the edge of the box, went to head the ball and missed, falling flat on his front in the area, just where the goalkeepers had churned the pitch to mud.

"My braces!" groaned Mr D who was still sitting on the bench. "Look what 'e's done to my braces! They'll not be the same again you know and I've 'ad 'em for forty years!"

Ron didn't care about his employer's braces. "Come on Shagsy!" he shouted from the touchline, to the annoyance of the linesman who gesticulated with his flag for the manager to sit back down. "Wake up will ya!" Ron continued undeterred. "You should've scored you toss-pot!"

The linesman came over to him. "You'll be made to sit up in the stand if you don't behave – now get back on your bench – you know you're not allowed to coach from the touchline.

Ron smiled at the official and made his way back to the dugout, ducking beneath the little shelter it provided from the rain which had now started to leak out of the murky sky in a monotonous drizzle. His Chairman sat sour-faced next to him, a tear in the corner of each eye. "Buck up, chief," said Ron jollily. "We'll be in the draw for the next round – you'll see!" and, in a matey manner, Ron jabbed Jack in the ribs with his elbow. Jack smiled a feeble smile and rubbed his side. He looked down and thought how bereft his trousers looked without support. He looked on the pitch and saw Sean's mud coated chest. He listened to the crowd who were singing "One-nil" again. He was depressed. He was having a bad day. It couldn't get any worse, so he decided to enjoy it.

"You're right, Ron!" he beamed at his manager. "We'll bloody do 'em second 'alf – an' I'll pay for all the drinks after!"

Ron looked at the Chairman, buoyed by his change of attitude, but worried by his last remark – had the old man finally flipped his loaf?

Every time Sean got the ball, Angela screamed and waved her scarf like fury, while Fiona sipped her gin and tonic straight from the thermos flask, glasses not being allowed in the stand. Sean twisted and turned in front of goal but was always tightly marked by the defenders, and only managed to slice a couple of snap-shots wide, the rest rebounding off legs and knees and bodies.

The referee blew two long loud peeps on his whistle and they trooped off for half-time. The music started again while some of the crowd filtered into a queue around the burger bar – voted second greasiest chips and stalest bun in a nationwide telephone poll only the previous fortnight – but it tasted grand when you'd been standing in the drips and drizzle for forty five minutes or more.

Quarter to four

"Right. Gather round you lot...... What was that fucking shite I just watched? And I had the Chairman sitting next to me on the bench! Do you think I'm going to get a new contract or a pay rise watching that crap? No, I don't think he'd even lend me the spit to lick a stamp after that bloody shambles. And you didn't remember about the team in white, did you? Where was Clarke, where was Lorimer? Back home on the bloody video, that's where *they* were. You've about as much resemblance to the team in white as my backside has with, with......" Ron frantically looked around the dressing room to see something which didn't look like his arse. The door opened and a trolley clanked in "......those three tea-ladies!" Ron announced triumphantly and the team all looked round to see what had appeared.

"Them three's got to be closest lookin' things to your arse in 'ere, gaffer," observed Tubsy. "Them's all 'airy an' all!"

"Sssssshhh," Ron hissed, holding his finger up to his lips. "We'll not be uncouth in front of the ladies.

"Come an' get it ducks," squawked Rustbucket as they started filling cups with the foul brew. Rustbucket left the other two ladies to carry on and came over to have a quiet word with Ron. "We noticed that one o' your lads was 'avin' trouble with 'is shorts, luv," whispered the cotton smock and apron clad defender. "We wondered if you wanted us to sew a new elastic in the waistband before the second half?"

Ron hesitated. "Well, I don't know – I had a lotta trouble getting those shorts back after you'd washed them – I couldn't find you anywhere – I had to get the groundsman to help – and we lost four pairs getting them down off the flagpole."

"Don't you worry duck," Rustbucket sounded very calming. "We won't need to dry them this time – just a little bit of sewing – nothing to worry about. What do you say luv?"

Ron was still unsure. "Well, those shorts he's wearing are actually the goalkeeper's – so you'd better ask him – they are his shorts so he'd better decide."

Rustbucket looked around until he spotted Piccalilli – then started to approach him. Piccalilli saw what he thought was a tea-lady, a

Scuntlepool tea-lady, homing in towards him. Terror gripped him! He panicked, screamed, leapt over the bench and the tea-trolley and bolted out of the door. Rustbucket didn't know quite what to do now. In his haste to get to the seat of Sean's problem he decided to approach the star player directly, but forgot to adopt his pretend voice.

Gruffly he said, "Would you like us to......" Suddenly he realised his mistake and finished his question in a really high voice, "sew up your shorts duck?" But Sean reached out and wrenched the wig straight off Rustbucket's head.

"You're not a bloody tea-lady at all!" he shouted. The other two with the tea trolley realised they were exposed. They fled from the dressing room, pulling the trolley across the doorway as they went, leaving the poor Rustbucket trapped and alone.

The Hetherington Sidney team made quick work of tying him up and suspending him by his ankles from one of the roof-beams. Then they wheeled the tea trolley until it was directly beneath him and removed the lid of the urn, so if he did manage to get free, he'd have no choice but to drop head-first into the vile liquid. This meant he'd have to wait quite a while for the tea to cool sufficiently not to scald him, before he could get down.

"Right," said Ron, looking at his watch, "Time for the second half," and they filed out of the room. Ron looked back with satisfaction at the dangling imposter, switched out the lights and closed the door. "Now remember," he ordered his players as they walked down the corridor leading to the tunnel, "You *are* the team in white!"

The second half

Ron Cliché assumed his position on the Scuntlepool bench ready to watch the second half, but immediately Backdoor and Wingnut came running over to him.

"Boss! Rustbucket's not on the pitch – he's been captured!" Wingnut jabbered in panic. "Shall we go an' find 'im?"

"No. Like I always say, football's a game of two halves. We'll just send on one o' the subs – go and tell the ref."

The two players looked at each other and shrugged, whereupon they heard the referee's whistle blow and knew it was too late to get the sub on for the kick off.

Backdoor and Wingnut ran back onto the pitch to join the game.

"Go on, get forward!" screamed Ron Conference from the away team dugout, wildly flapping his arms, knowing that the others were down to ten men. "Get forward! Go on Shagsy – get the ball, get the chuffing ball! That's it Tubsy – hoof it up field. Go on Sean. Go on my son...... Did you see that!"

Sean was upended by a wild tackle and the referee brandished his yellow card. This gave the Scuntlepool substitute the chance to take the field and Hetherington Sidney's personnel advantage had gone, but they still had a free kick thirty yards out and just to the left of centre. Sean writhed on the floor in agony and Phil rushed on to the pitch carrying his bucket. The sight of the freezing sponge made Sean leap to his feet, trying at all costs to avoid Phil's version of first aid. Feeling cheated, Phil splashed some water in the general direction of Sean's ankle anyway, then trudged off back to his seat on the bench, looking forward to getting a proper injury – nice bit of blood, perhaps, or a protruding bone splinter, something to get stretchered off about.

Sean went inside the area, Korma whipped in the free kick just out of the goalie's reach and, with his left foot high in the air, level with his head, Sean lashed it in on the volley.

Ron jumped up and down, screaming his delight, while the players all piled on top of Sean. The referee wrote down the goal in his notebook, then looked at Sean's back to get the number of the goalscorer. The majority of the ground was hushed, but the away supporters were singing "Up the Whippets" in their loftiest voices. The referee spoke to Sean, shook his head, then ordered a goal kick. The crowd suddenly went wild when they realised the goal had been disallowed – but what for? Sean came running across to the bench.

"What the buggery's going on?" roared Ron, looking like he was about to have a seizure.

"Ref won't give goal – says 'e can't read the number on me shirt cos o' them braces – they cover it up!"

"He can't disallow a goal for braces, for buggeration's sake. What is there in the rules about that?"

“I asked ’im that. Says ’e can do what ’e chuffin’ well likes.” Sean looked downcast. “I suppose we just weren’t meant to get through t’ third round, were we boss.”

Ron knew it was now time for action and not remorse. “Look, son, we’ll turn yer braces round – then they’ll cross over at the front and the back’ll be clear for the ref to see the number. Quick – come here.”

Ron made the adjustments while he carried on talking. “Now you must really show ’em. Make your anger count. Hit ’em where it hurts – in their area. Tell Tubsy and Dorksy to get that ball out as fast as they can into the opposition’s half. If Splutter or Gherkin gets it, tell ’em to run at them and put a cross in – I don’t mind if it goes wrong so long as you keep doing it – bound to get a good one in eventually, and I want you and Freddy and Billy to be on the end of it, all three of you. Drag the markers away if you can, get Billy to make diagonal runs away from goal to pull ’em out wide. And remember – *Lorimer* – you’re Lorimer and don’t ever forget it. Now get back on that pitch – good lad!”

He patted Sean on the shoulder after his pep talk and sent him back into the fray, then resumed his place in the dugout next to the Chairman, who had decided he liked being near the action. Mr Dugdale was joining in with the shouting and groaning that you have to do on the bench when his enjoyment was interrupted by his mobile phone ringing. He had a brief conversation, then switched it off and leant across to talk into Ron’s ear.

“That were the Chairman o’ Twigley’s ’Omes. He’s upset – says ’e can’t read the sponsor’s name on the front o’ Sean’s shirt now you’ve turned ’is braces round – an’ Sean is the one what everyone looks at.”

Ron turned in disbelief. “You’re fuckin’ joking! Do you mean he can’t wear his braces? Do you mean that the boss of Twigley’s Homes would rather we lost the game than cover up his name for half an hour? Do you mean he wouldn’t rather have his name appearing in the third round?”

“I don’t know. I think I’ll ring him back and explain.”

Just then, a shot by Freddy Bell was blocked by one of the Scuntlepool defenders. The rebound ballooned into the Hetherington half where Wingnut clipped it out wide right, Fergal O’Fishvan crossed it into the centre and Dorksy, in his rush to get back to his defensive position in front of goal, crashed into the ball and scored a great own-goal with a deflection off his left knee past his own keeper. The crowd went berserk and the chant was "Two-nil, two-nil, two-nil, two-nil......"

Ron buried his face in his hands. Fiona, feeling a little tipsy by now, had been fed up for some time with the Scuntlepool fan in front of her who kept shouting that Sean was a wanker, and she smashed her thermos over his head. This seemed to do the trick, as he no longer kept jumping up and obscuring her view; in fact, he lay quite still, slumped on the concrete terrace – his mates not noticing he had gone silent or, more likely, he just didn't have any mates. Angela and her friends were sobbing openly, their red and blue face-paint carried along in little streams by the tears rolling down their cheeks. The announcer busily announced that the goal had been scored by Sammy Capri, a Scuntlepool player, even though Dorksy was lying face down in the mud, unmoving, wishing he were dead. His team-mates patted him on the shoulder where he lay, offering words of encouragement. On the bench it was Jack's turn to motivate his manager. He put his arm around Ron. "Come on son, we can still do it. Sean can keep the braces!"

The Hetherington team continued for the rest of the second half to battle away on the claggy pitch, but only ten minutes were left and Ron was starting to believe it was all over. The crowd certainly did, singing and cheering as their side coasted to a comfortable victory by a two-goal margin.

With nine minutes to go, Sean got the ball on the halfway line and ran diagonally towards the right side of the opponents' penalty area. The defender marking him had got slightly caught out, and was behind Sean. He could see that if Sean made it into the area he might play a telling ball, so he grabbed Sean's shirt to hold him back but missed and instead got a handful of Mr D's braces. The defender fell over behind Sean still clutching the strap. It expanded and stretched as Sean continued running like he was on the end of an extendable dog-lead, until the strain was too great and the fastening gave way at the front of Sean's shorts. The elastic pinged backwards towards the Scuntlepool defender lying on the ground.

Just as Sean's equipment gave way, he hurdled a tackle coming in from another defender on his left. The braces, still attached to the rear of his shorts, exerted their full force downwards and, in a fraction of a second, the article of clothing zoomed down Sean's legs and completely off without him even breaking his stride. Suddenly he felt free, everything was easy, needing no thought. His training earlier that week clicked into place and he had only the goalkeeper to beat. He shaped to go one way, shimmied the other, then cut back again. Sean didn't bother to shoot – he just dribbled the ball into the net and carried on running straight into the mesh, grabbing it with two hands and pressing his face into the weave so his flesh protruded in squares. The referee blew his whistle and pointed to the centre circle – the goal would stand. Where in the seats and terraces around the ground there had been noise and expectation and a chorus of whistles, now there was hush. Where there had been quiet amid tears, now there was renewed hope and a lusty rendition of "Up the Whippets!"

After due adulation from his fellows, Sean went to retrieve his shorts and braces from their resting place in the brown ooze and tufts of grass which constituted an English December football pitch. Jack watched in horror from the sidelines as Sean held up the tattered remnants of his cherished braces: the dull broken muddy clasps clamped nothing but compressed topsoil between their plastic teeth. Sean studied them briefly, then tossed the whole lot, shorts and all, into the back of the goal where they were off the pitch, and ran to take his place in the centre of the field. The referee didn't seem to notice and blew for the restart, while the girls in the crowd shrieked their approval.

As had occurred in practice on a day that now seemed long ago, on a little training ground beside a stream in a town called Hetherington, Sean was transformed. He picked up the ball on the halfway line, beat three tackles and lobbed the keeper for the second. Then he completely silenced the home crowd by completing his hat-trick, rasping the ball in from an impossible angle ten yards to the right of the goal and almost on the bye-line.

He stood at the edge of the pitch with arms outstretched, facing Fiona up in the stand, while she blew kisses down to him.

As they stood clapping and cheering, Karen shouted in Fiona's ear, "I wonder what cream you'll need to remove the grit from under his foreskin?" Fiona laughed and the little band of away supporters sang

"Three-two, three-two, three-two, three-two......", mindful of the hateful looks surrounding them from across the dividing wire fences.

Two minutes of injury time saw both Rons leaping off their benches, hollering orders from the touchline and quickly retreating before they got caught by the referee or linesman. Back on the bench, they alternately clutched at their remaining hair and consulted their watches, Ron Conference's timepiece proceeding at a sluggish pace, each second lasting minutes, while it appeared to Ron Cliché that the hands on his chronometer would get a speeding ticket if they went any faster. Stuff Einstein; this was relativity in action.

The Scuntlepool team, with nothing to lose, had all their players bar the keeper camped in the Hetherington half, whilst the team who were in the lead tried to blockade the entire width of goalmouth with their eleven men. But you know how difficult it is to block all approaches, seal all the gaps – for example, in ice hockey the goal-minder is actually bigger than the goal, but they still manage to score! And so it was on a muddy day in drizzly Scuntlepool that a shot from edge of the area hit one of the massed defenders on the ear, took a slight deflection, hit the bottom of the bar and flashed down to the ground before bouncing into Piccalilli's sodden gloves. But had it crossed the line?

Every Scuntlepool player on the pitch's arm was held aloft as the home side claimed the goal, and the away team waited with dread for the referee either to blow his whistle and ruin their day, or to hold is arms wide and wave play on. But how could he do either? It was the ninety second minute of a cup-tie; the ball had ricocheted fast and low, briefly obscured behind the row of players just in front the of the goal line. If the referee got this wrong, the bullshitting male pundits on the telly later that night (whose only important decisions in life were whether to back Blue Blancmange in the 2:15 and whether to have a wank now under the TV desk or wait till they went home) would be merciless, heartless, vindictive. The poor old referee ran across to the touchline to consult his linesman, a swarm of anxious players following behind him like a band of nagging mother-in-laws.

For the first time in the game, the seagulls on the roof of the stand stopped bickering and showed an interest in proceedings: because the Scuntlepool half was entirely empty of people, the flock began to swoop down one by one and forage for worms beneath the churned turf, oblivious of the life-changing decision that was about to be made.

Fiona held her hands to her head.

Angela couldn't bear to look.

Sean felt a bit vulnerable with his dick hanging out, now that there was no play going on to distract attention, so he sat down in the centre circle while Piccalilli, in his goal-mouth and still holding the ball, ran over to Sean.

"Did you see if it crossed the line?" the referee asked the linesman.

"I reckon it did," replied the stern-faced flag carrier.

The referee blew his whistle, pointing and running to the centre circle. The crowd went berserk – there would be extra time!

The Scuntlepool players, all of whom apart from their goalkeeper had surrounded the linesman, celebrated off the pitch with their supporters. Piccalilli placed the ball on the centre-spot. The ref joined them and blew the whistle again. Piccalilli looked at Sean; he looked at Piccalilli – it was worth a try, wasn't it? The striker stepped back so he was behind the ball when Piccalilli tapped it forward. Sean ran onto it, then seagulls scattered in all directions as he drifted effortlessly across the thirty yards of empty space to the opposing goalkeeper who shouted vainly in protest before rushing off his line. Sean trapped the ball, waited for the keeper to slide in, then flicked it over the lunging body and into the open goal.

The celebratory tune of the home crowd instantly changed to cries of "Cheat! Cheat!" while Sean turned to look for the referee, who blew his whistle and pointed to the centre circle again. But was it for the Scuntlepool goal? Or had he allowed this one? Three-all or four-three? Ron Conference didn't know whether to pace up and down the touchline, or scream, or jump in the air as confusion engulfed the little football match that was nearing its conclusion that day. The referee took his watch from his pocket, stared for a couple of seconds, then blew his whistle two long blasts *peep peeeep* to show the end of normal time had been reached. Most of the home side's players hadn't realised what had happened – they were still congratulating each other behind the Hetherington goal when Sean had chipped the goalie for his fourth. The two sets of players and both managers now converged on the referee, and he whistled furiously to try and keep them back as they demanded to know the score.

"The match is over!" he cried, "There's no extra time!" This was the signal for Ron Conference and the Hetherington players to punch the air and fall about on the ground, playing with each other like joyful fox cubs. It also sparked a pitch invasion from the home fans' favourite end as the Scuntlepool players held the referee captive in the centre of an ever-tightening ring of angry flesh. The police started to rush from the stands and onto the pitch, forcing their way inside the cordon of threatening players to escort the referee back to his dressing room.

Jack Dugdale ran from the bench, his arms held wide, his hands open, ready to embrace Ron, forgetting his earlier magnanimity had cost him the support he valued most. He reached the touchline just before his trousers parted company with his corpulent waist, rucked around his knees and took him face-first to the ground better than any rugby tackle. Ron came over to him, dragged his boss's muddy face from the soily tangle of matty grass, and planted a great big smacker on his nose.

"We're in the bogging third round!" he bawled, right in Jack's ear, "The third bogging round!" and Ron hugged the clay-caked countenance to his chest.

The seagulls looked down on the frantic floodlit scenes below and, realising there would be a little wait before supper, amused themselves by pecking each other.

Sunday morning

SWING-FREE SEAN SENDS SCUNTS SCURRYING

Jack spoke the headline on the back of the Sunday paper out loud, even though he was the only one at the breakfast table. "What a bloody 'eadline!" He grinned as he spoke, then continued to read:

BUT MATCH ENDS IN CONTROVERSEY AS ANGRY CROWD INVADES PITCH.

The referee had to be given a police escort from the Scuntlepool ground at the end of yesterday's cup-tie after his decision to award a controversial goal, scored in the last minute of injury time by Hetherington Sidney's star striker Sean Shagdit, gave the away side victory by four goals to three.

Only moments before, the home side had been congratulating each other on their equaliser which had itself been the subject of a debate as to whether or not it had crossed the goal line. The Scuntlepool team thought it had, so they surrounded the referee and followed him off the field while he went to consult his assistant near the corner flag. The two officials gave the goal which was the signal for Scuntlepool celebrations to begin, extra time now being inevitable, but the referee immediately ran towards the centre circle and blew for the restart. The home players were still rejoicing off the field when, amazingly, young Shagdit and the Hetherington goalkeeper, Steve Piccalilli, found themselves alone with the ball in the centre circle. Piccalilli, tapped the ball to Shagdit from the kick off and left the striker with only the Scuntlepool keeper to beat, which he did with ease, chipping over the flailing body from twenty five yards as the goalie made a despairing dive at his feet.

Despite the opponents' protestations, the goal was allowed to stand, which prompted a pitch invasion by home fans, and fourteen arrests were made. A police spokesman said that the incident was managed very professionally by his officers, as they had been well prepared for minor trouble of this sort.

This is crackin' stuff, Jack thought to himself as he read on, relishing the story of the team's suits and shorts and the part his own braces had to play in the almost surreal events which had unfolded only the day before. *Could it have been a dream?* Not judging by the sad remains of the tattered Caravan Club trouser-holders which Jack held in his hands. But he'd see soon enough – that afternoon in fact when the draw was made for the third round. And it was worth it; what was the value of some sentimental elastic compared with going in the hat with the best football clubs in the land?

The newspaper report continued:

"*After the game, Scuntlepool Chairman George Bun was fuming at the result. 'Their last goal, if you can call it that, was an outrage. I've never seen anything like that before. We deserve a replay at the very least – we shall be appealing to the FA on Monday morning.' The referee said he could not comment on the game as to do so would be against FA rules. The Football Association themselves said they had received no formal request for an inquiry into the match and they would not be commenting further until after they had seen the referee's report.*"

Jack smiled. He imagined his old adversary George Bun smarting at the perceived injustice and, full of rancour, demanding that the wrong be righted. Jack closed his eyes and savoured the thought – it gave him huge pleasure. There was no way the FA would overturn the result – no breach of rules had been committed – the referee made his decision on the day. To set aside that decision would signal an end to the authority of every referee in the country.

"Jack."

He awoke with a jump as his wife called to him from the hallway.

"Jack – the BBC are on the phone – they want to know if Sean can go down to London this afternoon for the draw for the third round – they want to interview him."

"Aye," said Jack, almost in a dream, then he repeated, louder, "Aye, course 'e can!"

Sunday – 5pm

The TV picture shows Gary at the third round draw.

"You join us here at FA Headquarters where it's very nearly time to make the draw for the third round of this year's Football Association Challenge Cup, the point at which all the smaller clubs who've fought so bravely to get this far in the competition have their chance to be paired with the country's top teams for a January adventure that, win or lose, will never be forgotten. But before we actually make the draw, we've just time to talk to a few players from those clubs in the lower divisions, clubs like non-league Graffiti Town who've already knocked out two league sides and now wait to see if they can land a Premiership team like Jam United or Snotterham Tosspurt. So, if we can start with Neil Fourit who's scored in every round so far for Graffiti Town, what are your hopes for the draw?"

"Well Gary, I just hope we get a Premier team – that's the main thing."

"Because you want to test yourself against the best players in the country?"

"No, cos all the tickets are worth a lot more when we flog 'em on the black market."

"I see. Now, quickly moving on, let's get a word with someone from another non-league side, the Borington Chiphole goalkeeper, Ted 'Catseyes' Corunna. Who do you hope to get in the draw?"

"Well Gary, I'd really like a tie against me old club, Cheesily. Hopefully we'll stick one up 'em, cos they've got a load o' poofs playin' for 'em now."

"I see. And our final word before we start the draw will be with Sean Shagdit from Hetherington Sidney, and also with the stunningly scrumptious and stunning Fiona Opiumden who hasn't been out of the papers for the last six months, and I really fancy her. So Fiona, who do you hope for in the draw?"

"You of course, Gary."

"Really?"

"Of course."

"What, more than Jam U?"

"What could Jam U do for me, Gary?"

"Oh god – me microphone's got all sweaty. That's enough chat then – let's immediately hand over to the FA Chief Executive Alan Twatters and the two legends who will be withdrawing their balls from his little sack, Sir Bobby and Sir Jackie."

The TV screen is filled with the lugubrious figure of the FA Chief Executive.

"Ladies and gentlemen," he delivered his address in a monotone which presented a perfect contrast to the excitement of the situation. "We will now commence the draw for the third round of the FA Challenge Cup. The Home teams will be drawn by Sir Bobby, the away teams by Sir Jackie. So, if you would draw the first team please Bobby."

Sir Bobby shuffles the balls around, withdraws one and peers at it and tells the watching millions the number inscribed thereon.

"Number 7."

Alan studies his list and announces the home side.

"Number 7 is Blackbush Rovers."

Sir Jackie tries his luck at catching a small spherical object, then he too informs the world of those important digits.

"Number 82."

Alan flicks a page, searches the lower reaches of his list, and the very first tie of the third round is defined.

"Number 82 is Rogerham. Blackbush Rovers will play Rogerham."

"Number 60."

"Number 60 is Swithenscrote."

"Number 2."

"Number 2 is Anusoil. Swithenscrote will play Anusoil."

"Number 13."

"Number 13 is Cheesily."

"Number 9."

"Number 9 is......" *Alan raises his eyebrows and pauses to boost the suspense.* "......Borington Chiphole. Cheesily will play Borington Chiphole."

Cheers and applause as the camera cuts to "Catseyes" Corunna making an obscene gesture with his elbow and a pretend bottom.

"Number 1."

"Number 1 is Anton Gorilla."

"Number 53."

"Number 53 is Scrubberland. Anton Gorilla will play Scrubberland."

"Number 29."

"Number 29 is Lesstalent City."

"Number 35."

"Number 35 is Notclassy United. Lesstalent City will play Notclassy United."

"Number 81."

"Number 81 is Waste Sperm."

"Number 30."

"Number 30 is Lickyourpool. Waste Sperm will play Lickyourpool."

"Number 58."

"Number 58 is Snotterham Tosspurt."

"Number 32."

"Number 32 is Middleocre. Snotterham Tosspurt will play Middleocre."

"Number 23."

"Number 23 is ...... Hetherington Sidney."

"Number 25."

"Number 25 is .... Jam United. Hetherington Sidney will play Jam United."

Camera cuts to Sean and Fiona leaping from their seats, Sean picking her up and spinning her round in his arms, then to Gary's cheesy grin.

Ten past five

Back in Hetherington, the players and staff were excitedly gathered around the TV in the club bar when the suspenseful silence was terminated by mass jubilation.

Great bloody hairy bollocks – we've got Jam U at 'ome, we've got Jam U at bleedin' 'ome!" the Chairman boomed as he leapt in the air.

Jack launched himself into his manager's unsuspecting arms which supported him for a second before allowing him to crash to the floor, but Mr D was back on his feet without pause and engaging in another leap, this time onto Splutter's back from where he shouted at the dancing Smoggrate, "Get them bloody tickets on sale tomorrow, Stan!" The room housed an uproar of raucous bodies and rapidly deafening ears as the orgy of disbelieving excitement accelerated into frenzied pseudo love making such as is rarely seen outside of a Rugby Club Annual Dinner Dance. Tubsy even did one of his best and noisiest farts, but its rasp was insufficient to rise above the cacophony and therefore gave no warning of its potency, celebration quickly turning to protest as a large clearing formed around its erstwhile owner.

"Dirty bastard!" they all roared, but Tubsy defended himself.

"It weren't my fault – a bit of celebratory buttock clench and involuntary sphincter relaxation were to blame for that one!"

"Look you bastard!" Dorksy pointed to a tiny figure flopped between a chair and one of the bar tables. "You've gassed our Angela!" He went over to her and picked her up like a feather resting across his arms.

"It weren't me honest!" complained Tubsy, sounding flustered. I wouldn't 'urt our Angela – you know I wouldn't, don't you lads?"

"Ssssh, Ssssssssssh!" shouted Ron, "Gary's interviewing Sean!"

On hearing Sean's name mentioned Angela jerked her body rigid and sat straight up in Dorksy's arms.

"Sean?" she enquired, weakly. "Oh, where is Sean?"

"He's on the telly for goodness sake," said Ron while at the same time flailing is hands behind him to try and hush the noise. "Now sit down and listen to Gary."

"So...... Jam United in the third round at Sidney Park...... How do you fancy that then Sean?"

"Well Gary, it's every team's dream in't it?"

"And you'll have a bit of a chance too, won't you? A lot of teams have struggled on your ground, what with the massive slope."

"Aye. A lot of players 'ave trouble climbin' out o' the away dressin' room, but we provide ropes an' stuff now. After this match, you never know, we might 'ave enough cash to shore up foundations."

"And then there's the builders' trench by the corner flag with the cones round it – I'm told a player fell down that a couple of weeks ago."

"Aye, it's ever since the French bought the Pennine Water Board. They fixed the leak but discovered a snail colony around the pipes so now they're minin' them. Boss took 'em to court to get hole filled in but they counter-sued for crush injuries to livestock every time ball went in there, so now it's got a red an' white striped tent over top."

"I suppose it's the same for both sides though, so it is *fair. Now, Fiona, what do you think about the draw – it seems you've got Jam U instead of me after all."*

"It's fantastic Gary – I can't wait to see Sean play against them – I think they'll be quite surprised by his pace – I know I certainly was."

"Oh really? Perhaps you should explain."

"I think I'll leave it to your imagination thanks Gary. I hear you were quite fast in your day too."

"Where did you hear that? I wasn't fast, just always in the right place for a tap-in."

"Yes – I've heard that too!"

Gary, smirking to camera: "I think we'd better leave it there before the producer pulls the plug on the programme. Now back to Mark in the studio to give his thoughts on the draw."

"Well Gary, you're right about the hole – I can see that causing a few problems from set-pieces, and the dressing room cup of tea's gonna be a no no at 'alf time – it'll be over the rim and slopping in the saucer. But it's always the team from the higher division that's more nervous visiting a lower division club – they've got everything to lose – should be a cracker and we're all really looking forward to it.

"Now, Cheesily / Borington Chiphole – that's a mouth-watering prospect too......I hope I'm not boring anybody. I'm not boring anybody am I...... I don't think I am......I'm not a boring person most of the time......

The door of the club bar crashed open, cutting Mark off in full flow, and in walked the stern figure of Mr Stanley Dovehawk.

"Great news about the draw – I heard it on the radio as I drove in." He looked at all the curious faces staring backwards at him from their chairs in front of the TV, none of them but Smoggrate and Angela having a clue who he was."

"Mr Dovehawk," began Smoggrate, "It's very nice of you to drop in and offer us your congratulations – this is indeed a great day for the club, and for all the people of 'Etherington."

Dovehawk did not react to Smoggrate's greeting. During the long pause before he spoke, his bearing, if anything, became more uncongenial.

"As you quite rightly say, today is a great day for the people of Hetherington. But tomorrow will be a bad day for the people of Hetherington. For tomorrow, Mr Stanley Dovehawk will find out who is to replace him as parliamentary candidate for the constituency of Hetherington North, or to be more exact, which woman will replace him. And do you think that the new candidate will be interested in football? Will she have heard of Hetherington Sidney Football Club? Will she even, inconceivable as it may sound, have heard of Jam United?"

Dovehawk surveyed the scene before continuing, the faces still uncomprehending.

"As you sit here, on the finest day this club has seen in many a decade, it is unfortunate, most unfortunate, that I have to come and announce that there is a traitor, possibly traitors, in your midst."

Dovehawk stared at Smoggrate, making him squirm again, just like the first time they had met.

"I must state," gulped Smoggrate in an attempt at ingratiating himself, "that I have played no part in precipitating your apparent current difficulty."

"Ahhhhhhhhhhhhh," Dovehawk drew out the sound in a quiet but telling way. "Someone defending themselves before they have been accused. Most suspicious."

Smoggrate's mouth opened, but then he decided to close it again in case he buried himself still deeper in the mire. Instead, Jack spoke.

"I don't think it's right that you should barge into this club making allegations. I must ask you to leave...... And in any case, I think the time is ripe that we had a woman as our MP – as you yourself explained to the club Secretary – things move on, things change, nothing stays the same – we can't live in the past!" Jack could not hide a smile as he delivered the final words, but was surprised and slightly disconcerted when Dovehawk smiled too.

Dovehawk walked over to him and held out his hand, which Jack stood up to shake.

"I don't believe I've had the pleasure," smarmed Dovehawk in a buttery voice. "I assume you must be the club Chairman Mr Dugdale."

“Aye, that I am.” said Jack, put on the defensive by Dovehawk’s sudden charm.

Dovehawk continued, “You’ll be pleased to know that I’m leaving now, so you won’t have to throw me out. But just remember, although this is the day you drew Jam United in the cup, it is also the day you met Mr Stanley Dovehawk.” Stan never withdrew his steely stare burning into Jack’s eyes, even for a moment to blink. “And traitors have to watch over their shoulder...... day and night......”

Dovehawk turned and walked out of the room, the players and staff watching in silence the departure of the wounded man.

“He bloody threatened me – did you ’ear that?” stormed Jack. “Who does he think ’e is?”

Smoggrate concurred. “Aye. And it sounds like after tomorrow e’s goin’ to be even less than ’e thinks ’e is now!”

Monday morning, 10 o’clock

Dovehawk walked into 29 Cokedealer Street in a perfectly furious pique. Catching sight of Gerald leaning down talking to Margaret, the lady on the reception desk, Dovehawk snorted, “Is she here yet?”

Gerald tilted his head to look at Dovehawk and silently groaned. Then he stood up to reply.

“Er, yes, she is. I’ll introduce you.”

Gerald started to move towards the door at the back of the entrance lobby but Dovehawk halted him.

“Hang on, Gerald. I need a word with you first. We’ll go to my office.”

Gerald looked forlornly at Dovehawk as he braced himself to announce the next piece of news.

“We’ll find another room. You see, Adelina is waiting to meet you in your office – I thought that would be easier – she needed a bit of privacy to prepare herself.”

“Prepare herself! In my bloody office! What’s she doing then? She can’t get a bloody shower in there you know!” Dovehawk approached Gerald menacingly. “Or is she just going through my drawers?”

"Oh no, Stan, I'm sure she won't be doing that." Gerald reassured him.

"And why not? They're a meddlesome lot on the women's committee – they'll do anything for inside information: it's an aid to emasculation – I should bloody know!"

Gerald waited for the tirade to finish and then matter-of-factly stated, "She can't be going through your drawers because an old door resting on two piles of magazines doesn't have any." He looked at Dovehawk in the hope he wouldn't blow, before continuing, calmly, "That's all I meant."

Dovehawk growled a little, but managed to hold himself together.

"Come on Gerald, *drawers* are a metaphor! The point is, you've left her in my office the same as you did that blasted Pree woman. And she went through my metaphorical drawers like a piss-run down the inside of your leg when you forgot to shake it! Come on – I need a word – where can we go?"

"It's busy here. The only place that might be free is the loo."

"That'll do. I can think more clearly in those surroundings anyway. And I need a piss."

The pair headed off to the back of the house. Gerald saw the door to the toilet ajar and pushed it open.

"We're alright – it's vacant. Do you want to go in first? First one in gets to sit down."

"You can sit, Gerald. I prefer to stand when I'm thinking."

Gerald lowered the seat and took his place, while Dovehawk squeezed in behind. With not much room to spare, he trod on Gerald's toes while trying to make enough space for the door to swing, finally managing to get it closed. Dovehawk then slid the latch across with a clonk. Gerald frowned.

"Do you think we should be locked in here? Politicians have come to grief doing this you know."

Dovehawk smiled.

"Don't worry. I'm gay now. It's part of my strategy."

"You're gay now, and I'm not to worry! Well cheers, Stan." And Gerald folded his arms and crossed his legs. "What would you like to talk about then? Now we're cosy like."

"That's a daft question, Gerald. I should have thought it was obvious. We've got to work out what we're going to do."

"About what, Stan?"

"Are you deliberately being obstructive? Or do you only behave like this in toilets? Is the smell of bleach affecting your neural pathways?"

"I'm not trying to annoy you Stan, honest. I don't understand what you mean when you say *we*, as in, what are *we* going to do?"

"All right. A bit slowly for the hard of understanding then. What are *we*, that's you and me, going to do to make sure *I*, that's me, don't get de-selected by the bitches at HQ? Is that simple enough?"

"Perfectly. Now I can answer your question." Gerald looked pale and his voice quivered, "But you're not going to like the answer."

"Come on Gerald – you don't need to be shy of old Stan do you? We've been working together for six months now in the constituency, and I've only shouted at you a couple of times."

Gerald grinned. "A couple of times a day, aye!"

"So what's the problem then?"

"The problem is, I have to remain impartial. I'm the Party Agent for whomever is the appointed candidate for this ward – and I can't be seen to be supporting you to the detriment of another, even if she has been bounced on us at the eleventh hour."

"But that's the point isn't it, Gerald. By changing horses at the last minute they jeopardise the whole operation, make the Party, and me, look stupid. To switch candidates now would be farcical in the eyes of the press and the public!"

"I agree with you that far, and I have raised that very issue – I sent a letter, an e-mail, and phoned HQ to put my opposition to the possibility of a change on record. But, if the decision is made that there is to be another selection, despite my opposition to the process, I still cannot back one candidate. Let's face it, if Adelina wins, I'm out on the stump campaigning for her. She mustn't be of the opinion that I'm disloyal."

"Well I think that's exactly what you are!" Dovehawk blustered and fumed. "I can't believe I'm having this conversation. I thought we were a winning team you and me, Gerald, trusting each other's judgement, but coming to the other's aid should ever a gaffe be uttered." For the first time that Gerald had ever known, Dovehawk looked glum. "Judas," he muttered quietly but with consummate feeling.

Gerald felt very uncomfortable. "I'm sorry, Stan." he grovelled. "We are a good team. And when you overcome this little difficulty we still will be. But that's the bottom line. You have to win this one without me."

Dovehawk looked down at the bespectacled figure, all the more pathetic for being atop his porcelain perch.

"I can't believe I ever needed you from the start, Gerald. You do nothing but irritate me, like having a worm up the bum. When I triumph, I shall have a new agent. I shall have Angela Twogood – for what you're paid she'd be more than willing to walk round a few housing estates talking to punters. I shall cite *irreconcilable differences* as the reason for our separation. Now if you wouldn't mind leaving, I need a piss." And Stan proceeded to undo his fly.

Gerald hurriedly stood up and squeezed past the large volume in front of him. Grappling with the latch he heard the loud torrent of pent up urine striking the reservoir in the bowl. He slipped through the most minimal amount of doorway required for his exit and fled back to the reception desk in the front room, only to be confronted with the sight of Adelina standing chatting with Margaret.

"Hello Gerald," Adelina spoke in her lovely smooth West Indian tones. "I got tired waiting in that room all on my own. Has Mr Dovehawk arrived yet do you know?"

Her face and voice conveyed both passion and understanding, even when speaking on the most mundane matters. Gerald was convinced, even though they had only just met, that no one could ever be angry or sharp with Adelina as she seemed such an easy target that her castigator would immediately be filled with regret at having mistreated her. He hoped above hope that Dovehawk would feel the same way! On the other hand, Gerald was puzzled how someone like

Adelina could have become a politician. He suspected that her willingness to listen and self-effacement must conceal a strong protective barrier beneath, or she would have been swept aside by all the maniacal egos surrounding her. He felt himself secretly hoping Dovehawk might lose the forthcoming contest. A pertinent thought, as Stan's overbearing form chose to appear in the room at that moment, still zipping its trousers.

"Yes, he is here now Adelina," blurted the panicky Gerald in a belated reply to her question. "In fact," he said, turning, "This is him." And he stood aside and cast his arm in the direction of the post-ablutive neo-poofter.

"Stanley Dovehawk," Gerald announced, "This is Adelina Omov, your fellow selectionee and Chair of the Housing Committee on Bent Council."

After a very slight pause during which her large eyes sparkled wider and more endearingly, Adelina spoke.

"Hello Mr Dovehawk. I've been lookin' forward very much to meetin' you."

Dovehawk seemed unusually unable to find his voice. Gerald wished he would say or do something, just to remove the nervousness from the situation. But still Stan stood there, not even making the usual loud purr from his over-enthusiastic olfactory passages. The sounds of his breathing, Gerald noted as he strained to hear, were more like little whimpers, as a dog makes while awaiting the arrival from its owner's hand of a much longed-for biscuit. Gerald couldn't take the suspense, and so tried to encourage communication. *Bloody hell*, he thought: *it's like two tribes making contact in the Amazon for the first time*.

"Stan." He sounded the name brightly. "Adelina said hello to you. Would you like to say hello back?"

Gerald watched as Stan did nothing. Didn't move, didn't speak, didn't blink, didn't snort like he always snorted, didn't even remove his hand from his fly. Just stood there, staring at his adversary like a museum mummy-case staring at the visitors. Gerald, most embarrassed, looked at Adelina, expecting to see her discomfiture at the course which her first meeting with Mr S Dovehawk was taking. But he was amazed to see her eyes filled with sympathy and compassion as, without theatre, she opened her arms, crossed the no-man's-land between them and embraced the normally recalcitrant politician.

"It's all right my darlin' man." She spoke warmly past his ear, her head resting on his shoulder. "I know I can be a bit of a surprise for people; not quite what they expect." She then drew her head back and looked straight into his eyes. "But we'll get on fine, you and me. If you show me where is the nicest pub near here, I'll take you for a beer at lunchtime."

Gerald's stomach was in knots, still not knowing what would happen, as Adelina turned towards him.

"Mr Dovehawk is a bit shocked at the moment, so I'll go out for a while and do a bit of shoppin', if that's all right wid you, Gerald."

"Er, yes. Yes, Adelina, that's a good idea. I'll have a word with him while you're gone and maybe you two can have a chat later."

"Yes, down the pub. Men work better down the pub. I'll see you later then, Stan." She held his shoulders in her hands and stepped back to arm's length, looking at his face.

Then, surprisingly, Stan calmly uttered, "You're beautiful."

Adelina beamed at him, as the mouth on his expressionless face continued, "But that wasn't a chat-up line............ you've nothing to fear from me............ I'm gay."

Gerald was gobsmacked.

Adelina laughed, leaned forward and pecked Stan on the cheek and said, "That's good, cos I'm pretty gay myself." With which she turned around and stylishly floated across the floor, out of the front door and into the street, her long red coat brushing her body in all the right places as she went. In the room which she left behind, it was as if the lights went out and the heating turned off. Gerald noted that Stan was now purring and snorting once more, his hands clenching, his brow furrowing. Harsh reality had returned. He was going to blow.

"Gerald!" he stormed. "I want a word with you!"

"OK Stan. The toilet's still free I think."

Stan grabbed the poor Gerald by his jacket collar and manhandled him to the staircase.

"We'll use *my* office. The toilet stinks of piss."

They entered the room and were immediately assailed by a glorious smell, faintly lingering now, intimating greater strength earlier, but present nonetheless as a reminder of a pleasant memory. They both sniffed deeply, before each of them realised what the other was doing. After exchanging knowing looks, Dovehawk slumped down in his chair and cried despairingly.

"How can they do this to me, Gerald? I thought they'd send me a fully paid-up lesbo in dungarees with an ear-to-ear-beard and her nose chained to her dick. They can't do this to me! – she's gorgeous!"

"It's all true. Your office has never smelt so appetising. I only left her up here for half an hour. Her perfume, so piquant, like freesias in a vase on a sunny Spring morning when, in the shafts of light shining through the panes, you can see the dust hanging in the air, held aloft by the scent from the flowers." Gerald sat in the visitor's chair and closed his eyes, his head laid back against the cushion."

"What are you drivelling on about?"

"I don't want to be a politician's hack any more."

"What?"

"I want to write poetry. I've never written poetry. Couldn't string the words together without it sounding like: *at this moment in time, we are in negotiations over job demarkation lines and the erosion of differentials*. It's not really up to: *shall I compare thee to a summer's chuffin' day*, is it?"

Dovehawk looked at the reclined Gerald.

"This is bloody December, the only flowers are down the cemetery, I've got an opponent for my constituency who I can't be nasty to, and you're getting on my tit. Does your wife know about your fantasies, Gerald?"

"What fantasies?"

"Your desires, Gerald. Your delusions about poetry, your misplaced loyalties, and your infatuation with black female politicians who look like models and make you feel all warm inside when they speak. I think perhaps I should let her know a few truths about you."

"You're a heartless man, Stan."

"I prefer *ruthless* to *heartless*, but I suppose it's close enough. I am a politician, when all's said and done."

Dovehawk looked sharp again, the memory of Adelina fading fast as he tried to concentrate on the imminent threat to his position.

"Right then, Gerald. What's the procedure from here? Who's on the selection panel? How is the candidate selected?"

"Well. On Wednesday night there's an extraordinary meeting of constituency Labour Party members. The two candidates will each address the floor for a maximum of ten minutes, putting their case for selection, then there is half an hour for questions to the candidates, then there is a secret ballot of all the members present and the winner is announced. The decision is notified to Labour Party Headquarters, and the National Executive Committee can either accept or overturn the result."

"So if she wins the ballot here, I'm out for sure. And if *I* win, she can still get the nomination anyway if the result is overturned."

"That's right. But imposing a candidate is a serious matter. Pants have ended up down, if you get my drift, around ankles, so to speak, when the NEC has tried to impose candidates in the past. The local members don't like it."

"So you think that if I win the local ballot, there's a good chance the result'll stick?"

"It depends on how much Pree Puckering wants to chance her arm. It'll be a finely-balanced decision for her. She could be one of the ones who loses her pants."

"She bloody well will if she sits in my office uninvited again! She needs a bloody good seeing to!"

"So you've often said. But you're gay now, remember?"

"Only in public. I can still be straight in private. That reminds me, I'll need a DVD player and projecting TV at the meeting on Wednesday – I've got a video to show."

"A video of what?"

"Me and my boyfriend Marlon, on the job of course!"

"Are you sure this is the right strategy, Stan? Have you thought this through? Are you positive it won't backfire on you?"

"Course I have! Adelina is a woman, and she's black, right? So a white middle-class (but from a working-class background) male with a super-finely-honed libido is going to get de-selected before you can say 'Bent Council'. But if that super-finely-honed libido just happens to prefer other men, I don't see how they can further disenfranchise an under-represented section of the population."

"Everyone knows you, Stan. Especially all your ex-girlfriends. You'll never pull it off!"

"You just watch the pissing video, Gerald!"

Monday, just after 1 o'clock

The lunchtime crowd in the *Mole-strangler's Arms* were a noisy bunch, but they all went quiet when Dovehawk walked in with Adelina by his side. Stan was taken aback, because usually when he walked into his local there was the odd greeting of 'Eh up Stan' and they carried on talking and laughing as normal. Where he would often have to stand behind several people at the bar, waiting to get served, today a clear pathway opened in front of him, straight to the landlord waiting to take his order. And still there was hush. Stan went to the bar and started to go for his wallet, but Adelina stopped him.

"No, I told you, I'll buy these, Stan." She then addressed the landlord. "Two pints of bitter please, and whatever Stan's having as well."

And with that comment, the lounge bar burst into laughter and a loud voice, young and boisterous proclaimed, "You jammy bastard, Stan. 'Ow do you do it? Not only the most gorgeous lass outside o' 'ollywood, but she's buyin' you a pint an' all!"

Stan smiled bravely as he took his beer, and he and Adelina headed off in search of a secluded corner. The place was almost full, and they stood next to the giant fireplace, wood fire blazing nicely, next to some lunchers in suits who had their backs to them.

"So you're gay then, are you Stan?" asked Adelina with her gentle way of eliciting sensitive information.

Stan harrumphed a bit and then proceeded brazenly. "Aye, I'm gay as they come, me."

"That's funny," Adelina continued, probing, "Because I can usually tell a gay man." She took a sip of her beer before resuming. "But that's the beauty of this world, isn't it Stan: we're all different, special in our own ways – and God created you a very special person I think."

"Oh? In what way?" While he was asking this, Stan realised that everything Adelina said, whilst sweet and charming, was also disarming, as if designed to make him drop his guard.

"I have this feeling that you were placed in this world to give pleasure, Stan. Your care for others shines from every pore. I think the people of this town are very lucky to have you as their parliamentary candidate."

He couldn't believe what he was hearing.

"But they won't have me for much longer, will they. I mean, that's what you're here for – to take it off me. Right?"

Adelina smiled one of her smiles again.

"Why would I want to do that? No. The reason I am here is merely to give a choice of candidate. I'm not here to take it off you. If I were living here, I would definitely vote for you, Stan."

"What?"

"You are a lovely man." She tied to explain, but didn't realise she had reduced Stan to a gibbering pulp by complimenting him once more. "It's just a question of procedure the reason I am here. If they had had a proper selection process the first time around, there would not be any need for all of this. Your re-selection is a formality."

"But, but...... does that mean we need to bother with the vote on Wednesday at all then?"

"Oh Stan, that's the crucial part. We must have the vote so that people cannot accuse us of being undemocratic."

"But if we have a vote, you'll win! You're bound to win – I mean – you're bloody lovely – I'll probably vote for you meself!"

"Oh you are very kind, Stan. You see? I told you that you were put on this Earth to give pleasure. And you didn't really believe me when I said it. Come on, tell the truth, you didn't, did you?"

Stan responded coyly. "Well no, not really I didn't – I mean – I know I'm likeable, but I thought you were maybe laying it on a bit thick."

Adelina smiled, then downed her pint in one.

"You can buy me another one now, if you like."

Stan grinned, then downed the remains of his own.

"Aye, I bloody do like!" he bawled. "I bloody like beer, I like you, I like the world, and just for today I even like poxy Hetherington complete with that prat Gerald. He threw his arms around Adelina, gave her a hug that exhausted all the wind from her lungs, then headed off back to the bar, singing as he went. His mobile phone then rang and he was still singing when he answered it.

"Stan-ley Du-uv-hawk," he trilled into the mouthpiece.

"Hi, it's Fiona sweetie – you sound amazing – wish I was on what you're on. Listen – something amazing's happened – have you heard the news? It's only just been announced."

"News about what?"

"About the football – it's Jam U – they've announced they're pulling out of the FA Cup – said it was to help diplomatic relations for England's next bid for the World Cup – anyway – get this – they're entering the World FC Championship instead."

"What, you mean the World Football Club Championship?"

"No Stan luvvy – much more exciting than that – it's the World *Furry Cup* Championship – you know: *tongues* – it's held in Brazil – very popular over there apparently – well it would be wouldn't it – makes me go all squidgy thinking about it – anyway – me and Tamara are thinking of going – isn't it exciting?"

"You want to watch?"

"No we want to be in it – apparently girls can volunteer to join in – more the merrier – just think of all those scrummy South American footballers – yum – I hope they shave off their stubble first though…"

"So what happens to Hetherington Sidney in the cup?"

"Are, well that's the bum bit – Sean's terribly upset – Scuntlepool complained about the last goal on Saturday, so it looks like they'll just play that match again – poor boy – I think it's knocked a few million off his transfer fee."

"Christ – what a turnabout. Anyway, Fiona love, I needed to talk to you. This meeting I've got for my re-selection – it's on Wednesday – could you get that DVD whatsit thing copied onto a video for me – Gerald's a bit low-tech."

"Of course, sweetie. Sean'll be drowning his sorrows tonight. Fancy coming round?"

"You bet, love – I'll tell you all about what's happened today. The woman they've put up against me as prospective candidate – she's so understanding – she makes the world seem a better place. I 'aven't got a chance."

"Oh – you'll sort something out, Stan. You're a survivor, a shape-shifter, a chameleon; and they've got long tongues as well...... Did you want a temporary job as head coach at Jam U? You need to be able to speak in several different tongues!"

"Go on, get you off into that shower, or bath of ass's milk, or whatever you have, and I'll be there at the usual time."

Stan switched off his phone.

"Two more pints, please Doug."

Monday, just after 1 o'clock

The phone rang on Smoggrate's desk. He was adding figures in his head and tried to proceed, ignoring the interruption, but the persistence of the noise gradually broke his concentration as one by one the numbers fell into an irrational heap on the floor of his skull. Oh dammit! Now he was annoyed. Had he not instructed Angela that he wasn't to be disturbed? He picked up the phone.

"What is it, girl?"

Angela sounded flustered. "I know you're busy Mr Smoggrate, but the press keep ringin' up, and they're all outside the ground, too. Something terrible's 'appened!"

"God, no. Not Jack, surely? Not 'is 'eart? It must've been the excitement o' gettin' Jam United in the third round."

Angela carried on as if she hadn't heard him. "There won't be no Jam U in the third round, Mr Smoggrate. That's what the press are sayin'. Jam U 'ave pulled out o' the cup...... Hello. Hello Mr Smoggrate. Are you still there?"

"Aye Angela. Aye, I'm still 'ere. Well lass, there must be some mistake. I think someone's 'avin' you on."

"No, it's true – it's not just one – they're all sayin' it – I've 'ad ten national newspapers on the phone in the last twenty minutes – I knew you didn't want to be disturbed – but I 'ad to tell someone – oh dear – Mr D'll 'ave an 'eart attack!"

"Quite so, Angela, Quite so – I think I might be 'avin one meself. What are the symptoms?"

"Er, tight pain across the chest. Numbness an' pins n' needles down one arm, difficulty breathin', vision of room closin' in around you......"

"Aye, I've got all them all right. Look, don't worry Angela – I'm sure this can be sorted out – it's got to be a joke – just come in 'ere a sec love an' we'll think on what to do next."

"OK Mr Smoggrate."

The phone went click and the door separating the two offices immediately opened.

"Oh Mr Smoggrate," sobbed Angela. "What will we do?"

Smoggrate held out his arms and she ran into his embrace, soaking his collar with free-flowing tears.

"Eh lass. It's all right. It's only football, you know. No one's died."

Angela still sobbed. "What about Mr D? He might die. It's just so unfair."

Then she raised her head, renewed shock apparent all over her face. "Who'll tell 'im? This lot might be camped round 'is caravan site!" She pointed out of the window, and Smoggrate saw a dozen people next to the entrance to the ground, all talking on mobile phones.

“If they get to ’im first, it’ll be worse. And I didn’t tell ’im – oh no......” and she broke down weeping again. “I’ve probably killed ’im Mr Smoggrate!” she wailed, and collapsed again, Smoggrate’s other shoulder getting a soaking.

Trouble was, he thought he could do with a good cry himself, but his rôle as provider of support to the frail little body convulsing in his arms not only prevented him showing his grief: it also impelled him to take on the dreadful responsibility of informing the Chairman of this most unforeseen and wretched circumstance. While he paused for thought, he gradually became aware of the two phones in Angela’s office, ringing constantly, and they made him realise the hopelessness of the situation: it was impossible to tell Jack first – they would already have got to him. Oh well. Nothing could be done. Poor Jack. But, Smoggrate considered, it was no worse for him than it was for the fans, or the players, or for himself. He looked down. Or for little Angela. Yes, it was just as bad for everyone.

Angela sat up, looking a bit incongruous perched on the normally unapproachable Smoggrate’s lap.

“Right,” she said, “I’ve cried enough now.”

She stood up, adjusted her skirt and almost wiped her eyes with her hand, just stopping herself when she realised she had better use a tissue.

“Go and tidy yourself up,” said Smoggrate. “Put your lovely face back on, an’ your lovely smile, then we’ll go down an’ meet ’em. We’ll face the world, together, and we won’t let it bloody well beat us!”

He winked at Angela, and she smiled back at him through lips and runny cheeked mascara and eyes that were pink pools.

Monday, just after 1 o’clock

“Hello, caravan sales,” said Jack as he picked up the phone in his office at the caravan site.

“Are you Jack Dugdale, Chairman of Hetherington Sidney Football Club?”

“No. I’m Jack Dugdale in charge of caravan sales at Carefree Caravans. Which model were you interested in?”

“Hello Jack, this is Bobby Spark – remember me? – I write the *Talking Balls* column in *The Fun.* I wanted to know your comments about Jam United pulling out of the cup.”

“My comments are, if you don’t want to buy a caravan you can shove off!” And Jack slammed the phone down, only for it to ring again almost immediately.

“Hello, caravan sales,” he said, exhibiting a slight exasperation that might have spoilt that all-important first contact, should the caller have been a prospective customer.

“Hello Jack,” smarmed the gravelly too-many-fags-a-day voice at the other end. “Bill Norris here. So what do you reckon to this caper with Jam U, eh?”

“Look Bill. I don’t know nowt about it. An’ I’m trying to sell some caravans. You’ll ’ave to contact the club!” And again Jack put down the receiver, only to have it ring straight back at him again.

God, he thought, it’s *not* a hoax. He reached in his jacket pocket and switched on his mobile, and that also immediately began to ring.

What’s goin’ on? he wondered. ’As the ’ole world an’ ’is dog got nothin’ better to do than ring up caravan sales? He waited till the mobile took a message, then quickly he pressed the button to dial out and he rang the club, but only got the engaged signal. There was a crunch of tyres on the gravel outside his office. He looked out and saw the driver get out and saunter up to the door. It was Fred Bighill, the sports reporter on the local paper, the Hetherington Gazette. As Fred walked into Jack’s office, another car drew up outside, this time with two occupants, one with a load of camera equipment.

“Quick!” shouted Fred. “Lock t’bloody door and let’s ’ide somewhere! Whole o’ Fleet Street’s gonna be ’ere in a minute!”

Jack did as Fred ordered, just beating the latest arrivals to the door.

“Mr Dugdale!” the first one shouted through the letterbox. “Can we just talk to you for a couple of minutes? It won’t take long!”

Jack ignored them and joined Fred in the little kitchen round the back. He pulled all the curtains closed.

“So, is it true then? Jam U ’ave pulled out o’ cup?” Jack sounded like he didn’t want to hear the answer.

“Aye, Jack. But it weren’t really their fault. They were forced into doin’ it by the Sports Minister. Soon as he ’eard that the ’ole o’ FIFA’d bin invited to the Championship in Brazil, an’ that they were all goin’, ’e said that it were vital that the top English team attend too, to show our commitment to ’ostin World Cup. Fait accomplis – nowt they could do about it – a political decision.”

“To attend what? The World Football Club Championship or sommat?”

“No Jack, not the World *Football Club* Championship – FIFA turned that down in favour of the World *Furry Cup* Championship – it’s a crackin’ event so I’m told. All us football writers’ve already booked our plane tickets.”

“But that means there’s no Jam U for us int’ third round. They can’t leave us ’igh an’ dry can they Fred?”

“Look ont’ bright side, Jack. You’ll probably get a bye straight through t’ fourth round, that’s if Scuntlepool lose their appeal – and they certainly should do. If they don’t then worst that could ’appen is a replay at Sidney Park.”

“But I don’t want a bloody replay, or a bye t’ fourth round,” Jack wailed. “I wanna play Jam United int’ third round.” He shook his head. “We shall ’ave to fight this, Fred.”

“In that case, you’ll need support of our local MP. Like I said, it were a political decision, so you’ll need someone on the inside, someone who knows the rules and ’ow t’ get round ’em.” Fred looked thoughtful. “Shame we aint got a local MP at the moment. By-election’s not till after third round is it?”

Fred looked at Jack for a reply, but he was just staring straight ahead into space.

“DOVEHAWK” Jack mouthed the name slowly and resignedly.

“Aye. Mr Dovehawk – ’e’s the one you want to talk to,” said Fred, “’Ave you met ’im?”

“Briefly. I met ’im for the first time yesterday, just briefly.”

“Aye. Well you’ll ’ave to ask for ’is ’elp. I’m sure ’e won’t mind – give ’im a local issue to get ’is teeth into – something to get ’im int’ papers – they like bein’ int’ papers.”

"I don't think there's much chance o' gettin' Dovehawk's 'elp. You see, 'e blames me for stitchin' 'im up."

"Why's that, Jack?"

"Cos I stitched 'im up o' course. That's the trouble wi' these politicians – too bloody sharp – they spend all their lives lookin' out for people stabbin' 'em int' back."

"God. An' you 'ad to be the one to go an' do it! Oh Jack, no Jack, no." Fred looked and sounded terribly grave. "You shouldn't o' done that." He drummed the fingers of his left hand on the draining-board. "'E were probably your only 'ope."

"Well. If 'e's the only 'ope, then I'll 'ave to try an' mend some fences. Per'aps I can 'elp 'im win back his place in the by-election."

"'Ow the'ell will you do that? The re-selection meetin's on Wednesd'y night – that's only two days away! I know that cos we're doin' a special late-edition o' the paper on Thursd'y wi' the result."

"Wednesday is it? Well, I'll go to the meetin' an' speak on 'is behalf."

"Don't be daft, Jack. For a start you don't know 'im, so 'ow can you speak for 'im? And for a finish 'e don't trust you – with good reason. Why would 'e want you there? You'll just make things worse. Leave 'im to fight 'is own battle – I'm sure 'e's capable."

Jack pondered. "Aye, you're probably right, Fred. I should stick to caravans." Jack became agitated. "I wish those bastards'd stop knockin' on my front door! Can *you* get rid of 'em, Fred?"

"What? Get rid o' journalists? You must be jokin', now come on Jack. They'll be stickin' closer to you today than Shagsy's marker durin' cup tie!"

"What shall I bloody do, then?"

"I'll walk out o' front door an' call for hush. Then you tell 'em you'll be givin' press conference in one hour's time back at club, an' that you've no comment to make at this stage. Then we'll get int' car, drive over there an' sort out wi' Stan Smoggrate what you're goin' to say. Right?"

"I'm glad you're 'ere, Fred. I've 'ad dealin's with papers – but nothin' like this!" Jack peeked out of the kitchen door and through the window overlooking the yard where there now appeared to be at least six cars and another just arriving, although he couldn't see much because of four or five faces pressed against the glass, peering in. "Come on then. Let's get it over with."

"Let me go out first. I'll tell 'em to shut up an' listen," said Fred.

He undid the lock on the door and stood at the top of the two steps leading to the office entrance. Cameras whirred and clicked, and there were several calls of "Are you Jack Dugdale?" and "Who are you?" and "Where's the Hetherington Sidney Chairman?" and suchlike.

"Right!" Fred's voice boomed out over the cold car park, a puff of steam venting in a plume from his mouth. "Let's 'ave a bit of 'ush. Mr Dugdale'll be out 'ere as soon as you all shut up an' listen!" He waited, while the hullabaloo died down. "Right, 'ere 'e is then – Mr Jack Dugdale, Chairman of 'Etherington Sidney Football Club." Fred stepped to one side, allowing Jack just enough room to stand beside him on the little stair landing. The questions immediately started firing in again and Fred put his arms out in front of him, palms to the floor, and waved them up and down while calling for quiet once more. It seemed a long time before Jack was able to speak, and soon even the journalists were urging their fellows to be quiet so that the proceedings could get underway. Jack decided to get it over with quickly.

"I'm goin' back to the club to consult my staff. I've no comment to make until then. There'll be a press conference at the club at half past two – that's one hour from now – thank you very much."

Fred tried to protect him as Jack locked the door then descended the steps and headed for the local reporter's car. They were jostled a bit, but Fred managed to bundle Jack in the passenger door, telling him to lock it from the inside. Immediately, eveyone else leapt into their cars and hurtled off down the dusty track where, equally hastily, they screeched to a halt as they met other reporters' vehicles still arriving from the opposite direction, and the whole motorcade caused a blockage in the narrow access road which led away from Carefree Caravans.

"We'll not get out o' here wi'out an 'elicopter," stated Fred in a manner which didn't convey any sense of impatience. "D'you want a game of I-spy?"

"Not right now, Fred. I'm too upset for games. 'Ang on a minute. My car's still outside the office. Let's dump your car 'ere – that'll 'old 'em up a bit in any case – go back to my car and leave by the big gate at the other end o' the site – that's the way I bring the caravans in an' out – this track's much too small!"

"Sounds fun to me, Jack. Come on – let's abandon ship."

They both stepped out of Fred's car and started walking back down the lane, past three cars which were behind them in the queue. The occupants of these cars immediately jumped out and started asking questions, but Fred and Jack just continued to walk along the track back to the office, surrounded by the little huddle of reporters and cameramen. Once there, they got into Jack's wonderful old Rover 3500 and purred off between two rows of caravans. By the time the last car of the group managed to reverse back to the site office, turn round and pursue them, they were locking the fifteen foot wide iron gate behind them.

Monday, five minutes to two

As they drove into the club car park, a shout went round the massed ranks lying in wait for them, and Fred and Jack once again had to fight off reporters and cameramen to reach the entrance to the ground. Old Trevor, the steward on duty, had resolutely defended his creaking fortress against invaders and was observing the car park from a window in the back of the stand. He saw his Chairman's car arrive, went immediately to his station and prepared to unbatten the door and to face the enemy. He opened it a crack and looked outside, but there was no one near the building for they were all concentrating their attentions on the two gentlemen getting out of the Rover.

"Mind my bloody car!" he heard Jack shouting. "You scratch that paintwork an' I'll sue the lot o' yer!"

Trevor opened the door wide and waited for the ruck to descend upon him.

"Make way for the Chairman!" he ordered in the most authoritarian voice he could muster at his age.

Somewhat dishevelled, the said Chairman ducked down under arms and cameras and made his dash for sanctuary. As he dived through the doorway Jack managed to gasp, "Let Fred from the 'Etherington

Gazette in too, Trevor – there's a good lad." He stood in the dark lobby for a while, regaining his breath and composure. The air smelt of football boots and old socks but it tasted sweet to Jack – he thought that this was how a fox must feel that's escaped the hounds: back amongst the familiar smells of his favourite haunts. He heard Fred behind him shouting, "Geroff!" and Trevor doing his best with hoarse croaks of, "No more inside! You just wait 'ere!"

Still puffing a bit, Jack and Fred made their way to the stairs which led up from the base of the stand to the club offices. When they reached them, they were immediately startled by a shriek from above, followed by the clatter of high heels on the wooden treads.

"Oh Mr D!" Angela came running down the steps dangerously fast in her precarious footwear, but was too excited to exercise caution. "Oh Mr D – you're safe!" she shrieked as she tripped two paces from the bottom and flew into Jack's arms. "Oh Mr D she sobbed, undaunted by her gymnastic experience, or by the fact that this was the Chairman upon whom she was crying. "Oh Mr D......"

"Yes Angela, yes, so you've said lass." Jack hugged her a bit longer, getting slightly embarrassed, then put her down.

"Oh Mr D," Angela looked up into the old man's eyes. "We were scared you might of 'ad an 'eart attack or sommat – an' we couldn't get 'old of you to warn you! It would've been all our fault!" and she sat down on the foot of the stairs and started crying again.

Jack looked at her and decided he couldn't cope. Then he spotted the lurking Smoggrate.

"Smoggrate!" Jack roared, as people do when overwhelmed by a situation. "What've you done to this lass?"

Smoggrate had seen the Chairman in this state many times before and knew it was best not to say anything. He merely hovered at the top of the stairs, like a giant bumblebee atop a shed roof, buzzing over the world below.

It was the avuncular sports reporter who attempted to take the heat out of the situation.

"Calm down, Jack." Fred spoke kindly and with an outsider's detachment. "We're all a bit het up at the moment." He sat down on the stair next to Angela and put his arm around her. "We'll go upstairs, 'ave a cup o' tea – or per'aps somethin' stronger, eh Jack?"

and he looked up at the red-faced Mr Dugdale and winked, "An' then we'll sit down calmly and decide what the Chairman will say in the press conference. We've only got......" – he looked at his watch – "'Alf an hour."

He gave Angela a little squeeze. She dabbed her eyes with her becoming-soggy tissue and turned to Fred and grinned. "Thanks," she said. "I'll be all right now – let's get to work, Mr......?"

"Bighill." Fred helped her out. "Fred Bighill – sports writer on the 'Etherington Gazette."

"Oh, course you are!" Angela laughed. "I've only ever spoken to you on the phone before. I knew I recognised yer voice!"

Monday, twenty past two

Ron Conference was almost home after his morning's work with the team on the training ground. He drove his Skoda into the turning which led to his road, thinking about what he must do to make Tubsy more aware of his positioning in the heart of the defence. He gets sucked out to the wings too easily by forwards going wide. Then when a midfielder makes a run from the centre of the field and the ball is pulled back to him, Tubsy's not there to intercept and there's only the goalkeeper as the last line of defence. Ron turned into his own road. We'll have to work on that some more tomorrow. If an attacker goes to the wing, Tubsy's got to let the full-back take responsibility and hold his own space in the area in front of goal. His mind was still elsewhere as he drove up to his house and he only noticed the crowd around his front garden when he had difficulty getting his car onto the driveway. They surrounded the vehicle and cameras flashed all around.

Christ! he thought. I'm either famous, or something terrible's happened.

Monday, half past two

The Chairman and the club Secretary sat at the boardroom table, in the middle of one of its long sides, while on the opposite side the press were squeezed into the space between it and the wall.

Jack cleared his throat, and began to read from a prepared script. Fred Bighill stood in the doorway, near his fellow scribblers. He had no need of making a recording, or taking notes.

"Ladies and Gentlemen. As we have not been apprised of the facts by the other interested parties, we find it difficult to make a comprehensive statement. Therefore, I will merely state at this stage, that if what appears to be the situation, turns out, in fact, to be the truth, then we at this club find the current turn of events to be unacceptable, and we shall be doing all we can to get this decision overturned. Note that we shall be pursuing all avenues open to us in attainment of that goal. That's all I have to say in my statement, but I will answer a few questions."

A flurry of voices now all spoke at once. Jack sat there, unmoved and unanswering, until Fred called loudly, "One at a time!" and a single voice was heard sufficiently clearly over the hubbub to gain a response.

"What is your reaction to Jam U's decision to withdraw from the FA Cup and play in the World Furry Cup?"

Jack frowned. "If you want the truth, the honest truth – I think it sucks!"

Monday, half past two

Stan and Adelina emerged from the raucous surroundings of the *Mole-strangler's Arms* and into the dull, damp and now almost dusk-like December afternoon of the street outside, holding onto one another for support as they teetered down the road in a direction similar to that which would take them back to their campaign headquarters.

"We've had a couple, haven't we?" Stan chirruped brightly as he enjoyed the swoosh of his drinking-partner's coat against the side of his right leg.

"You've had *five* actually Stan," said Adelina in tones of mock reproach.

Stan thought for a second. "Well *you* must've had five as well then!"

"Don't you know it's rude to count a lady's drinks?" Again she admonished him, but in a way that just made him feel like a naughty boy, and he liked feeling like that.

"What aftershave do you wear, Stan?"

"Aftershave?" Stan chuckled. "It's only the bloody Conservatives who wear aftershave. A Labour man should smell of nothing but sweat and toil. Mind you, I did suck a Parma Violet this morning before I judged the baby contest – didn't want 'em all bursting out crying when they caught a nose-full of the night before's fumes. By the way – I've got to open a fête tomorrow. Will *you* be doing that now instead?"

"Can't we both do it?"

"I thought you'd say that. We can't be seen together in public all the time, you know. People'll talk. I'm supposed to be gay, er, I mean, I'm gay."

Adelina looked at him suspiciously as they walked, bumping into one another with each inaccurate step.

"Why do you keep mentionin' that? I don't think gay people go on about it all the time!"

"Don't they?" Stan looked taken aback. "I'll shut up then."

As they continued along the pavement, laughing and joking, the flustered sight of Gerald hove into view a the end of the road. He spotted the two figures and came running down the street, shouting to them before he reached them.

"Where have you been? You said you were going out for lunch. We've got the photographers booked for half past two – you've got to get your pictures on your manifestos, and the press are supposed to be here as well, but they don't seem to have turned up – I think there's something big going off in town."

"Yes, there is Gerald. Poor little Hetherington's lost its reason for living. No one's going to care about us, or about our silly little by-election, or about any photo that you could dream up in your entire lifetime...... Unless perhaps......" Stan looked at the lady on his arm. "A picture of Adelina. That might restore some spirit to the natives in their time of despair."

"My god, Stan. I've never heard you so cynical before. You should be ashamed – and you'd better not let anyone else hear you talk like that – not if you still want to be elected."

"I don't know?" Adelina's voice intervened between the quarrelsome twosome. "I thought what Stan said was rather nice." She nodded to him appreciatively. "Thank you Stan."

“My pleasure love. And I meant it! I’m fed up with petty party apparatchiks telling me what to do all the time!” And he glared at Gerald.

“Oh, poor Gerald.” Adelina now defended the faithful worker. “He’s doin’ his best for all of us. You mustn’t be dismissive, Stan. You couldn’t fight a by-election on your own, you know.”

“You tell ’im! Trouble is, he thinks he bloody well could!” Gerald was aggrieved. “Right, if it’s all right by you......” and he looked at Dovehawk with an attempt at contempt, “We’ll go back to HQ and put some wheels in motion.” He watched as Stan and Adelina started to move, taking a while to get in step and giggling as they went. “Looks like wheels is what you two bloody need, as well. Isn’t it bloody marvellous,” Gerald continued muttering as he tagged along behind. “Yesterday he wanted to kill her. Now they’re holding bleedin’ hands! Bloody sodding marvellous!”

Monday, half past two

Ron was lying face down in his wife’s favourite winter-pansy bed, crying.

A TV crew had just arrived and live round-the-world satellite transmission was occurring. The sound-recordist held the fluffy sock-thing covering his microphone as near as he dared to Ron’s mouth without causing further needless damage to any blooms, and was gratified to see the little volume meter on his instrument fluctuate in time with the distraught manager’s blubbering lips.

Unfortunately for Ron, the TV crew was Japanese, and his prostrate body was not providing the most exciting pictures imaginable. Tiring of the repetitive nature of someone sobbing into finely tilled topsoil, the Producer decided to introduce live wildlife onto the set. Fortunately for Ron, there were no scorpions or killer ants in his front garden, and even the snails had been seen off by a liberal dose of slug pellets, so they had to make do with a couple of toads from the ornamental pond. One sat on Ron’s head and croaked, but couldn’t be heard much above the commentator’s excited voice. The other hopped up the commentator’s leg which made Ron even less of an attraction. Someone must have called an ambulance, for while the commentator was screaming, rolling his trouser up and jumping about on one leg, the emergency vehicle arrived and took him away, leaving Ron, unnoticed, amongst the flowers. The TV camera crew followed their man, realising that this was much better for the ratings than some saddo passed out in a floral display. The toad croaked and headed off back to its pond, while Ron knew none of this: even the newspaper journalists' entreaties for a ground level interview passed over him. Each reporter tried in turn, hoping that his bedside manner might be seductive enough to get a response.

A passing St John's Ambulanceman on a bicycle saw the little gathering and leant his machine against the gatepost. From his handbag, he produced a bandage.

"Where's the wound?" he asked in urgency, approaching the casualty.

"He's not injured – just upset." observed one of the hacks.

The St John's man moved Ron's limbs around until he was in the recovery position, then took a blanket from his bag and draped it over his patient. "How do you feel, now?" he asked, mopping Ron's brow and dusting the peat from his nose.

Ron opened one eye and looked up aimlessly. "I want to die." he wailed.

"Right. I've got just the thing for that. You hold on there now." The medicine man ferreted in his bag again, and pulled out a half-bottle of scotch. He unscrewed the lid then, instead of pouring a measure, he stretched a teat, like one you get on a baby's bottle, over the glass neck of the spirit-holder and upended the whole contraption into Ron's mouth. Ron's eyes opened and grew wider and wider as the bubbles started to flow upwards into the airgap at the base of the bottle, which was now at the top.

"Now be sure to drink it all up and you'll feel much better."

Lying surrounded by pansies and with a warm glow beginning to pervade his body, Ron thought that the softly spoken man who was nursing him may just be right.

Monday, two forty five

Gerald couldn't believe what he was hearing. After they'd had their photos taken, Dovehawk said to Adelina, "You know you can use my office any time you want if you need to get on with some work. Or even if you don't." And Stan winked.

"That's very kind of you, Stan. Perhaps you could take me there now and show me where you can squeeze me in."

"Aye. It'd be my pleasure. Just follow me. Mind the stairs – they're a bit creaky – specially with my weight on 'em. Trouble is, as I expect you already know, the desk's only a door on two piles of books...... We'll have to see how best to......"

Gerald watched as the two of them left reception and climbed up to the first floor, Stan's voice growing fainter and fainter before dying away. He felt slightly nauseous.

"Now," said Stan, as he and Adelina surveyed the surface of the desk with its peeling paint and drawing-pin holes. "We'll have to share the phone too – although nowadays nearly everyone uses their mobile."

"Yes, I don't need a phone."

"And the computer – we'll take it in turns with that, right?"

"Stop worryin' Stan and come and sit down." Adelina sat in Stan's chair and pointed to the visitor's chair. "Bring that one round this side. We don't want to sit facing each other all the time."

Stan did as she asked and she shuffled to one side to make room for him, so that her legs were against the column of paper which was the desk-support.

"It's cosy isn't it?" purred Adelina as Stan sat down and drew his chair into the narrow gap beside hers.

"I'll get Gerald to move the piles out some more." said Stan. "That'll make it easier for us to get our legs in."

"Why?" Adelina spoke right into his soul. "Don't you like touchin' me?"

"I told you – I'm gay."

"I know – that's why I'm so interested in you. Men are fascinated by lesbians aren't they? They try to convert them. I want to convert you, Stan. I want to show you how a woman feels, what she's like to touch, to caress. The way her body moulds around your harsh manliness. Come on, Stan. Just touch me. Go on. Just touch me here, on my breasts."

She presented her perfectly formed chest for his palpation, the curves straining slightly at the buttons of her blouse. Tentatively, his hand reached out. Because he had to show some reluctance in performing this manual manoeuvre, he had unusual time to be aware of his moving hand, pulsing like a leaf with rain falling upon it, regularly, in time to a heartbeat, probably his own; but as he looked ahead to where his hand should alight, he could see her breast was jumping to the same rhythm. Were their heartbeats synchronised, he wondered, or was she transmitting vibrations through the tension-thick air which were then picked up by the hairs on the back of his hand, making it twitch in sympathy? While he watched his hand, she watched his eyes, listened to his breathing, then felt the first touch as his large palm flatly pressed against her breast. She took hold of the hand and returned it to its owner. Calmly, she undid the buttons of her blouse, one by one, slowly, until four were open, then five, and she pulled aside the two thin cotton covers to expose the black coffee skin of her breasts pressed together tightly-packaged in her white bra. She gathered Stan's large head in her arms and smothered him to her bosom, burying his nose so that his usual loud and blustery breaths could hardly be heard. Then she kissed the back of his head and whispered in his ear.

"I feel gay when I'm with you Stan. I feel gay, gay, oh so gay, like the rooster chase its hen or the turkey gobble his lady or the drake quack him his duck – that's the kinda gay I am with you Stan."

The silence between her breasts was very calming, but after a couple of minutes Stan could no longer breathe. Fighting for air, he pushed himself up against the weight of her embrace until, panting, he observed between puffs, "Dark down there isn't it?"

Adelina smiled. "You like my tan Stan?" She hooted with laughter as the phone rang and she answered it.

"Hello. Labour Party Headquarters. Can I help you?..... No, I'm not Mr Dovehawk's secretary but I can get him for you – I'll just see if – aaaaaaahhhhh......" she giggled, "......he's available." She pressed her hand over the mouthpiece. "Stop that!"

"I wasn't doing anything! Just trying to get my balance!"

"You're wanted on the telephone. It's the Chairman of the football club."

Dovehawk took the phone from her and growled, " What does he want?" Then he bawled his name into the receiver: "Dovehawk!...... Yes, I've heard about that...... Yes...... Jam United...... Yes...... You want *me* to help you?...... Are you sure? After what you did to me?...... I'm your only hope am I?...... That's a good one, that is..... If I'm your only hope, then I don't think you've got a hope, do you? I suggest you talk to my replacement...... she was the lady who answered the phone to you, but she's unable to take calls at the moment – she's busy trying to seduce me!"

Dovehawk smashed the phone back down and looked expectantly at Adelina, but she turned serious.

"Well Stan. What did they want?"

"They wanted me to help them with this Jam United business. And after they stitched me up, too. I told them to shove it."

"Stitched you up?"

"Yes. They were the ones who contacted Labour HQ and told them I hadn't been properly selected. So I got landed with you – all cos of Hetherington Sidney bloody Football Club, and I don't even like football!"

Adelina looked affronted.

"So, you've been *landed* with me have you? Well if that's how you feel, I think we should have separate desks!"

Dovehawk tried to placate her. "You know what I mean – it's the principle of the thing: they were meddling in what didn't concern them. That's what we have *politicians* for. We don't allow other people to do it."

"Well I think you *should* help them. After all, if it wasn't for the football club you would never have been sharing a desk with me."

"It's true."

"And are you still gay, by the way? Can I stop trying to convert you now?"

"I'm considering reserving my gayness for when I really need it; which in this instance is Wednesday's meeting where I intend to show a video of me kissing a large black willy. But now my façade has crumbled somewhat, I fear you may expose me."

“Sounds very fair,” said Adelina, “After all, at this moment in time I myself am most exposed.” She grinned mischievously and started to do up her buttons.

Stan sighed. “I can’t be bothered to do any work. Shall we go back down the pub?”

“What will Gerald say?”

“He can come with us. He can buy the bloody drinks.”

“I’ll drink to that, darlin’ – I’m just gettin’ my coat.”

They went downstairs to reception where Gerald was stuffing envelopes.

“Come on Gerald,” ordered Dovehawk jovially, “You’re coming down the pub to buy us a drink. It’s time you got out of this office.”

“What do you mean?” remonstrated Gerald. “I’ve been out on doorsteps for the last month, or hadn’t you noticed?”

“So a canvassing trip to the local hostelry’ll by right up your street, as it were.” Dovehawk chuckled at his accidental pun, the five pints he had already consumed putting him in a flippant frame of mind.

“Oh do come, Gerald.” Adelina joined in. “We hardly know each other yet. And we may be together for some time if I beat Stan on Wednesday.”

She looked so alluring, but Gerald felt inferior with Dovehawk standing there. He knew he wouldn’t be able to say anything to Adelina without having to endure Dovehawk’s barbed comments, sarcastic and vainglorious at ordinary times; but given extra edge by a copious fuelling of *Hetherington Fine Ales*.

“Besides,” Adelina continued, “If you’re with us it will stop Stan tryin’ to get my blouse off...... somethin’ which he almost succeeded in doin’ only just now!”

Oh god, Gerald thought – it’s going to be one of those days. It was bad enough being the political agent for *one* candidate, but why did they have to send him two? And worse than that, two that were going to gang up on him. Gerald wanted to go home. He also wanted to be near Adelina. Life was full of choices – but why couldn’t they be simple ones? There was a knock at the front door and Dovehawk, already on his way to escape from the office, pulled it open. A tall, tanned, curly-haired individual flashed a false smile and shook Dovehawk's hand. He reeked of stale tobacco and had obviously only just returned from a holiday in Tollymarinos.

"It's lucky you phoned," said the new arrival, refusing to release Dovehawk's hand while he spoke. "Our promotion's just finished in this area but I've driven here all the way from Halifax specially."

He relinquished his grip and breezed past Dovehawk into the centre of the room where he plonked his briefcase on the reception desk, opened it and took out a calculator. The others stared while he pressed a few buttons.

"This room'll be one and a half grand. I'll just go upstairs and have a look, OK?"

"No it's not bloody OK!" Dovehawk found his ability to speak had returned. "Who are you?"

"I'm Gary of course, I thought you knew." The individual leapt across to Stan and grabbed his hand again. "You phoned up for windows, and now I'm here, so I'll just go upstairs and have a measure up..."

Dovehawk tried to be patient, but knew he was temperamentally incapable of maintaining such calmness for long.

"Look, this is Labour Party HQ – we get lots of people playing practical jokes. Someone's rung up for windows and given our address – happens all the time......" Stan called his agent: "Gerald, sort him out and let's get out of here."

Gary's gloss of benign good humour turned to belligerence in an instant.

"I've driven all the way from Halifax," he thundered. "What about all the juice I've used?"

Gerald fidgeted uncomfortably. "Sorry Stan – I phoned up Gary."

"What for? Double-glazing? Christ – you'll do anything to get out of buying a pint. How did you know we were taking you down the pub? Have you got my office bugged?"

"You said your office was too cold. I thought I'd get the window changed."

"Just a heater that worked would have done, Gerald. Bloody hell!" He pointed to the salesman. "Give this man a cheque for his petrol and let's get out."

"But what about the windows?" Gary was angry now at the loss of a sale.

"How much was your petrol, Gary?" asked Dovehawk, as Gerald reluctantly got out his wallet and opened a chequebook.

"Twenty six quid should just about cover it."

Gerald grimaced, and wrote out the cheque for that amount, handed it to Gary and escorted him, fuming, to the door.

"My wife'll kill me! Gerald wailed as he looked back plaintively at Dovehawk. "That comes out of our joint account!"

"And you've still got to buy the drinks yet!" Dovehawk made no concessions to Gerald's matrimonial misgivings, while Adelina, laughing so much tears had started running down her face, suddenly realised that he wasn't seeing the funny side.

"I'll buy the drinks," she stammered between fits of mirth. "Poor Gerald – he was only doin' his best to keep you warm, Stan."

"I don't need some twonk who goes on sixteen holidays a year and smokes fifty fags in an afternoon to come and price me up for windows just when I'm gagging for a pint in the company of a sublime and sensual lady!" thundered Dovehawk "You just needed to ring up a sparky and get him to change the plug on my fire! Now are you coming Gerald, or not? And to give you a clue, the answer is not *not*." He slapped his hand on Gerald's back and guided him out into the street.

Monday, 3 o'clock

The Jam United training suite had wide-screen wall-size computer TV with digital fibre-optic microwave downlink from the Jam U private satellite orbiting the stadium, in which the latest schoolboy outing was being shown around the ground. Eating popcorn and swigging coke, the Jam U players were preparing for the World Championships by watching a porno film, each of them hoping they could be first in the bog at the interval, while the girl who brought the ice cream cones round wondered if she'd get many takers at half-time for a tub and half a pint of plasticy-tasting flat squash which, at two and a half quid a go, made the price of replica shirts seem reasonable.

The Jam U manager was in the sound dubbing cubicle where none of the others could see him below his waist, and although his running commentary annoyingly drowned out the fake orgasms on the surround sound system, they still couldn't understand a bloody word he said.

Aah... Aaah... Aaaah... "Ball!" *Aaaaah... Ohhh...* "Tongue!" *Ohhhh... Ohaaah... Ohaaaah...* "Ball!" *Wah Waah Waaah Waaaah Waaaaah...* "Final ball!" *Waaaaaah... Yarrooooop... Waheeeehh...* "Goal!"

At the end of the show, they all sat there, sticky, with grins on their faces, popcorn all round their mouths, coke slopped down their tracksuits.

"When are we gonna start proper trainin' boss?" asked the star midfielder hopefully, excited by the prospect. But as the lights came back up, the players could see nothing of their manager because the windows of the sound dubbing cubicle had all turned milky.

Monday, 3:45

It had been a busy day at the Citizens' Advice Bureau and the adviser, Mr Tone, had dispensed so much information he was a little fatigued by the time Jack, one of his regular customers, came to see him.

"We don't get many enquiries like yours I'm afraid, Jack. In fact we don't get any, so I'll have to do some research." Mr Tone, was puzzled yet interested. "Are you sure you wouldn't be better off talking to your solicitor?"

"Solicitor? Never! They cost money you know – and they're less use than a telephone box wi' a turd in it. No, no – I always come 'ere – y' get much better service... an' it's free." Jack delivered his report on the doughty volunteers of the C.A.B. as a eulogy. "All I need to know is whether I can have Jam United excluded from the Furry Cup."

"Have you got any shopping to do?" Mr Tone elevated his pupils until they were almost hidden beneath his eyelids, leaving only his spectacles still looking at Jack. "If you come back at half five I should have some news for you."

“Would you? That’s grand – but I’m ’avin’ a bit of ’arassment from the press.” Jack spoke gravely to Mr Tone. “D’you think I could stay here? They didn’t see me sneak in.”

“OK then, you can sit in reception. You can get a cup of tea from the machine if you like. I’ll call you when I get anything – but I’ll have to see my other clients first.”

“Aye, I understand. Thanks very much. I always appreciate your excellent ’elp y’ know.”

Jack returned to the waiting room, followed by Mr Tone who called the next person into his office.

“Mr D! Mr D!” a young girl’s voice called out and Jack was surprised to see Angela was there fidgeting excitedly in front of him. “I’ve got some good news – I came straight ’ere to tell you! Scuntlepool’ve lost their appeal – we’re int’ third round! Isn’t that fantastic?”

Jack pondered, his depressed state making him slow of thought so he had to take time to consider whether the news he was hearing was indeed fantastic. Angela waited, eager, intense, and when she didn’t see the expected joyful reaction in her Chairman, her cheery little face saddened.

“Eh, cheer up lass!” said Jack, putting his hand behind her head and giving it a gentle squeeze. “O’ course it’s good news – me mind’s not right at the moment – poor old Jack’s gettin’ slow in ’is old age.” He saw her smile reappear, though not possessed of the same excitement. “It’s *fantastic* news!” he said, and pulled her head to his chest where he snuggled it into his jacket. “Here,” he fished around with his other hand for his wallet and took out a few tenners. “You take this and go down the shops – buy yourself a new pair o’ shoes or sommat. That’ll cheer you up. I’ve got to wait ’ere to see Mr Tone – he’s ’elpin’ sort out this other business. Go on lass – off you go!”

Angela took the notes – there looked to be about four or five of them – and her face lit up.

“Eh, thanks Mr D! New shoes to celebrate bein’ int’ third round!”

Monday, ten to six

Jack had sat patiently for a long time when Mr Tone poked his head around the door, although he had quite enjoyed watching the variety of life passing through the C.A.B. that afternoon. He lifted himself carefully from the plastic chair which had become harder and more uncomfortable by the minute.

"Sorry I took so long. If you'd like to come through now," said Mr Tone, almost brightly.

"Any news?" asked Jack eagerly, feeling the onset of pins and needles in his bottom.

"I believe so – and quite interesting too." The two men walked together into Mr Tone's room. As his host shut the door, Jack gingerly lowered himself into the chair provided for the client, which, although padded, exacerbated the tingling in his buttocks.

"And good news it is, I 'ope." Jack could feel his heart beating in an expectant manner which, combined with the nether numbness, made him feel like he only possessed the top half of his body.

"That'll be for you to judge." Mr Tone referred to his notes, unheeding of Jack's uncomfortable shuffling. "During my research I've found something unusual. There seem to be two world governing bodies for the sport to which you referred: the *Consejo de Lenguas Internacional Tiesas*, which is Spanish for the International Council of Stiff Tongues, and their great rivals, the *Taquiner International Conseil de Langue*, which is French for the Council of International Tongue Teasing. Although deadly enemies, C.L.I.T. and T.I.C.L. have in fact cooperated in the organisation of these World Championships to stage an ultimate showdown, a winner, *un enfrentamiento último*. It appears that each half of the draw will have entries from countries whose national ruling bodies are affiliated to one world council or the other; then in the final, the contest will not only be between the two countries involved, but also between the two organisations. There's a lot of pride at stake."

"Aye, I can see that."

"Now, we come to Jam United's, or to be more precise, England's involvement. As you know, England has only taken up the sport for the political expedient of aiding its attempt at hosting the World Cup, so there's no English governing cunnilingual organisation in existence."

"None?"

"Well, none except for an amateur body, the Red Rim Raiders, or 3-Rs for short – and as you can deduce for yourself, they are not entirely applicable."

"You're sure about this."

"Oh yes – I looked it all up on the internet – their website's a disgrace! Now comes the interesting bit. Because there is no English national body, Jam United are not affiliated to any organisation recognised by either of the world's governing bodies."

Mr Dugdale leapt from his seat and punched the air. "Yes – got 'em!.....I knew you'd come up with the goods, Mr Tone. You always do!"

"Not necessarily. They've been given honorary membership of the Spanish body."

"Oh no!" Jack was crestfallen. "I thought we 'ad it there." He slumped back down and instead of suffering the spikes of the pins and needles, he now felt like he was sitting on a lumpy, despairing old mattress of a bottom.

"But," Mr Tone's tone remained unchanged, conveying that all was not lost, "Listen to this. The French, not to be outdone, immediately offered honorary membership of their own, thereby creating a political dilemma for Jam United." Jack raised his head again and Mr Tone fixed him roundly with his lenses. "Interesting, eh?" The two cusps of his lips were close to hinting at a smile. "They can't turn down one offer in favour of the other for obvious reasons – it would be perceived by the rejected party as a slight. And they can't accept both because they wouldn't know which half of the draw they should go in, or whom they would be representing if they got to the final. See? Stalemate."

"Bloody 'ell. I almost feel sorry for 'em." Jack guffawed and then paused dramatically. "But I *don't*!" he shouted and gripped his hands tightly into fists, as if recalling the pugilistic spirit of his youth. "'Ow come none o' this 'as been mentioned on the news?"

"Who knows? I expect it will be – the press must be doing the same research as me."

"'Ave you any suggestions 'ow to proceed?" Jack forgot all the stresses in his wracked body while he watched the cog-wheels turning within the glazed cranium that presented itself so mystically across the other side of the table: *the apotheosis of a forehead*, thought Jack, *the place where dreams are crystallised into facts*. The heat rose from Mr Tone's furrowed frontal lobes for one minute, one whole minute and then two, followed by three. Through the waiting, Jack drifted off gently into the transcendental world, his vision becoming first blurred then dark; while unkind dreams played upon his mind, dreams of fear, and even hopelessness. When his sight gradually returned, his viewpoint was filled with Mr Tone's pink-cloaked skull, unprotected and vulnerable, and Jack knew he had the answer – straight from Mr Tone's head without the need to converse; it was big and pink and it needed to be protected.

Midnight

Angela had gone to bed just after eleven o' clock, but after lying there for fifty or more minutes she realised that sleep would not come easily. The thoughts of let-down and hurt would not go away, and she knew that Mr Smoggrate and Mr D and Ron and all the players and groundstaff would be feeling just the same; it was just so unfair. And poor Sean. Just imagine what he could do against the best team in the country – and now that's how it would remain – in the imagination. The smudges of tears on her pillow became cold against her cheek, so she turned it over and threw her head down into the soft dry side. Poor Mr Smoggrate. He was a bit of a berk, but she still felt sorry for him, and he had been so kind when they left the club to come home, giving her a lift to her house and telling her to get some rest, try not to worry, and they would fight another day in the morning. "Mr D'll think of something!" he had assured her confidently. "You know he always does!" She had pondered this through the raw stinging of her tear-flooded eyes.

Many times Mr Smoggrate had told her the story of when the club had almost gone bankrupt, all those years ago when she herself was just starting at her very first school. He told her how Mr D had paid all the wages from his own caravan business until he had managed to balance the books. Compared with those difficult days, this situation was unimportant, just one game in a whole season. Yet it *was* important. It meant everything. Angela prayed that Mr D would succeed. She felt the crispness of the unused side of the pillow and wondered if Sean had managed to get any sleep, or if he too was lying awake with these same thoughts......

Just after midnight

Fiona went into the bathroom for a pee and found that in order to carry out her intended function she would first have to remove Sean's head from down the toilet bowl.

"Out of the way, sweetie," she asked breezily. "I've just *got* to go."

She leant down and took his shoulders, but his body was so slumped that his was a dead-weight and difficult to move.

"Well, darling – I hope you're listening because I've got three choices." The smell of vomit burned the lining of her nose as she bent forward to speak loudly in his ear. "I can flush." She tried to see a reaction, but his head only rocked in time with his breathing. "Or I can piss on your head." Again she sought a reaction, but in vain. She stood up and looked at the shower. "Oh well." Fiona slipped out of all her clothes, adjusted the temperature of the spray, climbed in and sighed with relief as she felt the trickle of warmth down her leg being washed away almost as quickly as it arrived. She dried herself and slid back into her knickers just as she heard the doorbell. She gathered her towel around her and took a look at Sean before tripping off to the front door. Through the spy-hole, the fish-eye lens encompassed the broad figure of Dovehawk, bringing the whole of his perspective into view, making him smaller and unimposing.

"Stan sweetie – you're early!" said Fiona gleefully as she opened the door and his true expanse filled the threshold. She pulled the gnarled old head to her lips and pecked hard at its cheek, her breasts falling from the parting curtains of her towel. She gathered them up again and called to Dovehawk excitedly, "Come and look at this!" She took his hand and pulled him down the lobby to the bathroom door.

Dovehawk saw the prone figure and chuckled.

"You'd never think *that* was worth five million quid would you?" said Fiona with a pert irony. "Grown defenders quake in their boots when they see him coming!"

"Luckily a sight which I shall be spared," said Dovehawk with a twinkle in his eye and a jowly grin.

"I know what you're thinking," she said. "You're all bloody schoolboys at heart, even at the age of fifty three."

"Now come on lass...... fifty two! It's on the first page of my manifesto if you don't believe me!"

"You mean there's something in your manifesto that's true! You amaze me! If I had carte blanche to lie like that, the first thing that'd go would be my age!"

"It's not that simple – they're hot on birthdays. You can promise sixty billion extra for the NHS and a new school in Scrogmorton quite wantonly and without recourse; but misinform the powers-that-be about one's date of birth and you'll be disqualified from standing in the by-election in seven seconds flat."

"Politics and football – amazing aren't they? They make no sense whatever – yet I've become mixed up in both of them."

Dovehawk tutted. "You say that, but it's no different from any other profession. You can't tell me there isn't blatant self-seeking and mendacity in the world of modelling – not to mention the number of slimeballs you have to sleep with!"

Dovehawk immediately regretted what he'd just said, realising its implication, but instead of expressing pique, Fiona merely withered him with her look, before saying as she bent over to pick up her tee shirt, "I suppose I can't argue with that really, having slept with *you*."

Although insulted, Dovehawk was overjoyed that she had floored him with a retort rather than gone into a fit of the sulks or even thrown him out into the cold night. He looked at the back of Sean's head and chirruped heartily, "What a lucky lad this boy is! You're bloody gorgeous, Fiona!"

"I know," she said as she evaded Dovehawk's lurch and outstretched arms, sending him tripping over Sean's feet which were sprawled across the bathroom floor. "But always remember," she advised him curtly, leaving him in no doubt of her resolve "- I don't *have* to be!"

"I'll never forget it again," said Dovehawk from his resting place in the bidet, his fat veiny worthless legs entwined with those costing over a million pounds apiece. Looking up he saw Fiona's long long limbs standing tall and straight above him, and it occurred to him that in this strange world, hers were probably valued at only a fraction of that sum. *I wish she would be nasty to me*, he thought, *the women round here aren't natural – they're all too bloody nice – it's not what I'm used to. I might take a holiday in Scuntlepool – that'll sort me out. Or sleep with that ghastly Pree bitch... in Scuntlepool!*"

"Come on then," breezed Fiona. "You can stop thinking about what you're thinking about...... I'm sorry to tell you I'm getting dressed and we're going to Tammy's."

"Eh?" Dovehawk's mind returned to his own body, an unfortunate resting place. "Oh right – I wasn't thinking about *that*, honest. I was just thinking how nice you were."

"It's the same thing. *Nice* one minute, *I want to shaft you senseless* the next – both those thoughts are exactly identical to you lot."

Stan looked at Sean, what he could see of him, the top end of his arched body disappearing, from Dovehawk's low viewpoint, down the bell of the great china tuba. "I wonder who shafted *him* senseless then?"

"He manages that all on his own sweetie. Help me get him into the recovery position before we go – it'd be a waste of a rare talent if he choked while I was out."

Dovehawk, after struggling mightily first to disentangle himself and then to stand up, found the task of supporting Sean's head altogether easier, while Fiona dragged him onto the floor unceremoniously, flipped him over onto his elbow with a practised grace, then kissed him lightly on the forehead. She gathered up her clothes from their little heap in the corner of the bathroom, flitted off to the bedroom and when Dovehawk knocked on her door only thirty seconds later she was brushing her hair and sitting in front of her mirror fully dressed.

"D'you know, my wife used to take hours getting ready to go out; no wonder I smoked so much in those days. It was like awaiting a birth. In fact she spent less time in labour than she did polishing her bloody nails."

"I have to spend such a long time in make-up every day for my work, I just can't be bothered when I go out socially. You'll have to put up with me looking scruffy."

"Scruffy'll do me fine." Dovehawk noticed the comatose body on the floor. "Heh – seeing Sean like that makes me fancy a drink. I'll book a taxi to take us so I don't have to drive back."

Fiona looked at Dovehawk in her mirror, stopping in mid brush. "So, you're up for a party tonight then, eh Stan?"

"I think I might well be," he said.

Nine in the morning, Tuesday

Dovehawk became aware of a rattling sound and, as he slowly awoke, became aware that he was in a strange bed. It was huge. In fact, it had no end, mainly because it was round, but also because the edge was so far away that its horizon blended fuzzily with the walls of the room. He noticed how the Georgian window extended right from the window-seat at the floor almost to the ceiling twenty feet above. And the three other windows in the room were the same, each being curtained with a mustardy yellow material which let in enough light to see clearly, even though it was the dull middle of winter. Dovehawk remembered setting out for Tammy's party in ebullient mood. Had the taxi forgotten to take him and Fiona home he wondered?

Somewhere in the bed, at sort of "ten to" if you imagined it as a clock face and Dovehawk was the twelve, there was a lump in the covers. He sat up to investigate and was distracted by the sight of a real fire burning brightly in the grate and, alongside it, on his knees and bearing a shovel, a gentleman wearing black. *Oh my god – it's the Grim Reaper!!!* was Dovehawk's first thought. But as the man took another shovelful of coal from the scuttle and carefully placed it in the centre of the blaze, Dovehawk realised that it was the sound of stoking which had awakened him.

"Excuse me," said Dovehawk, tentatively, unused to the trappings of grandeur and not knowing how to address someone who tended fires.

The servant remained in his kneeling position while he turned his head, noted Dovehawk and stood up, facing him directly, his back held perfectly straight. He nodded before speaking.

"Good morning sir. I hope you spent a comfortable night."

"Yes, thank you. It must have been most comfortable as I don't remember any of it." Dovehawk raised his wrist to consult his watch but it was missing, and for the first time he realised he was naked. "Do you think you could tell me what the time is?"

The man withdrew a pocket watch from his jacket, flicked open its cover and consulted. "It is three minutes past nine," he informed Dovehawk serenely, "Which it would be, for I tend madam's fire at exactly nine each morning." And he looked over his shoulder to reassure himself that the flames were frolicking in the hearth.

The beginnings of a headache and a parched throat told Dovehawk that he'd had more to drink than usual the previous night. He looked around, trying to spot his clothes. "I'm afraid I've overslept – I need my jacket – I've got an appointment somewhere but I can't remember where or when – I need to look at my diary."

"Quite so, sir, but I'm afraid I don't have your jacket. Would that be all? I shall arrange for you to have breakfast in a quarter of an hour, if that's convenient."

Dovehawk fussed around in the bed, knowing he couldn't get up to look for his things because he felt too uncomfortable prancing about naked with the servant still in the room. What would his Labour Party chums say if they knew he was getting free breakfast in a stately home? It would have to be declared on the Members' Register of Interests; should he ever become a Member – and that outcome was gravely in doubt.

"Thank you," said Dovehawk, trying to sound like an effete Lord from a fifties British film. "That will be quite all – you may go now."

The man nodded his head again and left the room, drawing the double doors closed while walking backwards, which indicated to Dovehawk that he must have appeared in the same movie.

"Right," said Dovehawk loudly as soon as he heard the catches click shut. "Come on Fiona – we've got to get going. I think I've got to be somewhere at ten. Do you know where my clothes are?" He looked at the swelling in the quilt but it remained unstirring. "Fiona? Please love? We've got to make a move." He implored the bump, but still it was unmoved, so he leant across and lifted the heavy eiderdown – it *was* the middle of winter in a house that was three hundred years old – and there, on the lady's tummy was the lovely birthmark he'd kissed the week before. "Oh bloody good god!" wailed Dovehawk out loud, the butterflies freeing themselves from the chrysalises in his stomach, this was *Tammy's* bedroom! He remembered it now from his assignation with the magnificent Marlon.

Two gluey eyes opened, just barely, and a grin reassured him that his presence in the Mistress of the House's bed had not been accidental or, worse, unsolicited.

"Oh, you naughty little Labour chappie." Tammy's expression of affection was delivered through a yawn. "I'm glad you're still here." Her words were sleep-filled and soft. "Last night you kept going on about having to be up early for an engagement – some nasty Trotskyites – they sounded ghastly – I've never met *one* of them with a sense of humour." She closed her eyes and relaxed with a shudder, trembling her way into the mattress, her breasts rippling in time with her undulations. "I'm glad you decided to stay with your little Tammy-poos."

"Oh my bloody good god," repeated Dovehawk, daunted.

"I do love these cold mornings," she continued. "Especially with a man in my bed to keep little Tammy warm. Now you're sober, you can tell me all about the squalid little things you have to do to become successful and powerful, so you can make all the little people pay their taxes." Her voice changed suddenly to one of exasperation. "Oh, bugger it. I need a wee and I don't want to get out of bed." She slumped even more, if that were possible.

"Tammy." Dovehawk spoke gently. "I've got to go. Do you know where my clothes are?"

"Oh don't go darling. I'll get Bargreaves to bring us breakfast – we can eat it in here – it'll be lovely – you can lick the crumbs off my tummy."

"But it's like you said – I *have* got an appointment. I'd love to stay – but I can't – I need to find my clothes."

Tammy huffed with annoyance, her eyes still closed. "Fiona undressed you," she said, uninterestedly. "You'll have to ask *her*."

"Fiona? Well where is she?" Stan's urgency bordered on panic.

"She's gone to Opium Haul – to see her grandfather. It's the anniversary of his liver transplant, darling."

"Oh no!" gasped Dovehawk.

"Not at all," said Tammy, reassuring him on the matter. "It refreshed his drinking career so utterly that now he's an unchanged man – to look at him you'd think he'd never had to lay off. The operation was so effective he hardly remembers his hiatus of enforced abstinence."

"My clothes, though. Where are *they* now?"

"Don't you remember anything Duvvy? You took us *both* on, darling, me *and* Fiona. In the taxi. It was a hell of a squeeze" She rolled over and hugged his leg. "But don't worry. You were just marvellous, darling; I'm really quite sore. It's the first time in a cab that I've ever got a bigger tip than the driver."

"So why am I back here?" Dovehawk was lost in confusion.

"Like all men darling, you fell asleep straight away afterwards. By the time the taxi dropped off Fiona, we'd forgotten you were there. I had to wake up my gardener at four in the morning just to help drag you out onto the drive."

"So why were *you* with us in the taxi?"

"Oh, I always see Fiona home. You never know what nasty fiends might try and seduce her in the dead of night."

Dovehawk shook his head. "I don't believe any of this. I just want my clothes. And a phone – I need to call Gerald to find out what I was supposed to be doing. Oh god, and my head hurts!" He clutched his poor throbbing skull. "I'll wake up in a minute. And when I do, it better bloody be better than this!"

"I should have known," said Tammy, turning her back with a flounce. "You socialist oiks are just ungrateful! I'm ringing for Bargreaves to have you removed."

Tammy pulled the liana-like rope hanging beside her bed, although it wasn't beside any particular side, the bed being a circle.

Dovehawk was amazed at how quickly the doors opened. He assumed Bargreaves had been listening outside.

"Mr Dovehawk's leaving. Give him some clothes and the use of a phone. Oh, and before you do, pass me the potty."

Bargreaves walked to a cabinet, retrieved the chamber-pot and placed it on the bed beside Tamara. Dovehawk was amazed when she immediately heaved herself, starkers, on top of it and tinkled away with both men watching. When the sound stopped, Bargreaves handed her a tissue with which she wiped herself before sliding gratefully between the covers once more to assume her most coveted and comfortable position.

Bargreaves took the pot in his right hand, and with the other beckoned Dovehawk.

"If you would care to follow me, sir. I should say you would take a 44 inch waist and 17 inch collar – am I correct?"

"Near enough," grumbled Dovehawk, grabbing a pillow to hold in front of him while he walked behind the butler, his bare arse wobbling all the way to the door. Tammy looked up, raising only her head, unable to resist taking in the view of the humiliated politician's big white floppy backside which looked so ridiculous that she had to giggle. Dovehawk heard her laugh and looked round just in time to catch a glimpse of her pillow flying through the air towards him. Tammy, sitting up now, screeched her amusement, while Dovehawk's look of shock was obliterated briefly as the airborne object hit him in the face, then dropped to the floor. Forgetting his own modesty, he launched his own pillow at Tammy but it missed by some margin and she didn't even have to duck. Annoyed at missing, he lollopped over and threw himself on top of her, all his weight horizontally impacting her soft curves, trapping them between the expanse of his chest and belly and the soft eider mattress beneath.

"Go Bargreaves! Now!" shrieked Tamara between giggles.

Bargreaves retreated backwards through the doors, his precious cargo of piddle clutched in his hand. His wife often asked him what went on up at the house, but he preferred to forget work when he was at home.

Five past ten on Tuesday morning

Gerald was sitting at his desk in the foyer as usual when Adelina came down from her office.

"Where is Stan?" she asked with concern.

"I've no idea," said Gerald resignedly. "I've rung his mobile phone and the person who answered asked me what time I wanted a taxi for."

"He does know that the Minister's coming to make sure we give out the correct figures for tax and spending and unemployment targets?"

"Course he does," said Gerald in irritation. "He's just buggering us about like normal." He looked at Adelina, admiring her dark green jacket and skirt. "Stan has no respect – that's his trouble. And yet people still like him." He cast his eyes down to his papers and wrote on his pad. "It's a mystery to me. Everyone says *Good old Stan* and he's no respect for any of them."

"He's a character. Larger than life. And he's fun to be with. Manners don't count for anyt'ing when you have a magnetic personality."

"Well it aint bloody fair then!" Gerald looked despairingly at the infinitely desirable Adelina and inwardly cursed the inertia of his predicament. "No one wants to shag me!" he muttered despondently.

"Stop feelin' sorry for yourself, Gerald. You have a wife who loves you – that's worth more than anyt'ing as shallow as you're contemplatin'."

"It may be worth more, but it isn't *fun.* Stan spends the whole time bulldozing his life from one climax to another and everybody congratulates him for it! If I tried it, I'd get picked up on the first day and thrown in the cells. Then they'd let me go with a caution – I can imagine – so humiliating – *Don't you think you're old enough to know better sir? – Now don't let us have to catch you doing anything as silly as that again.* It's like spending your whole life being treated as a schoolkid."

"You have got it bad today, Gerald. Let me try Stan's mobile phone again – are you sure you got the right number?"

"I phone it up ten times a day. Usually to find out what he's up to. Here, you can try if you want." Gerald pressed the Stan button on the phone and handed it to Adelina. He listened as she said, "Hello, is Mr Dovehawk available." Then he saw her face become quizzical. After some time without speaking, she looked at Gerald and raised her eyebrows. "Yes, OK," she said, "The address is 29 Cokedealer Street, Hetherin'ton."

Adelina handed the phone which now smelt strongly of her perfume, back to Gerald.

"He said he's got my husband's clothes and he'll bring them round straight away, but only if I pay the price for the cab in both directions. I agreed. I hope that's all right with you, Gerald?"

"I didn't know your husband was a taxi driver."

"He *is* actually, but not here. In Hackney."

"Oh, how apt."

"Indeed. But the taxi driver I was just speakin' to, he has Stan's clothes."

"Oh for god sake. Has that man no control of his bodily faculties?"

"I think you're bein' very disparaging. What if he's been hurt? Mugged? Kidnapped?"

"That'd be the day, when something *bad* happened to Stan. If he got plastered and fell in the gutter, he'd get rescued by some nympho rock-starlet and the next day the Government would announce that mud-streaked piss-heads were being made eligible for Government grants."

The door opened and someone in a suit walked in, waving his arms and trying to organise everybody.

"The Minister's just arrived," he trilled, "I'm Abigail Cramfull his press secretary. Come on – everyone outside on the pavement for the photo-opportunity."

"But you're a bloke! Why are you called Abigail?" asked Gerald, astonished.

"Oh, haven't you heard?" said Abigail, tainting the slightly smoggy morning air with garlic fumes. "We need to cut out sexual bias in the Labour Party, but we want to do it without taking on any more women. So I thought up the solution this morning. You're now called Geraldine by the way."

"Oh. Thanks for letting me know."

Gerald whispered to Adelina as they made their way yonder into the grey day, "Are you going to stand for that? You're on the bloody Women's Committee."

"Sounds like you will be soon, too," she said with a smirk. "Here, let me straighten up your rosette.

She fiddled with Gerald's pin for a bit, then they joined the small gathering on the street, the Minister beaming effortlessly for the half-a-dozen cameras that were trained upon him while at the same time giving off vibes of subsurface irritation at the fact that no one else was ready.

As Adelina walked through the door, he immediately grabbed her hand in his and sparkled his delight for the press as he gushed, "Hello there Adelina! Very good to meet you! I'm Mandy." Gerald shuffled alongside and tried to look unimportant, at which he succeeded, but he also looked out of place as well. The cameras clicked. After a minute or so it became apparent that Dovehawk was missing. The Minister, smile still clamped firmly in place, leant down to Gerald.

"Where's Stan?"

"Er... ill," said Gerald, thinking quickly.

The Minister looked less than pleased. The smiled twitched at the corners and almost fell off his face. "You should have warned me!" he said with malice. "These situations can go badly wrong. Nothing can be left to chance. Now we're going to look foolish!"

"Is Stan Dovehawk boycotting this event?" quipped one of the journalists, his voice displaying to all that he intended to give the Minister a bumpy ride.

"No, no... not at all," chortled the Minister in a display of flippancy. "His agent was just telling me that he is, most unfortunately, not well enough to attend. Of course we wish him well – and we hope he will join us shortly."

"Seeing as you've got just the one candidate stood by your side right now, I'd like to know: has Stan got the shove already?" asked another voice

"No. As I said, Stan is ill." A brusque edge to the Minister's voice now made his inner turmoil apparent. "I shall be meeting him as planned, even if it has to be later and in private."

"Why is it that only four weeks from the by-election, you still don't have a Labour candidate? It's a farce isn't it?" The questions were now firing in without a gap.

"Not a farce at all. It's democracy. That's what happens in a democratic organisation like the Labour Party. The members get a choice and must decide. No quick fixes. No rigged ballots. Democracy in action, that's what you get with the Labour Party, and that's what you don't get with the other Parties."

"But you've 'ad a candidate for the past two months. And now you 'aven't got a candidate. It's a cock-up in't it? Either that or you don't know what you're doin'!"

The Minister was about to offer another riposte when a car drew up behind the small cordon of pressmen in the road and stopped. The driver wound down his window and roared, "Is Mrs Dove'awk 'ere?" He paused for a response, but there was a hush, and no one even breathed let alone made a move. " Well, if she is," he continued, "Tell 'er I've got Mr Dove'awk's clothes!" And with that he opened his door and emerged carrying a dishevelled suit on a hanger and a brown parcel tied with sellotape.

"Oh shit!" groaned Gerald under his breath, and looked away.

Adelina strode forward and a murmur rumbled through the huddle.

"Bloody 'ell!" The driver said as he presented the garments to Adelina, laying the suit across her outstretched hands. The Minister, looking so shocked that now, finally, the smile had disappeared altogether, rushed to her side and took the parcel. The cabby ran his eyes up and down her body as the scent of her breath turned to steam in the crisp morning air. "If I was married to you, I wouldn't be out doin' what 'e was doin' at four in the mornin'!" he said, then held his hand out towards her, palm upwards in readiness to receive his fare.

Adelina looked at the empty hand, and turned to the gentleman on her left.

"Minister," Adelina drawled in her most alluring voice. "I've left my bag inside. Could you, do you think?"

"What?" The Minister read her pleading eyes. "Ah, yes, of course. Er, how much?" he asked the cabby, thrusting his spare hand into his pocket.

"Fifty three quid."

The Minister looked slightly askance, but then, unfazed as a politician always should be, withdrew his hand from his trousers and counted out three twenties, placing each note in the taxi-driver's hand whilst saying loudly, for everyone to hear, "I think I should get two of Stan's suits for that amount ha ha ha!"

The crowd loved the remark; cameras clicked and guffaws echoed from the walls of the terraced houses on either side of the road, amplifying the sound. Adelina and the Minister walked back to the front door of the Party HQ. She tapped the cowering Gerald on the shoulder, making him jump as he turned round in trepidation. She then delivered the suit into his arms while the Minister dumped the parcel on top. Gerald scuttled off inside to get rid of them.

"Can we take it that Mr Dovehawk will be following along, shortly after his clothes, Minister?" called one of the journalists mockingly.

"I have no comment to make about the arrival of Mr Dovehawk's clothes. I'm sure there will be a perfectly logical explanation, but I am not party to his itinerary – you'll have to ask his agent, Geraldine, when he reappears through the door behind me."

The Minister gestured to the door, wishing that it would indeed open and, like a large red mouth, swallow him quickly inside.

"If the two candidates are married," another press-man asked, "Does this not compromise your position of no quick fixes or rigged ballots Minister?"

The Minister grinned. "I think I'll leave it to Ms Omov to answer that."

Adelina nodded and addressed the audience. "We're not married. Just good comrades... or colleagues... whichever way you in the media like to put it nowadays. We shall fight for the honour of representin' this constituency for the Labour Party, and whoever wins, that person will devote themselves totally to makin' sure that they get the most votes at the by-election by supportin' and helpin' the people of Hetherin'ton."

The Minister's smile relocated itself more jollily on his physiognomy, signalling his pleasure at the last remark. He spoke hurriedly to head off any more questions.

"That'll be all, ladies and gentlemen. We're going inside now for a meeting – then we shall be taking a walkabout through the town centre at noon. Thank you for your time."

He held up his hand in farewell, but a sixth sense among the journalists alerted them that something was afoot and all the cameras turned from the Minister and pointed towards a Rolls Royce which floated silently down the street towards them. When it stopped, the driver got out, opened the rear door, and there sat the stately figure of Stanley Dovehawk, looking like an undertaker in his long black suit and top hat.

The Minister, brazenly exuding confidence while under duress, rushed over and took Dovehawk's hand, just as he had Adelina's ten minutes earlier. Stan, thinking that the Cabinet Member was offering him assistance, gratefully accepted and hauled on the proffered limb, resulting in the off-balance Minister tipping forward and banging his head on the car roof.

"Christ Stan!" Mandy blurted, rubbing his head. Then, remembering where he was despite the pain he instantly recovered his composure: "Lovely to see you, Stan. Are you feeling better now?"

Stan extracted himself and stood erect, replacing his topper which had become dislodged during the fracas.

"Better than you by the looks of things, Minister. Would you like me to get Gerald to arrange an ice-pack? That could turn into a nasty bruise."

Mandy furtively sneered at Dovehawk, making sure it was out of camera-shot. He then put his arm around his candidate, or possible candidate, and escorted him with false bonhomie to stand next to Adelina and Abigail at the front door, through which the skulking Gerald had yet to reappear.

"Nice car, Stan!" came the first remark from the press-men. "Why didn't you share the taxi with your clothes?"

Dovehawk grinned. "My clothes were unavoidably engaged elsewhere other than on my person. At this moment I have no knowledge of their whereabouts."

"They're in a brown parcel – your agent's just taken them indoors." A reporter supplied him with the missing information.

Stan looked supremely in command, happily engaging in the repartee. "In that case, they're in safe and trusted hands. I shall retrieve them in time to open the Primrose Primary School fête at half past two."

"Did you know that you owe the Minister fifty three quid for getting them back?"

"No, I didn't – thankyou for pointing that out. I can assure you, if he considers them to be worth that sum, I shall allow him to keep them."

The Minister slapped Stan on the back, pretending he could take a joke, while more people had stopped to watch what was happening, and two policemen were making their best efforts to keep the road clear for traffic.

"Right!" shouted Mandy. "I think we're causing a bit of a disturbance out here. As I said, we shall be doing a walkabout at noon – if you'd care to rejoin us then ladies and gentlemen – thank you very much for your time."

"'Ave you been sacked, Stan?"

The questions came faster now time was running out. Mandy had already turned to head back inside, followed by Abigail, leaving Stan and Adelina standing together like comrades in arms, facing the onslaught.

"You all seem to know more about what's going on than I do! You tell me!" said Stan, enjoying some verbal jousting.

"What were you doing at four o'clock this morning, Stan?" asked a young reporter.

A loud vacuum of expectation numbed the clamour and silence fell. Stan paused, playing with the crowd, looking around at each of them before speaking.

"First tell me what *you* were doing at that time?" he asked, glowering at his inquisitor.

"I was asleep," said the blondish tousle-haired young lad sheepishly, like someone in the audience at a comedy show fearful of saying anything, knowing that whatever he did say would be turned back against him.

“There you go!” blasted Stan triumphantly. “You’re a *journalist*, aren’t you? If you were doing your job properly you should *know* what I was doing at four in the morning, or at least have found out by now! I’m not going to make it easy for you by telling you.”

Everyone laughed and Abigail, having popped his head around the door to see why the others had not followed the Minister into the sanctuary of 29 Cokedealer Street, marched up to Stan to try to urge him to wind up.

“As I suspect you all know,” said Stan, revelling now in this impromptu press briefing, “This is the Minister’s press secretary. He not only knows the answers to questions you haven’t yet thought of asking, but also what the weather will be like next week, and whether I shall develop piles during the election campaign. He no doubt also knows who will be the Labour candidate at this by-election, so I suggest you find that out right now...... And then please tell me!”

Dovehawk doffed his topper, graciously held the door ajar for Adelina to pass through, then followed her, leaving the floundering press secretary securely stranded in the clutches of the antagonistic mob.

“Ah, Stan,” spat the Minister with the inherent vileness of someone freed from the restraint of public scrutiny. “Are you deliberately being obstructive? Or is it just your objectionable nature which makes you neither amenable nor amiable?”

Gerald smirked in the background, and Stan noticed him doing so.

“If you are referring to my lateness, Minister, I can only beg your forgiveness. It was due to circumstances of a delicate political nature which overran their allotted span somewhat. I assure you that no insult to your good self was intended, either in the fact of my absence, or in the manner of my late arrival.”

“So you’re sorry then?”

“Deeply. But not sorry enough to accede to the purpose of your visit: which is to sack me.

“Staaaaaan.” The Minister’s manner changed to chummy indulgence, as if a switch had been flicked. “You know that’s not true. I’m here to help you with the campaign – press a bit of flesh, let the cameras get a few shots of you with someone whom the public recognises.”

Stan put on a display of hurt for those around him to see, but he congratulated himself within on having neatly switched from defence of his own tardy position to attacking the motives of his avowed helper.

"Are you sure about that? I mean, have you consulted your press secretary on this matter?" he said, timorously playing the victim.

Mandy looked bemused. Why was Stan was so untrusting? He put his arm around Dovehawk in an act of consolation. "I don't need to consult my press secretary," he said softly, "I can tell you honestly that I'm here to help both you and Adelina with the campaign."

"Oh that's good," Stan said, "Because all the papers say that Abigail Cramfull tells *you* what to think."

"Oh no no no," the Minister laughed nervously, "I can think for myself. Don't you worry on that score, Stan."

"I've stopped worrying already. Thank you Minister." Dovehawk gushed with obsequiousness. "You can't believe how much better it makes me feel, knowing that Abigail Cramfull has no influence on you whatsoever. I wonder what he's telling the reporters?"

"What?"

"He's outside, with the press."

"No, no!" gasped the Minister, "He can't be left alone with journalists! Lord knows what he might say!"

Half past ten

Jack sat in his office at Hetherington Sidney Football Club, waiting for the phone to ring, which it did, often, but never with the person that he wanted to speak to at the other end, so he was becoming more and more agitated. *Right, I've given 'em an hour – I'll ring 'em back meself,* he thought. He dialled and waited, staring at the stark headlines on the back page of his newspaper: *JAM U PULL OUT OF CUP*. He read on while he continued to wait: *Sensation rocked the football world yesterday when Jam United gave in to pressure from the England World Cup Bid lobby and withdrew from this season's FA Cup competition to play instead in what has been dubbed "The Furry Cup Final" in Brazil. Their manager said "We have not taken this decision lightly, we have given it a lot of..."*

"Department of Health," came the chirpy voice on the phone, interrupting Jack's reading.

"Hello. It's Jack Dugdale 'ere, Chairman of 'Etherington Sidney Football Club. I rang at nine this morning and spoke to the junior under-secretary's secretary, Doctor Mary O'Gosh. Is there any chance I could talk to 'er again? – only it's urgent.

"Just trying to put you through...... You're a drug-dealer did you say?"

"No, that's me name Mr Dug-dale." He pronounced the two syllables distinctly.

"OK – I'll put you in the queue. We're not very busy but my managers are trying to encourage people to use e-mail so that I can be made redundant. Thank you for calling."

He commenced the long wait listening to Rachmaninov, but this was soon interrupted by an exhortation to log on to NHS Direct STD Services at www.spottydick.com. Jack yawned. His life was in their hands. He began to doze off.

Twiddle iddle diddle boink Peep Thank you for holding. If you want to contact us about joining a waiting list, you can mail us at waiting.ages@nhs.com. Twiddle iddle diddle boink Peep Thank you for holding. If you are already on a waiting list and want to move up a few places, mail your credit card number to us at hardcash@nhs.com stating the amount you wish to spend – £50 per place on the list. Twiddle iddle diddle boink Peep Thank you for holding. If you want a new hip you can Click "Hello, this is Dr O'Gosh's secretary – can I help you?..... Hello? Hello?"

"Ah, hello – er... Jack Dugdale 'ere – er... are you a real person or another message?"

"I'm Dr O'Gosh's secretary – how can I help?"

"Ah, grand. I spoke to your boss just over an hour ago and she said she'd ring me back – it's about the World Furry Cup Championship."

"Ah yes, that rings a bell – I think that's why she's dashed out of the office – gone to try and get tickets. I've got a note here on my desk somewhere. Ah yes, here it is – she says she can't formulate policy on her own – it'll have to wait for the next meeting with the Minister and the Permanent Secretary – but she says you could try the Health Education Council – they're not accountable to anyone so they can do what they like. Is that any help?"

Jack boiled over and snapped back, "It would 'ave been an hour and an 'alf ago! What's their number?"

"Oh haven't a clue. It's best to look them up on the internet."

He groaned in dismay. "Is that your answer for everything?"

"We don't use the phone much now, you know. They're trying to save money by making all the call-centre staff redundant."

"Aye, I can tell that! Thanks for your 'elp!"

Jack thumped the phone down and it immediately rang so he picked it up and shouted into the mouthpiece without listening who it was: "And *you* can go and *bollocks*!"

"'Ang on a minute, Jack – that's a bit strong – I 'aven't said owt yet!"

Jack recognised it was his friend, the reporter from the local paper.

"Oh, sorry Fred. What's up lad?"

"'Ave you 'eard, Jack?"

"'Eard what?"

"Eh, graaaand! – I thought I might be first to tell you...... Jam United's manager's left the country – gone on a fact-finding tour to Brazil 'e 'as. Took overnight flight to Rio, then train to Belo Horizonte, then bus ride up the precipitous crags into village o' Clitalickabudal – the 'ome o' the event – up int' mountains, that's where 'e's gone – important to get altitude trainin' you know."

Jack realised he wasn't understanding much this morning, and it wasn't getting any better.

"But 'e's the manager – why should 'e need altitude trainin'?"

"I suppose 'e thinks it's important that 'e shouldn't pass out ont' touchline. Mind you – the team didn't get to go with 'im – 'e's sent them for a week int' Lake District. But last time I went there I can't remember 'avin' to pop me ears that often – the 'ills in Cumbria just aren't that 'igh."

"World's goin' mad in't it Fred? Thanks for lettin' me know, mate. What are you doin' now any road?"

"Ah." Fred sounded cagey. "I was just comin' to that. I'm writin' up my view of yesterday's events, y' know, spendin' my time wi' you as story broke, holed up together in your office, our excitin' drive to the club, press conference, all that jazz. I was wonderin' if you'd mind me makin' a bob or two floggin' story t' Nationals? There'd be a drink or two in it for you o' course!"

"Heh – I know you Fred – do I 'ave any say in the matter – you'll go and do it anyway won't you you old bugger – it's your job."

"Aye I know. But I thought I'd ask you first – just out o' politeness – an' it's best to stay mates wi' Chairman o' local club."

Jack thought for a bit.

"Aye – OK then – you can sell your story with my blessing – but I don't want you puttin' words in my mouth what I never said – an' I want fifty percent."

"Fifty percent! – come on Jack – I 'ave to make a livin'! Ten percent."

"Forty."

"Twenty."

"Thirty"

"Twenty five."

"Done," said Jack, "An' don't flog it for less than fifty grand. If you can't get that for it then we'll make up some stuff what didn't 'appen an' get a better story."

Fred spluttered. "You amaze me Jack. OK – I'll see thee."

Jack replaced the phone and again it rang straight away. He'd given up on his mobile ages ago and switched it off – this one was getting just as bad. What was Angela doing putting all these calls through to him?

"What now?" he muttered gruffly.

"Ah Jack," came a silken Irish tongue. "It's Doctor Mary here, from the Department of Health – you rang me earlier, remember."

“Aye!” Jack said excitedly. “Course I remember. Any joy?”

“Joy? Oh yes – I can get the flight to Rio all right, but I was wonderin’ Jack, do you think you could tell me the name of the venue? – I’m havin’ a bit o’ trouble workin’ out the journey as I don’t know were I’m supposed to be going.”

“But what about the points I raised when I spoke to you earlier – aren’t you going to denounce it?”

“Oh Jack – I couldn’t do that – it’s not in my remit. Didn’t you get my message now? The Health Education Council – it’s right up their street – they love interfering. Now if you could just tell me the name o’ the town where it’s being held?”

“I don’t believe this. *Calm down Jack, calm down,*” he muttered to himself, but it was audible to Mary at the other end of the phone.

“That’s a good idea Jack. I think you should calm down and have a little cup of tea and a cigarette.”

“A cigarette! I thought you were supposed to be the department o’ ’ealth!”

“Oh, come on now Jack – we don’t want to be like that, do we? A little cigarette every now and then just to calm the nerves – what harm can that do? So if you could just tell me the name of the place, Jack......”

“OK. Here’s what I suggest. If you give me a telephone number, a direct line, to someone important in the ’Ealth Education Council, I’ll tell you the name of the place.”

“Well why didn’t you say that before? You want to try Professor Ciara O’Gosh – she’s my twin sister – 07990 682916 – she advises on what to put on all the Health Education posters.”

“Grand. 07990 682916 you say?”

“Yes.” Her silky smooth voice started to sound menacing. “Now where is it Jack? I’m getting impatient.”

“I only just found out – I can’t really remember – it’s something like Flicalicabudal.”

“How do you spell that?”

“Well I don’t know – it’s foreign – it’s near Bell Horizontal or some such place – ’ere – I’ll give you the phone number of my mate Fred – ’e’s the one what just told me the name of it – he’s on ’Etherington 2510 – it’s the local paper – ’Etherington Gazette – got that?”

“It’ll have to do. But I was really hoping for more from you Jack.”

Jack was amazed at how such an inviting voice was simultaneously laced with threat.

“Oh were you?” He countered, gruffly. “Well the same could be said for me with you. I’ll talk to your sister. Bye bye doctor.”

“Later Jack,” she signed off abruptly and the phone went click.

Jack flicked the cradle, just for long enough to get the dialling tone, pressed the button for an outside line, then dialled the number he had been given by Doctor Mary. The mobile phone rang and a voice answered which was exactly the same as the one he had just been speaking to.

“Professor O’Gosh,” said the voice.

“Hello professor,” Jack effused, “I ’ope you don’t mind me ringin’ – my name’s Jack Dugdale – I was given your number by your sister Mary – it’s about your job with the ’Ealth Education Council – I wondered if you might ’ave a position regarding safe sex?”

“Are you gay or heterosexual.”

“Heterosexual o’ course!”

“What positions have you tried already?”

“Pardon?..... Oh, no – sorry love. What I meant is, do *you* ’ave a position regardin’ ’ow safe it should be to ’ave sex with lots o’ different women?”

“Oh, now I know what you’re talking about, Jack...... you need our *Sure Whore* scheme...... it’s a list of approved prostitutes – all tested by the Ministry and guaranteed free from germs – if you give me your e-mail address I can send it to you.”

“What?..... Oh no, no – that’s not what I meant either. Sorry. I’m not makin’ this very clear. It’s about the World Furry Cup Championships to be ’eld in Brazil. It’ll involve unprotected sex won’t it, so I thought you might ’ave a view – maybe express disapproval of the event, you know, do a poster and try to stop the Jam United team from participating."

"Oh *that* – you mean the *Furry Cup Final* as we like to call it. My sister told me about it already this morning so she did; it sounds like a good crack. She's tried getting us the tickets but said she'd have to ring some eejut to get the name of the place where it's held."

"Oh did she?" Jack bit his tongue. "So what about the safe sex then? Will they 'ave to wear condoms over their 'eads, or are you goin' to ban it?"

"Oh no – that won't be necessary. I did a bit of research after Mary phoned. The event's sponsored by the Terror del Fuego Mentholated Lozenge Company. Apparently they have great antiseptic qualities, as well as heightening the sensation for the girls. The competitors are supplied with them free – a fresh one must be sucked before every round. They're supposed to work miracles on the ladies, and the men don't get clap of the mouth. According to the literature there's a 99% success rate at preventing infection."

"Oh bollocks!" said Jack, uncaring. "So you'll not do anything then?"

"As I said – we're getting tickets. Hmmmm......" Ciara paused for thought. "I'll have to have my bikini-line done...... must get an appointment. Oh – and I expect we'll carry out a double-blind controlled study on the Terror del Fuegos – see if there really *is* any benefit – you never know – they could soon be on prescription over here! I can imagine the poster now: *Suck this...... before you suck this......*"

"This is madness. I 'aven't managed to get any sense out of anyone for bloody days now – I'm at the end of me tether."

"Is that right. I'll send you the poster about all our helplines then – if you'll just give me that little e-mail address of yours......"

"Bollocks!" Jack snapped again and slammed down the phone. It immediately rang, annoying him even more.

"Hello!" he barked.

"Hello. This is Adelina Omov – I'm standin' as prospective Labour candidate in the Hetherin'ton by-election and..."

Jack interrupted her: "I'll not be votin' for you bloody Labour lot! An' I'm not in the mood for talkin'!" Then he realised what she had said. "'Ang on...... Who did you say you were?"

"Adelina Omov – prospective Labour candidate in the Hetherin'ton by-election."

"Does that mean you're standin' against that Dove'awk bloke?" Jack slowly savoured his words "And you could kick 'im out?"

"Yes. I was goin' to say that when I heard about your little problem in the FA Cup, I wondered if there was anythin' I could do to help?"

"Help! Oh yes, help – that's exactly what we need. Don't you know I've tried everyone: Dove'awk, the government, 'Ealth Education Council – they're all mad – all stark starin' bloody barmy – and they're all off to Brazil as well!"

"Yes. Well it sounds like a bit o' fun, doesn't it?"

"Christ, you're another one! Is everybody missin' the point 'ere, or is it just me who's daft?"

"Oh come on. If you'd read my book *Black Feminism for the Future*, you'd know I'm a libertarian at heart. You can't stop people enjoyin' themselves."

"I agree with that. But what you're talkin' about isn't enjoyment – it's indecent and amoral! And it could lead to the downfall of our national game!"

"That's my point – all those indecent things are fun. Life would be dull without them."

"A lot of 'elp you're goin' to be!" Jack's disillusionment deflated him again.

"Don't despair. We must think of a way to approach the problem without appearin' to the public as killjoys."

"Well *I* can't think of a way – an' believe me I've tried."

"Well. I think we should ask the Jam United players' wives what they think of it."

Jack was briefly again revitalised, but there had been so many false hopes that he immediately tried to look for flaws.

"Aye, that's certainly a good idea. But you y'self said we mustn't appear to be killjoys. That's what we'll be if we try to get the event stopped."

"No, not killjoys at all. We'll just arrange a rival tournament, to be held in England, specially for the Jam U wives! We'll get all the famous and best lookin' men in the country – your Sean'll be one of them – to take part in a competition to pleasure the Jam U lady-folks."

"Eh?" Jack thought about it. What were the pitfalls? The wives might not agree – but there was no harm in asking. "Sounds magic. Can you arrange it then lass?"

"I should certainly think so – the only pity is, we'll have to hold it indoors; England in the middle of winter: it's not Brazil is it?"

"Aye. I tell you what. We'll 'old it in one o' the big conference centres in their own city – that way their lasses'll not 'ave far to come, an' we'll get all their masses o' supporters – they probably won't bother goin' to Brazil when they know they'll 'ave better entertainment served up on their doorstep! Oh, an' we'll need to get 'old o' some o' those special throat sweets what blow the gussets out o' yer tights."

"They sound amazin'. I'll start phonin' the wives as soon as I get their home numbers, or their mobiles."

"I've just thought – all you need to do is tell one of the tabloid papers what you're doin' – give them an exclusive an' they'll do all the phonin' for you – we need to compose a press release."

"I've still got the Minister here at our headquarters. As soon as he's gone I'll come over to you and we'll write it over a drink in the club bar. What do you say?"

"I'll look forward to that. I'll go an' tell the doorman straight away that 'e's to let you in when you arrive. What do you look like?"

"Oh. Just like any other little old black lady from North London – you know – bright clothes, lots o' shoppin', very friendly."

"You sound lovely. Well, bye bye then lass – here's to a successful partnership."

"Goodbye Mr Dugdale – I assume that it is you who I've been talkin' to – I never asked."

"Aye. Jack Dugdale it is. You must call me Jack."

"And you must call me Adelina. I'll be about an hour and a half. See you soon Jack."

"Aye, see you soon lass."

Jack heard the line go click and put down the phone for the umpteenth time that morning. "Yes!" he exulted. "At last somethin's gonna 'appen!" *Ring ring...* went the phone.

The first Saturday in January – Third Round Day

Adelina looked around the arena. To her immense relief it was full – fifteen thousand people all seated and undercover and happily buzzing with expectation, while the huge banks of video screens above the tiers of seats on either side gave a magnificent magnified view of the bed in the centre of proceedings, too small to be seen by the unaided eye from anywhere much further away than the tenth row. The Grazedknee Colliery Band were offering a fast rendition of themes from Porgy and Bess to get everyone in the mood, while the large shining contraption looking like an overgrown fruit machine around which they were marching proclaimed itself in vivid flashing illuminated letters: *Terror del Fuego – "la Pastilla del Amor"* (Terror del Fuego – "the Love Lozenge").

At 3pm precisely, the band filed out of the auditorium, the blinds on the skylights whirred closed, the house-lights dimmed to nothing, and all attention was focused on the illuminated stage and giant screens. The Master of Ceremonies walked on, bowed to each point of the compass, then took up his position in an elevated pulpit overlooking what was to be the scene of the action: it was Jack, wearing top hat and tails, looking like a ringmaster in a circus, the light bedazzling from his glitzy costume.

"Welcome ladies and gentlemen. We have here, today, for your delectation and titillation, at the first event of its kind in English history, three footballers, four pop-stars, two actors and one business tycoon fighting it out to impress our gorgeously desirable women-folk with their sinuous oral gymnastics. The ladies whom these most desirable male-athletes will be trying to please come from many walks of life and backgrounds, as you will hear at the beginning of each round...... So let's not waste any more time – I'll introduce you straight away to your two judges – whose decisions are final and the only ones which count – may we have a big round of applause for Adelina Omov and Stanley Dovehawk.

The cheers were generous as the two judges smiled at each other between taking their bows.

"Before we get the action started, we just need to explain the rules," said Adelina, her radio-microphone picking up her silken voice and echoing it around the cavernous building. "The first rule is: no beards or moustaches. Our guest crimper, Algernon," she opened her arms towards a smiling man with no hair, "Has taken up his cut-throat razor for the day and has been practisin' on our competitors' designer facial hair, so that none of them has an unfair advantage. But me, I don't like the beard anyway – thick one too tickly, thin one too prickly – I mean – how you gonna concentrate wi' dat goin' on? Now, here's Stan to tell you how we award the marks."

Dovehawk carved his crustaceous cheeks and chin into a grin a mediaeval mason would have been proud to chisel upon a gargoyle.

"Marks are awarded in ten categories with a possible ten marks for each: *delicacy of build-up*, *attention to detail*, *area of coverage*, *complementary finger-work*, *crescendo*, *height of pinnacle*, *duration of attainment*, *sound level*, *relaxation*."

Adelina turned and looked at him.

"That's only nine, isn't it Stan?"

"Oh yes," said Stan, poring over his notes. "What could the tenth one be, Adelina?"

"Oh. I think I know what that tenth one is Stan," She turned her head back to the audience. "Finally, for the tenth category, the lady herself can award marks out of ten accordin' to her *satisfaction*. That is if she can speak. *Struck dumb* will count as an automatic eleven!"

"I'll second that, Adelina," joked Stan. "Right then, we'll now hand back to Jack to introduce the contestants."

The two judges sat down.

"Thank you Adelina and Stan. Now ladies and gentlemen, onwards with the proceedings. To get us off to a swingin' start, the first ten lady volunteers are all nurses at the big 'ospital just up the road. They're all local lasses who like a good time – an' most of 'em go to

Ibeeza on 'oliday – so they know what it's all about. So get your 'ands together for Jackie, the first o' the nurses!"

A huge roar and whistles greeted Jackie who was wearing her uniform, her hair clipped up neatly in her little hat.

"Now. None o' that you dirty buggers!" Jack bellowed jovially to the audience. "We're goin' to spin this 'ere spinner to find who is the lucky contestant to prise open the charms of the beautiful Jackie." He spun a giant arrow on a clock-face which had only ten numbers. It stopped at number 7. "Number 7 is... Sean Shagdit! Who'd o' believed that, eh? Me own irrepressible star striker. Come on Sean – and don't forget your lozenge lad! That's it – take one from the machine and put it under your tongue, while you Jackie lass, you just make yourself comfortable on the couch."

Jackie beamed to the audience and winked at them, then sat on the bed and modestly swung her legs onto it, keeping them tantalisingly tightly clenched.

"Right, are the judges ready?" Jack eagerly pressed on with the script. Adelina and Dovehawk both nodded. "Silence then, seconds out: GIVE IT SOME, LAD!"

All the lights went out except for those illuminating the delectable Jackie. Sean knelt next to her black stockinged calves and, with a crisp movement, swung the nearer one over his head. The crowd cheered, while Adelina and Stan patrolled around the foot of the bed, peering purposefully at the proceedings.

"Ooohh!" shrieked Jackie. "That tongue's mean 'ot!"

"Ho ho!" chortled Jack. "The old Terror del Fuegos are doin' their job!"

Marks from the judges started to flash up on the screens – *delicacy of build up*: 6, *attention to detail*: 8. Jackie shuddered and groaned and the judges were obviously impressed for the marks mounted steadily – 9 for *complementary finger work*, 7 for *area of coverage*. Then Jackie fell silent for ten, twenty, thirty seconds – time ticked by with only her hands clenching and unclenching by her sides. Tension in the crowd was immense as forty seconds elapsed, a whole minute. Had she gone numb? Peaked too soon? Was this going to be a blow-out? Sean knew he was in trouble, but suddenly Jackie's back arched like an aggravated centipede, forcing her tummy up in the air.

Adelina and Stan immediately seized their opportunity for a low-level decision, both managing to get their heads beneath Jackie's taut body, one on each side. 9 shot up on the screens for *crescendo*, and none too soon for the judges had to leap for cover as Jackie crashed back down. While she squalled and whooped the marks piled up with matching frenzy: *sound level*: 8, *height of pinnacle*: 8, but her hollering quickly subsided and 3 was displayed for *duration of attainment*. As her body fell limp and flaccid, Sean stood up and raised his arms in the air to acknowledge the adulation from the masses – then manfully strode to the dispenser and withdrew another mentholated lozenge.

"Aye – that'll tek taste away son," recounted Jack wistfully, trying to remember a holiday he'd once had in Blackpool.

Adelina rearranged Jackie's dress for decorum, then picked up a microphone from under the bedcover and held it near the snoozing nurse's mouth. "Can we have your marks for *satisfaction* please darlin'?"

Jackie opened her eyes weakly then closed them again. "Fockin' ten," she whispered with a breathless charm.

"Shit!" grumbled Sean. "She's cost me a point!"

"Mmmmm," hummed Adelina, surveying the slumbering figure. "And it's got to be ten for *relaxation* as well – don't you agree Stan?"

"Oh aye. Ten for certain."

"Right then," said Jack. "So the grand total on the computer is: seventy eight out of a possible one 'undred 'n one. That's a crackin' score an' no mistake! Eh, look at the state o' that lass – she's goin' to remember Third Round Day for the rest of 'er life. Just to keep everyone's appetites whetted, I can tell you that in the next round the ladies will be nine of the Jam United players' wives, plus – as a late entrant – and you won't want to miss 'er – the Jam U manager's daughter – wow! Then to finish, as a stiffer test for our boys, to find out who is genuinely at the top of their game, we have ten novices from the convent who won their places in this contest in a Benedictine raffle – bet they thought first prize were a bottle – ha ha! Right. Settle down everyone. If you could just wheel Jackie off, Stanley, we'll get a new bed set up an' I'll introduce our next lovely nurse – Stella."

The spot-light shimmered across the stage as a black long-haired beauty clopped into view in her high heels.

Adelina watched the girl approach, her white uniform crisply brushing the silken stockings, her eyes sparkling, the crowd holding their breath in awe."

"Aaaaaaaah! It's me. It's me. Aaaaaaaah! That nurse is me! I can't do this! I'll lose the nomination!" Adelina screamed and felt herself falling, fainting. Jack spun his pointer to choose the number of the next contestant, then, right in front of Adelina's face, it changed to an ordinary clock again. Half past three in the morning. Oh god – what a nightmare! She sat rigid in her bed, the feel of the pumps from her heart bashing wildly against the inside of her head like boat-wash against a river bank. I wonder if this was such a good idea? she thought. But she knew it was too late – the editor of the paper had been most impressed when she had spoken to him on the phone; another day, another front-page already printed. My goodness – after today everyone in the country would have heard of Adelina Omov. How scary can that be?

Wednesday – seven o'clock in the evening

The back room at the Hetherington Working Men's Club began to fill, both with people, slightly damp and unaired from the fog of the December streets, and also with expectancy amid uncertainty. *Was this really happening?* they wondered as they smoothed their raincoats under their bottoms before sitting down, squishing the air from the old seat-cushions, sending dank musty messages of familiar surroundings to those already seated around and about. The stage was a low one, no more than eighteen inches high. The table at its centre was unspectacular, having three microphones installed in front of three chairs, with three glasses of water to be filled from a jug wearing a red rosette – a nice touch – perhaps to alleviate the drabness of the grey curtaining which formed the backdrop. But hell, it didn't matter what the scenery looked like – this was exciting stuff for Hetherington – the possibility of the chosen Labour candidate being de-selected? It was unheard of. It was a travesty. It was brilliant fun. There had been a buzz around the pubs and clubs in the town as Labour Members, not normally animated, discussed the pros and cons of having a woman MP – a woman MP who, judging by her picture on the flyer and her appearance on a brief walkabout in town with the Minister looked like she could melt anything in her path. Anything male that is; the women Party Members and the wives of their masculine counterparts were not so keen: much too stunning; too designer-clothed; too out of place on a bus. She may have got onto Bent Council but she'd never make it onto the committee of the Shirley Crabtree Appreciation Society, and she'd never be able to wing a burglar with a well-aimed Eccles cake at three in the morning, and neither could she carry three hundredweight of provisions home from Ecclesby Market unaided (it's amazing what northern lasses can carry so long as you make sure they're evenly loaded).

One lass arrived in the hall and said hello to her friend Dahlia while shaking out her brolly. The canopy of an umbrella can be quite elastic when it wishes; although most of the water droplets simply splotted around the vicinity of Dahlia's and Betty's ankles, just one catapulted in an arching vaulting trajectory towards the stage. Gerald was fiddling with the PA system, tapping this and that, satisfying himself that the combatants would be heard. The droplet passed over his head without him noticing and seemed harmless enough until it tumbled through one of the ventilation slats on the amplifier. An almighty bang wrought the air, causing the Salvation Army man (who had been given permission to attend) to drop his collecting tin noisily. This was followed by a loud staccato crackling from the loudspeakers that made everyone think Gerald had let one rip in front of the microphones, which of course he had as soon as he heard the initial bang, but it had been silent and he didn't see why anyone should have been any the wiser.

"Chuffin' 'ell!" said Gerald, trying to divert suspicion from his bottom, "I wonder what that was?"

"'Tent my fault," protested the Salvation Army man from his position just in front of the stage, "If folks weren't so mean as to give all coppers an' no silver it wouldn't 'ave made such a racket!"

"Eh up," laughed Dahlia. "That were you shakin' your umbrella did that Betty!"

"I just shoook it out – that's all I did."

"I know. But I saw the water drop in the light – shot right in t' machinery it did."

"Oh golly, no. D'you think 'e'll know it were me?"

"No, course not."

Dovehawk peered in from the wings, saw Gerald tapping a lot of dead microphones, chuckled and disappeared again. Gerald fished around in his toolbox and withdrew a screwdriver. He then pulled the mains plug from the socket on the wall and proceeded to dismember it. He didn't notice Stan and Adelina and the Chair of the Constituency Labour Party, Mr Rumbleon, walk onto the stage and take their seats.

"Good evening ladies and gentlemen," opened Mr Rumbleon. Gerald turned, gasped, frantically thrust the plug back where it belonged and rushed around tapping microphones again. "This is an Extraordinary General Meeting of the 'Etherington Constituency Labour Party which has been called to choose our candidate in the forthcoming parliamentary by-election. The two candidates are, on my left Ms Adelina Omov, who, as you can see, is a lady, and on my right, Mr Stanley Dove'awk, who, as you all know, is a gentleman...... sometimes! Ha ha ha!" and Mr Rumbleon chuntered away at his own joke, which was also to the amusement of most of the assembled personages.

"Objection!" uttered a shrill intrusion from way behind everyone in the room, so far behind that it seemed to well up from the narrow end of a megaphone and plant itself loudly and objectionably in the ears of all those present. Mr Rumbleon frowned as he tried to focus on the cause of the interruption. "'Ang on," he said, "I 'aven't got to the *if anyone knows of any just impediment* bit yet! Ha ha ha!" and again he enjoyed his own patter to the full.

"Oh bloody hell, no!" muttered Dovehawk. "It's that woman again!"

Adelina just sat where she was, noncommittally. Pree walked down the side of the chairs towards the stage. "I must insist," she said in an insisting manner, "That you, Mr Chairperson, present the candidates impartially. All this matey pally stuff with Mr Dovehawk lays these proceedings open to an accusation of prejudice."

Pree stood there, an imposing figure in her smart cream suit, skirt just below the knee, expensive strappy beige shoes, shimmering make-up, simmering eyes, scintillating soft brown hair. Mr Rumbleon coughed nervously, beckoned his two partners closer and whispered something. After listening to the answer, presumably to the question "Who on earth is that?", he coughed again before speaking aloud.

"This meeting is under *my* control, and I'll only take objections from the floor when they are indeed objectionable, as I see it. In this case, while I think that your objection lacks impartiality, you being here to support one candidate over the other, I shall attempt in future to be equally matey and pally, as you so put it, with Ms Omov. In fact," Mr Rumbleon looked across to Adelina, "It will be my pleasure to do so. Ha ha ha!" And he was off again.

Pree stood her ground. "I accept your answer as indicating that you intend to be neutral. I must remind the Chairperson that this meeting is to be conducted according to Labour Party rules and, as I am an accredited Party invigilator, I may report any procedural discrepancies to the National Executive Committee who may order you to do the whole thing again, or even take the decision out of you hands."

"Right!" blistered Dovehawk, unable to contain himself any longer. "That does it! You, you zealous bitch, know damn well that the National Executive can do just what the stuff they like with any decision reached at this meeting and, whether it's unbiased or not, it's still a thousand times more representative than your bloody lot who just think whatever Downing Street tells them to think!"

"And I shall be reporting that outburst, Stan, to the NEC at their next meeting." Pree sounded frighteningly calm.

"'Ang on a minute, Missus," croaked Mr Rumbleon, "I'm afraid you can't address one of the candidates by 'is first name as that could be perceived as familiarity by people with a trivial nature. Ha ha ha!"

Before Pree could reply, Adelina stood up and addressed the gathering.

"Now you hear what we women in the Labour Party are up against," she purred, unashamedly milking any sympathy that was going. "Whenever there's more than one of us, the men think we're ganging up on them and harangue us with insults which they disguise as their so-called humour."

Mr Rumbleon stopped sniggering in order to defend his so-called humour. "I'm not just putting this on cos you two lasses are 'ere y' know. I've been funny for years; always funny I am: 'Send 'em 'ome from Party meetings 'appy,' that's my philosophy. You ask any on em sittin' there just 'ow funny I am, go on, I dare you!"

"Oh just get on with it!" Pree dismissed him as an idiot. She returned to the back of the hall to sit in a vacant seat, then she took up a notebook and pencil.

Looking like he'd just had a skirmish with a swan, knowing a bite from something looking that elegant shouldn't hurt as much as it did, Mr Rumbleon gathered himself for an assault on the crux of the evening's business.

The candidates will now each 'ave ten minutes to address the floor. So," he looked to each side, not wishing to be told off again, "Who wants to go first?" Gerald hurried over and tapped on a microphone again, but still it was dead. He looked depressed and disappeared back into the mess of wires he had made in the rear corner of the stage.

"I don't mind," said Adelina.

"Nor me, " said Dovehawk.

"Right – well we'll toss a coin then – I think that's best. 'Ere we go – now which of you wants to call?"

"I don't mind," said Adelina.

"Nor me, " said Dovehawk.

"Right – er......" Mr Rumbleon tried to see Pree at the back of the hall, hoping for some guidance, an indication from her, as it had been some time since he'd read the rules on the conduct of Party meetings and he really didn't want to be told off again. "Is *ladies first* all right?" he ventured timidly?"

"What for?" Adelina asked innocently. "The tossin'? Or the speakin'?"

Mr Rumbleon's optimism was under duress. "Er, the tossin', actually, if that's all right?"

"I'll call *tails* then, Mr Chair." She looked satisfied.

Mr Rumbleon took a two-pence piece from his pocket. So as to make sure there was no perception of cheating, he flicked it high in the air. Gerald whooped a great shout of "Hurray!" behind him, just as he flicked, and the coin went even higher than he had intended. He watched it all the way as it attained full altitude before starting its downward plunge, slightly in front of where he was sitting. He hurled himself forward to catch it, but it was going so fast he missed it and it landed straight in the jug of water, splash-down, like a space capsule into the sea. A droplet of water ejected from the jug flew straight over Gerald's shoulder and into his equipment, making another loud bang. As Gerald disconsolately trudged off to the plug socket to check the fuse again, the three heads belonging to the people seated at the table all banged together in their urgency to see how the coin had landed. "*Tails*" said Mr Rumbleon, authoritatively. "Right." Then he had another feeling of unease. "Right. That means Ms Omov has won the toss. Er.....? Does that mean she goes first? Or does that mean she chooses where she would like to go?" Mr Rumbleon felt even more depressed when he looked down the hall and saw Pree making notes.

"She can choose," said Dovehawk, displaying magnanimity in the face of adversity.

Adelina stood. "Thank you Stanley," she acknowledged graciously. "I think that, as the latecomer to this contest, I shall go first so that you can have the final word – that seems only fair to me."

She swapped the order of a piece of paper with another one on the table in front of her as an indication that she was about to begin. The silence afterwards was complete; everyone awaited her address, hardly daring to breathe.

"My name is Adelina Omov. It's now thirty seven years since I was born in the back bedroom at 12 Beaumont Rise, Hornsey, North London which, for those of you who've not heard about it, is just down the road from here...... the A1 road that is!"

A couple of titters struggled from the audience, the male audience anyway; the female audience glowered venomously.

"My grandparents came here from Antigua in the Caribbean and immediately fell in love with the English climate. *None o' dat havin' to take shade all the time under de palm trees*, they said. *Now we can feel nice an' cool every day, and we get a shower as well so no need to wash in de marnin'!*"

A better surge of merriment from the audience this time, and Dovehawk chuckled heartily. Mr Rumbleon meanwhile looked like he had lost his sense of humour.

“Then, one day, granddad discovered that great invention: the umbrella. *Ah*, he said, *A portable palm tree what you shelter under when you want a cigarette – to stop it goin' out in de rain!*”

Adelina reached under the table. “And *here* it is,” she said, holding aloft a withered black gentleman's umbrella with a cane handle.

“This is granddad's umbrella – you see?” She opened it and held it up to the light, which immediately shone through a myriad of small holes, like the pricks of light from stars in a night sky. “You can tell he musta smoked a lot a cigarettes under dis umbrella – look at all de burn holes – if my grandmother had seen dis she woulda killed him!”

Now they all laughed.

“And to think – this is my inheritance.” She looked at it quizzically. “Our only family heirloom and it's got more holes than the Tories got backsides to talk out of.”

And they laughed some more.

“O' course, poor old granddad: he died o' de lung cancer. Cos you know, you were allowed to smoke on de buses in those days, an' bein' a conductor he needed a puff regular to get him up an' down those stairs nine hundred times a day.”

Then they groaned sorrowfully.

“So, I look at this old umbrella and it reminds me o' granddad, cos I think his lungs must ha' looked just the same as this! All full a holes!”

But were transported involuntarily into laughter again.

“My grandmother had a part-time job at the Edmonton Power Station – cleanin' the coal. Don't laugh! It was a very important job; you hose down the coal with the water to keep the dust from blowin' away an' gettin' up the residents' noses! O' course – you didn't need to do it when it was rainin'...... like I said – it was a part-time job! So, just imagine, in the mornin' in our house: grandma an' granddad get up an' take their first look out o' de window; if it's rainin' – mum make the tea an' de breakfast – get de kids ready for school – then she go off down de 'Olloway Road shoppin', while granddad he put up his umbrella, light up his cigarette and walk off to the Bus Depot; if it's not rainin', granddad leave his umbrella rolled up an' he whack grandma round de bum with it to get 'er off to work on time, then he light the cigarette at 'ome – an' de kids all get a bit late for school and get the tellin' off from de teacher. O' course, grandma always found out somehow, so my dad got a whuppin' from her and granddad felt the umbrella round *his* bum for not gettin' us ready on time. Life was simple in those days. My parents and grandparents didn't have to make choices all the time cos they did everything the same, every day, just like everybody else; and they were happy. Look at the world now! Choices all the time – so many – and worryin' about makin' the wrong one – we're all de nervous wrecks. Politicians say that givin' people choices improves their lives – you may agree, or you may take the opposite view. This contest for example may be givin' you a choice that you didn't want to make. Stan here was your candidate and runnin' an excellent campaign – the canvass returns all showin' he had more than fifty percent support – so why do you need someone like me rollin' into town at the last minute, tryin' to steal his thunder? Well I'm only black; I'm only a woman; but as I hope I just showed you by talkin' about my family, hopefully without borin' you too much, I have passion."

She placed her hand on her heart.

"I am a passionate woman. And that is what I will give to the people of Hetherin'ton, should I be lucky enough to be selected. I talk passionately, I live passionately, and I love passionately."

She looked across at Stan who grinned a flabby grin. The men in the audience couldn't think or move or make a sound, while two of the women loudly tutted their disapproval.

"And as an example, I'm sure you all must have seen this mornin's headlines in the papers. I will do everythin' I can, use every ounce of my strength, to support our lovely football club in their time of great sadness and loss. Even though my own loyalties lie with Snotterham Tosspurt – I supported them, you understand, only because my two brothers supported Anusoil – I can displace them in my affections completely for a friendly club like Hetherin'ton Sidanee FC."

Hooray cheered the clapping audience. Dovehawk looked a bit pallid, like he'd just been told that the beer was off and the only thing left to drink was goat's piss cocktails. Adelina sat down.

Dovehawk waited for the applause to dwindle, which seemed to him to take an awful long time, then stood up. He knew he was in trouble. The women in the audience looked up at him with hope and expectation in their hearts that he could put a riddance to the strumpet. The men watched Adelina sitting at the table, her hair shining in the stage lighting, her soft eyes beckoning, as if to each, on his own, especially. And they all felt gladdened.

Dovehawk cleared his throat. In apparent mimicry of his opponent's earlier actions, he grabbed a hold of his papers on the table, but instead of just shuffling them about, he held them up and theatrically ripped them apart, replacing each smaller sheaf upon its opposite half and tearing them again until they were made up of a hundred small pieces of paper the size of postage stamps. He then tossed them in the air, showering the assemblage of people behind the table, Mr Rumbleon looking up at Dovehawk as if he had gone barmy while at the same time dusting himself down to remove the unwanted confetti.

"I shan't be needing those!" Dovehawk expounded confidently, "As Ms Omov's speech has rather moved the goalposts!" And he noisily congratulated himself, Rumbleon style, at his wit, embroiling his audience who joined in with loud hilarity. Adelina clapped.

"I was born in Edgbaston, lots of years ago, so I'm a bit of an immigrant to the north of England meself. My father was – dare I say this? – a Union man. I don't think we're allowed to mention skeletons like that in our cupboards now we're New Labour, but it did instill in us the value of joining together in a unity of purpose, the feeling that a shared goal is much more attainable than an individual's solo aim."

He paused to draw breath, then sighed.

"But now I'm in this politics game, I find that unity to have deserted me. In this business, teamwork is your cover while you find out what the other bloke's up to, then denounce him and pinch his job. It's a lonely place from my perspective, standing here. Unity of purpose is espoused by Parties and the pursuance of policy towards a common good is their reason for being; but the nitty gritty is that of individual aims, hundreds of them, all with self-inflated opinions, big ideas, big egos and big publicity machines; and I don't seek to defend myself from being labelled with those characteristics: we have to be like that or we sink. I love life, love the joy of living; every day for me is an experience of sharing time, ideas, hopes. But I also *survive*. As a politician, to survive is all. But here, today, you've heard a remarkable lady who, I confess, I cannot criticise harshly, even though it's my job to do so. Which is why, just for today, I want to leave self-interest behind even if it does cost me my position, and instead try to remember my old father and his ideals of fellowship and mutual assistance.

"Obviously, I have been thinking about this speech for several days now. I've changed my mind countless times over what I was and wasn't going to say, and then when all seemed settled, changed it again. But then, last night, I had a dream!"

"Hallelujah!" cried Gerald as the PA system hissed back into life, then looked shamefaced as everyone burst into laughter. Adelina looked intently at Stan, remembering her own dream of the previous night.

"I couldn't have put it better! Thank you Gerald!" Dovehawk paraded his new-found evangelism. "Remembering that this was before I knew anything about Adelina's little scheme for a rival contest to Jam United's planned shenanigans, I found myself surrounded by an audience, much bigger than this one – thousands of them, in a great big hall, full of light. And at the focus, where all the light was converging, in the centre of this arena, there was meself, and Adelina, and Jack, the football club Chairman. He was the master of ceremonies, and announced that we were taking part in the competition which had been arranged to coincide with the third round of the FA Cup, Adelina's competition, and myself and Adelina – we were the judges. Isn't that incredible?"

Adelina looked nervous for the first time, thoughts rushing around her head. She hadn't told anyone about her dream, had she? Was there any doubt? No of course not – she definitely hadn't mentioned it, so he couldn't have found out. Which meant – oh gosh – he had had the same dream at the same time! Sharing desks was more risky than she had thought. She reasoned Dovehawk had downloaded her memory banks from just a brush against her thigh, and a touch of her breast.

"And we were team-mates, on the same side, working together, me and Adelina, and we had a great time doing the judging and then I woke up. And that was it. I didn't care any more for this crazy contest – me against her. I forgot all about my plans for my speech. I thought I would present myself as what I am – a man living in a world where he meets so many people, and yet is marooned in loneliness. It made no sense to me, so I thought I would present it here and see if it made sense to you. So, to conclude, I'll give three cheers: one to the people of Hetherington, one to the football club in their hour of need, and one to Adelina for having the courage to be counted when all I could do was dream...... Thank you everyone," said Stan, and sat back down, while all clapped except Mr Rumbleon who took up his position to introduce the next instalment.

"Now we'll take questions from the floor," he intoned. "So who wants to start us off? Hands up anyone? Ah, Mr Smidgeon, please go ahead."

The raised hand of Alf Smidgeon, a small man of about sixty, had been spotted by the sharp-eyed Mr Rumbleon despite the fact that he was sitting in the total eclipse of a large Lady Member on his left. Although he had been called upon, Alf appeared reluctant to commit himself to the onerous job of launching this next phase of the proceedings, and his unease was steadily aggravated by the mounting impatience displayed on the Rumbleon features.

"Well? Let's 'ave your question then, lad." Mr Rumbleon bullied poor Alf with both speech and look.

Apprehensively, Alf stood up, just failing to reach the height of his immediate neighbour's hairdo. "I'd like to ask the candidates what they would do about the police......" Alf began timidly. "Down our road last year......"

Rumbleon strained his body forward, almost lying across the table in his effort to hear. "Speak up lad. What did you say? Police?"

Smidgeon broke off from elaborating on his question and nodded to Rumbleon in the affirmative. Rumbleon sat back. "Right Ms Omov – Mr Smidgeon wants to know what you'd do about the police. And quite rightly too in my opinion – what about all these kids runnin' around swearin' at everyone and pinchin' cars?"

Adelina spoke. "As with everyone else who works for government run services nowadays, the police spend so much time filling in paperwork and reporting statistics they don't have time to be doin' what they're there for – patrollin' the streets."

Mr Smidgeon, still on his feet, raised his hand again, but Rumbleon glared at him.

"Let the lady finish 'er answer, then you can reply."

"I've finished," said Adelina. "I'm not one o' these people you see on the telly who only like the sound of their own voice."

"We're glad to 'ear that. Do you want to say anything Mr Dove'awk?"

"I just want to say that the law stops police from doing anything about juvenile crime. They're not *allowed* to stop the underage criminals from indulging in their hobby; I'd change the law so we can lock 'em up, same as any adult."

"Right, next question. Who wants to go next?"

"'Ang on!" Alf found a vocal volume of which he had hitherto seemed incapable. "I actually wanted to ask what the candidates thought about the police answerin' emergency calls and drivin' like maniacs, knockin' everyone over in their path! I saw a police car come down our road at ten to nine int' mornin' when all kids were goin' to school, an' he must o' been doin' sixty mile an hour in the thirty limit. They go on about drivin' safely, drink drivin', etc, but *they* drive like bloody lunatics themselves!" Feeling glad to have got that off his chest, Alf sat down.

"That was very assertive Mr Smidgeon – I can see that the subject affects you deeply. Very well done." Rumbleon looked to his left then his right. "Any comment about that from the candidates?"

Dovehawk nodded. "I must say they took two days to turn up to my house when I was burgled. The only time they use the blue light and the siren is when they're late back at the Station for their tea-break."

Lots of people in the audience laughed, and Rumbleon glared at Dovehawk for having the temerity to make a successful joke.

"I would favour the police and the ambulance and fire services to obey speed limits, even when they are on an emergency call – there's no point in getting someone to hospital three minutes quicker if you kill a child on the way."

The crowd applauded Adelina too.

Now, if that subject's quite finished with, I'll take the next question from...... ah yes – it's Stan Smoggrate – what a surprise that isn't! Ha ha ha!" – I thought *you'd* want to cross-examine the candidates, but don't be too long about it."

"Aye, that I do," said Smoggrate, standing up to avail himself of some fresher air and a clear line of sight along which to aim his interrogation. "I would first like to tell everyone 'ere that Ms Omov 'as been most 'elpful in respect of our little predicament at the football club, comin' up with new and unusual ideas; in contrast, I must add, with the stubborn uncooperation of Mr Dove'awk who seems to care little for the club or its supporters, despite me showin' 'im around the boardroom and its associated memorabilia."

Smoggrate looked at Dovehawk to check his reaction, but none was to be seen, the surface of the gruff politician remaining impassive.

"Yes, yes, all right – that's enough of the speech Mr Smoggrate. We want a question that these two up 'ere can answer – not a bloody sermon! Ha ha ha!"

Smoggrate waved his arm dismissively at Rumbleon, no doubt having much previous experience of his haranguing nature.

"All right, Rumble-Grumble, I'm goin' to ask a question to Mr Dove'awk personally. Should you become reinstated as our candidate for Member of Parliament, do you intend to assist 'Etherington Sidney Football Club in its fight to force Jam United back into the FA Cup?"

Dovehawk stood to deliver his response.

"Thank you Mr Smoggrate for giving me the opportunity to talk about this issue which is so dear to our own hearts, and the hearts of the inhabitants of this brave town." Dovehawk surveyed his audience keenly. "Or is that true? Let me see a show of hands of who would be deeply upset if Jam U didn't play here in the third round of the FA Cup, remembering of course all the crowds, and the drinking, and the fighting, and the noise, and the police on the streets, and the sirens, and the pubs with their windows lying on the pavements, and the queues at casualty."

Smoggrate waved and gestured wildly. "That's unfair!" he bellowed.

"You've had your turn!" Dovehawk bawled even louder. "You see everyone – this is the sort of reprehensible behaviour you get from football supporters – and Stan Smoggrate's supposed to be respectable." He skewered the wretched Smoggrate with his gaze. "You'll let me answer the question, or I'll ask Mr Rumbleon to have you ejected from the meeting. Mr Rumbleon's quite capable of such decisive action!"

Rumbleon glowed beneath Dovehawk's laudatory shower, quite unrealising that he was being roasted on a spit of faint praise. "Aye, that I will! I suggest you sit down Stan Smoggrate an' let Mr Dovehawk finish!"

Smoggrate sat down, wondering why his every encounter with Stanley Dovehawk put him in the wrong; it was so unfair!

"Please continue, Mr Dovehawk," grovelled Rumbleon.

Dovehawk looked to the back of the hall before he resumed, and noted that Pree was no longer scribbling dispassionately in her diary, but instead was transfixedly staring in his direction. He could feel, even at that great distance, her nervous energy willing him to make a fool of himself, while she also was excited at having no inkling of the outcome.

"So, as I said, hands up those who'd really *like* to have Jam United and their heaving hordes here, defiling this neat unflustered town with their litter and lager and language. Come on then. Are there any more?"

Stan watched as Smoggrate, one hand raised, furiously waved the other, exhorting the rest to join him. Some of the football supporting men-folk with their own arms raised looked sternly at their wives, tapping them with their elbows to urge compliance; a few women reluctantly acquiesced by raising an indifferent arm to half-mast.

Dovehawk, understanding every nuance of his Chairperson's sensibilities and frailties, aired his sycophancy once more.

"If you could do us the honour, Mr Rumbleon, of exercising your wise and impartial mind, what proportion of the audience, would you say, has its hand up?"

"I've already counted, Mr Dovehawk – it's less than half. Forty percent, I'd say."

"And how many of those are lady Members?"

Rumbleon scanned the dimly lit seating area again, this time taking longer. "Only two or three!" he eventually announced, although a few hands had wilted due to lack of blood supply to the arm.

“Good,” said Dovehawk, in a strangely optimistic way. “Now I don’t want anyone thinking I’m trying to score points here; I just wanted to inject some fact into what has become a very emotive argument. I can assure everybody in this room, that I will represent all persuasions and colours and genders among my constituents equally. I shall not be latching onto a particular issue just to gain cheap political capital. I feel quite able to support the football club while at the same time representing great swathes of the community who couldn’t give a toss about it, especially, of course, all the lovely lasses out there who think football should be practised more literally: that is, by regular connection of the toe-end of a high-heeled shoe with a tender spot in their other-half’s trouser region!”

Even Pree smiled as the ladies in the audience all clapped.

“So that’s it. I’ll always be glad to help out with any scheme which has the support of the community.” Dovehawk picked a newspaper up from the table and held it up so that the large headline could be seen by all: *JAM U WIVES TO BE GOBBLED ALIVE!* “In fact, I’d be honoured to assist Adelina with the judging – she knows she only has to ask.”

Dovehawk sat down. Mr Rumbleon, going out of his way to be scrupulously fair after his earlier admonishment, looked to his left to enquire if Adelina wished to make any comment. She acknowledged him with a nod.

“I welcome Stan’s, er...... Stan Dovehawk’s that is, support for the event – it should be a lot of fun. But I dreamt it up with the sole intention to shame Jam United into fulfillin’ their obligation to play Hetherin’ton Sidney in the third round o’ the cup.” Smoggrate and the football supporters cheered. “And talkin’ of dreams – I confess I had the same dream as Stan last night! It appears that exposure to each other durin’ this contest has provoked identical repercussions in our twilight thoughts. An’ I tell you – that’s scary! Thinkin’ the same thoughts as Stan can lead a person astray! I mean, it was only the day before yesterday when he was tellin’ me that he was gay!”

A murmur thrummed among those of the watchers who had not fallen asleep, and those who had were immediately wakened to be informed by their neighbours of developments. A look of shock came over Gerald’s face and he stared nervously at Dovehawk who gave him the thumbs up signal.

"I didn't believe him, of course. But then he told me he was going to show a video at this meeting. So I'm waitin' to see it!"

"Oh aye. I almost forgot about that," said Dovehawk nonchalantly. "Do the honours will you Gerald? Or have you blown up the whole of the electricity supply, the TV and the video as well?"

"No, I think they're working again now," Gerald replied mutedly. Then he went over to Dovehawk and whispered, "Are you sure you want to do this? It'll ruin any chance you've got, and Adelina knows it. At the moment you've got half the Members on your side; but while they're divided more or less evenly on football, there's one thing that unites them: they all hate queers."

"That may be true Gerald." Stan was grinning smugly and Gerald felt sorry for him. "But not me: I love 'em!" And Dovehawk held out the tape.

Gerald shook his head as he took the tape, trudged to the back of the stage and drew the grubby curtains aside to reveal a giant television. Then he ambled to the video machine and gave Dovehawk one last chance to save himself. Dovehawk gestured for him to continue, then sought Pree in the audience, but she had moved. He looked around and eventually spotted her seated right near the front, flagrantly seeking a better view, her mouth agape. Click went the video, Gerald switched off the lights, and the screen glowed its random snowfall pattern while the tape wound itself into position and started playing. There was a disco, lots of young people dancing and drinking. Then there was Marlon, with his friends, stripped to the waist and cavorting. Then there was Dovehawk, making his way through the crowd. Then there was Tammy, with Dovehawk being introduced, and laughter as they examined her stomach. And then there was Dovehawk, on his knees, kissing her tummy, the camera zooming in as he inscribed little circles with his lips.

"Right," said Mr Rumbleon for the umpteenth time that evening, "I've 'ad ebloodynough of this – switch that thing off Gerald, put the lights back on and let's get on with the votin'." As the lights came up, Stan was laughing, while Gerald's glasses had steamed up. "Now," continued Rumbleon, "When you've cleared your minds of all that smut, I want everyone to show their Party cards to Mrs Jessop who's sittin' at the table at the side o' the 'all – and remember, only Hetherington constituents can take part. She'll give you a votin' slip which you take behind the screen. Mark a cross next to the candidate you want, then deposit it in the ballot box which is next to Mr Filkin's wheelchair. When you've all done, we'll count up the votes and announce the winner. Then there'll be sausages and chips out in the main 'all, and a karaoke session while the loser drowns 'is or 'er sorrows at the bar."

As the voting commenced, Adelina went over to Dovehawk.

"Very good, Stan," she said, generously. "You hooked me like a fish."

"Aye. But don't worry love – I only do it in fun!"

"I know. That girl on the film – who was she?"

"That's Tamara Toker-Spankbottom. I only met her last week."

"Her birthmark, on her tummy – it looked like a willy to me."

"Aye, well, I said I'd show a video of me kissing a big one, and that's just what I did."

"You're incorrigible, Stan."

"I know. Do you fancy a quick one while they're counting the votes?"

"Drink or shag?"

"We tossed up to see who'd be first to address the meeting; let's toss for this one as well."

"I got to choose who went first. Now it's your turn."

"I like doing both. Heh, watch out – Pree Whatserchuffiname's coming over. *She* fancies me as well you know."

Adelina roared with laughter. "She hates you Stan. You're everything she despises: you're horrible, have no morals, are a blatant opportunist, treat everyone with disdain, and yet they all love you. It pisses her off so much. You know, the reason she wanted me to run against you was to test you out, see how you'd cope with someone who wasn't your stereotypical idea of a member of the Labour Women's Group. I'm not really Chair of Bent Council's Housing Committee. I'm not even *on* Bent Council. I just work for them, runnin' a group helpin' kids to get off the streets. She asked me to do this in return for gettin' more money for my unit, so I did."

"Well I'll be bollocksed!" Now it was Dovehawk's turn to realise he'd been duped. "Well you took *me* in, I can say. That's bloody brilliant."

"But don't tell Pree you know any of this – she'll cut off my funds."

"What? Oh aye. You bet. I'll not say anything. It's bloody great this is. Better than real life!" Stan made his last comment loudly so as Pree, who had just mounted the stage, could easily hear it.

"What's better than real life, Stan?"

"I can think of many things," said Stan, "But a life without you in it would make an excellent starting point."

"You're so charming. Does he say sweet things like that to you, Adelina?"

"Of course he does. You won't change Stan. That's his style." Adelina winked at him as she spoke.

"No. We won't change him. But we can *replace* him...... hopefully!"

Dovehawk rose to Pree's verbal tilting with his usual alacrity. "It's good to hear your completely unbiased viewpoint – honesty is not something I'd ever come to expect from you. Adelina and I were just going to the bar for a drink. Would you like to join us? We could talk about sweet things – flowers, and walks in the park, holding hands with loved ones, feeding the ducks – or *you* could choose the subject – whatever turns you on – I can make small talk on the bitchiest of subjects if the social occasion demands it."

"And also if it doesn't." Pree enjoyed being brutal and her body resounded with pleasure, proud and perky. Dovehawk surveyed the thrust of her hips flaring her cream jacket outwards, the matching skirt narrowing with the taper of her legs until bare shins and calves continued the gracile line to her flamboyant yet unsubstantial shoes. He couldn't stop himself wondering if Pree's knickers were as sparse as her footwear. One day, he thought, one day.

Pree watched his excursive look and saw in it his desire, so salivatory and base that her body was consumed by smutty nascent ecstasy derived from the contentment that her put-downs had forced the stubborn old curmudgeon to succumb to elemental male instincts which he was unable to satisfy in any place other than his imagination.

"You're a frustrated man, Stanley. Your body tells me that and your mind knows no way to escape from it...... It's eating you up!..... isn't it?"

"Bo-llocks!" said Dovehawk with such feeling that he made a single word sound like a poem.

"See? You've more of those in your head than you have in your trousers! Your mind is impotent!"

"Oh stop it you two!" Adelina admonished them cheerily. "Can't you be nice to each other for once?" She put an arm around each feuding despot and felt their dudgeon, hot and arrogant, oozing from their bodies like a corrosive fluid, meeting in a stagnant pool of contempt right there in front of her. She felt like a referee separating the contestants in a boxing bout; yet wasn't it she herself and Dovehawk who were supposed to be the adversaries?

"Well? Are we going for a drink or not?" she said, sandwiched between their rancour. A glance around the room told her that the queue to vote was quite short and counting would begin soon. "Come on, or we won't have time."

"There's always time for a drink," Dovehawk chuntered amiably, "Especially when you're in pleasant company, and half of the company I'm in at the moment is very pleasant. Please allow me to accompany you to the bar, Ms Omov, where I shall purchase you a beverage of your exact desire and specification."

"Pree?" Adelina sought the intentions of her mentor.

"Yes, I think so." Pree lightened up so markedly that one could be forgiven for thinking she always sounded friendly. "I can't think of anything nicer than relieving Stan of the price of a gin and tonic, garnished with liberal helpings of his subtle wit and invigorating bonhomie."

Dovehawk responded to her taunts merely by taking both ladies' waists in his arms and escorting them down the couple of steps from the stage, Pree swaying her body provocatively within his grasp, enjoying what she must be doing to the mental state of such a lecherous rogue as Stanley Dovehawk.

They had been at the bar for thirty five minutes when Gerald scurried through the door which led to the meeting hall and peered around, myopically searching for the trio. "They're ready, they're ready – you're to come back in now!" he babbled excitedly.

"Calm yourself, Gerald," urged the avuncular Dovehawk, now mellowed by a touch of good cheer. "There's no rush – they can't start without us, can they? I'll get you a drink."

Gerald knew Dovehawk would not be content with a fobbing off. "Oh, all right Stan, I'll have a half o' mild – but I'll take it through with me if you don't mind – they'll be waiting for us!"

"You'll sit down here with us and be convivial...... Half a mild please love – and not in a girl's glass," he asked the barmaid. Dovehawk returned his concentration to Gerald. "I was just telling Pree how lovely she looked this evening. Don't you agree?"

Gerald was taking his first sip of beer and almost choked, while even Pree couldn't subdue a smile. "Yes, she does, very nice!" spluttered Gerald, some spots of new-laid froth efflorescing on his spectacle lenses.

"You see? When she smiles like that, she invites the world to reach out and hug her." Dovehawk's hyperbole was so over the top that those present waited in fearful expectation of the dagger-thrust which would reveal its hidden intention.

"I must stop drinking this stuff," mused Dovehawk, holding his glass up to the light before swigging it back. "Come on – drink up Gerald – let's get this over with. Are you excited, Adelina?"

"As a Frenchman who's just noticed the English eat *fish fingers*."

"Is that one I told you?"

"No. Mr Rumbleon thought I'd like it."

"And do you?"

"No, but I thought *you* would."

"Rumbleon's jokes are like him – boring. Are you coming, Pree?"

"I wouldn't miss this for anything." She gathered her handbag from next to the chair-leg, stood up, leant down to finish her drink and planted the glass emphatically on the counter, like a metaphor, Dovehawk thought, for the crushing blow which she hoped her protégé was about to deal him.

“That’s it girl,” Dovehawk patronised Pree, “Gather your spirits.” He then took Adelina’s hand in his and squeezed affectionately. “Let us go forth into the arena, our pride before us, thoughts of defeat cast behind us, and lay ourselves bare to the whim and prejudice of the pigeon-fanciers, bingo junkies and amateur horticulturists that constitute the cutting edge of New Labour.”

“Yes, Mr Dovehawk. Let us do that. And let us be pleased for the winner, whoever that turns out to be.”

“Aye. I can drink to that.” And Dovehawk raised his hand to try and get himself noticed at the bar.

“No you can’t,” said Adelina, pushing his hand back down and dragging him off, protesting. “You just want to put off knowing the result, don’t you?”

“Well of course I do! You don’t think the condemned man urges haste in his passage to the gallows do you?”

When they re-entered the hall, all eyes were upon them, Stan and Adelina hand in hand like father and daughter in a bridal party, Pree the eternal bridesmaid. As heads craned round for a view over backs of seats already filled, Mr Rumbleon, sitting on his floodlit perch like a gastroenteritic parrot, looked fully jarred-off by their delayed appearance, and even though his wait was now over, his humour was not improved when Dovehawk strode up onto the stage and slapped him cordially between the shoulder-blades.

“Hope you can bloody count!” he ribbed the Chairperson loudly so everyone overheard.

“Actually,” Mr Rumbleon replied condescendingly, “We’ve re-counted twice.”

“Must be close then,” said Adelina excitedly.

“Come on Rumbleon: let’s hear it!” bawled Dovehawk. Now he knew he hadn’t taken a spanking in the ballot, he decided he wanted to get on with it. Rumbleon thought this request for haste was a bit of a cheek, seeing as it was the two candidates who had kept them all waiting for the last ten minutes. He scuffed his chair backwards, grating it on the wooden floor of the stage as he stood up and unfolded a small piece of paper.

"Ladies and gentlemen," Rumbleon began solemnly, "The result of the contest is as follows. Stanley Portland Dove'awk: seventy two votes. Adelina Jasmina Omov:" Rumbleon took his time to increase the suspense. "Seventy two votes."

A roar gripped the crowd, some scant applause breaking out amongst a general energetic chatter of disbelieving tension. Adelina's hand at first went to her mouth in a display of shock, then she covered her eyes. When she finally looked again, Dovehawk reached out to her and they shook hands, poignantly symbolising the evenness of their positions.

"Which means," Rumbleon struggled to make himself heard, "That the result is tied, and so I, as Chairperson, 'ave the casting vote!"

"Are you open to bribery?" quipped Dovehawk.

Rumbleon frowned. "As I've already been accused of partiality this evening, I find myself facing an impossible decision." He looked at Pree like he could rip her limbs off one by one. She remained stony faced. "So my only course of action, it seems to me, is to toss another coin."

An empty gasp of surprise drained the room of its hurly-burly.

"Come 'ere Gerald." Mr Rumbleon called the agent to his side. "You flip the coin, and I'll call: 'eads for Omov, tails for Dove'awk."

"Hang on a minute. Did the Salvation Army man vote?" Dovehawk pointed to the uniformed character who was just coming through the door from the bar having been around the whole premises with his tin. The object of this attention sat down and started counting his takings, not knowing that his conduct was being discussed at the highest level.

"I don't bloody know," grumbled Rumbleon, thwarted in mid-decision. "Is 'e a member?"

"We'll ask him," said Adelina. "Gerald, nip down the back and enquire, will you?"

"What? Oh, aye. Of course Adelina." And Gerald left the stage, while Mr Rumbleon drummed his fingers and fidgeted about, unchuffed at how events were being dictated by others, and not by himself.

"What relevance does this have?" said Pree harshly. "If he hasn't voted already, then he's lost his chance."

"Ah, good point," said Rumbleon, pleased to be able to reassert some authority. "Come back here Gerald!"

But Gerald was already conversing by now, and soon headed back under his own steam.

"He says he's a Liberal," said Gerald on his return. "But he once voted Raving Looney."

"Good!" Rumbleon said good because he had a good grasp of the situation. "Take this tuppeny bit Gerald, and remember it's 'eads for Omov, tails for Dove'awk. Is that what I said before?"

"Aye, I think so." He knew all eyes were upon him, and felt like they were too. There was no delaying it further; Gerald took up the tossing position; tensed his muscles; a flash of a camera from the auditorium blinded him; the coin rose on a steep circumvolution of the lighting accessories tethered to the Working Men's Club ceiling and set off towards a rendezvous with the front row seats and in particular Mrs Skulmongreley who used to be known to all her schoolmates as *ferret face*, which was quite a compliment in these parts. Gerald realised that despite having feared the worst from the moment he had been called upon to perform the tossing task, he had not been adequately pessimistic and that he was now embroiled in a "worse worst" scenario than his imagination had catered for. He launched himself after the elusive twinkling spinning coppery pinpoint of light which flitted above him.

"Have that photographer removed!" barked Rumbleon. "The press were told this was a closed meeting...... No, 'ang on a minute – 'e knows the result of the ballot now so he'll go back to 'is mates an' spill the beans. We'll 'ave to lock 'im in that cupboard!" And he pointed to a small door at the side of the room, while at the same time the photographer tried to make a dash for freedom. "Stop 'im, stop 'im!" trumpeted Rumbleon, "Oh *well done* Gerald – I didn't know you played rugby. What a great tackle that was, lad! Is it 'eads or tails?"

Gerald, his glasses askew, the press photographer sprawled out beneath him, Mrs Skulmongreley flopped on top of him, gurgled "I've got it!"

"No you haven't," squawked the pressman shrilly, "What you've got in your hand – that's not *it*!"

Pree looked at poor old Rumbleon, all his hopes of aggrandisement lying dashed amongst the heap of collided flesh that bedecked the orchestra pit.

"Yes, I know," Rumbleon said to her, "You'll be reporting this back to your bloody committee."

Thursday, six thirty in the morning

The string had only just been cut on the bundles of freshly-delivered newspapers when Dovehawk picked up his copy and started to read.

CHOICE OF HETHERINGTON CANDIDATE RESTS IN PRESS SNAPPER'S TROUSERS blared the banner headline. *The new Labour candidate in the Hetherington by-election was selected last night amid scenes of chaos. The press were not allowed inside the meeting, but we were later told by those present that the ballot of members resulted in a tie. Because the Chairman, for reasons of impartiality, didn't wish to exercise his casting vote, he decided that the outcome would be determined by the flip of a coin. This task fell to the Party Agent, Gerald, who ineptly tossed the vital 2p piece into an escaping press photographer's trousers. When the surprised snapper stood up and shook the errant monetary unit from his trouser-leg, it landed heads up, thereby ousting sitting candidate Stan Dovehawk to be replaced by ultra left-wing feminist Adelina Omov.*

There it was, in black and white – he was out, OUT, cast into the wilderness, just like Hetherington Sidney FC. Stan didn't much care for football, especially since the little club had been his downfall, but despite that he felt some bond with it now they were both cut off from their destinies, their reasons for being. Perhaps he could make amends. If he got the third round tie reinstated, his profile and stature in the community would be supremely elevated. Maybe he could force a re-run; but even that was unlikely, and presupposed that something could be done to get Jam United back in the competition. Stan flicked through his paper until a small headline caught his eye.

Jam United manager taken ill in Brazil

News just in that the manager of Jam United had to curtail his fact-finding tour of Brazil when he suddenly became unwell. He was taken to a hospital in the town of Belo Horizonte. No details have been released about his condition.

I wonder what that's all about, thought Stan. I'll contact the local press when their offices open and see if they've got any more details. But first he had more than two hours to kill with nothing to think about but the dreadful prospect of clearing his desk.

Half an hour later

Jack sat at the breakfast table reading his paper, chuckling at the outcome of the events of the previous evening, when the phone rang. He got up to answer it, expecting another pestering call from the media, but it turned out to be Fred from the Gazette.

"'Ave you 'eard, Jack?"

"'Eard what?"

"Eh, graaaand! – I thought I might be first to tell you...... Jam United's manager's 'ad to come 'ome! Got took bad in South America."

"Is it Lassa Fever?"

"No – turns out he's allergic to Terror del Fuegos – brought his whole 'ead out in a bright orange rash. Crackin' colour by all accounts! Lad who took photo of it before they got 'im bandaged up's made a fortune sellin' picture – it'll be ont' front page of all tomorrow's dailies – like one o' them fluorescent footballs what they use when pitch is all covered in snow."

"Where is he now?"

"Still ont' plane at the moment – then he's goin' to be moved under quarantine straight to Centre for Study o' Tropical Diseases in London – very 'ush 'ush."

"I thought you said he 'ad an allergic reaction to a lozenge?"

"That's what the 'ospital in Brazil said."

"So why's 'e goin' t' tropical disease centre then?"

"Eh, you're right! I'll get on the case and let you know. See you Jack."

"Thanks Fred."

Half 8

Dovehawk walked into the offices of the Gazette close on the heels of the receptionist who had just arrived for work.

“Is your sports reporter about, love?”

“I think everyone’s ’ere today – we’re doin’ our special issue to commemorate the fall of Mr Dove’awk. Just let me get me brolly down an’ then I’ll tell ’im you’re ’ere – what’s the name?”

“Dovehawk.”

“Oh... Right... I’ll tell ’im quick then... Are you sure you want Fred? I think our news editor would be the one you want to see.”

“If you let a news editor anywhere near me lass, I shan’t be responsible for my actions. What’s the sports reporter’s name?”

“Fred Bighill. I’ll get ’im for you.” She tapped out three numbers on the phone. “Sorry, e’s engaged – they’re always on the phone these journalists.”

“Take me to his office please love. Don’t mess me about – I’ve had a hard day.”

“OK, come on then. You know, we all feel quite sorry for you,” she said as they walked through to the middle of the building and up some stairs to the offices. “All the people ’ere who’d met you said you were a really nice bloke... for a politician, like.”

“I do me best.”

“I can see the attraction meself, actually. An’ I suppose you’ll be famous after today.”

“A loser’s fame lasts less time than it takes a Frenchman to light up a Gauloise after shooting his load.”

“I don’t get it, Mr Dove’awk.” She looked at him squeamishly.

“What I mean is, I won’t be famous tomorrow, so if you want to go out with me you’ll have to do it today.”

“I’ve got me lunch break between ’alf twelve an’ ’alf one.”

“Tell me, are you a normal girl, or are you one o’ these ones who’s nice all the time?”

“Oh, I’m a right cow if I don’t get me own way.”

“Thank god for that. No I won’t go out with you.”

“You bastard! You did that on purpose! Here, this is Fred’s office.” She knocked and went in. Fred was sitting amongst a cloud of smoke, his ear glued to the phone. He nodded to the girl and she shoved Dovehawk inside and sat him in a chair only just visibly projecting above the clutter. “See you at ’alf twelve then Mr Dove’awk – me name’s Glenda.” She blew him a kiss and left. Shutting the door disturbed the smoke into a swirling flurry which picked up dust from the unharvested desk and the mixture inveigled itself into Dovehawk’s chest making him rasp like a pop-up toaster on rapid refire.

“What you say?” Fred chattered amiably down the phone. “No, that’s not me desk crackin’ under the strain, that’s... er... Mr Dove’awk... Bloody ’ell, it’s Mr Dove’awk! I’ve got to go now Martin. See you mate.” He put down the phone. “Eh, Mr Dove’awk, what are you doin’ ’ere?”

“I want to ask you about the Jam U manager’s little problem.”

“Eh, funny you should ask that. That was Martin Snakespit on the phone – ’e writes the *Load of Balls* column in the *Daily Filler*, so ’e should know what ’e’s talkin’ about.”

“What did he say about Jam U’s manager then?”

“Sod all, but ’e reckons Shagsy’s worth six million now ont’ transfer market. That’ll pay for t’ new stand and ’alf decent burger stall at ’Etherington Sidney ground!”

“I need to know what’s wrong with him.”

“No one’s sayin’. I’ve been tryin’ to find out for more than an hour now. Plane touches down in...” Fred looked at his watch, “About five minutes from now, then it’s straight off to ’ospital for tropical diseases in London under police escort.”

“Don’t you think that’s suspicious?”

“Very. But I’ve got me contacts in place. Don’t worry Mr Dove’awk – soon as anythin’ ’appens I’ll know about it within minutes. Give us your mobile number an’ I’ll keep you informed of developments.”

“Have you been in touch with anyone in Brazil?”

"Aye, the 'ospital. But they just said 'e 'ad an allergic reaction to Terror del Fuegos – they're the antiseptic sweets they suck out there like fruit gums."

"Thanks Mr Bighill – I've got to go now. Here's me number. You must let me know if anything happens."

Dovehawk made his way out into the cold and wet of another unexceptional English December morning and made the un-longed-for walk to his ex-campaign headquarters. He shoved the door open and saw Gerald, beavering away as usual, such a dedicated Party worker, and now under new management. He looked up from his work and Dovehawk could see the emotion in his eyes, the pent up fear for this moment making him more furtive and awkward than normal, so that Dovehawk even wondered whether he might try ignoring his old boss altogether. But he didn't.

"Hello Stan," he managed, a tear almost perceptible behind a lens.

"Come on Gerald, I'm not finished yet – you know me!"

"Aye, I guess not. Have you come to say good bye?"

"Yes, that and to clear me desk me old mate." Stan slapped him on the back.

"Er, are you sure you wouldn't rather come back tomorrow?" Gerald blinked, concealing his unease only indifferently.

"Why?" barked Dovehawk, suspicious of any attempt Gerald ever made to thwart his actions.

"Er..." Gerald floundered.

"Oh never mind," Dovehawk routinely dismissed him and headed off up the stairs for a last visit to the power-centre which was his office. The door was shut and he barged straight in, expecting it to be empty, or to see Adelina arranging some trinkets to cheer the masculine mood of the place up a bit. The first thing that struck him when he opened the door was the warmth, always missing during his own period of tenancy, but now forming a picket of cosiness across the doorway. The second thing that struck him was the vision in primrose sitting at his desk, a bad dream revisited, mouth, lipstick, hair, stare, all there as remembered. The third thing that struck him was the thought that that bastard Gerald must have mended his heater just in time for his unplanned vacating of the premises and that the first buttocks to luxuriate on a warm chair belonged to his nemesis.

“Sit down, Stan,” said Pree, her condescension held in check but only just.

“I’d rather stand,” grunted Stan.

Pree looked up at him but still managed to remain superior. “Oh we did all this last time – it’ll be so much easier if you just sit down – you know you will eventually.”

“I’ve come to clear me desk, and to do that I need to sit where you are.”

“You really think I hadn’t thought of that?” Pree laughed disparagingly. “All your seamy little things are in that cardboard box over there in the corner behind you.”

Dovehawk turned to look at the collected works of his campaign life and felt sad to see that they fitted into such a small space.

“And there’s a disk in there with your sexist screen-saver on it too.”

“Oh? And what have you replaced it with? A picture of our esteemed Leader perhaps?”

“I shall only do that when our Leader is a woman. For now I have to make do with Winnie Mandela.”

“You’re the only one who does.” Stan went to pick up his box, but Pree called him back.

“Come on Stan, just sit down a minute; I want to talk to you.” She sounded grotesquely smug, but what the hell Stan thought; he might have a laugh now he had nothing to lose. The visitor’s chair was not contoured to his posterior, but at least now the heating was fixed it didn’t feel like he was perched on a marble slab.

“What are you doing here?” He started resolutely by undermining his tormentor’s position. “This is Adelina’s office now.”

“Oh, she’s very inexperienced. I shall be running her campaign for a couple of weeks until she gets the hang of it.”

“Oh I see; she’s too nice you mean? I realise it takes a complete bitch to run a campaign to your high standards. Are you going to train her up?”

“Oh don’t bother insulting me Stan until you can manage better than that. You won’t have realised what I’m about to tell you because, being a man, you’ve had it all handed to you on a plate, but I’ll try to explain it to you anyway. A woman politician not only takes abuse and criticism to her face, but also has to put up with behind-the-scenes denigration and character assassination; your poor male ego would crumble under even one tenth of the brickbats which we fend off with grace and decorum.”

“Exactly! Adelina has grace and decorum. She’s a *woman.* You’re just a bloke in a skirt!”

“If that is how you feel, then I’m afraid you only have yourself and those like you to blame. You have made me what I am!”

“But you’ll never make Adelina change into a monster like you!”

“In that case she may fail; that is the chance we all take. But I am a winner, Stan.” She shifted her posture to appear even more upright, more taut: a soft womanly body pumped with pride and predominance into a rigidly ascendant form. “And *you* are a loser!”

Because the desk was just a door rested on piles of old papers, Dovehawk could see her legs, neutral-coloured fine denier tights covering the smooth skin, his view drawn from her ankles to her knees at which point it was halted by the darkness of that confined space beneath her skirt where her thighs began. She continued chiding him: “And *that*, I am proud to say, is the way it should be after one hundred years of feminine struggle!” He could take it no longer. He stood up and strode around the desk to behind where Pree was sitting, her expression turning from power to puzzlement. Firmly but gently he took her under the arms and pushed her forwards over his desktop, at the same time kicking the chair away with his knee. He lifted the primrose skirt high in the air until it was over her back, the hem around her neck, her lovely full-hipped arse arching upwards as her hands grasped the other side of the dusty old door to maintain her balance. “What are you doing?” she demanded testily, but without making any attempt to mitigate her vulnerable position by struggling to wriggle free.

“The men’s committee has taken note of your observations,” Dovehawk said, relishing his words as he eased the waistband of Pree’s tights around her hips and, in one swift movement, down to her knees, “And has decided to lodge a complaint at your next meeting," he continued as he dropped his trousers, pulled her panties to one side and aligned himself with her entrance, "At which I shall be presenting the object of my grievance most forcibly to the Chair of the women's committee."

Whump......

From the reception area downstairs, Gerald heard a loud gasp of air and then groans, muffled, but definitely from somewhere in the building. He sighed and continued with his canvass returns. Five minutes later, Dovehawk appeared at the bottom of the stairs, carrying his cardboard box. He dumped it down on Gerald's desk, crushed the poor little agent in his arms and planted a sloppy wet kiss on his face. Gathering his box up again, he danced out into the dismal street wearing a lopsided soppy grin which would only be removed by prolonged exposure to grim reality. Gerald realised he wasn't in the same league as people like Stan, and that perhaps that was a good thing.

Just outside the door, Stan met Adelina on her way to work.

"Good luck, girl!" he shouted to her as she arrived for her first day as prospective Labour MP for the Hetherington Constituency. "Good bloody luck!"

"Where are you goin' now, Stan?" she said, in a subdued tone for someone normally effusive, tangibly displaying the strain of her close victory and embarrassment at her friend Dovehawk's unwitting vanquishment.

"I'm going to take my packet of highlighter pens and magic markers which I have here in my little box and I'm going to write *Just Shafted* all over Pree's car."

"Oh, Stan, you didn't?"

"She said I was too old!"

"Oh Stan, you're not too old."

"She knows that now! Where's her car?"

"She comes up on the train."

"Oh well, it was a nice idea. You know she's pinched your office? You're going to be sitting next to Gerald in the hallway."

"Gerald's all right."

"You're too accepting. Watch people don't shit on you."

"*You* never did, Stan, and others have told me that you're quite good at it!"

"Flatterer! Right, I'm off. Good luck again, Adelina!"

"Good luck Stan. You seem happier now than when you were still the candidate."

"There'll be another day for Stan Dovehawk, love. I just hope I'm there to see it. Give us a kiss." Stan dropped his box on the pavement; some of the pens and pencils scattered off the kerb into the flowing gutter, others up onto the weeds bordering the houses. He grabbed his replacement around the waist and hugged. "Now I've put her straight on a few things," Dovehawk assured Adelina confidently amidst their cuddle, "Don't let her make you cynical like the rest of us. If you can avoid that, you'll triumph like a snowdrop in the harsh winter soil."

"Stan, you're poetic."

"I like to think so. Others spell it differently. Go on – get yourself inside that building and give 'em hell."

Adelina looked at him one last time. "Thank you Stanley," she said with a purr, "I think I will."

Ten

Dovehawk sat on the train heading up to London. He held his mobile phone to his ear and listened while it rang at the other end.

"'Etherington Gazette, Glenda speaking," came the faint voice from the earpiece when it finally answered.

"Hello lass! Stan Dovehawk here. I can't share your butties with you at dinnertime love – I've just found out that the National Executive Committee's meeting this afternoon to confirm my de-selection – so I intend to put in a surprise appearance. I hate to let you down, love, but my career hangs by a thread."

"That's OK Mr Dove'awk; when I told this lot 'ere about our date they told me you were a lecherous old git anyway!" (Despite the sentiment, Dovehawk could hear in her voice that she sounded un-put-off.)

"It's all true lass. Thanks for being so understanding. If I'm ever allowed to show me face in Hetherington again I'll buy you a cup of Bovril."

"I'll look forward to it. I've never tried Bovril."

"I've never tried Terror del Fuegos – but I think I'm about to."

"What?"

"I'll explain next time. See you love, and tell Fred Bighill to keep me posted."

"OK Mr Dove'awk, see you love."

Dovehawk removed the phone from his ear, pressed a couple of buttons and rang Fiona.

"Hello Stan sweetie. What terrible news – are you very sad?"

"Sad? No Fiona love, I'm not sad. Listen. Can you meet me at Heathrow Airport at seven o'clock this evening? We're going to Brazil."

"Brazil? But I thought we were going in January. Why now?"

"Because something funny's happened out there that they're not telling us about. So I'm going to find out for meself. And if you want your Sean playing Jam U in the cup in January, then you'd better come with me."

"Oh come on, Stan – you just want me to pay for the flights."

"And that as well!"

"Can Tammy come too? She can pay for all of us and she's such good fun on a beach."

"Why? What the bloody hell does she do?"

"She walks up to the boys with her tits out, and tells them she doesn't see why they shouldn't show her what *they've* got as well!"

"Mmmm... Sounds fair I suppose – so long as *I* don't get asked."

"Oh, she's seen yours sweetie – she's only interested in novelty. I don't think she's been to Copacabana."

"We're going up in the mountains – her nipples'll get frostbite."

"Oh, she's a wizardess on the slopes."

"OK love, you can bring who you like. So long as you'll order the tickets and meet me at seven, yes?"

"I'll get Tammy's credit card number."

"Good girl. And can you ring Fred Bighill at the Gazette for me and ask him if there's any news on the Jam U manager's condition?"

"OK. Is there anything else you want? And have you ever considered getting a secretary?"

"I am currently without portfolio! My newfound lowly status hardly warrants a secretary."

Quarter past four that afternoon

The torpid proceedings of the Labour National Executive Committee drivelled inexorably from one low-point to the next, the discussion of the Hetherington by-election scheduled last in order to provide at least a minor crescendo of excitement at the end.

"Next item on the agenda – the ratification of the selection of our new candidate in the Hetherington by-election," droned the lady Chairperson in a teacher-like auto-pilot. "Ms Omov won the contest by a narrow margin. Would anyone like to debate this? Or shall we move straight to a vote?"

There was a knock at the door and a Party official walked in and went straight to the Chairperson. "Mr Dovehawk's outside," he whispered in the Chairperson's ear. "He says he would like to present his case in person and to make himself available for questioning while you are discussing this resolution."

"Oh. Does he?" The Chairperson sounded haughtily displeasured at the prospect that her urge to urgency in the matter of dispatching Dovehawk to the political dustbin may have been confounded. "Well. I suppose we'll have to have a vote on whether we want to hear him. Wait here while we have a show of hands, Georgina – then you can inform Mr Dovehawk if his presence is required." He nodded politely, acquiescently accepting his gender-altered sobriquet in line with latest Party policy.

"All those in favour of hearing Stanley Dovehawk, hereinafter to be known as..." she consulted her ready-reckoner which worked out the name changes... "Staniella – we'll call him Stella for short – raise your hands. OK, keep them there – looks like that's carried. Go and get him please Georgina."

"Yes Madam Chair."

Thirty seconds later, the peerless figure of a fully post-caring Dovehawk lumbered into the room. Ms Chair gestured to the spot from which he was to deliver his valedictory. Dovehawk smiled graciously.

"Begin when you're ready Stella," said Ms Chair without looking up from her agenda.

Dovehawk looked at her, wondering to whom she was talking, but, unenlightened, he decided to start anyway.

"Thank you Madam Chair. I appear here today, not as a victim craving your sympathy, nor as a bad loser who cannot accept the result of a democratic poll, but as a representative of a significant, proud and vociferous minority, already sadly under-represented in the House of Commons, and still more so should you rubber-stamp my de-selection as candidate in the Hetherington by-election. For I am that thing most sought-after in the Cabinet ranks of any major modern political party – I am your earnest gay – unflinching in my support for *all* Government policy, even that which could be considered illiberal, while lending stupendous amounts of credibility to the slow, some might say almost stationary, pace of change."

Madam Chair, perhaps taken aback by what she was hearing, now found Mr Dovehawk's countenance more intriguing than her paperwork.

"Are you sure you're gay? I remember you made an indecent suggestion to me at Conference."

Dovehawk, realising his past must be swiftly re-evaluated, stammered an instant reply. "Ah, yes. That's because I thought you were a man." The roar of instantly-stifled laughter which consumed the meeting around him let him know that he at least had a chance; let him know that the creature sitting at the top table was not wholly loved by everyone in the chamber. "Of course, I only go for very pretty men," he said in attempt at redemption, "As you will see from my video."

"Video?"

"Yes. I've brought along a very touching video of me and my friend Marlon."

"Marlon? We can't have that!" Madam Chair consulted her list. "He'll have to be called Marion from now on."

"I'm sure he won't mind." Dovehawk turned to play to his audience. "May I show you my video?"

"Show of hands please – all those in favour of seeing Stella's video indicate now... Carried... Could someone call Georgina to set up the TV and draw the blinds please."

They all watched the video in the darkened room, like a load of pervos from the Board of Film Censorship: fascinated, but considering it fit only for their own consumption.

When the showing was over and the light restored, Dovehawk took a bow in honour of his starring role. "See," he said, "Marlon's very sexy isn't he?"

"Yes he is, in places," said Madam Chair, quite flushed and flustered. "So Mr Dovehawk, are you telling this Committee that you have *never* had sex with a woman?"

"Never," said Dovehawk reverently and with elements of solemnity.

On cue, the door opened and there stood Pree, looking unusually cheerful; even jolly.

"*Never* Stan?" She winked at him. God, he felt himself almost fancying her.

The Chair banged her gavel on her desk. "Will you please remember to address the plaintiff by the correct misnomer Ms Puckering – namely, in this case, Staniella, or Stella for short!"

"Stella?" Pree winked at Stan again, her eyes casting up and down his porpoise-like form. "How fetching – it suits him."

"Ms Puckering. Are you here to testify that *you've* had sex with Stella?" The Chairperson couldn't remain sufficiently dispassionate to hide her burning interest.

There was a long pause before she answered. The arena was agog with expectation.

"Yes." Sharp intakes of breath were heard all around the room as Pree took a hanky from her sleeve and dabbed at a mock tear, while being mindful not to blemish her perfect foundation. "Sad as it may seem, and even though he's too old, I did allow myself to succumb to his attentions." Then, feigning hurt she added, "And he is rather rough!"

Madam Chair looked shocked. "And you did this even after seeing the video?" Ms Chair seemed concerned at her co-committee-ite's judgement; or lack of it.

"Video?"

"Ah." She realised from Pree's expression that her knowledge of Stella's alter ego was scanty. "Pass her the tape please Georgina – I think Pree should watch it at home when she's sitting down."

"With a stiff one in her hand," said Dovehawk, inelegantly embellishing the Chair's sound advice.

"That's quite enough from you, Stella. It would seem that you've brought nothing to this deliberation except your mendacity. You should be ashamed!"

"Indeed not!" Dovehawk, still indefatigable under fire, hoisted his bravado for one last assault. "I appear here today, not as a victim craving your sympathy, nor as a bad loser who cannot accept the result of a democratic poll, but as a representative of a significant, proud and vociferous minority, already sadly under-represented in the House of Commons..." He looked around at his audience, feeling their impatience at his repetition. "...Even more so than is the gay community. For I am that thing most sought-after amongst the ambivalent majority of any major modern political party – I am your middle-of-the-road-bisexual – unflinching in my support for *all* Government policy, even that which could be considered decisive, while lending stupendous amounts of credibility to those policies which leave us sitting firmly on the fence."

Madam Chair, again bemused by what she was hearing, seemed to have trouble formulating her next line of enquiry, while Pree appeared to be hugely enjoying the moment, the climax of Dovehawk's final unprincipled grasp at tenure.

Madam Chair floundered, making those present feel empathetically uneasy at her discomfort, worrying for her safety against such a deft adversary as Stanley Dovehawk. She became pale, twitched...... she grimaced...... she braced herself......

"Stella," she finally said in a soft manner designed to put him at ease and let him know he could be truthful without fear of reproach, "Have you ever had sex with animals?"

It was a blow which Dovehawk had neither thought of nor anticipated, but he knew he could not afford a stumble.

"Christ! You haven't got a bloody sheep outside in the corridor as well have you?"

Uproar. Unconfined.

"Vote!" shouted Pree. "Move to the vote Madam Chair!" She yelled as raucously as she could, trying to make herself heard above the pandemonium.

The Chair banged her little hammer. "All those in favour of accepting the decision of the Hetherington Constituency Labour Party to adopt Ms Adelina Omov as our candidate in the Hetherington by-election, show now," she shrieked. "Carried! End of business... thank you everyone!" She gathered her things into a neat heap, slid them into her briefcase and zipped it closed.

The forlorn figure of Stanley Staniella "Stella" Dovehawk shrugged its shoulders, then looked to Pree, to fix upon her flaunted features of unchained and unchecked victory; but... and he stared for longer to make sure... it wasn't there... no tormenting petulance could he see... no smugness could he detect. He went to her and her eyes, where lacerating shards of broken glass would have been in character, instead were melting, welling up with real tears. She opened her arms and he slumped into them, hearing her whisper into his ear as his chin rested on her shoulder, "It's over Stan... it's over..."

Ten past seven that evening

"Oh Duvvy Luvvy, pick up one of my bags will you darling? Bargreaves can only manage seven on his own and I've split a nail."

"What do you need all these bloody cases for?" grumbled Dovehawk, realising that travel with Tamara was going to be fraught with tantrum.

"Oh Duvvy – one has to be prepared on holiday. It's like setting off for a war-zone: the right equipment makes all the difference."

"Well I'll carry the bag with your beach stuff in it – I've seen the size of your sunbathing attire and I reckon I can just about manage that even with a bad back."

"You think of nothing but my underwear do you darling? Never mind, my little Duvvy – you won't have to imagine for long. I've packed some specially scanty items for you to mess up. But you'll have to wait until I've shagged every barman called Alfonso in Propacrapapebble, or wherever you said we were going."

"Oh come on Tam you old tart! Hurry up," shouted Fiona.

"I will if you get someone to help with my bags. It's all right for you Fifi darling – you've got *legs*, so you don't need any clothes."

"I have requisitioned a trolley ma'am," said Bargreaves from within his immaculate suit. "We can make our way to the Departure Lounge without delay."

"Thank god for that," said Dovehawk. "Have you got room for her thong-bag on there as well?"

"Of course, sir. All madam's things can be accommodated."

The party made its way to check-in and Bargreaves stacked all the luggage on the scales.

"I'm afraid you have two hundred kilos excess baggage," said the young lady at the desk.

"Oh that's all right, darling," said Tammy, "I'll pay the extra."

"I'm sorry madam, but your flight has a rather special passenger which means that the plane is fully laden. I'm really very sorry, but you'll have to leave half of this behind – we'll arrange to have it delivered back to your home."

"What?" Tammy couldn't believe it. "But *I'm* a special passenger, too. I always pay Excess Baggage."

"Our special passenger is an elephant – he weighs three and a half tons – that means there's no spare capacity for Excess Baggage."

Tammy looked around her and pointed to one of the nearby check-in positions. "Look – there's a fat woman there: she must weigh twenty stone! I only weigh eight stone, so with my baggage I still weigh less than she does with only her hand luggage. And I'm First Class – there's plenty of room – I could take all my stuff on the plane as hand luggage and that will leave more room in the hold for the elephant!"

"Oh no madam. The elephant is First Class too. "The Bumjob of Rumjobpoor is very particular about the comfort of his elephant on all his trips. You'll have very little room for hand luggage."

Bargreaves sighed with relief; the prospect of carrying eight heavy bags of hand luggage into the plane on his own was undelightful.

"An elephant? In First Class?" Tammy was becoming squawkative.

"It's all right, Tam." Fiona put her arm around her friend. "I'll help you sort through – we'll just take the things you really need."

"Oh don't be silly Fifi – you know I need everything – you know I can't cope without my wardrobe! I'll just have to wait for the next flight," she pouted. "You and Duvvy can go with the smelly old elephant."

"I'll tell you what I'll do." The girl at the desk was trying her best. "I'll put your stuff with the elephant's food – we allowed for a ton and a half of hay for the journey but he's only brought a ton."

"Hay did you say?" She took Stan's hand before giving her orders to the check-in girl. "Tell you what. Me and Duvvy'll go with the elephant food – you can put my luggage on our seats."

21:00 hours GMT

Dovehawk sat in his spacious First Class seat, sipping Champagne and reading his Evening Standard.

MANAGER'S MYSTERY ILLNESS said the headline.

The Centre for the Study of Tropical Diseases in London refused to speculate about the condition of the Jam United manager who was taken ill in Brazil yesterday. They issued a statement saying he was still undergoing tests to try to determine his ......

And that was as far as Dovehawk got before his paper was grabbed from him. He looked up just in time to see a small portion of the back page disappearing between Jumbo's giant molars.

"Sorry about that Mr Dovehawk," said the hostess, attentive to his every need, "I'll go and fetch you another one. That's four that Jumbo's eaten already – it's lucky we brought extra copies on board."

"Aaaaaahhhhh!" came a shriek from the next seat, where Tamara held her glass to one side as if to protect it.

"What's the matter Miss Spankbottom?" said the ever-helpful hostess.

"It's that ghastly elephant. He's pinched my bottle of Moet. Look. It's in his trunk – he's tipping it into his mouth. Where's the Bumjammer of Ramthepoor? Can't he control his greedy pet?"

"It's all right madam – I'll get you another bottle."

"And some hay for the brute too please. That might take his mind off the drinkies."

"Aaaaaahhhhh!" came a shriek from the next seat, where Fiona held her hands to her breasts to cover them.

"What's the matter Lady Opiumden?" said the delightfully unflappable hostess.

"The elephant's eaten my top!" giggled Fiona, incoherent with laughter.

"It's all right madam – I'll get you a complimentary tee-shirt. You can cover yourself with my tea-towel while I fetch you one."

"Thank you," said Fiona, draping the airline's monogrammed cleaning cloth across her chest.

"Oh how annoying!" said Tammy, looking at Fiona with unconcealed irritation. "She looks better wearing a naff old tea-towel than I do in my silkiest sexiest bra!"

"I don't know," said Dovehawk conciliatorily. "You might look better than she does if you were wearing just oven gloves."

"Right Duvvy," said Tamara, rightly offended, "That's the last time you get to play with my birthmark."

"No matter love, your bum's nicer than Fiona's any day; hers is all bony."

"Oh yes sweetie?" Fiona spoke with vicious calmness. "You obviously don't want *any* fun on holiday."

"No matter," grunted Dovehawk, "Jumbo still loves me; look – he's trying to remove my trousers."

"Well he won't get much sustenance there," said Fiona.

"And it's the only part of you which is more wrinkly than your face," said Tammy.

"And the elephant's," said Fiona.

"That's more like it girls. Have a go at old Stan. That'll make you all feel better; and it'll help you take your mind off the elephant."

"He's got a very small willy," said Tammy thoughtfully.

"Who, Stan has?" said Fiona.

"I was thinking of the elephant."

"Looks big enough to me," said Fiona, peering.

"I mean compared to the rest of him, darling. I bet Mrs Elephant's a bit frustrated. I bet she has a bit on the side."

"Perhaps he's good with his trunk," said Fiona, screwing up her face. She reclined her seat into its bed position, stretched out her long legs for comfort and adjusted her tea-towel for modesty. Before she closed her eyes, she noticed that the elephant looked intently at Tammy, never flinching in its gaze, unblinking. Was there lust in that look? She rolled her head slightly to her right and saw her friend reciprocating the animal's stare, but with concern and irritation painted all over her face.

"Oh that beastly beast!" Tammy wailed. "Why does it keep looking at me like that?"

"Because you said it had a small dick of course," observed Dovehawk astutely. "From the look of him I think he wants to show you what a good little squirter it is."

"Oh no! Do you think so? Now you've said that I shan't be able to close my eyes for a second on this journey without the fear of being rogered by an over-inflated rhino."

Dovehawk sniggered. "You'll need to worry more if he decides to give you a fingering first!"

"Do you think he's going to be able to go the whole of the flight without needing the lavvy?" said Fiona from her relaxed position. "I don't want a shower until we get to the hotel."

"I think you'll find the keeper's round the back with a large bucket," said Dovehawk.

"I hope it can pee straighter than Sean then," said Fiona ruefully. "And come to think of it *you* as well Stan!"

"Oh this is just worse and worse," Tammy said, flustered. "I shall have to see about being moved. Why do we have to have the elephant anyway? Why can't it go with the common people in Third Class?"

The hostess appeared carrying all sorts of stuff. "Your paper, Mr Dovehawk. Your Champagne Miss Spankbottom. Your tee-shirt Lady Opiumden. And a jeroboam of bubbly for you, Jumbo." She handed the elephant the huge bottle of fizzy wine which it took with its trunk and poured into its mouth, guzzling the entire contents in just a few seconds.

"You see," said Dovehawk, "That's why the elephant goes First Class!"

"Oh dear," said Fiona as her head reappeared from the innards of her freshly provided upper clothing, "Now it'll definitely need a pee before we get to Rio."

"Four gallons," mumbled Dovehawk to no-one in particular. "That's how much they do when they get going. I rather suspect that bucket's only good for half a tank-full."

"Eeeee!" squeaked Tammy as the elephant extended its trunk towards her new bottle. "It's thirstier than a Frenchman chewing a tampax. Go away!"

9pm back in London

Ron Conference was a desperate man; or was he a broken man? He couldn't decide. Desperation was his driving force at this moment, keeping the nervous breakdown in check until the time when overriding hopelessness would consume his soul. Perhaps Ron was desolate yet determined.

He had spent all Monday night and most of Tuesday morning recovering from his hangover induced by the plenteousness of the potent potion administered by the Good Samaritan in his garden. Feeling nauseous in body and mind, he had resolved that to do nothing, to rely on hope alone, would diminish him in the eyes of his players, the lads, his boys; he keenly felt the burden of knowing how they looked to him for leadership, incisive purpose, decisive action, coruscating wit. Well, perhaps not the last bit; they did always take the piss out of his jokes. But when the world is grey, nothing is funny, and here he was, Ron Conference, the Manager, up to the job, parking his car in readiness for a maraud into London's last leper colony: the Centre for the Study of Tropical Diseases, to plead in person with a fellow footie boss to resist the lure of an all-expenses-paid trip to sunny tongue-tied titillation and instead to play a simple game of football on a cold January day in the north of England. With a choice like that, Ron felt sure there could be only one response.

He arrived outside to see the press were there in force, milling around, waiting for news of the manager's condition. How was Ron to get into the building, let alone to see his opposite number? Luckily, Monday's events had prepared him perfectly. The toads in his garden pond were not of the common indigenous variety. As he walked towards the crowded entrance, the sight of the weeping red wheal on his forehead sent the assembled hacks running in terror, leaving him a clear path to the guard at the gate.

"My name's Ron Conference; I rang earlier today."

The guard looked at his sheet of paper and nodded. He then radioed the hospital and, after a time, scribbled down a note on the sheet next to Ron's name.

"Go through the main entrance, turn right, up the stairs, Ward 7. Here is your welcome pack – it tells you all the facilities available to you while you are in quarantine. Have a nice stay." He pressed a button and a small person-sized gate opened next to the guardhouse. Through this entrance was a turnstile; as he pushed through and the mechanism click click clicked, Ron felt quite at home.

Ron walked across the small compound, in the entrance, up the stairs and spoke to the nurse sitting at the desk beneath a Ward 7 sign suspended on two flimsy looking strings.

"Mr Conference," she said, "You are in bed 3, just down there, next to the Japanese gentleman."

"Japanese gentleman?" queried Ron. "I thought I would be in isolation."

“It’s perfectly all right,” the nurse assured him, “The Japanese gentleman has the same complaint as yourself. He came to grief the same as you, in your own garden! You can discuss your symptoms together – it’ll be more fun for you than being in a room on your own.”

Ron saw his roommate with his leg exposed to the air, horribly defiled by cankerous buboes which became ever more engorged in a double-line from ankle to groin, like footprints. Ron’s hand went instinctively to his own meagre pustule, checking that it had not suddenly quadrupled in size.

“Christ. Did Percy do all that?” he asked the fellow sufferer. Ron was shocked by the evidence of his own eyes.

“Corumbian Crapping Toad,” the Japanese enunciated in a slow, harsh voice, nodding vigorously.

“Yes,” said Ron, “That’s right...... Percy’s his name, and he is indeed a Columbian Clapping Toad. But how did your leg become so swollen? I’ve never seen anyone come out in a rash like that before.”

The Japanese shrugged. “I just sclatch,” he said. “So they give me these!” He held up his hands, showing them to be completely shrouded in white mittens. “Broody agony!” The deep feeling conveyed in those two words told Ron he wasn’t exaggerating!

6am Friday, local time, Brazil (09:00 GMT)

The railway station in Rio was just bursting into life in the pleasant sun of an early morning. Tammy looked delicious in a floppy white hat to shade her from its rays, but she didn’t feel delicious.

“Duvvy! I’m not going on a smelly old train! I was promised a beach!” She was complaining again, but Dovehawk knew her bluster too well by now and enjoyed winding her up all the more. “Fiona. Tell him. Go on, tell him *now*!”

Dovehawk went to put his arm around the protesting Miss Spankbottom.

“Get off!” Tammy swung away from him. “The next time you touch me it’ll be to rub sun lotion on my bronze baked body languishing on soft sand under a sweltering sun!”

“Oh come on Tam – don’t be such a misery!” Fiona pleaded. “It’ll be nice up in the mountains. We’ll find out what Stan needs to know, then afterwards we can spend till Christmas on the beach! Come with us...... Please......"

Tammy looked at her friend and felt mellow towards her. Then she looked at the people with their animals, boarding the already over-full train. "Where's First Class?" she screeched. "I need to see the travelling conditions before I decide."

9am Friday, London

Ron had been wondering ever since his arrival in hospital how he could find out where the Jam U manager's room was. He was pondering that very question when he suddenly realised he had lost the train of thought, interrupted by the refectory noises coming from the bed next to him where Kendo, the Japanese TV presenter, was munching heartily on his slug sandwich.

"D'you want some salt with that?" Ron asked, slightly nauseated at seeing some grey antennae poking out from between the crusts.

Kendo looked round at him, paused from chomping and shook his head. "No no......" he said animatedly, undisguisedly excited by his subject. "Salt make srug crurl up very small. Srug not rike salt. Kendo not rike unhappy srug." He grinned, satisfied with his explanation, then popped the escaping head and tentacles between his incisors. Ron couldn't help imagining what the tussle between muscly tongue and squirming mollusc would feel like. The thought was revulsive but also involuntary and inescapable; Ron could feel the recoiling eye-bearing feelers wedging in his molars, the slime cloying in his throat, the glutinous sheathing seeping from the corners of his lips, the part-digested dinner from the gut greenly delineating a patina on his hard palate.

Antennae, he thought, absent mindedly tonguing the fissures between his teeth. *Mmmm – that gives me an idea.* On his way to the toilet, Ron took care to study the nurse at her desk: her telephone, but that probably wouldn't help him; her panic button for emergencies, not really suitable – that would only get people running to his own ward. He needed to see her use the hospital's public address – then there could be possibilities.

7:15 am local time, Brazil (10:15 GMT)

The train growled and grumbled its way along the track from Rio to Belo Horizonte at a steady twelve miles an hour.

“So exactly what sort of bird is that, Tam?” Fiona asked with two large glints of mischief in her eyes.

“I don’t know. But it’s got a beastly beak – look at the horrible thing. If you had a heart you would let me sit where you are.”

“Next to the alpaca?”

Tamara looked at the moth-eaten creature opposite, its bottom wedged between Fiona’s and the somewhat larger version fitted to the Brazilian Indian woman occupying the adjacent seat. It winked back at Tammy.

“Oh yeuuuuuugghhhh!” She turned her head away in disgust, but it was a mistake, for lunging instinctively at a glint of light from the diamond stud, the rhea (for such was the bird) pecked her ear.

“Aaaahhhh!..... That’s it!..... I’m moving!”

Dovehawk and Fiona both laughed. Bargreaves fiddled around in his pocket. “If you’ll allow me madam,” he said. Getting up from his seat next to a goat with bad breath, he went over to the errant bird and stretched one of madam’s elastic hair bands onto its beak, winding it around several times for tightness. “Will that be all madam?” he enquired as if he were waiting on her at breakfast in Throginthroat Hall. Tammy saw the bird still had an evil expression, but noted that its beak was now firmly clamped.

“Yes thank you Bargreaves,” she replied. He bowed his head deferentially and resumed his seat, first having to remove from it an anaconda which had slitherously disencoiled the front portion of its length from around its owner’s neck and was heading for the next carriage via Bargreaves’ vacated position. The rhea stared at Tammy accusingly, giving an irritated hiss every now and then, its two little nostril holes fibrillating at their edges as if in annoyance at its tight-beaked predicament. The alpaca belched. Dovehawk, having been lucky enough not to find a vacant seat on embarkation, stood at the side of the compartment with his head out of the window. He felt the squeeze of hands with long nails digging into his waist.

“Move over Duvvy. Let me share your window. All those animals hate me. And they smell. I need some fresh air.”

He jammed his head to one side of the small window, allowing sufficient space for Tammy to get hers out, brushing his cheek on the way, her hair tickling his face and nose. She then puffed hard on a cigarette and the smoke made Dovehawk's eyes water, little bits of ash stinging his cornea.

"Here," he grumbled, "We'll swap sides – then all your hair and fag smoke'll go downwind.

"Oh stop moaning all the time!" Tammy puffed hard again.

"Moaning all the time?" gasped the dumbfounded Dovehawk. "And *you* haven't complained about anything at all, I've noticed!"

"If I was on the beach where I belong then I wouldn't be complaining."

Dovehawk grunted, "Right," in a menacing tone which Tammy plainly didn't recognise, for she stayed perfectly still, her head remaining out of the window as the politician withdrew his, took one step back and planted a stinging smack from the palm of his hand across Tam's right bum cheek. As she shrieked she straightened; the crack of her head hitting the top of the window frame shocking even the animals into silence as they all stared, waiting to see what would happen next. Tammy, too stunned to scream at that very moment, turned around to face her assailant, rubbing her head and kneeing him between the legs at the same time. Dovehawk crumpled, his head by his thighs, his hands nursing his groin, but Tammy had no mercy. She jumped right on top of him, flattening him to the floor on top of all the legs and wildlife between the two banks of seating. He felt a large rodent infiltrating its prickly whiskers into the back of his neck. What do they keep under these seats? thought Dovehawk. He lashed out at the offending wildlife and heard a woman shout at him. Christ...... they don't shave much round here do they? he thought while expressing his regret to the offended lady: "Perdón señora!" – after which he just lay still while Tammy sat on top of him.

Bargreaves, always on hand to assist, took another foray into his pocket full of useful nick-nacks and arrived on the scene with a sticking-plaster.

"If madam would kindly present her injured bodily part for my attention, I shall dress the offended area with this adhesive application."

Tammy looked up at him impishly. Saying nothing, she undid Dovehawk's trousers and exposed the top of one of his thighs. She then took the plaster from Bargreaves and stuck it tightly to a part of the sensitive inner-leg which had a covering of particularly fine hairs.

"There," said Tammy jubilantly, "I'll remove it later – that'll be something for Duvvy to look forward to." She bent down and whispered in his ear, "Won't it darling."

"Would madam care for another plaster for her wounded head? Or perhaps one for the gentleman's other leg?"

"No thank you Bargreaves. I'm feeling much better now. That will be all."

"Thank you madam." He nodded and went back to marshalling animals into their correct places so he could sit down.

Noon local time, Brazil (15:00 GMT)

It was high summer in Brazil. Belo Horizonte bus station glared whitely and too brightly, the hot haze streaming upward from its arid loading bays distorting the straight lines of the concrete buildings into diffuse shimmering curves. The bus to Clitalickabudal waited where it presumably always waited. It had an essence of permanence about it, a strange and perplexing feature in a device dedicated to transit, especially if one were a prospective passenger, worse still one in a hurry. There was no one aboard; the vehicle had cast its shadow for such a time that the dusty tarmac was cool, Providing pleasant shade and seating for a farmer and his troupe of Amazonian monkeys. Not that the monkeys had any intention of enjoying the shade, preferring to cavort on the roof until the blazing metal, hot enough to fry an egg, scalded them sufficiently to force them to take refuge within the umbra at the side of the vehicle, down below. The driver also sat, leant against one wheel, reading his newspaper, disturbed only now and again by a monkey using his shoulder as a ladder, to which his response was a whack with a swish of his arm, aimed unerringly at the errant primate, and usually connecting with it too.

The quartet of travellers which was Tammy, Fiona, Dovehawk and Bargreaves had just negotiated tickets for Clitalickabudal using Fifi's best Spanish which she had gleaned from her many Mediterranean modelling assignments; and it seemed to have worked, for they had parted with money in return for the driver's assurance that he would transport them to the village of that name, albeit at a time of his own choosing. Unfortunately, strings were attached to the transaction which meant Tammy had another pout on. She took out her anger as usual on Dovehawk.

"But you don't understand! It's quite simple; even for someone as plebby as *you*: I'm not going to pump up the spare wheel on the bus!"

Dovehawk tried to explain the situation to her without hurting her feelings, yet only managed to sound like a frustrated parent urging action from a recalcitrant offspring. "But according to Fiona, the driver said it's the local custom for tourists to carry out routine maintenance on the vehicle before it leaves. That way the bus company can't be held responsible for his own laxness if he drives it off the cliff."

"You do it then." Tammy's voice lost all decorum as she became hysterical.

"I'm checking the wheel nuts."

"Well Fiona can do it then."

"She's checking the oil. Be fair Tam – we gave you the easiest job – look – you've got a nice pump." He pointed to the grubby object with several rusted arms and levers hanging from her grasp, she having rashly accepted it without realising either its purpose or the implication of her taking it. "It'd clean up all right with a bit of Brasso."

Tammy felt it was time to spell out her agenda, slowly and forcefully.

"I came on this trip to get drunk, to get tanned and to get shagged." She now sounded more authoritarian than Dovehawk, the reaching of the end of her tether having calmed her. She glared at him. "I also came on this trip with *you*...... Do you think that the fact I haven't achieved a single one of those things could possibly be down to your presence?"

"I think you're being a little unfair."

"Good. That's how I like to be...... Here you are......" She handed the rusty tyre-pump to the corpulent politician, whose vascular system was already having trouble coping with the heat, making him leak like a clapped-out condom. "You can do it – it won't take you much longer – and in any case the rotten old bus doesn't look like it's about to go anywhere.

"If you'll allow me, sir." Bargreaves, without a single bead of sweat on his brow despite his formally dressed condition, held out his hand to relieve Dovehawk of the antiquated air-blowing contraption. "I have finished adjusting the brakes, greasing the propeller shaft, fixing the bonnet catch and ascertaining that we have sufficient fuel."

Dovehawk handed him the device, looking very sanguine.

"Well done Bargreaves. You are without doubt both resourceful and invaluable. Would you like to work for me? You would make an ideal political agent. And my current one is a little withered.

"You don't actually need a political agent any more, do you Duvvy?" Tamara reminded him of his sadly diminished situation.

"I shall when I find the secrets of those hills," said Dovehawk poetically, staring up to the ice-capped mountains only a bus-ride away. "I shall be in every newspaper in the country."

"I'd like to be on every beach in *this* country." Tammy spoke with resignation at the prospect of even seeing one. Then one of the monkeys pinched her hat and took it up onto the roof. "Now I shall get sun-stroke," Tammy wailed.

The driver, not having moved a muscle for an hour except to receive their cash, without consulting a watch or a clock, on receipt of no signal obvious to those around, suddenly got up, went to his cab and started the engine, sending great clouds of blue/black smoke swirling through the windless heat-laden air. The monkeys all started chattering excitedly, rushing about and looking over the sides of the bus, maybe to check if it had started to move off. The four tourists rushed through the door into the sweltering saloon, tripping in their haste to avoid being left behind, while the farmer unhurriedly followed them. After a clatter and crunch of an attempt at finding a gear, the charabanc took to the road, swinging around the exit from the compound, leaving plumes of dust and fumes in its wake.

3:53 pm, London

Ron had spied on proceedings all day, biding his time, learning the protocols, sussing the equipment. Now, with the nurse away from her station to get herself a cup of tea, his moment of opportunity had arrived. He installed himself at her desk, pressed the button on the base of the microphone and spoke in clear, unruffled tones.

"Emergency. Emergency. All doctors and nursing staff to the Jam United manager immediately."

Then he went to the door leading from his ward and waited. A member of staff soon came running past him, entering the code on the keypad to let herself out. Ron followed her, unnoticed in the commotion. He joined the general swarm of people rushing down the corridors, noting all the time where he was, the direction they took, the number of the wards, until eventually everyone rushed through a door with a security guard standing outside. In the centre of the throng he slipped in undetected as they entered a ward which seemed empty of patients. They were each handed a biological suit, including galoshes and mask, which the doctors and nurses quickly slipped over their clothing. Ron took his and did likewise. Now he was indistinguishable. They all walked through a door and into a long shower cubicle which liberally hosed them down while they continued moving, drying them off with hot air before they emerged at the other end. As the staff rushed through another door into a darkened room, Ron just had time to notice an eerie orange glow escaping from it before he ducked aside from the crowd in search of a good hiding place in which to lie low until the furore had died down. Then he could have a little chat with the Jam U manager, just the two of them. He hoped he could kindle camaraderie rather than rivalry; commiserate with the poor man; maybe nip out and get him a bag of jellies or other desirable treat.

4:21 pm

The nurse on duty in Ward 7 frowned at the empty bed. She had just got back from the other side of the building where, it had become apparent, the Jam United manager's condition had improved slightly rather than deteriorated. She was as puzzled as the rest of the staff at the message which had been delivered earlier on the tannoy. Now she returned to find one of her beds was vacant.

"Kendo?" She spoke softly to avoid startling the dozing Japanese. "Kendo? Can you hear me?"

He opened one eye.

"Kendo. I'm sorry to wake you. Do you know where Ron is? You know...... Mr Conference – in the next bed."

"Oh yes," said Kendo sleepily. "Lon in next bed."

"Yes – that's where he's meant to be. But he isn't. Have you seen him?"

At this point, Kendo remembered what Ron had asked him to say if one of the nurses asked where he was. He sat up and grinned before delivering his line. "Lon in toyret." The look of satisfaction on his face was all-encompassing – his whole head exuded delight in his rôle of accomplice; he decided to stay awake now and see what transpired, be ready to embellish the story as best he could to maintain the excitement.

As the nurse trotted off to check all the lavatories, her dark hair tied tight beneath a crisp white cap, Kendo listened as her starched uniform rustled against her legs in time with her purposeful step. He liked that very much.

4:22 pm

Ron crouched behind a washing machine in a room off a corridor which led to lots of other rooms: doctors' studies, a small kitchen, a TV room, etc. He had decided that he was least likely to be disturbed in the wash-house, and now he was straining his ears to try and detect the last signs of agitation amongst the staff departing the scene of the false alarm. Slowly he stuck his head out – the room was empty. Should he try to get to the Jam U manager's room unseen, or should he be brazen and walk straight in without hesitation? He was, after all, wearing the correct garb, and he couldn't wait too much longer because his absence from his own ward would soon be noted. On the other hand, if someone was already in the room with the patient, he couldn't make overtures without blowing his cover. He decided he had no time to dally. Ron marched out of the door of the wash-house, into the corridor, then through a door on the right which led to the reception area of the ward, including the nurses' station. As he walked past the nurse on duty, he was thankful that she was wearing the full biological suit the same as his. She glanced up as he passed and his stomach jumped with apprehension. "Hi," he chirruped jovially, hoping that the nurse would assume she knew him – the masks prevented recognition at any distance greater than intimacy. He carried on past – straight up to the door which the medics had scuttled through earlier. He looked through the small window in the door, and there was that orange glow again, spookily pervading the room. He could now see that it came from one end of the bed, the end which was against the wall. He peered, straining to accustom his sight to the dimness, but he saw no one inside the room. Without looking behind him, he pushed on the handle, slipped inside and closed the door behind him.

What a weird place; what strange sensations gripped his thoughts as he stood aghast at the sight of the man lying in the bed, his head swollen and pulsating like that of a creature from a sci-fi movie. Ron's feelings were of curiosity and repugnance mingled; he was eager to see more yet fearful of what he might uncover. And on top of all that, he felt like he was on the bridge of a starship – there was equipment surrounding the place, all of it covered in knobs, switches and lights. He went to the prostrate man and knelt next to him.

"Can you hear me?" Ron asked in hushed voice so as not to cause suffering to the luminescent head next to him.

"Aye."

Ron was relieved that communication was possible. He had worried that an illness such as this might be incapacitating in any number of ways, including speech or hearing. Now he needed to establish his own identity.

"Can you see at all?" Ron carried on his line of questioning.

"Aye," responded the mouth from the inflated flesh around the famous manager's skull.

"Good," said Ron, and took his mask off to reveal his face for examination. "I'm Ron Conference – manager of Hetherington Sidney Football Club."

"Oh aye?" replied the head, its orangeness fluctuating in time with lip movements.

"How did you get like this?" Ron said as compassionately as he could.

"I was in Brazil – caught some fancy disease."

"Were you playing a friendly?"

"Aye – you could say that...... It was very friendly anyways."

"That's nice. Er...... I can't hide the reason for my visit; I'm here to ask you if you would reconsider your decision not to play in the third round of the cup. The whole of our town is very sad and disappointed. It would be a gesture of great courage and understanding if you were to change your mind."

4:26 pm

Kendo was sitting upright against his pillows, fully alert when the nurse returned. The soft sound of her chubby little thighs rubbing against each other symphonically beneath her uniform made his taste buds water.

"I've searched all the toilets, Kendo. Are you sure that's where he went?"

Her large brown eyes made it difficult for him to lie; but somehow, when using a language that's not your own, it seems easier, as if engaged in a performance rather than real life.

"Ah...... I remember. He saw me eat food. He rike to tly. He gone to get himself srug sandwich!" Kendo spoke with aplomb, his face lighting up with joy, but the content of his utterance betrayed him, for the nurse had earlier heard Ron grumbling about his neighbour's revolting eating habits. She briefly waggled her finger at him in admonition then rushed off to her desk where she grabbed the microphone.

"Patient Ron Conference, number 6867786, has absconded from his isolation unit. All staff please check your areas and report any sighting to Ward 7."

4:28 pm

The nurse on duty in the serious isolation block was already suspicious that the figure who had greeted her five minutes earlier had not emerged from the Jam United manager's cubicle. On hearing the public address she rushed to the room and found a mystery person beside the bed, his head no longer protected by a mask.

A quarter of an hour later, Ron was in solitary confinement in a different room, no longer with his Japanese friend, a guard standing outside the door. Now there would be no escape, and he had been told that the possibility of cross-infection meant he would have to remain in the hospital all over Christmas, when the team had several important league games. It seemed he had ruined everything.

Ten to two in the afternoon local time, Brazil (16:50 GMT)

Tammy had realised soon after the start of their bus journey that sitting next to the window was a mistake. The cliff edges were so close on occasions that you couldn't see them at all, the side of the coach giving the impression of floating, its tyres off the road and scrabbling at thin air. Aside from this terror-inducing illusion, the monkeys, who were happily riding on the roof, oblivious of their proximity to a doomed fate on the rocks and cataracts below, leant down and reached in through the windows every now and again, grabbing whatever came first to hand on the person sitting there unprepared for such invasion. Tammy therefore cowered in the central aisle of the saloon, sobbing inconsolably, too petrified to move even though her friends now assured her that their destination was in sight and that the roads had broadened to an extent that the distance from edge to edge was now greater than the width of the bus. There she remained as they lurched noisily into the main street of Clitalickabudal, chickens scampering for their lives. The driver drew his rattlebone contraption to a halt outside a wooden shed which doubled as waiting-room and bar (necessary considering the length of waiting involved prior to any travel in these parts), hopped spryly from his perch and straight inside for a refreshener.

"Come on Tam," Fiona said, cuddling her friend, "It's all over; we're there now."

Tammy sat and shook, staring at the floor as if she found fascination in woodworm. When she spoke, all that came out was a timid request, "How far is it to the beach?"

Sensing that the bus would not be commencing its return journey for some time and that they were therefore safe to leave Tamara where she was, Stan and Fiona set off to gather information from the locals, leaving Bargreaves dabbing at his mistress's head with a hanky dipped in cold-cream.

The monkeys were already in the bar, drinking from a large bucket of water kindly provided by the proprietor, but they mostly enjoyed dipping their hands in it and flicking it over anyone who walked through the door, Fiona and Stan making excellent targets.

Dovehawk looked at the bar's patrons – six of them, plus the driver, all men. "Ask them how we get to the World Furry Cup Championships," said Stan.

Fiona frowned. "I'm not asking *that*. It's embarrassing! And anyway – it's not something you learn in Tenerife."

"Oh? I rather thought it was......" Stan raised his eyebrows. "Well what *can* you ask then?"

Fiona thought about it. "I can ask where the girls are."

"That'll do. Go on lass."

By this time, having discussed their way out of their quandary, they had attracted the attention of the human inhabitants of the room as well as the monkeys.

"Donde está las chicas por favor?" Fiona tried her luck in Spanish, but she had no idea what dialect they spoke up here in the mountains.

They looked blankly at her, shaking their heads. It wasn't promising. She turned to Dovehawk and shrugged.

"We'll use sign language," he said, and strode to a central position between the tables and chairs. "I'll need to use you love – just to demonstrate what a girl is." He beckoned Fiona to join him. Presenting her like a prize fishing trophy, he boomed loudly, "Ici chico!"

The men all burst out laughing, spluttering on their drinks.

"What did I say?" asked Stan.

"Well you started off in French – but that wasn't really a problem. I think the bit they found most amusing was you referring to me as a boy."

"And what's wrong with that? You're a tasty looking boy. This lot just wish they were gay like me."

It was true; the men had stopped chattering and now focused lustfully on the Honourable Fiona – not that they were aware of her provenance. However, being cognoscenti of the female figure in these parts, it was probable that her five foot eleven-ness set her apart from local woman-kind and made her exceptional, even to an audience subjected annually to an over-exposure of the feminine form.

"What shall I say then?" Dovehawk, not normally lost for words, found himself frustrated by a situation which deprived him of vocabulary.

"Oh I don't know: they probably speak an Indian dialect up here – Incas and all that."

"Might as well get a drink then. What are you having love?"

The door opened and Tammy walked in.

"Bloody hell," said Dovehawk, "Look at the timing on that! Would you like a drink Tamara?"

"Would a Frenchman like me to tie him up and pull out each of the hairs on his scrotum one by one with my teeth? I'll have a piña collada."

"You'll have a half of llama piss like the rest of us. Heh – look at that!" Dovehawk pointed to an advertising plaque on the wall. "A sign for Terror del Fuegos! At last I'll get to try one."

Unusually, they sat in near silence, drinking their drinks, Tammy calming her nerves from the terrifying journey, Dovehawk trying to extinguish the flames in his mouth brought about by a single Terror del Fuego, Fiona just taking in the scene, a beautiful bloom between two withering leaves. Every now and then, Dovehawk stopped slopping cold liquid into his mouth just long enough to grumble – but the fire quickly rekindled and he was forced to resume hosing-down operations.

After ten minutes or so, the door opened and Bargreaves stood in the entrance.

"May I come in, madam?" He used only a very slightly louder voice than normal to project across the distance separating him from his mistress. "I have some information to impart to the gentleman."

"Yes, come in, come in," said Dovehawk excitedly, usurping Tamara's authority. Bargreaves, however, didn't enter until Tammy nodded her approval.

"I have made enquiries at the *Oficina de Correos*; that is, the *Post Office*," he said as he joined the little group.

"Have you found the girls then?" Dovehawk noisily dragged another chair over to their table and plonked the poor butler down on it, then leant right into his face to be sure he didn't miss anything.

Bargreaves coughed affectedly against the back of his right hand, then cleared his throat, in the manner of pre-oratory ritual. "There are no girls, sir. Well, not exactly." He looked into the eyes of the politician and saw them boring into him from too-close range. "The girls that there *are* are in here."

"Where?" Dovehawk gesticulated wildly around him like a rotary clothes dryer in a breeze.

Bargreaves indicated the monkeys. "Apparently the girl girls have to be rested, ready for the event proper – they mustn't become over-strained beforehand; or should that be beforetongue?" Bargreaves' mind meandered inconclusively. "No matter which, all the practice sessions take place using lower primates of a more hirsute disposition."

"Bloody hell!" snorted Dovehawk, "Is that legal?"

"The Catholic Church frowns on all sexual pursuits which cannot result in progeny; therefore, from their point of view any bestial practice is futile and is therefore a sin. The secular authorities, however, take a different view: they are keen to reduce human population growth, so animal associations are not necessarily discouraged."

"How do you keep your monkey still?" asked Fiona.

"You speak as if you are consulting someone versed in the arts, whereas I can only pass on information provided by others, ma'am. Having said that, I believe you give it a banana."

"Ohhh!" huffed Dovehawk. "Now *that's* definitely illegal!"

While Dovehawk got caught up in the trivia of legalities, Fiona was eager to seek any conclusions that could be drawn from Bargreaves' revelations. "So the Jam United manager," she said, "What happened to him? Was he really allergic to Terror del Fuegos?"

"He had a bad reaction to them. But it wasn't that that made him so unwell."

"I suppose he shagged a monkey did he? It's the sort of thing a footballer *would* do." Tammy noticed her friend and remembered her attachment to Sean. "Oh, no offence Fifi darling."

"It would appear that the gentleman in question did engage in a deviant pursuit with a sub-species closely related to homo sapiens, but of a more oral nature than madam has postulated. It was his allergy to Terror del Fuegos which precipitated his downfall, for I am informed that he refused to suck one before his training session, and within an hour of his encounter had started to exhibit the unmistakable signs of a disease to which most of the indigenous populace are immune, but which can affect foreigners when they partake of the local customs unprotected: namely *orange monkey disease*."

"Bloody hell!" Dovehawk was at last paying attention, but failed to add substance to the debate as he slowly pondered the implications of what he had just heard. "Is it contagious?"

"Highly!"

"I've got to tell Fred Bighill of the Hetherington Gazette!" Dovehawk took out his mobile phone and looked despondently at the signal level indicator which refused to indicate no matter where he held it or at what angle it was pointed.

"I've arranged facilities for you to call England at the Oficina de Correos straight away; if you would care to follow me sir, I'll show you where it is."

Twenty five past five in the afternoon in Hetherington – almost going home time

Fred Bighill was, as usual, sitting in his office, gassing away on the phone when the door was flung open and Glenda rushed into the room and started talking to him so fast that, with the phone going as well, he couldn't understand any of it.

"It's Mr Dove'awk on the phone, from Brazil: he says it's really important – you've got to take the call Fred!"

"What? 'Ang on a minute – Bill – are you still there? I'll ring you back – there's some kind o' panic goin' off 'ere – cheers mate." He put down the phone. "Now what is it lass?"

"Mr Dove'awk – from Brazil – I'll just go and put the call through!" And she sped off again.

Six seconds later, Fred's phone rang. "Mr Dove'awk? Is that you?..... OK OK – I'm listenin'...... What? Are you sure?..... No – none o' the papers here 'ave got that story...... the journalists couldn't speak the language, and none o' the locals could speak anything else...... You were dead lucky to be out there with a polyglot butler...... It's catchin' you say?..... Right...... But not the same disease? 'Ow d'you mean?..... So let me see if I've got this right: he's got orange monkey disease, which makes your 'ead swell right up an' glow bright orange – an' it 'as to be kept cold. But anyone who comes into contact with 'im gets green monkey disease, which makes your 'ead swell right up an' glow bright green – but it 'as to be kept 'ot. Is that right?..... OK – I'll write the story now and get it to the dailies before closing time. Eh, you know what? – I reckon Jam U'll 'ave to pull out o' this now – if what you say is right an' all the trainin' rounds for the participants will be with the monkeys too, they're as good as back in the third round. Well done Mr Dove'awk!"

Christmas Day

"Mmmmmmm – this is so lovely," cooed Tamara, "I can't think why anyone would want to spend Christmas freezing to death in England when they could be lying here on the beach at Copacabana. Rub some more sun tan oil on my shoulders will you Duvvy darling."

Dovehawk lay in a reclined posture, his head propped up against a pile of clothes, reading his paper. Tamara and Fiona both lay face down on their beach towels, soaking the sun into their near-naked bodies, only up-the-bum bikini bottoms and factor ten for protection.

"Whenever I lean over to oil you, Fiona complains that my svelte body blocks out all her sun!" said Dovehawk, wishing to remain in his comfortably undisturbed position. "You'll have to come over here."

"Oh but Duvvy! You wouldn't make your little Tammy get up would you? That would be unkind."

"Where's Bargreaves – can't he do it?"

"No, I sent him off for a paddle. Anyway, I don't want Bargreaves, I want *you*. I want to feel the coldness of that first splash from the bottle, followed by the warmth of your harsh manly fingers burning into my clavicles. Don't you want to make your little Tammy feel all warm?"

"Oh for god sake," Dovehawk muttered as he cast his paper to one side and strained at his elbow joint until it was sufficiently straight to roll his body onto its side, a very ungainly exercise that made him look like a woodlouse that had become marooned on its back and was trying to curl up to free itself. He managed to get into a kneeling position, then crawled over to Tammy where he threw one knee across her body and straddled her back. He reached into her beach-bag for the sun lotion, then sat down on her bottom in preparation for his task.

“Ohh!” she yelped, “Something’s scratching my hip!” She reached behind her to examine the source of the irritation and felt where Dovehawk ’s thigh pressed against her. “You’re still wearing that plaster I stuck on you in the train aren’t you?”

“Yes,” said Dovehawk in a manner which indicated that the fact he was still wearing it was obvious.

“How horrible! It’s been on there for days – you should take it off.”

“I can wait.” Dovehawk undid the cap from the bottle and liberally splashed the cold liquid all over Tammy’s back.

“Ooooohh that’s cold,” she shivered as she spoke. “Would you like me to take your plaster off for you?”

“No thank you.” He began smoothing the balmy fluid around her ribs and shoulders while Tammy groaned in ecstasy beneath him, but he then became distracted as a tiny vortex of wind spiralled along the sand, fluttering his paper – a two-days-out-of-date copy of the *Daily Filler*.

“Duvvy?” Tamara sounded all woozy – but had that demanding note in her voice which presaged a question to which the correct answer must be provided. “Is it exciting lying on a beach in Brazil with your little Tammy?”

There was no answer, and the circling motions of his fingers impressed less upon her flesh.

“DUVVY?”

“WHAT?” Stan was a little short with her and realised he didn’t mean to be so. “What?” he repeated with tenderness.

“I just asked you, is it exciting lying on a beach in Brazil with your little Tammy?”

“Oh. Yes it’s lovely; except I’m not lying on the beach – you made me get up!”

“I made you get up so you could make love to my spine with your fingers; but you seem to have stopped; are you listening? Duvvy? DUVVY?”

"What now?"

"There's no need to be like that." She was all sulky and petulant. "I was only complimenting you on the way you make love to me with your fingers."

"Hurry up Stan," came a voice from his right, "You're keeping the sun off me."

"Sorry. Sorry to both of you...... It's just that I've spotted something in the paper."

"Oh you nasty little Labour proley person – you're supposed to be on holiday, titillating your little Tammy, and instead you'd rather read a boring old newspaper."

"Sorry Tam – I'll finish you off in a minute – you'll be interested in this. Listen. It says here that Mr Squiffy Spankbottom of Throginthroat Hall has kindly offered the services of his daughter, Miss Tamara Toker-Spankbottom, for the pleasure of all the Hetherington players, should they win their cup-tie against Jam United next Saturday!"

"Really?" Tammy looked around at Stan. "Gosh – daddy is *so* naughty! Does it say that the Jam United players can have me if *they* win?"

"Afraid not. I think you're in for a celibate week-end. You'll just have to fit in as many Alfonsos as you can before we go home. Have you had any yet?"

"Only three. I also found a Federico who was rather attractive, but he got a bit narky when I screamed '*Oh Alfonso!!!*' as I came."

"Oh – I find it's best to go for a neutral sounding scream when I come," offered Fiona sweetly, "Something like: oh ooohhh ohhhhhhhhh ooooohhhhhhhhhhhhhhh YES!" She considered the matter. "On the other hand, sex is such a personal thing – you know – their thingy, your hole – I suppose we should keep it dignified by at least attempting a name."

"By the time I've done the oh ooohhh ohhhhhhhhh ooooohhhhhhhhhhhhhhh bit, I don't care what they're called," said Tammy.

"Very wise," said Dovehawk as he re-commenced massaging operations to Tammy's torso, causing her speech to tail off into a series of gurgles which became lost in her towel.

"Me next when you've finished her," said Fiona.

Dovehawk looked at the perfectly proportioned bottom on the prone Honourable Lady Opiumden, deliciously inviting him to be its next occupant of the day.

"I'm never going to get a chance to read my paper am I?" he groused.

"Oh come on Stan!" said Fiona mockingly, "You've been reading it for hours!" She thought about what she'd said for a moment then decided to modify her statement. "Well no; actually you haven't been reading it have you? You've just been staring at the front page because it's got your picture on it!"

"Ooooooooooohhhhhhhhhh!" cooed Dovehawk with equal disparagement. "Do I hear a note of envy there? When was the last time *you* graced the front page? Getting a little nervous that they might not be so interested in you any more?"

"Well we all came on this trip together. I don't see why we shouldn't take equal credit for uncovering the *orange monkey scandal*," complained Tammy.

"Jea-lous! Jea-lous!" sang Dovehawk mockingly, fluttering the *Daily Filler* in front of Tammy's nose.

"Oh just bog off!..... You're pathetic!....." Tammy gave a violent wriggle which shook the crowing Dovehawk from his buttocky perch and deposited him like a giant jellyfish helplessly stranded in the sand, slimily palpitating with the kind of mirth which renders limbs useless.

"Yes, he is pathetic isn't he?" said Fiona. "But he hasn't seen the front pages of yesterday's newspapers yet!"

"What?" queried Dovehawk, his irrepressible humour suddenly quenched as if the tide had come in. "We haven't got yesterday's papers out here yet. How do you know what's on the front page?"

"I know because *I* gave them the story!" She couldn't help ending the news she had just imparted to Dovehawk's ears with a little twist of implied threat, simply to worry him.

"You had to resort to making up your own story just to knock me off the front page? And you call *me* pathetic?..... Hmmmmppphhhh!" Dovehawk gave a louder than normal rendition of one of his usual snorts.

"You can insult me if you like," Fiona said in her smoothest manner, refusing to give him the satisfaction of a raised voice or elevated temper, "But you will end up having to apologise again, as usual."

"Why should I?"

"You'd better go and get the latest papers – then you'll find out."

Dovehawk took a glance at his watch, although this was not at all necessary because he had been counting down the minutes to the time when the English editions of the Christmas Eve newspapers would arrive. "They're not here for another half an hour yet; go on Fiona love – tell us what you said – please......"

Fiona sniggered at the ex-politician's plight – his desperate desire to know making itself apparent in his anguished pleading.

"No. You can wait." And she rolled her head to face away from him. "You can apologise to me now if you want – you might as well if your pig-headedness permits. Or you can leave it till the last moment when you're thoroughly beaten and ashamed as usual – in which case I shall make sure that your contrition will be much more humble and degrading...... Either way, you can spend your waiting-time topping up the sun oil on my back......"

Dovehawk spluttered as he hauled himself up then flumped down onto the pert aristocratic bottom.

"And you can stop spluttering."

"That's what *you* think," spluttered Dovehawk, annoyed at not knowing what everyone back home would have read hours and hours ago at their Christmas breakfast tables. He splashed the syrupy liquid about Fiona's body liberally like he was shaking sugar on his corn flakes, but his mind wasn't properly on the job in hand.

After five minutes of receiving his sub-standard attention, Fiona told him he could go. Stan gathered his shoes and socks and headed off up the beach towards the town and the news-sellers.

Twenty minutes later he was rejoining the girls, holding *The Fun* in front of him for their inspection.

"Oh – what does it say?" said Fiona eagerly, leaping up into a sitting position and adjusting her sunglasses against the glare of the white newspaper. "Bring it here quick Stan!"

"It's all right – I'll read it out to you; are you ready for this?"

Dovehawk began to read:

"*MY NIGHTS OF LUST WHILE SEAN SLEEPS!*

LADY FIONA REVEALS 54 YEAR OLD STAN'S SORDID SEX SECRETS"

"Oh gosh! Does it?" said Fiona. "Where could they have got that from?"

"Crikey!" screeched Tammy, "What does it say next? Do hurry up and read it out Duvvy or I'll wee myself!"

Dovehawk failed to hear her, for he was busy turning purple. "I'm going to sue for this!"

"It's not that bad is it sweetie? You're still on the front page like you wanted. I'm just sharing it with you."

"This is terrible," he continued muttering, "They've got my bloody age wrong!" He looked accusingly at Fiona. "Did *you* tell them I was fifty four?"

"Well," said Fiona innocently, "I knew I was only one year out when I said you were fifty three and you got all cross."

"Hurrrrffffffff!" snorted Dovehawk.

"If you don't carry on reading, Duvvy, I'm going to pull your plaster off," said Tammy as she quickly slid her hand up his leg and grabbed the piece of decaying pink plastic. The feel of the sand stuck to its curling edges made her briefly nauseous before she very gently pulled and Dovehawk roared in pain.

"All right! All right!" he screamed, throwing his legs about, trying to shake her off, and he hurriedly began reading again:

"*Lady Fiona Opiumden yesterday told of nights spent making love with sacked Labour politician Stanley Dovehawk while her boyfriend lay on the floor beside the bed, unconscious through drink.*

Bloody hell – you didn't have to tell 'em the truth did you?" he said as he broke off.

"I just can't help it – I go all red when I tell a lie."

"Is that right?" said Dovehawk ironically. "Then what colour did you go when you told them this next bit?:

Fiona described how the ageing politician......

AGEING POLITICIAN!...... What a bloody cheek!" he stopped to moan again.

"Oh shut up," said Tammy, shouting down his complaint, "And get on with it!"

Dovehawk grumbled some more and then continued.

"*Fiona described how the ageing politician was so turned on when she wore her fiancé Sean's Hetherington Sidney football kit that he insisted she wore the full strip including the boots during love making sessions.*

You managed to come out with that line without a blush I suppose?" Dovehawk challenged Fiona.

"Of course not – I never mentioned what happened in bed; I mean it wasn't really worth mentioning was it? The papers make that stuff up – that's what journalists do. We provide the essentials and they fill in all the little details."

"Oh I love the little details," shrieked Tammy. "Keep going Duvvy – I want to know what else it says!"

Stan cleared his throat, the bright sun glaring off the paper making his eyes turn everything into a giant rectangular green blob when he looked away.

"You finish it," he said, handing it to Tamara.

She snatched it before he let go then tittered and screamed as she digested the scurrilous article.

"So, what do you think?" asked Fiona, looking Dovehawk straight in the eye.

"Aside from a few factual inaccuracies that I suppose I'll just have to live with......" He paused, then grinned at her. "......It's blinkin' wonderful!" he shouted, and grabbed her into a giant hug.

"So you're going to apologise for being horrid to me?"

"Oh, I suppose so." He shifted himself to assume a position of kneeling prostration before her, then delivered the well-practised speech. "I am truly and most deeply sorry for ever having doubted you. There is only one thing better than being on the front page of the newspaper, and that is being on it with you." He bowed his head until his forehead made an impression in the sand, just in front of Fiona's knees, while two men ran up to the little party on the beach, one of them snapping away with a camera, the other shouting out questions:

"Mr Dovehawk! Lady Opiumden! Can we have an interview? How long will you be staying in Brazil? Have you spoken to Sean? Will you be going to the Jam United game? Have you got anything to say about your relationship?......"

"Excuse me!" Tammy peevishly tried to get herself noticed. "There's someone else here too you know...... Hello...... Yes *me*...... And I'm much richer than these two!"

"Oh sorry love!" said the newspaperman. He pressed his dictaphone in Tammy's direction. "Tell me love. Has he had both of you? Was it three in a bed?"

She waited, the look of mischief flowing across her face like sunlight chasing along the ground behind the shadow from a cloud. "It was in a taxi actually."

The reporter jumped in shock, unable to believe his luck.

"And *I* don't remember a thing about it," said Stan, "But I'm informed I was rather good."

"Only my gardener said you were good!..... A good *weight* that is!" Tammy was enjoying being the centre of attention at last, and sensed her own chance to get on the front page of the paper. The reporter meanwhile was becoming confused with all the new characters being introduced into the story and was wondering how he should angle the final draft.

"And another thing," said Dovehawk. "You can announce that I plan to stand as an independent candidate in the Hetherington by-election...... I shall be standing as *Real Labour*. That's *Real Labour*, not *Real Madrid*. *Real Labour*. Got it? Put that on your bloody front page!"

The reporter's mouth dropped open, and that was all. Movement ceased. His body became petrified while his brain assimilated what was happening to him: *two scoops from a speculative trip to a beach on a foreign shore; was this benign coincidence? or was god conspiring to give him all his good fortune on one day, turning the rest of his life and career in journalism into an anti-climax?* It was too terrible to contemplate. He fainted.

"Oh bugger," said Tammy. "Trust me to find the only journalist in the world who can't cope with a juicy story!"

"Don't worry," said the photographer, throwing his camera down and grabbing his colleague's notebook and tape-recorder, "I've got all the pictures of yours and Fiona's tits that I need. I'll handle this story!"

"What about *my* tits?" asked Dovehawk, offended, pulling aside the buttons on his shirt.

Boxing Day

The front page of *The Fun*:

STAN THE STUD'S THREE-IN-A-TAXI ROMPS

AND HE SAYS HE'LL STAND AS "REAL LABOUR"

Hot on the heels of the Sports Minister's resignation over the orange monkey scandal, the man who caused his downfall, Stan Dovehawk, has announced that he will be standing as an independent in the Hetherington by-election under the banner of "Real Labour". This news comes at the same time as more details of his lurid sex life were revealed, this time from the mouth of multi-millionairess Tamara Toker-Spankbottom (pictured below).

Third round day

Fiona's imitation fur coat was all-enveloping, the matching hat and gloves leaving only her eyes and nose and mouth exposed to the deep chill which had besieged the north of England since the beginning of January. Her body which had so recently been toasting on Brazilian sands was warmly protected beneath layers of jumpers, jeans, boots, socks and thermal knickers.

Dovehawk had never seen Fiona wearing thermal knickers, and he'd never been to a football match either – not for years anyway; not since as a nipper he had accompanied his father to watch Anton the

Gorilla a couple of times, but all he could remember about that occasion was that he had crossed his legs for the whole match rather than go for a piss because the bogs smelt so bad...... Oh, and that they had won the FA Cup thirty seven times but the most recent triumph was so many centuries ago that no one was old enough to remember it. Dovehawk wore thermal knickers. Some would call them long johns, but it didn't really matter what they were called so long as they were warm which, as he sat next to the delectable Honourable Fiona in the Stanley Park home supporters' stand, they indeed were.

The temperature at eight minutes past two on this Saturday afternoon had failed to climb to zero. And how did Dovehawk know this? He knew because the manufacturers of the under-pitch heating system had thoughtfully installed four flashing displays, one on each side of the ground, which alternately indicated degrees Celsius and Fahrenheit so that the public would be impressed by the muddy consistency of the pitch on days when, unassisted, it would have been as hard and white and spiky as an inverted artexed ceiling. Dovehawk recalled Smoggrate's words from all those weeks before when he had first been invited to visit the club in his capacity as Member of Parliament elect: "Costs five 'undred a day to run when it's switched on, you know; but worth every penny if it means we can play all through January and February, specially third round day, eh Mr Dovehawk?" And here was the proof – the pitch in all its slimy glory, the epitome of a third round pitch from the lower divisions, waiting, vegetative yet sentient, like the open pincer of a Venus flytrap waiting to bamboozle, crush and digest the meat of an illustrious Premier League club. Maybe.

The grandstands were filling up nicely. With fifty minutes still to go to kick-off, three sides of the ground seemed about eighty percent full while the Jam United end already looked chock-a-block, an ocean of red which shone with cheer, the beams from the floodlights highlighting the culmination of five thousand puffs of chanting breath rising into the crisp chill air like dancing aurora. And how appropriate: the northern lights, pride of English football, the mightiest team in the land paying a visit to one of the lowliest, replete with past glories, but fallen upon harsh economic times. To draw Jam U at home in the third round was like winning the lottery only better because it brought joy to thousands instead of just one or two, and although the joy it would bring to Smoggrate and his bank-balance was incalculable, that wouldn't stop him trying to calculate it so he could show off to Mr Dugdale.

When the Hetherington Weavers' Band made their pitch inspection earlier in the day, they were concerned about the gloopiness of the playing surface, so they now marched onto the field wearing wellies. The Bandmaster had instructed them to keep moving at a lively pace to avoid becoming bogged down, and the programme of music he had chosen would be played at a keen allegretto or quicker so they should not be too imperilled by an unwitting rallentando. However, the sight of them almost jogging around the ground drew much raucous amusement from the stands and they had to blow and bang quite hard to make themselves heard.

Angela was nervous with over-excitement, scared at the waiting and wishing the time would pass, but she was also trying to remember these moments for the future so they could be cherished and not wasted. Angela was very lucky today for she had been rewarded: Mr Dugdale had told her that, if she wished, she could wear Hetherington kit and lead the team out onto the pitch at five to three. She would be there with Sean at her side, her ultimate wish come true, but the suspense was making her feel faint.

Fiona was also looking forward to seeing Sean, having reassured him that her undiluted dalliance with Dovehawk was merely the means to keep her in all the tabloids. Her absence from him over Christmas had made her heart grow fonder and she knew that, although he was a bit of a flop in the bedroom department, his speed and power and grace on a muddy field always sent shivers through her. In a few minutes time he would test himself against the best and the fans would either be dazzled or disappointed but either way it wouldn't matter – the beauty of the unknown gave everyone the biggest buzz imaginable and now, at last, they were going to find out.

In the Directors' box, Tammy shared a space at the bar with Fiona's grandfather, or rather, Fiona's grandfather was attempting to occupy the same space as Tammy and using every available handhold which happened to avail itself on her very handleable body to assist him. Further along the bar, Jack chatted to Sir Bobby, but their conversation was punctured every twenty seconds or so by the Hetherington Chairman looking at his watch, itching to see whether it was time for them to go to their seats ready for the start of the match.

Poor Mr Rumbleon had taken up his seat in enclosure C, only to find to his horror that he was in the centre of a little cluster of Jam U supporters with non-existent haircuts and tattoos on their teeth. Rumbleon realised that they must have picked up their tickets on the black market, but he knew that this block of seats had all been allocated to fellow Councillors, Labour Party members and Rotarians. Surely, they wouldn't have? Would they? He decided to hold an enquiry on Monday morning into the whole scandalous affair. He also decided, as a safety measure, temporarily to support Jam United, so he quickly studied his programme to find out the names of all their players'.

Smoggrate was putting the finishing touches to showing Adelina around the boardroom. Compared with Dovehawk, she had been a revelation: she hadn't harangued or humiliated him once, nor made a single impertinent suggestion. She looked like a million dollars and sounded like treacle on ice-cream and made the pompous Smoggrate, when extolling the virtues of Dibbsey and Needham, feel like he was describing the Pyramids. What a lovely lady, he thought. I'll have to put it to Mr D that she should be offered a place on the Board.

The South Stand was a cold and barren place, shaded as it was from even the feeble rays of winter sun, while acting as a funnel to channel the harshest and nastiest north east winds into its confines, so it was not surprising that this was the place designated by Smoggrate for use by the TV commentator, on a special ledge, prominently exposed to the weather's violent vileness. There had only been one TV commentary on a Hetherington game in the last five seasons and that was for a last day do-or-die relegation fight with Arthritics Athletic. But with today's game being the plum tie of the third round, television coverage was obligatory and competition had been stiff amongst the commentators to avoid the assignment, the story of the Sidney Park ground's commentary position having been so over-elaborated and exaggerated at each re-telling that its reputation filled telly verbal-drivel-land with dread. But the editor decided that this match warranted top billing, so a top-drawer commentator would be winched to the rickety perch in the sky atop the South Stand; his creaking bones liberally insulated with layers of TV Corporation-subsidised thermal undies, his hat fleecily lined, his gloves pre-warmed in the microwave, his hip-flask fully charged, his voice silken and lubricated with the finest Kendal mint-cake. Not only that, but he would be assisted by no less a personage than Ron

Accrington – Hetherington Sidney's ex-manager and notable TV pundit.

Twenty past two and Lord Opiumden brushed the rim of another large glass of gin against Tammy's lips, tipping it up just as it passed its intended target and delivering an ice-cold trickle of clear fizzy liquid down her neck. She grabbed hold of the stem of the vessel to right it before any more of the contents spilt out and yowled in semi-drunken anguish, partly at the discomfort of something freezing disappearing down her blouse and partly at the thought of all that gin going to waste. The Noble Lord staggered and swayed, giggling as he finished the contents of his own glass, then ordered more drinks to be added to his slate. Lord Opiumden's bar bill was a remarkable affair; a life-long affair; a love affair. Each day when he woke up, assuming he woke up, he had dark thoughts which quickly needed to be subdued or else he would succumb to depression; but his gloom never lasted more than a couple of minutes, for that was all the time it took him to remember his bar bill, his glorious Hetherington Sidney FC slate, always with a couple of blank lines available at the bottom to be filled-in with the price of the tipple of his choice. Life was a wonderful thing and Fiona's grandfather lived it to the full. His new liver had settled in well to its vigorous schedule of blood-cleansing, and when his doctors revealed it had belonged to an abstainer and so had very few miles on the clock, Lord Opiumden resolved to give it a thorough workout for the remainder of their time together and see which of them first reached their timely demise.

Looking at Tammy, he remembered her as the little girl who used to come over to play with Fiona, rushing around the corridors and catacombs of Opium Haul, dressing up in the old clothes they found in the attic, hiding in the suits of armour, opening up the dusty cobwebby trunks of junk in the basement and making ghostly wailing sounds in the crypt. Now though, through his alcoholic haze, she was a big little girl with curvy sticky-out bits that he found hard to resist. He gave her bum a grand-paternal pinch; she gave His Lordship's moustache a fearfully painful tweak in retaliation; but neither of them could feel much under gin-induced anaesthesia and were just doing it for fun.

Half past two and Angela jogged up and down on the spot to try and keep warm in the freezing lobby outside the dressing rooms as she waited for the players to emerge, for her tiny body and thin legs made her susceptible to the cold. By contrast, Wally the groundsman was sweating like a goodun as he emerged from checking the under-pitch heating boiler and spotted Angela hovering there. He tutted, causing disapproving puffs of smoke to eject from his roll-up. Shaking his head, he grabbed Angela's tiny arm just below her shoulder, his hand easily closing right around it, and dragged her into the bunker which housed the appliance, a welcoming rush of heat blasting out at them as he opened the tiny door through which even little Angela had to duck. He sat her down on the grimy dust-impregnated seat-pad of the chair he used for monitoring the equipment, easily in reach of the big brass power regulating handle next to the temperature gauge which hovered in a mid-position showing that things were cooking nicely. Wally showed the frozen waif where she could place her hands to warm them without risk of being scalded, then he went around the contraption for another look at the oil dipstick, the pitch mud-depth-detector and the boiler water-level sight-glass. He patted the pale-blue painted cast iron contraption affectionately, thinking of all the years gone by when he would have been sweeping snow and frost from the grass on the morning of the match, just before the referee's pitch inspection, hoping that the blanket of white crystals would have protected the surface sufficiently to allow the game to go ahead. How much more civilised this was; and how much warmer too.

Twenty to three and just by the corner flag one of the band-members suffered a high speed blowout in his euphonium, an easily remedied occurrence, merely requiring the removal of his dentures from the instrument's mouthpiece which, in a normal practice-room or quadrangle environment, could be performed without difficulty. But in freezing weather conditions on muddy grass, the same set of actions became fraught with danger, requiring quick thinking, deft handwork and improvisation. Now remember, there hadn't been any weaving in Hetherington since 1971 so the band members were no spring chickens, and the Second Euphonium was a sprightly ninety three years old, which gave him plenty of experience of eupho-orthodontic rectification, but also meant his wellies were leather-soled and offered minimal grip on the slimy surface of the Stanley Park football field. Weaving was the last thing on the Second Euphonium's mind when he began to retrieve enamelled tombstones from the narrow brass hole in which they had become wedged, but unfortunately for the poor old chap, weaving was exactly what he did, building up to a zig-zag slide which culminated in him tripping the Third Cornet in front of him who was felled like a sapling. The ensuing pile-up took several minutes to clear, even with the help of police and ambulancemen. It was eight minutes to three by the time they re-assembled and as they trudged off the field, their rendition of the Souza march being played at the time of the accident sounded a bit more gravelly than before, but no less spirited.

Jack consulted his watch again. “It’s time for us to take our seats gentlemen,” he said. “Are you coming Lord Opiumden?” He gestured to the old man who appeared to have his hand inside the front of Tamara’s dress and, judging by the manipulations he was performing to foil her attempts at removing it, it seemed to Jack unlikely that he would be joining them to watch the match. Then Tammy smacked His Lordship one round the left ear which straight away did the trick, his arm retracting instantly to soothe the outraged auricle, and onlookers must have wondered what all the fuss was about. She picked up her coat and handed it to the Lord who, still rubbing his ear with his left hand and carrying his drink in his right, had to work out what to do to take hold of it. He decided to finish his drink first, which he did, then dropped the glass on the floor before grabbing the coat and dutifully holding it open for Tammy to insert her arms. Having wriggled inside the coat and hugged it tightly around her, she felt sufficiently wrapped and fuelled to face the cold, and went to take her place next to Fifi and Dovehawk in the stand, leaving Fiona’s granddad trying to procure another drink, convinced he hadn’t had the last one.

Five to three and the referee and linesmen came out of their own dressing room and knocked on the door of the one belonging to the home side, shouting that they were ready to go. They then went to the other side of the tunnel where the concrete in front of the away dressing room had cracked and subsided. The youngest official, having been delegated to perform the job, crawled carefully to the top of the precipice, before abseiling down the tortuous path to the door using the ropes provided, there to knock and announce the same message. Wally, who had been keeping an eye out for signs of readiness, disappeared back into his boiler room to gather up Angela who, hot as toast, ducked out of the door and skipped over to the start of the tunnel to be ready at the head of the queue. Ahead of her, all was darkness beneath the grandstand, the structure drumming noisily to the sound of a thousand shuffling feet above her head.

Beyond the gloom, the contrasting brightness from the floodlit pitch was funnelled towards her by two lines of policemen forming extensions to the tunnel walls, many of them peering back at her to see if the procession was ready to move. Behind her, the referee chatted to his assistants. Then there was a clattering sound as the two dressing room doors opened and the players' metal studs ground their jumbled rhythms on the concrete floor, the Jam U footballers hurling themselves up the cliff-face like practised marine commandos, dragging the linesman after them, to join the home side who were already lined up behind Angela. With a ball under his arm and a club pennant in his hand, Dorksy stood by her side, gave her a friendly squeeze with his spare hand and grinned, the stubble on his chin separating into bands of light and dark where it was alternately stretched and folded as it followed the contours of jovial flesh.

"What a day this is, eh lass?"

She could only grin back at him, looking like a bit of a Doreen but not knowing what to do about it.

"'Ere – you can 'ave this – give you sommat to do." Dorksy handed her the pennant which she took without even registering that she had done so. The Jam U players were now lined up on her other side. She cast them a glance and felt as if she was going to faint: shutting her eyes and breathing deeply, she prayed that she wouldn't. Dorksy looked down at her from fully a foot higher and saw the discomfort written in her contorted face and trembling body. As the referee shouted "Go!", Dorksy grabbed Angela's hand and held on tight while they walked out into the artificial glare of the freezing afternoon, keeping her from falling and dragging her along so that, whatever happened, she would at least make it onto the pitch. The police at the end of the tunnel pushed back with their arms outstretched, widening the gap for the entourage to get through, and this was the signal for everyone in the ground to start cheering and whistling and shrieking and shouting, loosing off their firecrackers and blasting their hooters and throwing their streamers up into the air.

Dorksy threw the ball onto the pitch, but still hung on to Angela while walking to the centre circle. Behind him the rest of the Hetherington players dispersed as soon as their boots hit the grass, running off to the home end of the pitch where they had a kick-about, while Jam U did the same at the other end. The referee, clutching the match ball, checked his watch and examined his notebook and pencil to make sure they were fully functioning. As Sean ran out, he noticed a massive placard draped over the fence opposite the tunnel. *SHAGSY WEARS THE TROUSERS!* it proudly asserted, a statement which for the time being was true.

The TV commentator went through the team sheets, the camera picking out each player who might have a crucial influence on the outcome of the match, these being Sean for Hetherington Sidney, and the whole of the Jam United team. But viewers were bored with hearing about Jam United, so Sean got top TV billing, the accolades pouring upon him being twice as numerous and three times as fictitious as those for any other player.

"He's had a new haircut specially for the match! Look at that; fantastic. And a baby on the way too we understand – only seven months to go; fantastic! And we hear that he may be on his way to joining his opposite numbers here today, Jam United, in a transfer deal worth six point five million pounds! Wouldn't that be incredible if it turns out to be true?..... What do *you* think Ron?"

"I'm not taking sides cos as you know I've managed both these clubs – (well, I've managed every club in the country actually) – but it would be nice for the underdogs to get something out of the match, and this boy holds the key to that. Anything they get I feel is going to come through him. And he's a smashing lad too. And there on your screen now you can see his gorgeous girlfriend – Lady Fiona. What a cracker she is. And if this transfer rumour turns out to be true, then he's got the lot hasn't he?"

"Indeed he has Ron. You can't argue with that!"

When all the players had finished disgorging onto the pitch, the clubs' backroom boys followed. For Jam United there were trainers and physios and doctors and acupuncturists and faith healers and astrologers and assistant coaches by the bucket-load; for Hetherington just Phil with his sponge. And surrounded by these ancillary staff, at the centre of each huddle (albeit a small huddle on the Hetherington side) walked two men with bandages swaddled about their heads. Their presence was immediately picked out by the TV cameras who provided close-ups for the stay-at-home matchgoers, those actually present in the ground having to make do with their own eyesight because the Whippets' budget had yet to extend as far as equipping Sidney Park with TV screens.

"Yes!" shouted the commentator in his eyrie, forgetting that five seconds earlier he had been upset when his nose ran and froze into a small icicle attached between the nasal fluff and his top lip, "The managers are both here! We wondered if they would be allowed to attend on medical grounds...... Well...... Now we have our answer!..... What do *you* think Ron?"

The Jam U manager had a plastic bucket attached to the top of his head which was brimful of ice, shining orange in the glare of the lights and plain enough for all to see.

"Perhaps that's where they've got the champagne chilling for the after-match celebrations!" Ron Accrington wittily joked for the admiring listeners at home.

Accompanying the Jam U manager was a tracksuited man carrying spare ice in another bucket, this one made from galvanised steel and of two gallons capacity.

The Hetherington manager on the other hand had a portable sun-lamp installed above his head, held fast to his body by a waist-belt and shoulder straps, which cast its plentiful beams upon his cranium from where they were reflected back with a greenish hue.

"He can't be getting his hair done, that's for sure," quipped Ron Accrington, "Cos I know for a fact he hasn't got any!"

Alongside him, Phil carried his sponge bucket in one hand and in the other a gas-powered hair dryer which he was careful to keep pointed at his boss's forehead as they slowly made their way to the home dugout. When they got there, they carefully sat down, making sure that the radiant heaters installed in the tiny concrete bus-shelter of an edifice were all on full and were all trained on Ron Conference's green head. The two dugouts were right next to each other. Next door, a fan was blowing cold air onto the Jam United manager's incandescent orange brow.

"You'd better not shout too much today," advised the Jam U assistant coach, "You'll overheat if you do!"

"You'd better start shouting now," said Phil in Ron's ear, "It's the only thing that's going to stop you cooling down in this weather!"

Three o'clock and Angela handed her pennant to the Jam U captain, took his in return, then waved to the crowd on all four sides of the ground in turn. She then went to Sean and kissed him, just a peck, before running off to her seat in the stand where Jack was waiting with her coat.

Phhheeeeeeeeep. The referee blew his whistle and they were off.

"Hit 'em hard!" roared Ron Conference. He stood up outside the dugout to shout, but an icy blast of winter wind cooled his head and he felt sick. Phil grabbed him and repositioned him in his hot-spot. "You'll have to yell from a sitting position," he told him as he aimed the hair dryer and switched it on full.

"The only way they'll get a result here is to hit 'em hard, then catch 'em on the break," pronounced Ron Accrington sagely. Ron Accrington didn't feel cold at all. Jack had kindly provided him with a foot pump with a pipe running directly from the club bar into a holding-tank on his lap, from which a drinking-straw protruded to his mouth, providing internal warmth and comfort while de-icing his lips.

Korma, running flat out, saw the ball go into the possession of a mean United midfielder. He decided to close his eyes and crunch straight in. The outcome could be a broken leg, a yellow card, a red card, studs up the goolies – it was definitely best that he didn't look. Then amazingly, half a second later, he found himself sliding across the sticky surface with the ball lodged between his shins. He jumped up immediately, looked to his right and there was Sean on the touchline. *Donkkk* – he sweetly connected the ball with his left foot and it speared off towards the space in front of Shagsy who was already running on to it. The ball hit the turf five yards to Sean's left and instead of bouncing nicely to him as the Jam U defender coming to intercept it had expected, the heavy ground made it stick and it only rolled a few feet. The defender missed it, while Sean swerved and collected it with his left before immediately shooting from six paces outside the penalty area. The ball came off the outside of his foot, slightly mis-hit, and across the face of the goal where it rebounded off one of the Jam U central defenders straight to the goalkeeper who whacked it down the other end of the field. Piccalilli, the Hetherington goalkeeper, saw it go high in the air like a planet; so high it went above the scope of the floodlights and became entirely invisible. The Hetherington defenders gathered at the spot where they thought it might land, with a couple of Jam U strikers at their sides trying to jostle them out of position. Suddenly, the ball reappeared from the sky like a comet, hurtling down for an impact with Earth, straight where Piccalilli was standing. He jumped up and grabbed it thankfully, then landed heavily, tripped, somersaulted and backward flipped, the pair of them (ball and goalkeeper) ending up in the Hetherington net.

"Yeeeeeeesssssssss!" screamed the away fans who were behind Piccalilli's goal.

Phhhheeeeeeep went the referee's whistle.

"Bollocks!" went Ron Conference.

"Ooooooohhhhh!" went the commentator. "Oooooooohhhh oooooooooohhh ooooooooohhh!" as he waited for someone to tell him in his headphones who had scored and what the score was.

The Jam U manager jumped up and down and danced around with his cohorts, then had to be calmed down and cooled off with some freezer spray.

"Oh dear," bemoaned Ron Accrington from his elevated viewpoint as assistant commentator, "Just what the home side didn't need – a lucky goal like that! It'll be hard for them now. If Jam U score again, it's all over; but worse than that, Hetherington have *got* to score now, and we know how difficult it is to get past this defence."

"Ooooooooohhh!" went the commentator. "And the goalscorer was Wreckham – what a lucky bounce! Oooooooooohhh! One-nil to Jam United!"

"Just remember!" screeched Ron Conference from his dugout as he watched his team line up for a second kick off barely two minutes into the game. "Remember who you bloody are! Bremner, Lorimer, Gray, Charlton, Clarke, Giles, Hunter, Madeley!"

"That were Leeds, boss!" shouted back Gherkin who, being the left wing-back, was the only one near enough to the bench to converse with his gaffer. "You know they always got beat in the FA Cup!"

"Not in the bloody third round they didn't!" screamed Ron, "And don't be cheeky! You're Reaney – and don't bloody forget that, OK?"

The referee blew for the restart, Shagsy tapped the ball in front of Billy Bell who drilled it back to Nobsy in central midfield. "Plan B!" he roared, and hoisted the ball almost vertically into the air. Everyone on the pitch bar Piccalilli rushed into the Jam U half, just as had happened a minute earlier at the other end. Nobsy barged his way through the scrum, not taking his eye off the ball, then launched it again from half way inside their half, at the same time colliding full on with a Jam U player, leaving both of them lying in a dazed heap on the floor. The referee held his arms out wide to signal play to continue as the ball gathered altitude again.

Into the goalmouth everyone charged, sensing that this was where the ball would ultimately reunite itself with terra firma. The cosmopolitan Jam U goalkeeper uttered "*sacre mama-mía fernando SOS*", or some such latin oath while he watched the small round object becoming bigger and bigger, spearing towards him. He jumped to meet it as it arrived, placing his hand beneath its trajectory, hoping to push it over for a corner. *Splat*. The ball landed at sixty miles an hour directly on top of the crossbar and on the goalie's hand, completely crushing the gloved fingers, numb from the cold, between ball and woodwork, then bouncing back up into the air again, almost as high as before. The linesman stood on the bye-line, straining to see whether the ball remained in play, ready to raise his flag should it stray over the line, blown by the wind. The goalkeeper fell to the floor, holding his poor hand, but unless the linesman flagged to signal the ball was out of play, the referee could not blow his whistle. Straight up the ball went, up and up, then it started down again. All eyes were upon it. The defenders, the attackers, the linesman, the referee, Piccalilli, everyone except the prostrate Jam U goalkeeper, who, by a double dose of misfortune, now had all the players clambering on top of him to get into the best position for the header. The crowd were silent. No one dared to breathe. The goalkeeper's screams carried clearly across the frosty afternoon, but nobody heard them above the noise of their own beating hearts.

The ball fell from its great height, seeming to take a long time which was of course an illusion generated by the expectation in the onlookers, and just before it landed the shoving and pushing crowd beneath it got insuperably tangled up with each other and fell over en masse. At the end of its plummet, the football blasted into the scattered bodies like a stone falling into soft sand, burying itself completely and failing to re-emerge. The hillock of flesh seethed and distended like a slime-mould while the referee, waiting and waiting for the ball to reappear, finally had to blow his whistle. It was stalemate – he would restart the game with a drop ball.

The players extricated themselves from their tangle one by one, until only the goalkeeper remained on the ground where he had been lying now for quite some time. The Jam U medical staff brought on a stretcher and took him away, leaving his bodily indentation clearly marked in the goalmouth mud. As the events on the pitch started to take their toll, steam started rising from the Jam U manager's head and more ice had quickly to be applied. Meanwhile, Ron next door was feeling a little shivery. "Hey Phil," he said," Go and tell Wally to turn the under-pitch heating up a bit will you. Every time I stick me head out of the dugout it starts to get too cold."

The Jam U centre-forward put on some gloves: to him had fallen the dreaded task of being temporary goalkeeper.

The referee asked for one player from each team to stand on either side of him. The Jam U player was almost on his own goal line, and the whole of the rest of his team were packed into the goal. Sean, the appointed player for the Hetherington side, stared at his opposite number keenly as he waited for the referee's arm drop and the ball to fall from his grip. When the ball was dropped, both players immediately went for it with their knees, cracking them together harshly whilst missing the ball altogether. It fell on the muddy ground and stopped just long enough for Tubsy, who was standing behind Sean (the theory being that he was wide enough to stand a good chance of a rebound) to prod out his leg and knock it towards the line. One of the Jam U defenders standing inside the goal smashed the ball out as hard as he could. Like a squash ball hitting a wall, it ricocheted off Tubsy's nose and rocketed into the top corner of the net. The theory had worked! It was one-one!

Phheeeeeep went the referee's whistle as the crowd roared.

"Magic!" went Ron Conference in his dugout, with so much glee that his sun-lamp got a fit of the shakes and he had to sit down in case the bulb blew.

"Magic!" went Ron Accrington in his commentary position, "That's just what this match needed!"

"Bollocks!" went the Jam U manager, his temperature taking another lurch upwards as his doctor measured and listened and shook his head sternly. "You won't make it through to half-time if you keep getting so excited," he warned his patient.

It was the second restart of the afternoon, and Jam U kicked off just as snow started to fall.

"Did you get the heating turned up Phil?" asked Ron on the Hetherington bench.

"Aye," replied the unflappable sponge man.

"Well get him to turn it up some more – we don't want the match abandoned – we'll have to pay back all the ticket money. This snow mustn't settle."

"OK," Said Phil, and headed back beneath the grandstand again to see Wally.

The snowflakes tumbling through the intense beams from the floodlights made the setting for the match look quite beautiful, like the proverbial Christmas card, except there were *ten* men on view dressed in red instead of the usual *one* with a few reindeer.

Ten men, thought Ron. *They're down to ten men. We should do something here*. He called his captain over to the touchline.

"Dorksy son, they're down to ten men – chase them – push up – don't defend too deep – push up into their half and make them give the ball away!"

Dorksy nodded then rejoined the fray, but although Hetherington struggled mightily to exert some pressure, nearly all the chances were created by the opposition and when the referee blew for half-time, the score was still one-all.

Because the snow only settled in the gaps between the hot water pipes running under the surface, the pitch had a series of white bars across it, going from one touchline to the other, making it look like a giant shove-halfpenny board. Ron was still concerned about the possibility of the match being called off, so he asked Wally to turn up the heating yet again; the gauge on the boiler was now three quarters of the way around the face.

When the Hetherington players came out for the second half, they found that the Jam U goalkeeper had been repaired and was back on the field, which was now starting to steam in places as a result of the heat being pumped into it from below. Indeed, when the game was resumed, the ball was reluctant to roll at all in the hot lines between the dustings of snow, making passing almost impossible. It was "boot it and run" stuff, and this didn't suit the Jam United manager at all. It was clear to all that he was rapidly losing his cool; in more ways than one.

Ron Conference meanwhile was feeling the ill-effects caused by the snow falling on his head. "It's no good," he moaned, "I need to keep warmer, especially when my head's out of the dugout."

"You shouldn't have your head out of the dugout then should you," said Phil unhelpfully.

"I can't shout at this lot with me head in here," retorted Ron, "Go and tell Wally to turn it on full power."

"Are you sure?" Phil looked shocked. "The manufacturers said we shouldn't run it above half way except in exceptional circumstances!"

"I know, I know. But these are exceptional circumstances. Just get him to whack it up for a bit."

Phil trudged off to give Wally his new instructions just as Stainsy lost the ball in midfield. The Jam U player hoofed it upfield, chased after it then slid in for a tackle against Tubsy. The ball broke free, Dorksy gave it some leather but for the second time that afternoon it hit Tubsy and rebounded into the net. His own net.

The red contingent in the crowd went mad, and the Jam U manager leapt from his dugout and on to the steaming pitch, the ice in his turban spilling in all directions as he hugged his players.

The referee blew his whistle for the goal. He then blew it again and went running over to the Jam U manager, telling him to get off the pitch. He flourished his yellow card at the team boss and wrote his name in his little book, the first time he'd had to use his pencil in earnest since the match began.

The Jam U manager, enveloped by steam from the pitch and with his ice all toppled about him began to glow bright orange as his fury rose. His doctor, seeing the warning signs, rushed out and grabbed him, jamming him headfirst into the freezing galvanised bucket which had been reloaded at half-time. More steam sizzled into the air as the manager's hot head was quenched under the glacial surface of the water.

"That was a close thing," said the doctor as he removed his charge's face from the bucket to allow him to breathe. "You must calm down!" And with those words, he thrust the gasping gaffer back into the dark and icy depths.

"Bollocks!" said Ron on Phil's return. "Did you see that?"

"No. Actually I didn't," said Phil, condescendingly. "You keep sending me on daft errands!" He didn't usually dare express his annoyance with his manager so openly, but at the moment he was in a superior position in terms of health, and he was also supremely fed up with the way his afternoon was going.

"Another bloody lucky goal!" roared Ron. "I can't believe how lucky this lot are! It makes me bloody sick! Jammy Jam United – they're living up to their name again!"

The pitch was now almost a bog, with noxious gases bubbling from its surface like a rotting swamp. "Two-one, two-one, two-one, two-one," sang the visiting fans, while the players sank ankle deep into the mire, as if they were playing footy on a foreshore.

Ron shouted and bawled at his players, but no one could make even one accurate pass in the conditions and the grass was completely obscured by a low lying stratum of fog, so even finding the ball was becoming tricky.

"Don't you think we should turn the under-pitch heating down? Or off perhaps?" Phil had to ask the question, even though he knew what his manager's reply would be. He looked at Ron, who just shivered.

"I'm too cold, Phil...... you can't turn the heating off now. Look." He held up his arm for his sponge man's inspection. "I'm shaking like a leaf – I can't stop it."

Suddenly, amongst the mist, there was a roar from the players, but the crowd couldn't see what was happening beneath the man-made mist cloaking the pitch. The referee blew his whistle and Ron saw his players heading disconsolately back to the centre circle. When Hetherington kicked off again, he knew it was three-one and so did the spectators who roared and jeered in equal measure, depending on where, or with whom, they were sitting: Mr Rumbleon clapped politely; Tammy headed back to the bar.

Ron rushed onto the pitch to confront the referee about the goal, for he had not seen it himself and therefore didn't believe it should count. As his feet touched the turf, there was a *bang* from behind him and he was hit in the back by flying debris. Like a soldier crossing no-man's-land on the Somme he was felled as he ran, swallowing hot mud as his face hit the pitch, but had no idea what it was that had happened; all he could think of was that the under-pitch heating boiler had exploded. *Oh no! Mr Dugdale and Mr Smoggrate would kill him! It had cost a fortune to install and now he, Ron Conference, through his own selfishness had broken it!*

Unable to move, he felt a trickle of something warm oozing down his neck and fear gripped him when he realised he might be fatally wounded. To reinforce that thought, he became aware of someone in the stadium screaming, then of more joining in, soft at first, subdued by shock, but becoming louder and hysterical, like caterwauling. He reached around behind him, just below his bandaged head, and scooped some of the thick liquid into his hand. He knew that any time now he could pass away into the next world...... *wherever that might be*, he pondered, *but it certainly wasn't the fourth round! Ha ha ha......* He was amazed by that thought. How could one enjoy humour at such a moment as this? He rubbed his fingers together, feeling the texture of the blood, but he didn't care to look at it; he didn't want to know.

He now became aware of his players rushing over to him, surrounding him and tending to him. Now he was not alone he decided to look at his hand, and what he saw made him feel sick. So sick he passed out.

4:37 pm, Third Round Day

With a look of professionally detached concern on his face, the TV presenter interrupts the live Rugby League to make an announcement:

"We're just getting reports of an incident at the third round FA Cup tie being played this afternoon between Hetherington Sidney and Jam United. We're not sure yet exactly what has occurred, but we can go straight to our cameras at the Sidney Park ground where, as you can see, there are ambulances and medical staff on the pitch, working amongst scenes of carnage...... Those things in your picture now are in fact the team benches, and we believe that is the area where this incident occurred...... You can see the doctors and ambulance personnel working on somebody there, while the spectators are all in a state of shock: you can se the horror written all over those faces...... These are truly shocking scenes at Sidney Park this afternoon...... We shall, of course, be returning to this story as soon as we have more information, but for now we go back to the Rugby League match where Hull K. R. were trailing to Wigan by 16 points to 11 when we left, but I can now tell you that they lead by 17 points to 16...... Oops! Sorry about that......"

4:37 pm, Third Round Day

Jack ran from his seat in the Directors' box, down the dingy fading painted corridors, leaving the smell of pipe-smoke behind, rushing through the aroma of hot dogs, past the toilets and into the odour of stale socks and boots near the dressing rooms. Policemen stood like sentries in various positions around the doors and the entrance to the tunnel, keeping out rubberneckers.

Jack shouted to anyone who could hear him "Have you seen my groundsman? He's wearin' a brown overcoat an' wellies. Anyone seen 'im?"

"I'm 'ere Mr Dugdale."

Jack looked behind him and saw an ashen-faced Wally standing in the doorway leading to the home dressing room.

"Oh, thank god you're alive!" Jack gasped. "What 'appened?"

"It was the boiler Mr Dugdale – it was on full!" Wally looked like an eldest son who'd borrowed his dad's car for the first time and stuck it in a hedge.

They were suddenly interrupted by an authoritative voice from behind them saying, "Hold up a minute gentlemen!" They turned round and saw one of the policemen walking over to join them. "I must warn you that anything you say now I shall record in my pocket book," the copper continued, "And it may be used in evidence at any enquiry or possible court proceedings arising out of this matter. I shall therefore read you your rights before you continue your discussion."

As the constable proceeded to deliver his oft-repeated homily, Jack decided to adjourn to a more private spot where the walls did not have so many ears. He took Wally into the home dressing room and the policeman ambled along behind them.

"I see they've taught you the latest techniques for tailing suspects then," said Jack loudly and facetiously over his shoulder at his pursuer. Then Jack whispered in Wally's ear, "Why was it on full?", but before his groundsman could answer he felt the policeman's cheek nuzzling between their own, trying to make it a threesome.

"What the bloody 'ell are you doing?" said Jack angrily.

"I'm gathering evidence from material witnesses."

"You mean you weren't givin' me a bloody kiss then? Well that's a relief. Kindly go outside now please, or I'll 'ave to 'ave words with your Sergeant!"

"I'm staying with you," the policeman said, dourly displaying his resolution. "If you two whispered a bit louder, I wouldn't need to come so close."

Jack couldn't believe what he was hearing and all his thoughts of indignation flooded out into speech: "This is *my* club paid for by *my* hard work selling *my* caravans and I can bloody whisper, or sing, or shout, or dance, or all the bloody lot at the same time if I want! Right?" He glared at the PC, then escorted Wally into the shower and turned the spray on, flat out, to drown out the sound of their conversation. "You can come in with us if you like!" Jack tormented the copper, "But your notebook's going to get soggy!"

The constable shrugged his shoulders and sat down on a bench, prepared for a patient wait.

Jack noted they were no longer part of a crowd and continued his gentle interrogation of the poor old groundsman. "Why was the heating on full then Wally?"

"It was the manager – he kept sendin' Phil to tell me to turn it up. He said the gaffer didn't want the pitch to freeze up after it started snowin'."

"Bloody hell," moaned Jack, "It'll cost a fortune to fix!"

Just then, Tubsy came into the dressing room, threw off his kit and jumped in the shower with them, surprising its two occupants. "Eh up Mr Dugdale, pardon me, I didn't know you were takin' a bath. I must get cleaned up meself – you should see the gore and guts on that pitch...... 'Orrible it is!..... Can you pass me the soap d'you think?"

"Oh lord." Jack sounded very downcast. "'Ow many casualties do you think there are then lad?"

Tubsy scrubbed and sudded his armpits unconcernedly. "Only the one Mr Dugdale."

Jack's head dropped. "Oh no, the poor bloke. And to think he was the author of 'is own misfortune."

"Aye, that he was," said Tubsy. "Completely 'is own fault...... If he 'adn't of sucked up to them shaggin' monkeys 'is 'ead would of never of gone off *bang* like that...... And now everyone's covered in this bloody orange stuff – its bloody ectoplasm – that's what it is!..... You should see the gaffer – smothered in it he is...... Now we'll all catch that orange monkey disease or whatever it's called and we'll all be sittin' with us 'eads in buckets of ice!"

"Then......You mean......" Jack tried to work out what Tubsy's statement *did* mean. "......You mean Ron's all right?"

Tubsy stopped lathering and stared at his Chairman in disbelief. "Well he's bright bloody shinin' fluo-bloody-rescent orange down the back. And he's all muddy down the front. And his 'ead's still all green. But apart from that, he'd win a chuffin' baby contest."

6 pm, Third Round Day

Ron Conference lay in his bed, surrounded by the paraphernalia required to keep his head at the correct temperature. A delicious nurse with long eyelashes dabbed at his body with cotton wool, which every now and then she re-saturated with surgical spirit.

An auxiliary nurse wheeled a trolley noisily to a halt outside and then he bellowed from the entrance to the ward, "Evening paper anyone?"

"Please," said Ron.

"That'll be fifty pence then please," he said, rolling up the journal and sticking it under Ron's pillow. He held out his hand to receive the money.

"I'm afraid I can't move at the moment," said Ron. "Can I give you it later?"

"Only joking," said the male-nurse, "We'll charge it to your room." He laughed and went off to the next bed shouting, "Evening paper anyone?"

Ron shook his paper out flat and saw the front page headline.

TRAGEDY STRIKES JAM U IN THE THIRD ROUND

Tragedy marred today's third round FA cup tie between Hetherington Sidney and Jam United at Sidney Park. The Jam United manager, only recently released from hospital where he had been suffering from "orange monkey disease", became so over-excited when his team's third goal went in that his head exploded, hurling large quantities of orange viscera all over the pitch.

The match had to be abandoned with the score standing at three goals to one in favour of the visitors, and an FA committee will now decide if the result should stand, or whether there should be a replay.

"Oooh!" squeaked Ron as the nurse applied surgical spirit to a tender spot. "That burns!"

"I'm afraid so duck," she said in a husky voice, "It's like using aftershave."

"Well that may be right, but I've never put aftershave on there before!"

"Well I can't 'elp it duck – your 'ole body looks the same to me – orange. 'Cept for your green 'ead that is. Eh, love, I've just 'ad a thought! If you 'ad a red bum you'd look like a traffic light!" and she slapped him appreciatively on his bottom with her latex-gloved hand.

"Most amusing," muttered Ron and turned to the back page.

UNITED TOO STRONG FOR GALLANT WHIPPETS

Ron closed his eyes and dreamily dozed, trying to sort his confused memories into sensible compartments in an attempt to make the best of everything. *Never mind*, he thought, *we played Jam United in the third round and we did our best and we lost. I'm not going to ask for a replay – they would have beaten us anyway.* Then his thoughts of magnanimity turned to melancholy. *I wonder where my dark suit is?*

I'm going to need it now and I can't remember what cupboard it's in.

6 pm, Third Round Day

Fiona sat at the Hetherington Sidney club bar, drowning her sorrows, waiting for Sean.

"Are you sure you don't want a lift home love?" asked Dovehawk as he stood with Adelina ready to leave.

"No, I'll wait for him. He said he won't be long – he's just getting cleaned up."

"Is he very disappointed?" asked Adelina. She knew how much Sean had looked forward to this match, but the sodden pitch had made it almost impossible for him to demonstrate any of his skills.

"A bit – but it won't last long – he soon bounces back. At least he got to play against Jam United."

"At least the club'll get to keep him a bit longer now," said Dovehawk, bending to kiss Fiona goodbye before escorting Adelina to the exit.

"How come you two are talking to each other?" asked Fiona, "I thought you were rivals again!"

"Oh we are," said Adelina. "But we had such fun durin' the last contest, we just had to do it again. Didn't we Stan?"

"Oh aye. That's right, aye." He pointed to Adelina. "Just look at the bundle of trouble that's been inflicted on me – and all because of this bloody football club!"

Sean entered the room and, seeing Dovehawk for the first time in sober light, glared at him and moved aggressively towards the fat politician. Fiona stood up and grabbed him, quickly turning him around to face the other way.

"Pick up granddad will you darling," she said, indicating to Sean a heap on the floor beneath two bar-stools. "We'll drop him off on the way home."

Sean looked at the collapsed body, then gathered the inebriated Lord in his arms and flopped him over his left shoulder. Mr Dugdale came in at that moment, saw his star player and patted him consolingly on his vacant right shoulder while Dovehawk made a hasty exit.

"Never mind lad," Jack said "You'll play for them lot soon enough." The Chairman tapped his nose meaningfully. "You mark my words." He leant forward and whispered in Sean's ear. Sean listened expectantly. "And not only that," Jack said soothingly, "We don't need to buy a new boiler either!"

Sean didn't manage to hide his disappointment.

"Don't look so sad, lad," Jack guffawed, "If we don't 'ave to buy a new boiler, there'll be enough cash to pay your wages for a couple o' month!"

9 am, Sunday – 11 days to go till polling day

Dovehawk felt a new man, and this invigoration caused him to recall how once he had felt old. Just the once – but it *had* happened. The experience was a little time ago and he chuckled at the memory. He had been getting over the flu and was booked to give a talk at the Selly Oak Naked Jugglers Association Annual General Meeting. There he had stood, on the rostrum, facing twenty seven naked jugglers in the audience sitting at tables while he himself did not have the luxury of a table or any other such protection. Having dispensed with his white-slightly-yellowing woollen pants on his way to the stage, on turning around to make his opening address he felt naked; which was unsurprising for he *was* bloody naked. Although consoled by the fact he was in company who shared his unclothed persuasion, the worst feeling as he stood there alone and exposed prior to starting was the dreaded expectation of hearing that first titter, a condescending chuckle from the audience. When he heard no such sound he thanked several gods and launched into his speech which proceeded perfectly, right to the end. Relieved, he inwardly congratulated himself as he asked if anyone had any comments or questions. A little skinny man with a sharp black 'tash and fine chiselled nose and crenulated ears stood up from behind his table, but Dovehawk didn't hear his question for, on seeing the little chap from the audience in his erect position, he gained at that moment the horrible realisation of what the Naked Jugglers Association was actually all about: they should have been called "The Over-Endowed Naked Jugglers". As he felt his already minor contribution to the full-frontal view shrivelling to nothing, he came to the inevitable and humiliating conclusion: he, Dovehawk, just didn't have enough to juggle.

On this Sunday morning, in the safety and anonymity of the car, he grinned as he remembered how his only thought at that time had been of escape, but his only action had been to stay put, standing there feeling very alone and ancient, waiting for something to come to his rescue. Eventually, someone thanked him for his interesting observations and, as Dovehawk had been a last-minute replacement for a lady speaker who at the eleventh hour had fought shy of exposing her collywobblers in front of negligibly-dressed jugglers, presented him with the bouquet which would have been hers should she have mounted the rostrum and revealed her rosy-cheeked charms to the members. Clutching his carnations, Dovehawk nodded briefly in acknowledgement and then fled.

Back in the present, Dovehawk sat in his car and pondered. He took a pad of paper and a pencil from the glove compartment and drew a line down the centre of one page to divide it into two columns. At the top of the left column he wrote *Things I Need*. The right column he labelled *Things I Have*. Then in the first column he penned some quick notes until it looked like this:

Things I Need	Things I Have
Agent	
Office	
Money	
Helpers	

He looked at the list, and couldn't help wondering if it should really be that small. He thought some more, but the only other thing he could think of that he needed was votes – votes and lots of them – yet that was looking a week and a half into the future.

An agent would be hard to find – Gerald had already made it clear that he would not defect.

The office – that would be no problem once he had some money.

Helpers – the vital ingredient – people to knock on doors – spread the message. Dovehawk wondered who would be willing to enlist. What group of people hated the Labour Party the most? Who had the government shafted utterly and irredeemably? *Teachers*! Yes, that's it – they're ideal. They knock off work at half past three in the afternoon, *and* they know all the parents. Most importantly, they detest New Labour.

Now Stan considered the right hand column, its emptiness gnawing at his brain more and more whilst he thought and yet nothing came. He tapped his pencil against his forehead, absent-mindedly staring into the car's rear view mirror where he saw another car parked up behind within which was the dim figure of a man in a dodgy mac. He then added to his notes:

Things I Need	Things I Have
Agent	Publicity
Office	
Money	
Helpers	

Yes, he thought to himself, that's what I've got – and it's the most important thing of the lot. The newspapers hate the Labour Party too, and I am their lone crusader, their talisman, their means by which they can make a boring by-election interesting for their readers.

Some movement in the mirror caught his eye and drew his attention again to what was happening in the car behind. The man in the mac got out, sauntered up the pavement and tapped on Dovehawk's window.

"Any chance of an interview?" he asked as Stan wound down the handle.

"Fire away," said Stan.

"Is it true that you're standing as an independent in the by-election on January the seventeenth?"

"Yes."

"And you'll be standing under the name of *Real Labour*, right?"

"Right."

"So what policies do you have which distinguish you from the official Labour candidate?"

"I am a *man*."

The journalist looked up from his notes, surprise on his face.

"That's not really a policy is it? More a feature."

"It's the reason that I'm having to do this – having to betray the Party I love and have loved for all my life!"

"But if you make that the sole reason for standing, won't you alienate the entire female population?"

"What do *you* think?"

The reporter looked him straight in the eyes. "I think you will."

"I'll ask you something," said Dovehawk, manoeuvring into an explanatory position. "How many women do you think voted for me at the selection meeting?"

"I don't know – the press weren't allowed in."

"Quite so – so I'll tell you. Most of them. It's not the women who I'm going to have to win over – it's the men."

"And how will you do that?"

"That's obvious isn't it? Blatant chauvinism! I shall invoke cooking, ironing, and Match of the Day!"

The man scribbled hard. "Christ – you really intend to win, don't you? Do you mind if I stick with you during the campaign?"

"Of course you can. Which paper do you work for?"

"Labour Weekly."

"Oh bugger off," said Stan, realising he'd been had. "You're not going to be able to publish a word of what I've just said are you? You're the bloody opposition!"

"No no – don't worry Mr Dovehawk – it's not a political magazine – it's for expectant mothers!"

Stan reached out suddenly through the car window and grabbed the lad, unsuspecting, by the collar using both his hands. He stared briefly at the fear-stricken youth before relinquishing his grip.

"Ha ha!" laughed Stan mockingly, then wound up the window and settled back down to compiling his list. *Never mind*, he thought, *the lad's only having a laugh at poor old Stan. I must remember to be nice to people*. He wound down the window again and stuck his head out to peer after the retreating figure. "Heh," Stan bellowed, "Who do you really work for?"

"Bloke called Gerald sent me – asked me to talk to you – I never met him before – he just asked me if I wanted to earn a few quid."

"Gerald!" Dovehawk exploded. "The slimy conniving little shit-house! How much did he pay you?"

"Well – he didn't yet – he said I'd get a bit when I got back with the story."

"I'll bet he did! Yes indeed – that's Gerald all right. Believe me, you won't get any money off Gerald – I've been trying to get him to buy a round for years." Dovehawk lurched himself sideways onto one buttock so he could thrust his hand into his trouser pocket. He withdrew a crumpled twenty pound note which had coalesced with the unsavoury contents of his handkerchief, so giving it a bottom-of-the-fridge lettuce-like texture, although luckily for the junior reporter the tatty sodden shred of paper still retained its full pecuniary value. "Take this," shouted Dovehawk, "And tell Gerald I intend to focus my campaign on bringing back trams to Hetherington, changing the colour of dustbins and a new uniform for lavatory attendants and park-keepers. Got it?"

"Yes Mr Dovehawk."

"Oh – and all members of the Women's Committee will have to send their dungarees to Oxfam and start wearing stockings and suspenders – you tell Gerald all that!"

"Yes Mr Dovehawk." The ersatz reporter grabbed the mouldy note from Stan's grasp, winced slightly at the feel of it, then trogged off back to his car.

Dovehawk's phone rang.

"Is that Dove'awk?" came a voice which sounded slightly familiar.

"It is," said Stan, unable to work out who it was, but knowing that he ought to know.

"Jack Dugdale 'ere." Stan, already in his euphoric heightened state, became even more alert. *I wonder what that bastard wants?* he thought to himself.

"Mr Dove'awk." Jack's voice sounded conciliatory. "I won't beat about the bush – I just want to say that I feel I've been, er, 'ow shall I put it? – *un'elpful* to you over the last few weeks, and I don't mind admittin' I feel guilty for what's 'appened."

"Your guilt is a great comfort to me," said Stan sarcastically, " But ten grand would serve me better."

There was a pause at the other end before Jack spoke again, hesitantly.

"Oh, right.... Well I can't give you any actual money..."

Stan broke him off...

"No, I didn't think you could – I'll just have to make do with your guilt then shall I? That'll cheer me up when I'm mortgaging me house to print a few leaflets!"

"'Ang on 'ang on – like I say – I can't give you cash because that would be a dangerous excursion into the political process – it could affect my business – I mean, I'd 'ave all the Labour lot and all the Tories, the 'ole lot of 'em against me... No, what I'm sayin' is, you'll need an office won't you?"

"Yes."

"Well... you can 'ave one o' my caravans."

Stan mused over the offer for a few seconds.

"Will it have a bog?"

Jack chuckled as he replied. "Oh aye – you bet it will!"

"And a desk?"

"O' course...... It'll be better than a proper office, I promise you. You can tow it around anywhere in the constituency, attend rallies, then kip in it when you're done of an evenin'."

"How about a shag?"

Jack spluttered.

"You *will* do anything for money won't you. I don't really go for blokes you know, 'owever famous they are."

"I meant the caravan, Mr Dugdale. Will it be suitable for entertaining my numerous personal assistants is what I was asking?"

"Oh aye... Aye – o' course it will – I'll even throw in a laundry service, for when things get a bit sticky like!"

"Yes, things are always a bit sticky in politics... Mmmmm..." Stan thought for some time while he was Mmmmmm-ing. "Here's the deal Mr Dugdale: I'll take the caravan, but on the following conditions: 1 – that you fit a tow-bar on my car so I can pull it; 2 – you get my Party slogans painted on the outside and 3 – you clean the lavatory out regular and hoover round every day... OK?"

"'Oover round! *Me*?" Jack baulked. "I can't be at your beck an' call all times o' the day to perform 'ousework duties!"

"I didn't mean it had to be *you* personally. Just as long as you send someone round each morning – I'll ring you up the night before and tell you where I'm parked. And I'll take the laundry service too."

"All right Mr Dove'awk. You're an 'ard man to work with. Now what about this sign-writin' you want – I'll 'ave to make a note."

"Oh – I haven't really thought yet. How about *Vote Dovehawk for Real Labour*."

"*Vote... Dovehawk... for... Real... Labour...*" Jack spoke the words slowly as he wrote them down. "It's a bit boring in't it? And it starts with VD. You really want a slogan that shouts out sommat memorable- you know – spells out a word with the initial letters, like: *Get Into Real Labour*?"

"*Get Into Real Labour*," said Stan as he thought about it. "That makes *GIRL* – I can't have that!"

"Why not? – it's a memorable word."

"But I'm not a girl though – if I was they would never have chucked me out in the first place and we wouldn't be needing to do any of this! Any more bright ideas?"

"Well it 'as to 'ave RL in it somewhere for *Real Labour*. Ow about, *Choose Hetherington And Real Labour – Awesome Teams – Always News*?"

"Very amusing," spat Dovehawk.

"Come on Mr Dove'awk – think hard – there must be loads o' gooduns."

"*Real People vote Real Labour.*" Dovehawk savoured the words as he spoke them. "Yes – I like the sound of that – that's what I want painted on the walls of my office."

"No no no!" insisted Jack. "You must be able to do better than that!..... 'Ow about *With Hetherington In Real Labour – We Inhabitants Need Dovehawk* – that makes *WHIRLWIND*!"

"No – *Real People vote Real Labour* has a grand feeling about it – that's what I want!"

"Fair enough Mr Dove'awk. Bring your car in, we'll fit the tow-'ook and you can pick it up with the caravan tomorrow afternoon."

"There's one more thing Mr Dugdale."

"Aye? What's that?"

"I want to borrow your Angela – I want her to be my agent."

There was a shocked silence for a second before Dugdale replied to the request.

"You can't pinch our Angela! She's only a snip of a girl – I couldn't let 'er get caught up in a nasty business like politics – I feel responsible for 'er!"

"I only want to borrow her, you know, to handle the press and the media – she's good at that. It's only for a week and a half. And I don't think you can say that politics is any more corrupt than football – especially the way you practise it."

"I take that as an insult."

"It was meant as one."

"I'll withdraw the use of my caravan."

"I haven't even got it yet!"

Dovehawk, embroiled in the midst of a childish argument, decided to put on his false voice of deep meaning and sincerity.

"Look – I'm going to win this by-election either with your caravan or without it. And I suggest that it is better for you that I am seen on polling day celebrating my victory from the verandah of one of your finest mobile homes!"

Jack thought for a few seconds. “Aye all right – you can ask our Angela but you’re not to bully ’er – understand? And no funny stuff of the horizontal variety either or I’ll ’ave it chopped off and mounted on a plinth.”

“Of course not – you know me. So she’ll need a desk in the caravan as well.

“What, so’s you can take advantage of her over it?”

“What do you think I am……? She’ll need a desk – fully equipped with a personal computer.”

“A personal bloody computer!” Jack shouted in disbelief.

“And broadband.”

“Broad chuffin’ band!”

“That’s right. And if you could cover the costs of her mobile phone for the week, that would be most helpful.”

“Cover the costs of ’er mobile bloody phone!” If Jack hadn’t just spoken, he’d have considered himself speechless.

“I assume that as you’re repeating everything I say, you’re writing all this down – it’s very important that a campaign be run with ruthless efficiency. It’s like a war.” Dovehawk concluded in a hushed and heartfelt manner: “And Gerald is the enemy.”

Now Jack was indeed unable to reply, a large lump of phlegm having plugged his throat.

“Right. I’ll be round to your caravan site tomorrow morning to take delivery!”

Dovehawk peremptorily concluded the conversation by pressing the red button on his phone. He then straightaway dialled Tamara. The ringing tone went on for ages before finally a groggy voice just managed to issue a noise which sounded a little like “Who’s there?”

“Stan!” Dovehawk cheerily blustered in his loudly bright and breezy manner. “What’re you doing you old tart?”

“Oh god – not now Stan – I’ve only just gone to bed.”

“But it’s quarter past nine in the morning!”

"Oh Stan – that's just so plebby always going on about what time it is. Ring me back when I'm awake will you?"

"Hang on Tammy – can I just ask you one thing."

"Not now." She was unimpressed, but Dovehawk was in such a state of haste and over-eagerness that he blundered on anyway.

"Have you got any money, Tam?"

She yawned before answering softly in her sleep.

"Oodles darling, but it's all in trust – I have to get by on a measly twenty thousand a week."

"Oh, right." Dovehawk sounded a little crestfallen. "So there's no chance of a few quid to print some leaflets then?"

At first, as Stan awaited an answer, he thought she was silently considering his request, but he soon became aware of the ripple of faint snoring in his earpiece, sounding louder with each passing second. Tammy had gone back to sleep.

Hearing her gentle slumbers, Stan now had a vivid flashback: he was still in his car, but those surroundings completely disappeared and he was by her side again in her big round bed. He lifted up the quilt and, seeing his bare hairy legs, and hairy other parts, he was gripped by panic at the loss of his trousers. He leaped out of the bed and ran around the room trying madly to find them but, as in all dreams, although everything felt completely real, his actions were in slow motion and nothing he touched was concrete. He felt himself falling and falling until he hit the floor of some imagined pit with a frightful jolt, that awful experience one often has at the conclusion of dreams.

He tried to wake up, to release himself from the nightmare and, after struggling to open his eyes for what seemed a very long time, he eventually managed to grope his way back to consciousness. He was lying on his back looking up at the sky. Where was the car? The ground under him was hard and uncomfortable; definitely not a nice plush car seat. He moved his head and focused on an object that was next to him. It was a lamp-post. As his lenses strained to bring the image into clear view, he was snapped out of his stupor by a wet and warm feeling burning into his chest. He saw the lamp-post and he saw the dog standing next to it. The dog was on three legs, its other leg being cocked. It was pissing on him. And, sure enough, it was a whippet.

“Bollocks!” groaned Dovehawk, rolling on his side to avoid the stream of steaming yellow fluid cascading and splashing about his person.

“Sorry Mister,” said the eleven year old girl at the other end of the dog-lead. “I didn’t think he ’ad no wee-wee left in ’im – e’s already done five lamp-posts in this street – but I spose it’s cos this one’s ’is special favourite.”

Dovehawk sat up on the pavement. He considered rubbing the sopping wet piss-patch on his shirt and then thought better of it. “How did I get here?” he asked the girl.

“You were runnin’ down t’street like you were scared – like you were bein’ chased by someone – then crash – you ran straight int’ lamp-post...... Shall I get me mam? She might lend you one o’ me dad’s shirts – ’e’s fat so she should ’ave one big enough as’ll fit you. An’ why aint you wearin’ no trousers?”

Dovehawk quickly cloaked his nether regions, but as he went to move and a jolting agony made him realise that his leg was hurt badly and he might not be able to get back to his car or even to drive the thing properly if he did. He nodded to the little girl.” Aye, if you could get your mum – that’d be great.” The dog slurped Stan’s cheek affectionately.

“Come on Sidney – we’ve got to get our mam,” shouted the child as she dragged the animal away and rushed down the path, disappearing through a gate just a few doors down the road, almost exactly opposite the place where Dovehawk had unwittingly abandoned his car at the start of his nightmare.

The woman who bustled out of the same gate and onto the pavement just thirty seconds later took one look at Stan and shrieked in delight. “Oooh! It’s Mr Dove’awk! Don’t move now, duck – just ’ang on a minute!” And she rushed off again without tending to him, only to reappear with a camera..

“Just a quick snap for the family album!” she said as she handed the camera to her daughter before kneeling down next to the stricken man and taking up a pose cradling Dovehawk’s head in her lap.

8 am, Monday – 10 days to go till polling day

In a splendidly foul temper, Pree barged open the front door to 29 Cokedealer Street and strode past Margaret the receptionist without glancing at her while simultaneously screeching "Gerald!... GERALD!..." in ferocious fashion.

Poor Gerald's heart dropped into his stomach and he wondered whether to make an immediate dash for the toilet and lock himself in. *Good god*, he mused, *I thought it was going to be less stressful round here with Stan gone.*

"Ah, there you are," squawked Pree, spying Gerald skulking behind the photocopier. "How did he do it, Gerald? Eh? Can you just tell me that? The first day of the new campaign... How did he do it?"

"How did who do what?" Gerald was genuinely puzzled, but noticed that Pree had a sheaf of newspapers under her arm. She dropped them on top of the photocopier and displayed the front page of the first one. It was *The Fun*. It had a picture of Stan on the front, lying in the street, his head nuzzled into a friendly lap belonging to...... Gerald couldn't believe it as he read the headline...... *Sean's Mum Rescues Stan – the Real Labour Man.*

Pree displayed the front page of the next newspaper. And the next. And the next...

"Am I getting through to you now?" she wailed at Gerald. "He's managed to get his picture and the banner headline on every front page of every daily in the land. Except for the *Daily Smut* of course, but he's even on page 3 of *that*!"

"Wow," said Gerald, his voice unable to disguise his admiration. "Who's he with on page 3?"

"On page 3? You want to see who he's with on page 3 do you? Well here it is Gerald look and study carefully – another masterclass in sexist slander."

She opened the *Daily Smut* on page 3 and there was displayed the smiling face of Stanley Dovehawk, beaming as he gave a retouched photo of Adelina's head superimposed on a stripper's body the benefit of his many years of experience in the pork sword department.

"REAL" ROGERS "NEW"! blared the headline. The article then continued:

Latest poll gives Stan the "Real" Man a 20 point lead over Omov the "New" Woman!

"What do you say to that then?" Pree looked stern as she waited for Gerald's opinion.

"Well, it's not exactly as per the Press Release we sent out, but at least our candidate has got her picture in the paper – and all publicity is good publicity so they say." Gerald knew that he was being over-optimistic.

"For god sake Gerald, what are we going to do? Is Adelina going to have to submit herself to the carnal lusts of the whole of the England team just to get a mention?"

"I don't know," murmured Gerald. "I'll give the England Manager a ring if you like, see if any of the players can fit her in."

She looked at him. "Gerald… You're not funny and you never will be…"

"Sorry Pree." Gerald picked up the papers and bundled them neatly into a pile, trying to make himself insignificant so she wouldn't shout at him again.

"Well, just you try and think of something, an initiative (although I realise that *you* and *initiative* don't exactly go together in the same sentence) to get us some publicity, while I go to the toilet."

She scrambled around in her handbag and left the room. A small slip of paper dislodged from her bag by her rummaging fluttered onto the floor, dancing in the eddy currents of scented air which she generated as she flounced out into the corridor. Gerald listened to the intense click clacking of her high heels growing fainter, then wandered over to retrieve the scrap. He glanced at it, saw that it was just a till-receipt, scrumpled it up and put it in the recycling bin. He than turned his attention back to the newspapers Pree had left behind. The back page of the *Daily Filler* announced:

FA TO DECIDE HETHERINGTON FATE

The FA will meet this morning to decide whether the FA Cup 3rd round tie between Hetherington Sidney and Jam United, which was abandoned in tragic circumstances on Saturday with twelve minutes remaining of normal time, should be replayed.

“Oh nooooooo!”

Gerald was startled by the female cry coming from somewhere in the building. He rushed into the corridor. On reaching the toilet door he could hear distinct sounds of sobbing within.

He knocked tentatively.

“Are you all right? Can I help?”

The sobs died down and Gerald heard the muffled blast of a nose being blown. Pree’s voice trembled from the sanctuary of the Labour HQ bog.

“No Gerald, I’m not all right. Please bugger off and leave me to weep.”

Gerald scuttled away from the door and into reception where Adelina had just arrived, the droplets of fog and light rain from the street glistening on her dark hair like the silver glitter dust on the Christmas cards which still littered the room.

“Adelina, can you go to the toilet please?” stumbled Gerald. “It’s urgent!”

“I think I should be the judge of that,” smiled the candidate, with a twinkle in her eye to match the shimmering radiance of her hair. “Is it blocked again? I’m wearin’ de wrong gloves for de plummin’”

“It’s Pree – she’s locked herself in the toilet! Shall we call the fire brigade?”

“Dat is a good idea, yes Gerald. Because when she finds out there are a couple o’ big beefy firemen in reception wi’ de big muscles she’ll be out o’ d’ere in no time.”

“OK Adelina – anything you say.!”

“But before you do that, I’ll go and ’ave a word. Firemen are better at getting’ cats down from de tree than rescuin’ ladies from outta de toilet.”

She wandered to the lavatory door and listened for a second. The sounds from inside were just audible: “It can’t be… It can’t be…”

Gerald meanwhile had returned to his photocopier. He took the newspapers from off the top so he could do some more copying and happened to notice the crumpled till-receipt lodged in the top of the bin. He picked it up, smoothed it out and read. *Good grief!* he blurted out loud and hurried off down the corridor again, clutching the shred tightly. He screeched to a halt next to Adelina and showed her. "This fell out of her handbag," he whispered as quietly as he could, "It's dated this morning. Look!"

Lord above! Adelina's thoughts burst out more loudly than intended as she read, "Boot de Chemist, Digital Pregnancy Test, twelve ninety nine! Well Glory be!"

9 am, Monday – 10 days to go till polling day

The Chairman of the FA rose to speak in front of the assembled committee members.

"As I'm sure you are all aware, this extraordinary meeting has been convened to debate the issue of the abandoned 3rd round tie between Hetherington Sidney and Jam United played on Saturday and to decide whether the match should be replayed or the result should stand. Who would like to start? How about Mr Dugdale as he is the Chairman of Hetherington Sidney who, remember, were trailing 3-1 at the time the game was stopped."

"Yes, thank you gentlemen." Jack scraped his chair backwards and rose to his feet. "Of course it will come as no surprise to any of you that I shall be asking you to vote for a replay. But I would like you to do so in the interests of the game, the fans, and the reputation of football in general. A replay will generate more excitement, more enthusiasm for the FA Cup – which has been waning in recent years – and a great fillip for our little club. I put it to you that a replay is in everyone's interest – ours to gain some much needed revenue, and for Jam U as a match *in memoriam* of their great manager."

"Thank you Jack. And now the Chairman of Jam United – would you like to have your say?"

"Thank you Chairman. As our club is in shock and mourning over our great loss, we feel it would be inappropriate to make our staff and players revisit such bad memories at such short notice. Aside from the fact that we would have won the game easily, the pitch conditions were not conducive to any sort of football that I or anyone else would recognise as skilful – so to thrust us into the uncertainty and heart-break of a replay would be both cruel and unjust."

"Thank you Luigi Georgi Andropov Romanov the Third."

The Jam U Chairman coughed in slight embarrassment before correcting the FA official.

"No – he left last week – I'm Miser Hilton Tightfist – we come from a long line of New York Tightfists."

"Well – thank you anyway – whatever your name is. Does anyone else wish to speak? Lord Opiumden? Would you like a word?"

"Yes, thank you Chairman. I can quite understand how upsetting it must be for the Jam United players to have to return to the scene of their tragic bereavement. So would it not be a good compromise on this matter to play a replay, and to hold the match at the Jam United stadium?"

"That sounds like an excellent compromise to me – would the Chairmen of the two clubs concerned be agreeable to that? Mr Dugdale, Mr Tightwad?"

Jack nodded his approval but Hilton Tightfist jumped to his feet. "No I sure as hell wouldn't! We won that game fair and square. There's no way they would have scored two in the last ten minutes!"

"Very well – in the light of your objection we shall have to put it to the vote. All those in favour of a replay at Jammy Trafford please show their hands… Thank you… Those against… Motion carried… Replay will be on Wednesday January 19th – kick off at 7.45pm… The meeting is now closed."

9:30 am, Monday – 9 days to the replay, 10 days to go till polling day

Stan was just on his way to Carefree Caravans to get kitted out with his new Campaign Office when his mobile rang. He looked at the handset and saw Adelina's name on the screen. Pulling quickly to the side of the road and parking his car, he stabbed the green button to take the call.

"Hello sweetie? Are you allowed to talk to me? Gerald will have a fit."

"Hello darlin' – how you getting' on wid your campaign? Got all your leaflets printed yet?"

"They're at the printers right now as we speak. How are you getting on? Is Pree interfering as usual?"

"How could you say that about the Chair of the Women's Committee? I couldn't possibly comment. Have you got a nice warm office sorted out?"

"Office? Oh yes – I'm on my way to pick it up – er, I mean view it at this very moment. Luxurious in all respects and very well appointed so I'm told."

"You won't be needin' your old fan-heater then wid de burnt-out plug? Only Gerald's got de latest in halogen cube technology for my office now and it's hot as toast – you should come over and we'll snuggle up in front of it together. Like de warm wind waftin' over a Caribbean island it is… I even got a palm tree for my screen-saver."

"It sounds very nice, but we'll have to leave it till after polling day – I can't be seen fraternising with the enemy."

"Which reminds me – the reason I phoned. You need to talk to Pree…"

Dovehawk spluttered. "I assure you I do not need to talk to Pree!"

Adelina continued. "Ordinarily I'm sure you're right in thinkin' dat way; but something out of de ordinary has occurred and she may want to tell you…"

"If she's got anything to tell me, I'm sure she'll find a way of doing it in the most obnoxious and painful manner she can devise. Why should I be the one to talk to her? That would be like meeting trouble half way!"

"Trouble, yes." Adelina mused out loud. "Trouble is exactly it. And I fear dat you've already met dis sort o' trouble half way, which is why it's de sort o' trouble which it is."

Dovehawk gulped. "What? I don't understand anything you're saying. What kind of trouble is it? And whose trouble is it? Is it hers or mine?"

Adelina laughed. "Both, you silly man! Dat's what I'm tryin' to tell you. Pree's in de family trouble cos o' you. At least, judgin' by the way she talking about terrible mistakes, an' suicide, an' abortion, an' feelin' so dirty, I'm assumin' it was you... Stan? Stan? Are you d'ere?"

"That's not funny Adelina. Did she put you up to this?"

"Oh no way, Stan. I'm doin' you a favour here as a friend. She'll sneak off down de clinic and you'll never know anything about it. I'm a friend, Stan. You ought to know."

"How do I know you're not winding me up? Did she tell you herself?"

"No – it was Gerald. He found her in de toilet screamin' and sobbin' her eyes out. She's very upset. The identity of de father of her unborn child has disturbed her whole way of bein', and only you could have that effect on her, don't you t'ink? After what you said happened that day I met you clearin' out your office, I'm assumin' it must be you."

"Can I ring you back? I need to think."

"I'm sure you do Stanley. Now don't do anythin' silly. You can call me whenever you want – I'll be here for you, in private that is. Of course, in public, I shall be rubbishin' your character and your policies and generally sayin' what a bad bad man you are! Which lookin' at page 3 of de *Daily Smut* this mornin' I should say you cannot deny!"

"Page 3? Yes, it is rather good isn't it – I shall have it on the wall of my new office. I might even have it as my screen-saver... Anyway, I'll call you back. And I suppose I should thank you, although I feel like I've been hit by a train."

"Pree look like she been hit by two trains!"

"She always did."

10 am, Monday – 9 days to the replay, 10 days to go till polling day

"Right. Gather round you lot." The Hetherington Sidney manager looked stern and subdued, as if he had some bad news to impart. "I've just had the radio on upstairs while you lot have been kitting up, and it's just been announced, by the FA, that..."

The lads stared at him, riveted to his expression, downheartened at the prospect of the news they were about to receive, almost not wanting to hear, but at the same time desperate to know.

Ron made them wait…

"We've got a pissing chuffing replay! At Jammy Trafford! How's about pissing chuffing that then eh?!"

They all started hugging and kissing and jumping for joy and screaming, just as they did when they found out they'd drawn Jam U in the first place.

"So get out on that pitch and TRAIN LIKE HELL!!! – you've got till a week on Wednesday!"

10 am, Monday – 9 days to the replay, 10 days to polling day

Stan drove into the Carefree Caravans site, parked in the space reserved for visitors and walked into reception. He was not surprised to see that the Carefree Caravans Office was a large caravan, such as the type you would rent for a fortnight at the seaside. He *was* surprised, however, to see that Angela was sitting at the reception desk.

"Eh up Mr Dove'awk – we was expecting you… Are you OK?"

"Er… yes… very OK thank you. It is good of Mr Dugdale to have organised things so well – I mean you being here and everything. Do you mind helping me out for a week with my campaign?"

"Oh Mr Dove'awk, it's a pleasure and an honour! It'll be much more fun than doin' the boring paperwork at the Football Club!"

"Don't get too excited girl," Dovehawk's voice sounded caution. "Politics can be very boring too a lot of the time."

"Oh not the stuff you get up to, Mr Dove'awk! I've read about you in all the papers! I don't think your campaign'll be borin' not one minute… Fame… Travel… All them celebrities… Beaches…"

"Yes most of them are…! Ha ha…!" He checked her expression but she didn't laugh, so he cleared his throat… "Hrruuumph…Well yes I do admit that lately I've had a run in the tabloids – but keeping up that sort of exposure is difficult, and sometimes a thankless task. We get more publicity for our cock-ups than we do for making a damn fine policy statement… Or having a rally with five hundred people turning up… Or raising five grand for the Mayor's favourite charity (which is usually himself by the way…)"

"OK Mr Dove'awk – but I'll risk it. I think for a week I might just enjoy the novelty of it before I go back to me photocopier…" She turned to the phone on the desk. "I'll ring through to Mr D to tell 'im yer 'ere – then 'e can organise the tow-bar to be fitted to yer car. You come with me an' I'll show you yer new caravan… er… I mean *office*."

"*Mission Control* I think we should call it Angela." Dovehawk beamed at her. "We're on a mission – and *you're* in control… I'd love to see it. In fact I can't wait! Has it got our slogans on it? Has it got a fax machine?"

"Good gracious Mr Dove'awk – 'old on a sec – I don't even know if it's got wheels!" Her tiny angelic face was rent by a giggly smile as she watched her little joke penetrate the harsh and hardened brain of the rumbustious old politician.

"Ha ha!" Dovehawk guffawed, but secretly had a nagging feeling that what if she was right?...!

"Ah Mr D – this is Angela – Mr Dove'awk's 'ere now – will you do 'is car? Oh… OK…" She looked up at Dovehawk. "Mr D wants to know what car it is…"

"It's the one with all the rosettes down the side of course. Couldn't miss it even in a supermarket car park."

"Ee says it's covered in rosettes down the side. You can't miss it…"

At that moment there was a mighty scrunching noise outside like someone's wheels skidding on the gravel, then a bang: *BANG*!

Angela and Dovehawk both peered out of the window.

"Mr D – it's Angela here still. Mr Dove'awk's car – someone 'asn't missed it! It's got a caravan jammed in the back of it! It's a right mess!"

"Whaaaaaatttttt!" boomed Dovehawk. "What shall I do now? Ask him Angela, ask Mr Dugdale if he's got a car I can borrow. Some twollock's just written mine off! There's rosettes everywhere! And bunting!"

"Ang on Mr Dove'awk... What you say Mr D? Is the caravan OK? It's a bit bent on the back corner. The lights are broke. But you can still read Mr Dove'awk's slogan: Real People vote Real Labour. I think it'll be right as rain with a bit o' gaffer tape to 'old it together at back…" She looked up at Dovehawk again.

"You didn't ask him about a spare car… And what about my caravan? I mean office?"

"E's put phone down – e's comin' out t' see for 'imself. Would you like a cup o' tea Mr Dove'awk? Or do you prefer a coffee?"

Dovehawk meanwhile had turned purple. He shook. He panted. He sweated.

Then there came the sound of Mr Dugdale's voice outside.

"What the bloody hell 'ave you done, Wayne?"

"Sorry Mr D – I was just fetchin' the old geezer's caravan and the rope slipped off the tow-'ook on the tractor. It rolled down the slope and *WALLOP*. That were it…"

Jack's voice lowered to a disbelieving hush: "WALLOP that were it." Then louder: "WALLOP that were it." And louder still: "WALLOP that were bloody it."

Dovehawk and Angela had by this time come out to join them and inspect the scene of devastation. Jack looked at them, then spoke, almost jovially. "Come back tomorrow Mr Dovehawk, we'll have you sorted out by then. I think Wayne will be working through the night tonight on your caravan. And for no wages!" He looked at the downcast boy. "Don't worry lad – everyone makes mistakes. And everyone clears up after 'em." He turned to Stan again. "I presume you can sort out another vehicle Mr Dovehawk?"

Dovehawk spluttered a little then, realising that nothing was going to change anything, least of all having a rage, he opened his car door and rummaged through the inside for his nick-nacks that he'd need overnight.

"Can you get me a taxi please Angela?" he asked politely.

"I can do better than that," said Jack jovially. "I'll give you a lift in my Rover. Where do you want to go?"

"29 Cokedealer Street," said Dovehawk.

10:30 am, Monday – 9 days to the replay, 10 days to polling day

"Good god," said Gerald. "If Pree catches you here she'll have your balls for breakfast."

"Apparently she already has," Chuckled Dovehawk.

"Oh, you know then…?"

"I have spies everywhere, Gerald. Especially in the toilets at 29 Cokedealer Street."

"Did you want to see her then?"

"Good gracious, no Gerald. Not even if she was the mother of my unborn child. How's she going to explain *that* to all her lesbian friends? Anyway. Dear Gerald. It's *you* I've come to see. *You* dear Gerald."

"Oh god, no! This is worse. Pree will kill me. You must leave, really you must… Please Stan… I'm not allowed to converse with you, or even make polite small talk…"

"Forget the small talk, Gerald. I want your car."

"My car!"

"You heard the gist of my request with stunning accuracy, Gerald."

"Why *my* car? Can't you hire a car?"

"Can you give me the money to hire a car?"

"Of course not – party funds are very tightly stretched…"

"Mmmmmm…" Dovehawk's mind wandered to Fiona's arse in a bikini… Then he looked at Gerald. "For god sake Gerald just give me the keys. It's only for a week. Please."

"But it's got Vote Labour stickers all over it. Pree'll notice… Please don't do this to me Stan!"

"Gerald, stop worrying. You can lend me a felt-pen. I can spell REAL."

"No Stan you're not funny… And you're not having my car… Not not not…"

"Oh you're like a child that won't share it's toys Gerald. I shall remember this display of recalcitrance when I'm MP. I thought friends were always there to help their old mates, but obviously chivalry has passed you by, Gerald. You're a jaded hack. I wouldn't have thought that you, a member of the Caravanning Club, could be so downright ungenerous, to me, your old pal, who just happens to be in need of a means of transport fitted with a tow-bar, such as the one which you yourself possess! Your selfishness reflects badly on all the other shed-draggers and gives them a bad name. I may have to write a letter to their quarterly magazine explaining how unhelpful you were. May all your urinals be blocked, and all your communal showers have turds in them. And may someone have shoved a used sanitary towel up your exhaust pipe."

Gerald looked white. He expected Pree to walk through the door at any moment. It would be worse than being caught with his trousers down – *in flagrante delicto* as it were with Dovehawk. Then he had an idea.

"The Caravanning Club. I know some of the executive committee. I'm sure they'll lend you a car if they know it'll be used for public duty."

Dovehawk fixed the poor Gerald with a demeaning stare.

"Of course they won't – they can't be seen to be political. They're the Caravanning Club. They sit in a field and drink tea. They say the weather's nice, even when it's pissing down. They crap in a bucket then carry it half a mile to empty it. They have teenage daughters who'd rather be getting shagged up against a wall than sitting under an awning with their parents. I'm leaving now, Gerald. You disappoint me. Tell Pree when you see her that I want half the Child Allowance..."

10:36 am, Monday – 9 days to the replay, 10 days to polling day

Dovehawk was on the phone, trying to wake up Tamara, when Pree emerged from a car outside 29 Cokedealer Street. She had to walk past him to get into the building.

"Good morning," gushed Dovehawk as she breezed past, blanking him completely. He watched her throw the door open wide, and just caught a glimpse of Gerald's nervous expression at the same time as the fresh Spring scent of her perfume hit his nostrils. She didn't look any fatter than the last time he had seen her. The voice in his earpiece said: *It has not been possible to connect your call; please try later.*

Bollocks, thought Dovehawk as he slipped the mobile back in his pocket, *I've got to get a car…* He looked at Pree's parked on the double-yellow lines outside Labour HQ, but it immediately roared off, her driver taking it round the side streets at the back to find a legal space in which to stop. Anyway, it didn't have a tow-bar.

He stared at the door of 29 Cokedealer Street, not really aware of the fact he was doing so, but doing so nonetheless. Then he was conscious, while not really acknowledging what it meant, of a hand gesture through the crack at the side of the door where it had not closed properly. He regained his alertness on seeing that it gestured him towards the building, so he went to investigate, and the polished nails and gold rings and fine bracelet told him that it was Pree's hand which was beckoning him hither. He nudged the door open and peered round, expecting to get a mouthful of undiluted abuse, but instead her face looked nervous, shocked almost, and she whispered, very gently, "Come in here a minute…"

He obeyed. She closed the door behind him, then proceeded up the stairs, not hurrying in any way, but moving efficiently, neat and tidy as was her way, like a shark through water, the perfect assassin. Gerald's mouth was almost on the floor as Stan winked at him and followed his nemesis up the stair-treads, behind enemy lines, his head level with the enemy's behind, so close he could nuzzle it, should he choose, which he didn't.

Another shock awaited him on entering his old office. Instead of Pree taking up her position of power behind his old desk, which now was a nice shiny new desk, she politely indicated that he should take the preferred seat, his old seat, except it was now a nice shiny new seat. She then pushed the computer keyboard to one side and sat on the desk right in front of him, her nylon stockings sizzling as she crossed her legs. The smell of her hit him once more. He knew he was powerless. She had won. This was the end. The feel of the lightest touch of her stocking-clad calf against his thigh made him like a schoolboy in front of the headmaster. Make that head*mistress*. She could humiliate him and spank him. He would be grateful.

"Stan." Her voice was melodious. This was wrong. He must have been really bad this time. To have upset her so much that she was opening on a kind and mellifluous note meant that the Death Penalty was not a sufficiently strong option. He was doomed. "Stan. Have you by any chance heard?"

Dovehawk allowed himself to return to the living; even if just briefly; it would be a remission.

“Heard about the…?”

“Yes Stan. About the... Precisely… I thought you would have. Adelina has been leaving hints. I suspected she might have communicated. What are your feelings about the…”

Dovehawk cut in before she was compelled to furnish the precise description.

“I believe in life…” He paused briefly then continued, “I know it’s not Women’s Group policy, but I don’t think they’d throw you out for keeping it!”

Her face suddenly took on a dark turn.

“Stan this has got nothing to do with politics, or the bloody Women’s Group, or your petty puerile sense of humour and ridiculous pathetic male ego! I asked you in here to try to be nice to you and ask you your feelings. FEELINGS! Yes I realise that I’ve wasted my time even thinking you might have any of those! If you’re going to act like a spoilt brat then I’ve no more to say and you can go to hell…! In fact, you can fuck off…”

“Pree! Pree! I’m sorry. I shouldn’t have said that... Let me start again… Please let me start again!”

His eyes begged for another chance.

“I want the… You know? The… I want you to keep the…”

“Baby, Stan. It’s called a *baby*!”

“I want you to keep the… I mean keep *our*… baby…”

Her face lightened again, although still it looked distinctly distrustful.

“I have to ask you this, Stan. So don’t be offended… Why do you want me to keep our baby?”

“Well because 1) it *is* ours, 2) it wouldn’t be right to get rid of it, and 3) it’s the only thing that you or me will ever have in common, but at least we will have that one thing, and we will both love it... There, I’ve said my bit. Now you can bite my head off again…”

He waited for the earthquake. Pree leant down towards him and kissed him on the forehead. The force of her leg against his thigh was excruciatingly sexy. "I hate you," she said matter-of-factly. "You are everything I detest. Yet it is with you that, at the age of forty four, I am having a child. Imagine what a politician she will turn out to be!"

"You're right!" said Stan. "He will!"

10:36 am, Monday – 9 days to the replay, 10 days to polling day

"Fucking referee's a blind See You Next Tuesday…

Tubsy. What is wrong with that sentence?"

"Has it got a verb, boss?"

"Oh it's got a verb all right Tubsy. The verb is the third person singular present tense of To Be. Which is *is*. The fucking referee *is* a blind See You Next Tuesday… any other ideas what is wrong with that sentence? Dorksy? Any ideas?"

"Is it cos you're a Southern poofter and you say *fucking* all posh like, whereas we up 'ere in't North say the fooking referee's a blind cu…"

"Enough Dorksy. It's nothing to do with the way you say it. So, my footballing misfits, what could possibly be wrong with that sentence? Korma? You have a stab at it."

"Nowt sounds wrong with it t'me boss. You'll av t' tell us…"

"OK. I'll tell you. What is wrong with that sentence, accurate as it is in almost all respects, both grammatically and in its meaning, is this: if you say it, you'll get sent off."

"Only if 'e 'ears yer!"

The others all started laughing.

"What was that remark Shagsy?"

"I said only if ref 'ears yer!"

"You're a wise head on such young shoulders aren't you my boy. But nevertheless, I don't want any of you saying that sentence, or anything like it in the replay on Wednesday, because the referee will be completely biased. It's well known that at Jammy Trafford all the decisions will go their way, and only one side will ever get a penalty, and only one side will ever get any players sent off. And I'm not going to explain to you which way round those sides are – cos even you lot couldn't be that thick, yes even you Splutter. So when the referee gives a crap decision. And then another one. And then another one. Instead of being tempted to use that sentence which I have just described, with the verb in it, and the two adjectives, and the two nouns, I want you to just smile, and walk back to your position, and play on without the slightest discouragement. Do you all understand?"

Ron looked around at the motley selection before him. Willing but uninspiring, he thought. But then again, he wouldn't swap them for the world. For the World Cup maybe, but not the world. They were his babies.

"Yes boss!!!!!!" they all chorused, like children at school assembly.

Aaaaaaaaah – my babies thought Ron.

10:46 am, Monday – 9 days to the replay, 10 days to polling day

Dovehawk thought *fuck*. He had parleyed with the enemy, and now a truce was in place. But only a private truce. In public, it was machine-guns across no-man's-land; and it was indeed no-*man's*-land. He had to thank the Women's Committee for that! He walked out into the street past the emasculated Gerald skulking behind the Party desk in the hallway.

The cold of the day hit him, yet he had nowhere to go; no office; no Party Agent; no campaign manager; well – he had Angela as his campaign manager but she was up at Carefree Caravans sorting out the wreck that was to be his office.

A Party Agent – *hmmmm* – he considered the position – his party didn't have any members – didn't officially exist. He needed to launch it. Where to do that? *Aaaaaaaahhhhhh, I've got it,* thought Dovehawk. *Down the pub! That's where I should launch the Real Labour Party, alongside the Real Ales!*

He had walked along the road a bit by now during his musings, and just there, right in front of him was... well it must have been an omen... The *Celebration Arms*. Yes, an omen. *Let's hope it's a good one,* he thought. It was coming up to 11 o'clock and the place was just coming to life. A man was outside sweeping last night's fag-buts from the pavement and a girl with a nice bum was leaning over the tables wiping them clean with a damp cloth. The door was open.

Dovehawk strode in. He had never been in this pub before – a strange omission. It smelt, as pubs do when they open up in the morning, of spilt beer and polish and a faint whiff of tobacco. The bar of course was unstaffed because they were busy with their chores, so Dovehawk made himself busy by studying the pictures on the walls, which is of course often the way to find out the history and theme of a pub, whether it be cricket, or rowing, or fishing, or dominos, or pigeons or whippets. Oh god, not whippets I hope, Dovehawk thought to himself; or football. But actually the pictures were of people dressed up in their finest having parties in streets. Street parties. Celebrations. The *Celebration Arms*! Obvious really, although it never is before you've looked and made the connection. Launching his political Party in a pub dedicated to and named after a Street Party! – the omens did appear to be all on his side. He studied the pictures and soon worked out that these celebrations were in aid of Queen Victoria's Diamond Jubilee, 22nd June 1897, not only the longest ever British reign, but also held on the longest day of the year (or possibly the day after as that often falls on the 21st, but it can be the 22nd).

Dovehawk was snapped out of his reveries by a chirpy voice.

"Y'all right there? D'you want a drink or owt?"

Dovehawk turned and saw that the possessor of the pert bum also had a sublimely pretty face.

"Oh, hello! Yes," blurted Dovehawk, "Yes please – I'll have a pint of bitter."

"OK," she chirruped and turned to go to the bar. Her bum really was… *Yes*, thought Dovehawk. *It really was. Something special…*

The sound of the liquid draining into the glass was the best sound he'd heard all morning. She plonked it on the bar.

"One pound fifty please duck."

Dovehawk fiddled with his pocket and extracted the necessary change, not one second taking his eyes off her dark silken hair and big round eyes.

"How come all the girls in Hetherington are so bloody gorgeous?" inquired the bumbling old politician.

The girl laughed. "To make up for all the bloody ugly ones that live in Scuntlepool o' course!"

While Dovehawk would have smiled and agreed with almost anything that she had said in answer to his question, her reply did genuinely make him chuckle.

"Don't you like Scuntlepool then?"

"Oh, I loov 'em. We beat 'em in't cup didn't we? If we'd o' lost then I'd hate 'em. But we stuffed 'em so I loov 'em. Till next time they beat us – then I'll hate 'em again…"

"I understand."

She pressed some keys on the till and threw in Dovehawk's one pound fifty.

"Can I ask you a question?" This was a ridiculous request, Dovehawk realised, because by asking it he had already asked one question anyway, so in order for it to make sense, he would have to ask if he could ask two questions.

"Course you can. So long as it is only one question." She stood there grinning. She was playing Dovehawk's own game.

Dovehawk paused. "Well I shall have to choose my question carefully then." He paused again before continuing. "Well the obvious question to ask is *what's your phone number?* That way I could talk to you again and stay in touch. And of course, to make conversation easier I'd love to know your name – but that would be another question. Hmmmmmmm…" He pondered. "Yet I also, at this moment, have a totally overwhelming and very impolite desire to know what colour knickers you're wearing…"

She giggled and turned away, wandering to the back of the bar to tidy up some bottles on the shelf.

"You better make yer mind up then, adn't yer?" she said cheerfully as she chinked the glass with her back to him.

"I tell you what," said Dovehawk, "Forget all those questions." He put his hand in his jacket, took out his wallet and pulled out a business card. "Here's my mobile number – just text me with your name and the colour of your knickers will you? – that way I get your phone number too!"

"Cheeky old git!" she chided him but did it laughingly, having fun. She took the card. Stanely Dovehawk, your Labour Party Candidate. It had "REAL" scribbled in biro front of the word Labour. "Gosh – I've seen you! On the front page of the paper – I recognise you now! You *are* a cheeky old git!"

"I am indeed," confirmed Dovehawk, proudly.

She propped the business card on the shelf at the back of the bar then, with a wicked glint in her eye, turned just her head towards Dovehawk, pulled the top of her tight tight jeans down her right bumcheek and revealed the waistband of her knickers.

"Red!" she proclaimed, like a naughty schoolgirl. "Red for Labour!"

"No, not quite," said Dovehawk, confidentially lowering his voice. "Red for *Real* Labour…"

2:13 pm, Monday – 9 days to the replay, 10 days to polling day

Dovehawk stayed at the Celebration Arms quite some time. He was arranging the launch of his new Party and the landlord was agreeable to holding it that same evening. The time that Dovehawk stayed at the Celebration Arms became perhaps a little too long, for his visit, by the end, had indeed lived up to the hostelry's name and had become, all by itself, a Celebration, and when he left he felt happy and at one with the world. The landlord's name was Martin, the barmaid's was Beverley. He hugged them both before he left and then lurched through the door and out into the cold air.

I love them two...! thought Dovehawk out loud, chanting to no-one and anyone as he swayed up the street. Dovehawk was pissed. Whatever he did, he must not go to 29 Cokedealer Street.

On entering 29 Cokedealer Street, Dovehawk nearly despatched the front door from its hinges.

"Gerald!" he proclaimed like a Jumbo Jet on take-off. "Gerald!" He held his arms out wide. "Gerald!… You're an old twat – but I love you!"

As he lunged for Gerald to give him a kiss, his prey feinted to the left, grabbed the phone and hovered his finger over the buttons.

"Stan!" Gerald shouted as firmly as he could muster. "If you don't leave I'm dialling 999!... Pree has told me that if you come in here making a nuisance of yourself I must call the police!"

Stan stopped in mid-lurch, wobbled against the edge of the desk, then fell across it, sending Gerald's monitor flying over the edge and dangling by its wire, bouncing it against the floor repeatedly with a nice *clicking* noise.

"Thank fuck for that!" boomed Dovehawk. "I need a fucking lift and they're cheaper than a taxi!!!"

He then fell off the desk and onto the floor, crumpling his rosette. When the police arrived he was asleep.

7:13 pm, Monday – 9 days to the replay, 10 days to polling day

Dovehawk didn't feel like a shag, so he knew he must have a hangover.

The WPC looked down at him disapprovingly. She had handcuffs strapped to her belt, plus a canister which must have been CS spray, and something else with wires on it that looked ominously like a Taser. Ordinarily he would have fancied the tits off her, especially if she cuffed him to the bed and treated him harshly. But now he could barely raise a smile…

"Mr Dov'awk," she spoke in tones that matched her look. "It's time to wake up now… You've been asleep for hours; what are we to do with you, eh?..."

Dovehawk suddenly panicked.

"God, what time is it?"

"It's a quarter past seven Mr Dove'awk."

"Quarter past seven? In the evening, or in the morning? Oh god don't tell me it's quarter past seven in the morning…"

"All right I won't then…" She laughed. "You're OK – it's quarter past seven in the evening!"

"Oh, thank you, thank you Officer. Only I've got to get down the pub for half seven… Any chance of a lift?"

"Blimey, you don't want much do you… First we rescue you from the floor of your old Party Headquarters where you have allegedly caused a disturbance, then we give you a lift to the warm friendly Police Station, then we provide you with a nice comfy cell and a bed for the afternoon, and now you want a lift down the pub…"

She looked down at him. She had the typical demeanour of a policewoman on duty: trying to look and sound harsh and in control, despite actually looking like a kissogram…"

"I'd be very grateful," said Dovehawk, his head throbbing. "You know that I always thank the local Constabulary most profusely in my victory speeches."

She stared at him and grinned.

"Can you put in a mention specially for WPC 359 Beverley then? I could do with a promotion."

"Oh, is your name Beverly too? Only the barmaid at the Celebration Arms, she's called Beverley."

"Me surname's Beverley, WPC 359 Beverley. Me first name's Sarah."

"Ah, that's nice. Mine's Stan. Pleased to meet you."

Stan tried to get up but his legs were like jelly.

"Are you sure you should be going back down the pub?" Sarah reproached him again. "Why don't you go home and get a good night's sleep – you'll feel better in't mornin'."

"Yes, but you see, I'm launching my Party and my political manifesto this evening. Well in fact in a quarter of an hour's time. The press will all be there. Maybe even television cameras. The Landlord of the Celebration is seeing to all the arrangements – I *have* to be there!"

"Don't you think that arriving in a Police Car might give the wrong impression?"

Dovehawk pondered. "It depends. Do the press know I've been arrested?"

"Aye course they do… You're a politician and yer all over the papers – they find out things before you even do 'em. The whole o' the front lobby's swarming with 'em an' there's satellite dishes all over our car park!"

"Well in that case, I can see no point in disappointing them. I shall need a blue-light escort for my own safety." He fixed the pretty WPC in a stare. "What's the chances Sarah?"

She thought about it.

"You need a wash and brush-up – I'm not takin' you in my Police Car lookin' like *that*. Any road, I'll just 'av to clear it with my Sergeant... You get yerself over to the washbasins and sort yerself out – there's soap in the dispensers – I'll bring you a towel..."

She went to leave, then turned back briefly. "And don't you go 'anging yerself wi' it – we're not allowed to give prisoners towels unsupervised in case they do 'emselves 'arm!"

"I assure you, Sarah, I have no thoughts of suicide, even with this monstrous hangover... I feel on the crest of a wave... I am about to meet my Party faithful."

"In the Celebration Arms, you'll be lucky to meet anyone who 'asn't got a criminal record."

She walked off and left him to his own devices.

7:36 pm, Monday – 9 days to the replay, 10 days to polling day

Dovehawk felt better. The cold water he had splashed on his face had woken him up and re-invigorated his intoxicated brain. WPC Sarah arrived at the washroom door and called him.

"Are you there Mr Dove'awk? We're ready to tek yer now..."

"Yes, yes I'm ready."

He dried his face and made his way out into the corridor where Sarah was waiting for him. She looked him up and down, then reached forward and adjusted his large red rosette which was slightly wonky on his lapel, and still crumpled from its mistreatment earlier in the day.

"That's better aint it Mr Dove'awk. You look ready to face the world again now. Not like when I first saw yer under that desk round Cokedealer Street."

"Yes, quite so," Dovehawk muttered embarrassedly, wishing to change the subject. "Is our getaway in order? The Sergeant didn't mind did he?"

"Well after he'd picked 'imself up off t'floor with laughin' he didn't mind. But he did make one stipulation..."

"Oh? What was that?"

“Don’t you worry yerself, Mr Dove’awk, you’ll find out soon enough! You’re gonna love this…”

Dovehawk couldn’t help feeling worried as he followed the WPC out of the back door of the Police Station into the compound where they kept all the police vehicles. Her handcuffs swung on her hips as she walked. He was getting in the mood now – he could tell his head was clearing!”

As they entered the compound, suddenly all hell broke loose on his left with flash-bulbs going off and people shouting questions. The WPC just carried on walking without looking round. Dovehawk, being a complete show-off, turned and waved. He didn’t notice Sarah had stopped in front of him and bumped into her. Being a trained Policewoman, she automatically responded to an attack from behind by flicking Dovehawk onto the floor in a smooth and well-worked manoeuvre, planting him squarely in the dirt while taking his arm behind his back and pinning him there. She then remembered that the forlorn and winded politician didn’t really constitute a threat to her well-being and tried to help him up. The cameras flashed like mad. She quickly got him onto his feet and bundled him into the back of the waiting police van, complete with inner cage and wire mesh windows.

“Holy shit!” said Dovehawk with as much breath as could muster from his compressed and deflated lungs. “I only bumped into you – I wasn’t trying to touch your arse! Why are you putting me in the Black Maria?”

“Sorry Mr Dove’awk – we respond without thinking to assaults about the unprotected rear of our personages. The police van was the Sergeant’s idea – that was his stipulation. It’s for your own safety – no press or photographers will be able to harass you, or me, until you arrive…”

“A fine bloody entrance this’ll be when I get to my Party launch party…”

“Do you want a lift or not? You can walk if you like through all that lot,” she said, pointing at the wire netting around the compound were the press hordes were baying for blood. “Yer lucky I didn’t cuff yer!” She finished off with a veiled threat.

Dovehawk grinned. “Now that really *would* get us on the front page of tomorrow’s papers!”

“I’ve got a horrible feelin’ that’s where we’re gonna be anyway – I’ll probably lose me job coz of you Mr Dove’awk…”

“Don’t worry, Sarah. I have many friends in high places. Any ramifications you suffer I shall address as sexism in the Force – they won’t dare harm your career on my account.”

“Thanks, that’s great news,” she said doubtfully, slamming the door on the van, insulating the flatulent Dovehawk from his pursuers, but unfortunately trapping his odours within the confined space of his mobile cell; she hated to think what smell would hit her when she was obliged to release him at the Celebration Arms.

She got in the driving seat, hit the starter, then switched on the blue lights and headed for the gate to the compound. A bobby was waiting there to open it for her. As he did so, swarms of press photographers crowded round, but there were no windows for them to get any pictures. Realising quickly that they would have to wait until Dovehawk’s disembarkation at his campaign party, the ran for their cars and set off after the van containing their quarry. Dovehawk listened to all the commotion going on outside, and felt a little queasy as the van swayed around the corners. *Oh god – I mustn’t throw up in the back of the police vehicle, he thought.* That would be so *so* bad…

The van drew to a halt. The driver’s door opened and closed again with a creaking metallic groan and a clunk. Dovehawk farted and felt better, although he was a bit wary of despoiling his pants. The back door rattled with keys and then swung open, while Sarah took a hasty step backwards to let some fresh air in before returning to unlock the central cage in which Dovehawk was temporarily incarcerated. the cameras flashed at him from all around, gaining a hundred pictures in less than a second, mainly of WPC Sarah’s very shapely arse. Dovehawk emerged and immediately had several microphones shoved in his face, each one covered with the fluffy lamb’s tail that makes you sneeze. He trudged to the front door of the pub, while a couple of police who had been despatched for the event tried to keep the press pack at bay. Dovehawk kept his head down and kept going until through the front door where the warmth and smell of beer and cigarettes hit him. Aaaahhhhhh – he breathed in deep breaths of the life-giving air. He was back at the pub, the place where he felt most at home. The policeman in front of him made a path through the throng so he could get to the bar. Beverley was there. And Martin the Landlord. They both wore big red rosettes. Martin quickly nipped off to get another one and pinned it on Dovehawk's lapel.

"There – yer ready now Mr Dove'awk – what d'you want to drink?"

"A pint'll do nicely please Martin. And Beverley…" He looked at the barmaid. "You looke lovely in your rosette, and a red sparkly top as well. Did you get it for the occasion?"

"Actually I 'ad it in me wardrobe, but I thought it'd suit – d'you really like it!"

"Yes, course I do. You look just the part. Is my Angela here?"

"Aye, she's up on the rostrum waitin' for yer."

"Good. I'll just get me pint, then we'll crack on…"

Dovehawk took his beer and fought his way through to the rostrum. An almighty noise crashed out as he mounted the two steps – he hadn't known beforehand, as he had been otherwise engaged with the Constabulary, but the Landlord had organised him one of the locals on his drum-kit to give him a drum-roll. He got up, tapped the microphone, and surveyed the scene. Angela smiled at him, standing at the back of the stage. A giant banner behind her, high on the wall, proclaimed *Real People Vote Real Labour!*

"Good turnout, isn't it?"

Some of the crowd roared, but most were press and stood there silent with cameras flashing and dictaphones blinking.

Dovehawk raised his glass. "Thanks Martin!" He looked to behind the bar where Martin nodded his appreciation. "And Beverley too…" He turned to look behind him. "And our Angela, my campaign manager… They've done an amazing job putting this on at such short notice, especially as I was not much help this afternoon, due to my fact-finding tour of the Hetherington Constabulary which, unfortunately, could not be postponed at such short notice, but was very instructive to me and will prove extremely valuable in my forthcoming role as your very own Real Labour MP for Hetherington…"

This time more hearty cheers rang around the lounge bar, even some of the hacks joining in, while another drum-roll added to the cacophony, augmenting the excitement of the occasion.

"I even got a ride in some police vehicles," Dovehawk continued ironically, with a gleeful lilt in his voice. The crowd jeered in a merry way. "Yes. Thank you WPC 359 Sarah Beverley for a most instructive insight into operational procedures... I was treated with great care and understanding and shall be recommending that our fantastic little local force should be held up as an example to others in how to perform their duties..." More cheers, while Sarah stood by the door, looking embarrassed.

"Now," said Dovehawk gravely, "Going on to more immediate matters, I must warn you photographers down there that I am prone to epileptic seizures, and ask you nicely if you could switch off the flash bulbs – that would be a great comfort." He looked down into the audience, hearing a muffled groan as the paparazzi muttered their displeasure. Dovehawk laughed. "Only joking," he chortled. "Take as many pictures as you like! Specially for the front pages!" They all started scrambling again and the flashes flashed as merriment rippled round his transfixed audience. "Here," he said, holding his arms out towards the doorway. "Here, Sarah, come and have your picture taken with old Dovehawk – they couldn't get a proper one when I was falling out of the back of your van!"

She shrunk back, cringing. "I'm not allowed Mr Dove'awk," she squeaked. "I'll get in trouble..."

The press shook their heads and said... *no... come on... go on Sarah...*, while at the same time moving aside to clear a path for her to approach the rostrum.

"Come on lass," said Dovehawk, "Don't worry – I'll clear it with your Sergeant... And the Chief Constable... He's probably here somewhere, with the rest of his Lodge!"

Go on Sarah... go on... the reporters all urged her to take the stage. She grinned and then strode through the human corridor, a wall of bodies flanking each side, until she reached the stage and Dovehawk reached down, took her hand, and whisked her up beside him.

"Now," he beamed, looking right at her right next to him. "What's me crime number?"

She giggled, then mouthed, "999."

"For those that didn't hear," said Dovehawk, "Sarah says my crime number is *999*!" He looked at her again. "Does that mean I'm a serious offender? Or is that the number you give out when the pissed-up lads ask for your mobile number on a Saturday night?" He gave her a squeeze while the flash photographers went crazy, then pecked her on the cheek before relinquishing his grip around her waist and allowing her to regain her place on the floor. She was clapped and cheered back to her dutiful position as doorkeeper, blushing madly.

"Now everyone." Dovehawk brought the gathering back to order. "As you know, I have suffered a slight setback in my efforts to represent you and your wonderful town and surrounding area as your MP, which is why we are here now to celebrate, in the Celebration Arms…" He looked at the Landlord and everyone cheered. "I hope that the name of the venue is auspicious… We are here now to celebrate the birth, actually I should say the re-birth of the Labour Party… The *Real* Labour Party…" More cheering ensued from the audience. "Now I don't need to stand here and tell you what the Real Labour Party stands for, because that will be obvious to all you hard working folk…" He looked around the room. "That is, if there are any hard working folk in here amongst all these ladies and gentlemen from the press… So I intend to throw this meeting open to the floor, and I'll just stand up here and answer questions. But before we do that, I just want you to meet my lovely lass Angela who will be running my campaign – and here she is."

Angela waved and the photographers all snapped away as she smiled nervously.

"Right… Anyone want to give me a question… Make 'em as hard as you like… You there… Oh hang on – I think he's from *The Fun* so this won't be anything to do with politics…" The room roared and jeered while the hack grinned. "Go on then lad – what do you want to know about old Dovehawk?"

"Do you think your arrest this afternoon for drunk and disorderly behaviour at the headquarters of your rival Party will harm your campaign?"

The room jeered again but soon became hushed, awaiting the reply.

"Right," said Dovehawk jovially. "You've got me there straight away – I wasn't expecting that one!"

The assembly exploded into laughter again.

"Right, what's your name lad?"

"Phil Tricky – political correspondent of *The Fun*."

"Ha ha ha!" roared Dovehawk, "political correspondent of *The Fun*. I like that one, ha ha ha!"

Everyone joined in while Phil Tricky also laughed, nobly and wisely disparaging himself in the process.

"Well Mr Tricky. I'm stood here talking to two hundred people. You've already spent the whole afternoon tapping a few hundred words into your mobile phone that will appear in front of nine million people tomorrow morning. So can you come here please and stand on this stage and answer the question? Cos you're the one who's already bloody decided – so we'd all like to know – we can't wait... Ladies and gentlemen, I give you Phil Tricky, political correspondent of *The Fun*, who will now tell us whether me falling asleep under a desk at 29 Cokedealer Street earlier on this afternoon will harm my campaign... Come on ***Phil***..." Dovehawk emphasised the name like they do on game shows when a new contestant is introduced into the action. His victim shuffled while the whole assembly stared at him, watching him, awaiting his response. Dovehawk had turned the tables. He would probably pay for it over the next week, for bruising such an ego as Phil Tricky's, but one thing was sure, the political correspondent of *The Fun* would never forget him, which was half the battle really when it came to maintaining press coverage.

Phil Twitter decided he had to play along. He mounted the rostrum while Dovehawk stepped back and gestured for him to take his place at the microphone. Phile Twitter coughed, as you do when confronted by an unexpected stage debut, then said in bashful journalistic tones, "Put it this way, Mr Dovehawk, I think that for once a political story has got the front page of our paper tomorrow..."

The crowd erupted.

"Good answer," bellowed Dovehawk, snatching the microphone back. Phil Twitter grinned along with him then went back into the mêlée. "You see," Dovehawk lowered his voice to a whisper as if delivering a confidential note to the audience, "Some journalists do have a sense of humour... Well done Phil – that's grand – and don't forget – you'll be on the BBC tonight as well... Your Editor will give you a rise after this. In fact, he may even give you some staff! The reason I say that is everyone, *The Fun* doesn't employ many people on its political desk. And you're looking at him..." Dovehawk opened his hand in gesture at the departing Tricky. "Now, for anyone who didn't catch the question that Phil just asked, and the answer that he provided to his own question, I shall reiterate... The question was: *Do you think your arrest this afternoon for drunk and disorderly behaviour at the headquarters of your rival Party will harm your campaign?* I actually take slight issue with the *drunk and disorderly* bit for I was merely sleeping, and I don't see how that can constitute *disorderly*. But nonetheless, that was the question, the answer to which, furnished from the horse's mouth, was that I, Dovehawk, Leader of the Real Labour Party, am on the front page of tomorrow's *Daily Fun*, just as I was on yesterday's front page, and the day before's! And the gentleman would like to know if it will harm my campaign!"

The roars and roars of mirth from the crowd almost took the roof off. When it had subsided Dovehawk continued.

"Next question please... Yes you from the *Daily Stale*..."

"With our huge budget deficit, and massive public spending plans, will you raise taxes in order to pay for all these commitments? And if not, where will the money come from?"

"Ahhh. A proper boring question... You can always rely on the *Daily Stale* for one of those, can you not ladies and gentlemen? Right, as you can imagine, since the formation of the Real Labour Party – oops, I nearly said *new* Real Labour Party then – how bad would that be?... Since the formation of the Real Labour Party yesterday, you can understand that the Executive Committee has not yet had time to meet to thrash out a detailed manifesto, which is why I'm allowing everyone to use their imaginations as to what the Real Labour Party will stand for. But one thing did occur to me last night while I was tramping the streets looking for suitable office premises. A new and untapped revenue stream is available, and is based on a model which has been completely successful in other countries around the world. This is, the licensed brothel. This will clear our streets of many people whom residents consider undesirable, while being able to be rigorously medically monitored, with safety for the girls, and a nice fat cheque for the tax-payer in the form of the licence fees. Of course, it would need to be properly regulated, so there would be a standards agency, which wouldn't cost any money because they would all be volunteers – I mean, who wouldn't volunteer for that job?... You, from the *Daily Smut*? I see you've got your hand up... You're second in the queue mate – remember I invented this plan!... We'd also have a rating system, same as they do for hotels. So we'd start off with a one-crab brothel... then progress up-market to a two-crab brothel, etc etc until the crème de la crème of the establishments would boast a full five-crab rating! What do you say to that?"

After the mirth died down he continued...

"Now, imagine trying to get that piece of legislation past the Women's Committee of the New Labour Party, which is actually, now, the old one of course... But here I am, unencumbered with such contrivances aimed at false perceptions of equality and emasculation, so you can all consider it a fait accomplis... You see *boy*!" He fixed the poor Phil Tricky with all the might of his steely-blue gaze... "You're going to need *two* front pages now aren't you?"

3am, Tuesday – 8 days to the replay, 9 days to polling day

Tammy's butler made his way discreetly and serenely across the dance floor, then stood next to his Mistress until she had finished prescribing some intimate circle with the long-haired Italian-looking Signor with whom she was cavorting.

"Your mobile phone, ma'am. It has just rung and you now have a missed call."

"Thank you, Bargreaves. Do you know who it was?"

"It was someone called Duvvy, whom I take to be your politician friend of the Labour persuasion."

"Oh yes! Thank you Bargreaves. Please ring him back straight away for me will you."

"Of course ma'am."

Bargreaves pressed a couple of buttons, checked that the phone was ringing, then passed it over to his partying employer.

"Duvvy, darling. This is a much more sensible time to ring me – you know I don't do mornings – well not normal plebby people's mornings anyway. What can I do for my little Duvvy-Wuvvy?"

"Tammy – I've just launched my new political Party. We had all the press and television down the pub. It was grand."

"What? Press and television? Why didn't you invite me? Oh you horrible little person – that's not funny… Are you going to be in the paper without me?"

"Tammy – you were bloody asleep. Anyway – you're lucky you're not in the paper with me this time – I'm on the front page, being dragged into a police van."

"Oh how exciting! Oh Duvvy, I do wish you'd called – I've never, you know, done it in the back of a police van, with all the sirens and blue lights and everything that must be so so sexy – I would have come simply loads."

"You'd have drowned out the effing siren! And I did bloody ring you – you hung up on me! So it's your own fault you didn't get a ride in the police van."

"Oh Duvvy shutup you nasty person. I don't know if I want to help you now. Politics is so sordid – what did you get arrested for?"

"Drunk and disorderly under Gerald's desk…"

"God that's boring. You could have at least been caught fornicating in a public place with me – how much better for your credibility than boring drunk and disorderly."

"Tammy, listen. I need a car – mine's buggered – some prat dropped a caravan on it."

"Oh Duvvy we've got simply loads of cars. Do you want a Rolls? Or a Ferrari?"

"I need something with a tow-bar on it – it's got to pull my new office."

"Mmmmm…" Tammy considered. "I shall have to ask the gamekeeper – he's got a Land Rover – that must have a thingy that you just said for pulling horse-boxes – I used to be a show-jumper you know – quite good."

"You like something wide between your legs?"

"What do you think Duvvy?"

"So when can I have it? – I need it in the morning."

"I'll try and remember to ask Mellors if you can borrow it..."

"Mellors? Your gamekeeper's called Mellors?"

"Of course. I fancied him from the age of twelve. I was fourteen when he took me over the fallen tree-trunk in the Lakehouse Spinney – I remember carving my initials in the bark while he was doing me – well I was bored... in both senses!" She giggled at her inadvertent joke. "Great big man, really small winkie. I've never regarded him in the same way again – a complete let down in the trouser department but he has got a Land Rover... And after that he owes me a favour..."

"You can say that again – you could get him bloody arrested."

"Oh Duvvy – what an idea! I could say it was you who took my virginity brutally at the age of fourteen! – that would get you on the front page again – how about that?"

"Yes but it would only be the once, wouldn't it... I'd find it rather tricky running my campaign while I'm on remand sharing a cell with some chavvy drug-dealer with five condoms full of crack shoved up his arse. Now can you get Mellors to drop the car round to Carefree Caravans at nine o'clock in the morning? Please Tammy, it's vital... Will you remember to tell him?"

"Oh Duvvy, Bargreaves is standing here next to me waiting for me to stop talking to some little lower-class chappie on the phone – I'll get him to contact Mellors first thing and drop the Landy round at the caravan place. Is there anything else you need?"

"I need cash. Lots of it. Well, up to my allowable election expenses."

"How much is that?"

"Twenty grand would be good."

"Oh Duvvy, I thought you said you needed lots. OK, I'll get Bargreaves to leave a wedge in the glove compartment. Do Land Rovers have glove compartments? I don't know, but if it hasn't then he can stuff it under the seat or something."

"It sounds like he should stuff it in Mellors' pants! Thanks Tammy, thank you thank you – you're such a different person at three in the morning – I can get some sense out of you – will you ring me when you get up tomorrow – you can come and see my caravan – I mean

Mission Control – and there'll be loads of press and TV reporters everywhere – you'll love it!"

"I'll be there darling, as soon as I've done my make-up and powdered my pussy… mwah!"

"Mwah… Pussy? Mwah mwah…"

Five to nine in the morning, Tuesday – 8 days to the replay, 9 days to polling day

Dovehawk surveyed his new office. Mission Control. It looked a lot tidier than the last time he saw it, embedded in his car.

A flurry of dust along the driveway indicated the arrival of motorised vehicle. Dovehawk watched it draw closer to him. He thought it a strange contraption to be visiting a caravan centre as, through the fog, he could see that it was very gaily coloured. As the dust cleared, he could make it out more clearly. It was a Land Rover. It was bright orange with brown tiger stripes painted on it. *Oh that's all right,* he thought, *it can't be mine – it's come from some zoo to pick up an old caravan to use as an animal cage.* It stopped near him and then the dust settled some more. There was writing along the side of the 4x4. He read it and his heart sank. "Spankbottom Safari Tours". *Bollocks* thought Dovehawk. *Real People Vote… Spankbottom Safari Tours. I don't bloody think so…*

Bargreaves got out of the passenger seat.

"Sir, your vehicle is delivered. I trust it is to your satisfaction."

"No it bloody isn't," moaned Dovehawk. "I'm fighting an election in the north of England not in bloody Botswana. I spose it's got a big fat bloody baboon in the back…"

"Not at the moment sir," Bargreaves sounded unfazed. "We'll arrange for one to be ensconced immediately. Mellors has hosed out the vehicle so it no longer smells of dung."

"Oh, well that's all right then." Dovehawk didn't sound unfazed; he sounded condescending. "Which particular flavour of dung did it present to the trained nostril?"

"I believe it presented quite a cocktail of assorted dung sir… Or should that be assorted *dungs*?"

Mellors climbed from the driving seat and approached them – he looked like a version of Tarzan carved from granite. From his insider knowledge, Dovehawk had a mixed impression. It really wasn't fair on the poor man.

"You'll 'av to watch it when yer drivin' Mr Dove'awk – t' puff adder went missin' yesterd'y an' we aint found 'im yet. If 'e is int' Land Rover, could you gi' us a ring?"

"A puff adder? I'll ring its bloody neck if it comes anywhere near me."

"No sir, don't approach it! Very venomous is yer puff adder. Just gi' us a ring an' we'll come up an' collect 'im. 'Is name's Poofter. Poofter the puff adder..."

"Does he respond to his name? Is he like a dog?"

"Oh yes sir... He always comes when yer shout 'Poofter... Poofter...' That's why we're so shocked he aint come back – we bin all over shoutin' 'Poofter'."

"Did you get any response? I should have thought wandering around a safari park shouting 'Poofter' might be a little controversial."

"Aye, we 'ad ter stop... 'Ealth an' safety or sommat..."

"Well I don't think I shall be going around in my Campaign Vehicle shouting 'Poofter' out of the window. It might draw a crowd. On the other hand, I was gay for a week myself..."

"You Mr Dove'awk! Gay? But yer always ont' cover o' newspaper shaggin' a different model!"

"Quite so. My gayness didn't work out. And this morning it's a WPC with whom I'm sharing the front page."

"Aye, I saw that you jammy bugger – I love women in uniform. They right do me 'ead in..."

"Yes, indeed they do," Dovehawk mused out loud, rubbing his sore cranium. "So, getting back to the matter of the loose viper – do you think Poofter the puff adder is *likely* to be in the Land Rover? Only perhaps we should search it again thoroughly now."

"I don't think there's no need for that..."

"But I'd like you to. Really I would." He looked up at the tough craggy features. "Just for me?"

"No Mr Dove'awk – taint necessary, honest – 'e normally turns up in one o' the toilet bowls in the park – it's nice an' cool in there."

"Well that's a relief. But just have one last check will you?" Then Dovehawk noticed something that looked like a brown coloured hosepipe lowering itself from the car door and onto the dusty roadway. He felt a quick jolt of fear pulsate through his system and immediately pointed at the dark shape which was now slithering towards them.

Mellors turned and spotted his slippery colleague. "Poofter me old mate. Where 'av yer been? We've bin lookin' everywhere for yer..." Dovehawk noted the gamekeeper's obvious affection for his lost pet with interest, then was aware of a loud shuffling and crash of long footsteps on gravel from his right. He turned just in time to see Bargreaves hurtling from the scene as fast as hid legs could travel, all his well-practised sombre serenity completely forsaken in his flight for safety. In fact Dovehawk amused himself to think that he had hitherto never seen Bargreaves do anything other than at a measured and sedate pace. Was the sight of a member of the snake species the butler's unique and particular flaw, the one thing that could make him lose all sense of propriety? But, Dovehawk remembered, he had been quite calm when handling the anaconda on the train in South America. Maybe it was only this one's venomous bite which made him react in such a manner of hasty self-preservation.

Mellors was unaware of any of the goings-on around him. He had picked up a stick and was tickling the snake under the chin, while charming him with a little tune, barely audible to Dovehawk across the ten yards or so which separated them.

"Nip round the back o' Land Rover and get out thick canvas bag will yer please Mr Dove'awk? 'E's nice an' docile now - we'll pop 'im int' bag wi' no trouble."

"What do you mean, *we*?" questioned Dovehawk, suspecting the worst.

"You jus' get bag 'an I'll show yer. There's nowt to worry about..."

"Lot's of people have told me that over the years. They're invariably liars."

“That’s cos you only talk to politicians Mr Dove’awk.”

“That is true…”

Dovehawk proceeded to get the bag and held the open neck towards the snake as instructed. Mellors wrapped the snake around the stick just as he would a piece of spaghetti around his fork and pushed the whole ensemble into the bag. He then took the bag and pulled the drawstring tight. Both men grinned at one another; then something caught Mellors’ eye, just over Dovehawk’s right shoulder. He pointed in that direction and the politician turned to look. In the distance, the two of them could make out the immaculately suited Bargreaves half way up the coarse-barked trunk of a large and noble tree, scrabbling to gain further height and safety.

“He doesn’t like poofters does he?” observed Dovehawk wryly.

Five to nine in the morning, Tuesday – 8 days to the replay, 9 days to polling day

Pree swooshed through the door of 29 Cokedealer Street. Gerald knew she would be coming, but was still terrified by her actual arrival. However, this morning he thought he held a trump card that might soften her anger. Pree fixed him with a withering glare.

“I assume you have seen the front pages Gerald!”

She sounded harsh but Gerald jumped at his opportunity.

“Yes Pree, yes! We’ve got him this time haven’t we…” It was a statement rather than a question.

“Oh really Gerald? Got him in what sense?”

“Well he’s been arrested and all the front pages have his picture with the Arresting Officer. That should lose him a few thousand votes don’t you think?”

“A few thousand votes?” Gerald heard from her tone that she did not agree with his prognosis. His heart sank as she continued. “It’s true that on the front page of the *Daily Stale* he’s pictured being led into the back of a police van, but he is smiling and waving to the photographers whilst doing so, and the WPC accompanying him appears to be enjoying the moment as well.” She threw the paper onto Gerald’s desk. “Then on the front of *The Fun* we have him emerging from the same van, accompanied by the same WPC, to make his triumphal entrance for his so-called Party’s inaugural conference at the Celebration Arms." She tossed *The Fun* down alongside the *Daily Stale*. "And on the front page of the *Daily Filler* there is a picture of him standing addressing his audience with his arm around his erstwhile Arresting Officer while he plants a big smacker on her cheek!...... It's another proud day for British journalism!" That paper joined the other two on Gerald's desk. "The broadsheets likewise have a similar range of coverage, all on their front pages." She flung the rest of the bundle down and paused to look at Gerald again. "And which is the first page in, for example, the *Daily Stale* to feature a photograph of our candidate?" She didn't wait for an answer. "Seven, Gerald. Page seven."

Two in the afternoon, Tuesday – 8 days to the replay, 9 days to polling day

Tammy rang Dovehawk when she woke from her slumbers as promised, then drove straight over to Carefree Caravans where Mission Control was now ready and waiting to roar away on its first assignment. Or, perhaps more likely, *rattle* away on its first assignment.

When she reached the bottom of the driveway she saw a large throng surrounding a small caravan, lenses pointing at the windows while hacks muttered messages into their recorders. A van with a satellite dish on the roof was parked next to Mission Control, dwarfing it and in the process making it look even smaller. When they heard the rumble of tyres they looked up the road expecting to see just another reporter arriving. But as Tammy's car drew closer a buzz went around the pack and they all hurtled towards her, cameras flashing like crazy as they realised this was no boring visitor of the journalistic persuasion. So close were they that she had trouble opening her car door, but eventually, after a struggle, she hauled herself from her vehicle and smiled for the cameras.

"Are you funding Mr Dovehawk's campaign?" came the first of a myriad of questions, thick and fast.

"Oh darling, just give me a few minutes with him and I'll be able to fill you in with more details. We need to thrash out our policy first... And she winked, walked to the caravan, banged on the flimsy door and shouted "Duvvy, Duvvy, let me in darling..."

Dovehawk gingerly opened the door and the cameras went bonkers again, while Tamara squeezed herself through the partially open portal and slammed it shut behind her.

"God Duvvy, how exciting! You said the press would be here, but I had no idea it would be like this! All this media interest – it really does turn me on you know." She grinned wickedly, then looked around the little room, noting the desk which took prime position in the centre. *Mmmm, that has possibilities,* she thought, picturing herself bent across it with her bum up in the air. A couple of filing cabinets converted from built-in cupboards disappointed her, but then she cheered up. "Oh look Duvvy, they've left the bench seats in at this end of your little caravan – they turn into a bed don't they? Don't they?"

"Yes, I believe they do," replied Dovehawk, although I haven't actually tried them out yet."

"Well now's your chance big boy," she gushed excitedly. Then she looked worried again. "Where's Angela? Is she here?"

"She's working for Mr Dugdale in the site office till I need her."

"Oh thank goodness Duvvy." Tammy ran to him and kissed him avidly on the lips. "Let's do it Duvvy, please. For your little Tammy… Let's christen the smelly old caravan! Quickly!"

"What? With all those reporters outside? It'll be in all the papers…"

She looked at him mockingly and spoke slowly as if she was talking to a child, "Yes… Duvvy… It… will…"

With that, she pulled her jumper over her head, slid out of her jeans and pulled his hand between her legs. "Put the silly bed together, Duvvy. I've got a little job for you!"

Three minutes later, the assembled press pack noticed the caravan had started rocking on its rusty springs. First they were puzzled, but then the penny dropped and some cheered while others tried to get their camera lenses through the perspex windows, but were thwarted by the closed curtains, while others had their fluffy muffled microphones jammed hard against the thin outer skin of the gyrating portable edifice, where they could pick up a muted soundtrack of the action taking place inside.

Tamara was on all-fours on the bed; she felt very naughty.

"Will the springs be all right? Oh I do hope we break them. It's so proley doing it in a caravan isn't it? I love to debase myself. I've been up-market so long the only way to get excitement any more is to go down."

"I'm trying as hard as I can. And anyway I don't want to break the springs; they're mine, they're all I've got between me and the street!"

"Oh you're so selfish Duvvy. Selfish selfish selfish. That's you all over. Don't you want to please your little Tammy?"

Dovehawk gave her bum a good slap and pounded into her with all his available vigour which, at the age of fifty two, wasn't what it used to be."

"Yes Duvvy, yes – like that – oh yes we'll break those silly little springs. Come on you old communist commissar and give it to me…"

"For fuck sake Tammy I'm fucking giving it to you as hard as I fucking can – *I'm* going to break before the effing springs give out! I'm right out of puff."

"I don't know what Fiona sees in you, Duvvy; she must be easily satisfied… Or is it that she's shagged you out before I got to you? You wait till I see her – I shall slap that 'oh-so-perfect' little arse of hers – she won't be doing any bikini modelling with a red-slapped arse, the little I'm-so-slim-and-gorgeous tart!"

"She's your friend…"

"She gets all the footballers and pop stars. I have to make do with her cast-offs. It's not fair. I'd rather be beautiful than rich."

"You wouldn't if you actually tried it for a few months. Beautiful wears off. Rich doesn't…"

"Oh Duvvy now you're lecturing me like some boring proley politician on the telly. Just shut up and fuck me. Like you mean it… Go on… Fuck my brains out…!"

"I'd be here all week trying to do that…"

"Aaaaaaaaahhhhh. What did you say Duvvy? That's it. It's over. I don't believe you said that. That's just so mean and nasty. I shall vote Conservative just to spite you! You see if I don't!"

"Oh come on! You were going to vote Conservative anyway! A stuck-up posh bitch like you would never vote Labour. Especially not *Real Labour*... Now come here you noisy arrogant po-faced little..."

Tammy tried to pull away from him but Dovehawk grabbed hold of her hips tight as you like in his big chubby hands and launched into her for all he was worth.

She squealed in shock, then immediately changed her tune. "Oh Duvvy – that's it, that's it! Oh Duvvy – you can be rude to me whenever you like if it does this to you. You... *baboon*!"

"Fuck the baboon," growled Dovehawk. "He's locked in the back of your Land Rover. I hope."

After a while, the press outside the caravan didn't know what to do while the caravan was bumping up and down on what was left of its springs. They had been trying to take photos and record the sounds of the events, but they knew they couldn't publish them anywhere so it was a waste of time. They had to make do with smirking at each other, some of them cheering while the others bade them hush so they wouldn't miss any of the erotic details as Dovehawk gave Mission Control a good seeing-to. Or should that be Miss In Control? Tammy suddenly started screaming like she was being murdered and the offside rear light of the caravan fell off and dangled on its wire, jiggling in time with the frantic motion. Then the springs stopped bouncing and she fell silent, as if she had indeed *been* murdered. Dovehawk emerged from the door to massive cheers and camera flashes, mopping his brow with a pair of satin knickers.

"Have you been discussing the future policy of the Real Labour Party Mr Dovehawk?" came the first question accompanied by multiple-orgasms of laughter from the attendant hacks surrounding his little wheeled shed.

"D'you know," said Dovehawk matter-of-factly, "I'd never realised that founding a political Party and commissioning its office was such a strenuous business..."

Tamara came out to join him, standing atop the rickety stair that gained access to the caravan door. She beamed for the cameras, having already dressed herself, readjusted her makeup and brushed her hair.

"Are you missing anything love?" one witty reporter quipped, pointing at the diaphanous string of material hanging from Dovehawk's chubby grasp.

Dovehawk, fresh from mopping, looked at the sweat-stained object and grinned. He offered his hand containing the intimate article to Tamara, who blushed beautifully. The cameras went berserk. Another front page was born.

Five to nine in the morning, Wednesday – exactly 1 week to the replay, 8 days to polling day

Pree swooshed through the door of 29 Cokedealer Street. Gerald knew he was in the shit.

"How does he do it?!" she stormed, throwing the papers down onto Gerald's desk. Each one featured, on its front page, the grinning Dovehawk handing a pair of incredibly small knickers to the supremely well-bread and exorbitantly rich Tamara Toker-Spankbottom. She fixed Gerald with her usual stare. "What did Adelina do yesterday?"

Gerald started be stuttering nervously. "Sh sh sh she visited a hospital…"

"Good. Very good. That's good publicity." Gerald could tell that she was humouring him. "What else did she do?"

"Sh sh sh she helped out in class at a Primary School…"

"Oh marvellous, Gerald. That's *so* original. And what else did she do?"

"Sh sh sh she joined the local campanologists and had a go at bell-ringing at St Sidney's Church…"

"Well, that must have been quite some thrill for the TV cameras. I assume we did have the TV cameras present?"

"Er er er not quite… you see," he swallowed, "They were all busy… at Carefree Caravans…" He looked at her hoping for mercy. Her gaze displayed none. "It wasn't my fault." He sounded like a child and, to complete the image, burst into tears. It had worked sometimes when he was eight.

"Gerald. If, while visiting the hospital, she had climbed into bed with one of the male patients, grabbed his penis and made groaning noises, we still wouldn't have made the front pages. If, while helping out in class, she had got one of the children to write BOLLOCKS in large letters on the blackboard, we still wouldn't have made the front pages. If while she was bell-ringing, one of the bells had come crashing down and landed on the verger, killing him dead, that would have been an act of God which *still* wouldn't have made the front pages, unless God herself put it there. And now, I think, God is the only one who can rescue us, and our campaign, in this dismal election. What do you think?"

Gerald just sat there and sobbed.

Eleven in the morning, Wednesday – exactly 1 week to the replay, 8 days to polling day

Airman First Class Kapowski, sitting in his gatehouse at the Hetherington RAF base which, since 1943, was home to the United States Army Air Force, closed his eyes and rubbed them. On opening them, he expected the disturbing image which had made him blink to have disappeared, it being only an apparition, an optical illusion, a mirage. It hadn't. It was orange and getting bigger all the time. It was still headed towards him and it looked suspicious. He was trained for moments like this. He had only seconds in which to act.

Dovehawk was sitting in the passenger seat as they chugged up to the guard's gatehouse, the Land Rover spluttering its way along as Tammy, who was driving, carefully towed Mission Control into this little piece of America slap bang in the heart of England. Angela was in the back with the baboon.

"Have you got hold of that monkey-thing, Angela?" squawked Tammy. "The beastly beast's a menace – it keeps trying to hug me. And it's got a frightful shiny purple bottom – I don't see why a lady baboon should find that attractive!"

"So she can see her face in it…"

"What Duvvy?"

"Women – they're always looking in bloody mirrors."

"That's very sexist. I thought politicians had to be Politically Correct."

"Only on television."

"We need to check our make-up."

"I don't know why you women always look at your face in the mirror – it's your arse we look at – not your face – men are scared of eye to eye contact – but if the seam in your trousers isn't lined up with your bum crack we notice straight away."

"Duvvy – you're so coarse… Oh look, the lovely soldier's coming out of his hut to meet us – he looks so smart in his uniform… Here he comes – oh Duvvy he's got a cap and everything, and what baby-face features… But. where's he going now?"

The Airman First Class flew from the shelter of his guardhouse, hurdled the chevroned barrier at the side of the road and disappeared behind a short concrete wall. Part of the road in front of Tamara's Land Rover reared up suddenly in front of them, blocking their progress. Then there was a massive explosion from behind them, and another and another. The occupants of the tiger-stripe safari-wagon crouched on the floor. The baboon, very frightened, saw the opportunity of hiding itself in Tamara's hair, whilst relieving itself among her expensively coiffured locks. The press cavalcade which had now arrived upon the scene rolled their cameras in disbelief as Mission Control exploded in a roaring sheet of white-hot molten flame, parts of its contents showering upon their cars. When the smoke cleared there was just a chassis-frame with some burning tyres.

"Duvvy!" Tammy's voice was very high. Her position in the footwell of the Land Rover was very low. "Going out with you was never going to be easy, but I think you've overdone it this time… Help me Duvvy. Just get me out of this alive and you can have anything you want."

"Two million…"

"What? How can you think of money at a time like this? I'm being blown up by beastly Americans and a monkey has its smelly bum in my hair. You really are selfish… Selfish… Selfish… Selfish…!"

"Shut up squawking you silly cow. Do you think I can ring the fucking Pentagon from here? Just quieten down – please… you're doing my head in…"

"Please Duvvy. Please get me out alive… I beg of you…"

"Tammy…"

"What?"

"I know that at times like this, when survival is all that matters, you'll promise me anything…"

"Yes it's true…"

"And you know you've got a lovely arse."

"Really?"

"Yes – better than Fiona's."

"Really??"

"Much."

"Really???"

"Yes Tamara… Really…"

"Gosh Duvvy. You've never said anything so nice. What do you want?"

"I want you to tell me why the whole right side of my body feels like it's on fire. Break it to me gently Tammy… Have I been hit?"

Tamara looked down to her left where Dovehawk was crowded into the passenger footwell. She saw that he was lying on his right side, and beneath him she could see what looked like a row of knitting needles all pointing up in the air, angrily. Some were hidden beneath his body, but they also would have been sticking out at the same angle and, Tamara deduced, would have been the cause of his considerable pain.

"Tell me I'm not dying!" groaned Dovehawk. "I have everything to live for: fame, fortune, notoriety… Is it a flesh wound Tammy? Or am I mortally wounded? Tell me the truth my angel… Or am I in heaven already?"

Tamara giggled.

"Duvvy," she whispered. "You've sat on Prickface the porcupine… He must have sneaked in while they were looking for Poofter the puff adder."

The baboon cackled, leaping off Tamara's head and jumping on Dovehawk instead.

"Get out of the vehicle!" came a booming order as if delivered by God itself from the sky. "SLOWLY, with your hands up!"

The watching Americans saw the door open. Out came a monkey with its hands above its head. Then Tamara, followed by Angela.

Dovehawk crawled for the daylight, pain coursing through his harrowed body. He looked up at the muzzles of guns arrayed around his head. "God bless America," he said enthusiastically.

Eight in the morning, Thursday – 6 days to the replay, 7 days to polling day

Headline from the *Daily Stale* –

REAL LABOUR OF LOVE ENDS IN FIREBALL

Arriving for a friendship visit to the American air base at RAF Hetherington, Stan Dovehawk, the maverick Real Labour candidate in the forthcoming by-election in the area, was yesterday mistaken for a suicide bomber and his cavalcade fired upon, his mobile Party Office being destroyed by withering fire from the Special Forces Unit deployed to guard against such events. The fifty five year old politician and his two female assistants were lucky to survive the onslaught, but all had later recovered enough to be photographed with the base commander who apologised profusely for the mix-up and promised the larger-than-life politician that he would do everything in his power to compensate for the unwarranted attack, even including a personal request to the American President that he might possibly meet with Dovehawk on his next visit to Great Britain and apologise in person for such a dent to Anglo-American relations.

The picture accompanying the text was of a fireball being towed by a safari Land Rover, with an inset of Dovehawk shaking the base commander's hand, while Tamara was draped around the rugged handsome Colonel, trying to snog his face off.

Pree read the front page report in a softly-spoken and resigned fashion, as if in acquiescence to the greater work of some deity which was conspiring against the Labour cause. Gerald cringed.

Eight in the morning, Thursday – 6 days to the replay, 7 days to polling day

Dovehawk was round Carefree Caravans bright and early in the morning. The lurid orange tiger-print Land Rover had survived Uncle Sam's anti-terrorism operation and, save for slight shrapnel damage to the rear panelling, was fully functional. Mission Control however was now an exhibit in the Imperial War Museum, a testament to warfare at the end of the second millennium; its twisted and mangled remains would be a joy for schoolboys to scramble over and schoolgirls to eat their crisps upon for the next thousand years.

Dovehawk descended from the vehicle and entered the site office followed by the baboon which scrorked happily at the adventure. Jack Dugdale was sitting at the reception desk.

"'Av you seen the mornin' papers Stan?"

"I bloody well have!" Stan was incandescent. "Fifty bloody five! They've got me down as fifty bloody five! Fifty bloody five it is now!... I'll sue…"

"For god sake Stan, act your age – it's not you I'm worried about – it's our Angela? Is she all right?" Jack talked to Dovehawk sternly while continually wagging his finger at him. "I told you not to put her in a position of danger… I bloody told you that… and I'm not 'appy!"

"Happy? You think I'm happy? I made a friendly visitation to our colonial cousins, which wasn't putting Angela in danger – well it shouldn't have been. But I got blown up! I got a baboon on my head! I got an arse full of porcupine quills! And they got my bloody age wrong in the papers! And *you're* not happy!"

"I'm not 'appy because Angela's life was put in danger AND… you blew up my caravan!"

"Yes. That's why I'm round here. I need a new one."

Jack's mouth fell open. The baboon sniggered and climbed up the curtain, screeching as it went.

"A… a… a… NEW one?"

"Yes, of course. A new one. That one was old and clapped out anyway – the springs were nearly gone."

"Aye, you can say that all right –the reason the springs were nearly gone was all over the front pages of yesterd'ys papers. You're a bloody menace you are Dovehawk. A bloody menace!"

"Indeed. We politicians do have a daring lifestyle which can lead us into interesting situations that the general public find hard to comprehend. But it's worth it if we can serve our constituents and help them with their problems. Plus of course the publicity is always good for business." He looked knowingly at the caravan magnate. "So, any chance Jack? I'll even say *please*. And that occurs about as often as I say *sorry*."

Jack thought.

"But I've only got a WindCheetah 9000 in the second-hand line that I can spare; it's got twin axles; very spacious; worth a few bob; will you look after it this time?"

The baboon cackled and jumped on Jack's in-tray, scattering papers all over the place.

"Jack," Dovehawk said earnestly, "You know me…"

"Yes," muttered Jack, "Unfortunately I do, along with your track record on the caravan-owning front."

"Good, so you'll get it sprayed up and kitted out then?"

"What? You want all those silly slogans painted on my nice caravan?"

"It'll be on the telly, Jack. Every day. With 'Supplied by Carefree Caravans' plastered all over it. You'll be laughing; you won't be able to supply demand… Can you have it ready by lunchtime?"

"Lunchtime?"

"Or just after – I know you're busy, but I'm in a rush – it's Thursday today and polling day's just one week away… *I*… I mean *we*… need maximum exposure… Isn't that what you want, Jack?"

The baboon picked up a pen and started signing cheques.

"Come back after lunch, and take this bloody animal away with you!"

Jack took a swipe at the baboon, but it hopped in the air and his hand whizzed harmlessly underneath.

Stan opened the door and saw a mass of journalists and photographers. The shutters immediately started clicking. Dovehawk gestured to the baboon to leave first, to clear a way through the jostling crowd. It ran gaily into the throng, squawking and screeching, jumping on shoulders and waving its shiny purple bum in their faces. Dovehawk tagged along behind as the hacks fell over each other trying to get out of the way, opened the door to his Land Rover and set off for town.

1.36pm, Thursday – 6 days to the replay, 7 days to polling day

Mission Control Mk2 looked very impressive. It was already surrounded with newspaper reporters by the time Dovehawk arrived back at Carefree Caravans. The cameras went ballistic once again as all four doors opened on the tiger-print transport and from thereoutof came not only Dovehawk, but Tamara, and Angela, and Fiona. They made their way to the front of the new Real Labour Office and posed for pictures. The baboon sat on the satellite dish on one of the TV vans and jiggled it with his toe, which made the picture wobble. The engineer shot out from inside to see why his worldwide broadcast had gone awry and tried to shoo him down. The baboon just laughed and did it with another toe to produce twice the shudder.

The glamorous trio and the unglamorous politician waited for a few pictures while Jack Dugdale came over to perform the key-giving ceremony to Stan's posh new edifice.

"It is with great pleasure," he announced to the assembled multitude, "That I present this key to Mr Dovehawk, the key to his new office, which we, Carefree Caravans, are lending him for the next week, while he fights…… And WINS!......" Jack looked all around, soaking up the attention. "Next week's Hetherington by-election!"

They stood for some more pictures, then Dovehawk tried the key in the door, opened it and, after a few parting waves, ushered the girls inside before him. He then made a large summoning gesture to beyond the crowd where the vehicles were all parked. The baboon immediately hopped down and ran to join him at the entrance to Mission Control, carrying the satellite dish. The engineer was by now at the top of the ladder and just climbing onto the roof of his TV van. He surveyed the empty scene, sat down with his legs dangling over the side and cried.

The door to Real Labour clomped shut behind Dovehawk and the monkey. Jack trudged unnoticed back to his Carefree Caravans office.

"Is he going to shag all three of them?" asked one of the reporters to anyone of his peers who was listening.

"I fucking would!" piped a middle-ish twenties hack, fag in mouth.

"He can't! He's too fucking old!" muttered one of the jaded older reporters in his forties.

"He's probably going to shag all *four* of them!" laughed another, who thought himself a bit of a wit.

"Oh no, not more monkey-shagging stories, eh lads? We done that to death with the Jam U fiasco!"

"I think you're all very childish!"

They all looked around at the young lady reporter who had dared to speak out in the midst of the male-chauvinist sentiment.

"Well you knock on the door an' ee'll like as like shag you too love – I mean, get the story from the inside – that's the best way. Make a fortune! You might as well use those tits while they still work for yer."

"You're disgusting!"

"And you'll regret it —————— Oh my god!"

There was a hush as every head turned to see the new caravan, on its now four little wheels, rocking feverishly to and fro. Shocked silence pervaded for several seconds, while jaws dropped. The all was cheers and clapping, while a few shouted "Lucky git!" and other such compliments. Meanwhile, inside his new office, Dovehawk had cleverly looped a piece of string around the catch that held the ventilator open on the ceiling. He held the end of the string in his hand while sitting at his desk. The other end of the string hung vertically down from the ventilator, and to the end of this he had attached a banana. Every time the baboon leapt up from the floor to retrieve this prized comestible, Dovehawk pulled the string so the banana passed through the ventilator and out of reach of the outstretched hairy hand. Each time the baboon landed back on the floor again, the caravan rocked. The two of them were having a great game. Every now and then the ape issued a screech of frustration which sounded not unremarkably like the noise Tamara made in moments of physical passion. Dovehawk carried on pulling – he could keep this up for hours.

Tammy and Angela and Fiona giggled as they looked up their fan pages on the computer. The reporters outside could hear their giggles and, alloyed with the cries from the monkey, were in a frenzy of delirium considering the outrageous fortune of the man.

2.36pm, Thursday – 6 days to the replay, 7 days to polling day

The poor baboon gave one final huge lunge, then Dovehawk released the string, allowing the poor beast to catch its prey, which it grasped while letting out the biggest and loudest screeeeeeeeeeech of the whole afternoon. He ripped open the skin and savoured the succulent flesh. The caravan stopped rocking.

"Time to pretend you've got a sweat on, girls," whispered Dovehawk so the prying ears outside could not hear.

"Let's all strip off," whispered Fiona. "That'll give them something to photograph!"

"Oh that's typical isn't it," whispered Tammy, but louder than the others so both had to Sshsssshhhh her. "You just like taking your clothes off because you look better than the rest of us!"

Fional looked hurt. "Just bra and knickers darling… I'm not doing a freebie you know… You look good in bra and knickers Tam… How about it Ange?"

"Oh god Fiona, I've never done owt like that – I mean you're a model an all – I'll look fat I know I will."

"Fat love? You're thinner than me – look…" Fiona stepped out of her jeans and pulled her jumper over her head, revealing her shapely and definitely not skinny body. "Come on girls, are you joining me? You only get one chance of getting on the front page of the papers Ange… Come on – just for me…"

"Oh all right then – but I'll be dead nervous… Can I stand behind you?"

"You can stand anywhere you like."

Angela did the same as Fiona, while Tammy humphed loudly. "Well I suppose I'm going to look even more stupid if I'm the only one who's dressed."

"Ha ha," laughed Dovehawk. "That *would* make a change for you! Ha ha!"

Fiona fixed Dovehawk with a harsh stare. "Don't know what you're laughing at Duvvy. Come on – off with those trousers!"

"What?" he grumbled in shock.

"Oh yes – you as well Stan!" chirped Tamara, and she and Fiona grabbed him by whichever bits of his apparel came to hand and harshly removed it while he moaned all the way through.

"Shoes and socks too!" said Fiona, ordering him to raise his foot so she could perform that duty.

"Why? You lot are still wearing your shoes! Why can't I keep mine on? Politicians look silly without shoes…!"

"We're keeping our shoes on because high-heels make us look so much taller – and improve our posture. You on the other hand will be fine, because no-one will be looking at you."

"Yes – I suppose so – I take your point."

The door opened and the baboon went out to welcome everyone. He threw his banana skin and it landed on the lens of the engineer's TV camera, blotting out the picture, just as Fiona, Tamara and Angela emerged from the gloom and into an array of floodlights and flash-bulbs.

"Whhhhhhhooooooooooooooooooo!" cheered the reporters. As Fiona had predicted, no-one really noticed when a shadowy portly figure shuffled out behind them. Not until the girls turned to notice him, then moved aside to reveal the … *thing* … in underpants…!

Dovehawk was a vision in just string Y-fronts. His rosette was tastefully pinned to the gusset. His mobile phone was tucked in the waistband. It rang. The assemblage erupted in mirth.

"Is it on vibrate Mr Dovehawk?"

Dovehawk withdrew the flashing beeping object and looked at its screen. "Oh god it's the wife!" he said in jest, knowing it would get a laugh.

"I thought you were separated!" shouted one of the hacks.

Dovehawk looked down at his pants. "Can you tell from there?"

They all laughed some more.

Dovehawk continued… "Oh you mean separated from the wife? Well if I wasn't, I bloody well am now… Have you seen the front pages lately? The things you lot write about me – it's scandalous!"

"Will you be suing then, Mr Dovehawk?"

"Suing? Not bloody likely. I think you all do a cracking job... Except..." Dovehawk looked stern while they all went quiet, except for the cameras which carried on clicking and flashing. "Except... none of you can get me bloody age right? Why is that? Look lads... if you *do* get it wrong, can you err on the low side – I mean – this morning in the *Daily Filler* – fifty five! Fifty bloody five! It's an outrage!"

"Girls!" shouted the reporter from the *Daily Smut*, "Is Mr Dovehawk good in bed? Did he satisfy all three of you?"

"They giggled and looked at each other, before Tammy spoke. "Oh god yes darlings – we can hardly walk..."

The cheers rang round again.

"Can all three of you turn round please so we can have a picture of your bums?" asked one of the photographers while lining up the shot. "Thanks girls..."

"Here, that's sexist," moaned Dovehawk. "Don't you want a picture of my arse too?"

"No thanks Stan... We want to encourage readers not put them off..."

"Bloody cheek. I'll tell you what though – they are three nice looking bums true enough." He himself turned round to get a look, thus providing a view of his own corpulent buttocks to the attendant paparazzi. They frantically changed to wide-anlge lenses.

Eight in the morning, Friday – 5 days to the replay, 6 days to polling day

Headline from the *Daily Smut* –

NOW IT'S FOUR IN A BED FOR STAN THE STAMINA MAN

Stan Dovehawk, the Real Labour candidate in the upcoming Hetherington by-election, arrived to pick up his new office yesterday accompanied by no fewer than three stunning beauties – The Honourable Lady Fiona Opiumden, her best friend and multi-million pound heiress Tamara Toker-Spankbottom, and the petite and shy Angela Twogood, his campaign manager, on loan to Dovehawk from Hetherington Stanley Football Club. To the amazement of onlookers, within just minutes of receiving the key to his plush new premises from Jack Dugdale, owner of Carefree Caravans, the four of them immediately got down to bonking. As you can see in our photo, they emerged an hour later scantily clad and grinning.

Pree looked at the picture, then dialled the number for the clinic. It started to ring. She hung-up and began crying.

Ten in the morning, Wednesday – the day of the replay, tomorrow is polling day

Dovehawk was out knocking on doors. The houses in the narrow streets were bedecked with bunting and flags in the red and blue Hetherington Sidney colours.

Adelina too was "on the stump", trying to pick up last-minute votes.

It was inevitable that they should meet and, when it happened, around a corner suddenly, at the junction of Acacia Grove and Asbestos Lane, they smiled copiously at one another, then stood side by side and held a posed handshake for the press photographers. Pree and Gerald hastily retreated from the scene. Dovehawk's little band of supporters whom he had managed to recruit during the previous week clapped politely as the two candidates exchanged pleasantries.

The two parties then headed in their respective opposite directions. When Dovehawk and Angela turned into the residential street where they had parked Mission Control, they were surprised to see a long line of people stretching from an open window on the caravan, along the pavement and halfway down the road. There must have been twenty of them and, on closer inspection, they were all children. All bar an incongruous looking gentleman at the back of the queue wearing a suit and carrying a briefcase.

"Ninety-nine please Mister," chirped the little boy at the head of the queue. Angela and Stan watched in amazement as the baboon chuckled happily while scooping a large dollop of ice-cream from a tub onto a cornet, slipped a flake in the middle and handed over the tasty delicacy. The boy happily trotted off, slurping the drips and snaffling the end of the flake, his total enjoyment displayed in the gobs of white and brown claggy liquid oozing from the corners of his mouth. The little girl behind him squabbled with a couple of her friends to be next; she managed to fight them off and the process was repeated. The baboon wore a little white pinny and a paper hat. After another ten or so customers had been satisfied, the baboon started to become agitated; he made hooting noises, becoming louder, and hopped up and down with ever greater annoyance. At that moment, a car drew up and from it popped Fiona and Tammy. They undid the boot and took out two more big tubs of vanilla ice-cream, a box of flakes and a packet of cones. The baboon ceremonially grabbed the empty tub from which he had been serving and placed it upside down on his head, indicating to the girls that he had run out. The children, who had been fearing the worst when the ice-cream had all gone, eyed the fresh delivery with keen interest and immense relief. Tammy and Fiona popped the supplies through the caravan door and normal service was resumed.

"Ninety-nine please Mister."

"Chuckle chuckle. Oooooooh oooooooh!" Ice-cream – cornet – flake. "Oooooooh ooooooooh"

"Ninety-nine please Mister."

"Chuckle chuckle. Oooooooh oooooooh!" Ice-cream – cornet – flake. "Oooooooh ooooooooh"

"Ninety-nine please Mister."

"Chuckle chuckle. Oooooooh oooooooh!" Ice-cream – cornet – flake. "Oooooooh ooooooooh"

The queue shuffled along in orderly fashion, the satisfied urchins hanging around and shlurping while some of them made monkey noises in imitation of their furry host. Several ninety-nines later, the man in the suit was next in the queue. The baboon looked at him expectantly, but no request for a ninety-nine was forthcoming. Instead, the gentleman reached in his pocket and produced a plastic laminated card for the monkey's inspection.

"I'm from Hetherington Council Environmental Health Department. May I see your Food Hygiene Safety Certificate please?"

The baboon looked at him perplexed. After a while it made a jabbering noise. Stan and Fiona watched with great interest, but stayed in the background to see how things would turn out. The press as usual had all their cameras trained on the scene.

The Officer continued in an attempt to be helpful. "Your Food Hygiene Safety Certificate – it's an A4 sheet of paper – it should be pinned up on the wall of your premises. Can I see it please?"

The baboon decided the best course of action would to be helpful. He chuckled and handed the man a ninety-nine. The Council Official baulked and took a step back. "Before I can handle any food produce, I must get changed!" He quickly retrieved a white paper suit from his briefcase and slipped it over his suit. He then donned a white disposable hat and galoshes, and finally slipped on a pair of sterile rubber gloves. He moved towards the hatchway again and the baboon profferred the ice-cream which the man now took.

"I note that you have rather hairy hands. Have you washed them before handling the food?"

"Arrrruuuuunnnnkkkkk," chirped the baboon, and proceeded to lick his fingers with his very long tongue.

"Yes, well," continued the man from the Council, "I shall have to make a formal inspection of your premises and submit a report. May I come in please?"

The ape swung through the window with the greatest of ease, leant around the side and pushed the door button allowing the door to swing open. The Council Official disappeared inside. Dovehawk began to laugh. "This is going to be some crack!" he chuckled to Angela and the other two girls who had now joined him. The baboon carried on serving the children who had been in the queue behind the Environmental Health Inspector. After ten minutes the man emerged, clutching a clip-board. He finished scribbling on it then handed the paper to the baboon, who wiped his bottom on it. The Official then took another piece of paper from his briefcase and stuck it to the door. The children who were still waiting strained to see what it said. The man stood among them and began an oration.

"After carrying out an inspection of these premises, I have found them to be in breach of several food hygiene regulations. I have therefore officially issued a Hygiene Emergency Prohibition Order. Now go home children – this outlet is now closed!"

The baboon looked at him mockingly while the children booed and hissed. The monkey balanced a cornet on his head and jeered at the Council Official. Then he grabbed a handful of vanilla ice-cream and launched it straight into the man's face. Everyone was now laughing while the poor bloke tried to wipe away the cold sticky mass which coated him, making him now the same white colour all over. Of course, working for the Council, he had a beard – so the sticky globules became particularly entrapped in the thick spiky hairs. Dovehawk wondered if there should be a law against beards for Food

Hygiene reasons, as yesterday's dinner was almost certainly concealed within its wiry tendrils, along with today's dessert!

"Aaaaagh!" grumbled the man. "Right! That's it!" He took his mobile from his pocket and hit a couple of buttons. As he talked into the mouthpiece he spluttered white sticky ice-cream over his phone. Looking smug, he hung up. Dovehawk decided it was time to get involved.

"What would seem to be the trouble?" he enquired in a friendly but formal manner.

"Are these *your* premises?" asked the Official.

"These are currently my premises, yes – until the day after tomorrow…"

"Good. In that case, you need to read this Emergency Prohibition Order which I have issued. It will tell you that you have no Food Hygiene Safety Certificate displayed on the premises, and that your staff are not sufficiently well trained and equipped to provide the service of comestible products. I am therefore condemning this food outlet and it will shortly be impounded." He looked even more smug as he spoke the last few words, knowing that he was exercising his just and draconian rights.

"That's all very well," riposted Dovehawk, "But I think your regulations cover the *sale* of food products. And I think you'll find that in this case no money has changed hands!"

"That's got nothing to do with it," harrumphed the Official. "As far as I'm concerned, you have supplied a whole street's worth of children with food which could be contaminated. This could prove to be the source of a major outbreak! Ahaaaaa! Here comes the towaway truck now!"

The Council parking enforcement vehicle operatives parked up behind the caravan, unhitched it from the Land Rover, then winched it onto their trailer. They drove off, the baboon waving and jeering from the roof of the caravan as it was carted away, the children joining in the baleful chorus.

"Where are they taking my Party Headquarters?" roared Dovehawk.

"To the Council pound. Here is a receipt for it. You can retrieve it on payment of a £475 reclamation fee."

"£475 reclamation fee! You can stick it up your fucking arse!"

"And that's another offence you have committed! Swearing at an Officer carrying out his Official Food Hygiene Inspection duties is a criminal offence. Plus your employee threw ice-cream in my face, which is physical assault and constitutes another offence. Plus he refused to answer questions."

"Look." Dovehawk glared into the ice-cream streaked eyes of the boring bureaucrat. "You're calling my primate friend uncooperative? You wanna try talking to any of your mates who work for the Council, then you'll know what banging your head against a brick wall is all about. Believe me, the ape makes a monkey out of all of you!"

"I could get you arrested Mr Dovehawk."

"And when I'm your MP, I can get you the sack."

Ten thirty, Wednesday morning – the day of the replay

"Right. Gather round you lot." The Hetherington Sidney manager addressed his players with hope in his heart; but the probability of a sound thrashing in his head. He looked at them and smiled.

"Nothing I can do for you now lads," he purred. "In nine hours time you'll be playing the best team in Europe, possibly in the world! Nothing I can say will motivate you more than that thought. So hold onto that thought, but at the same time don't be overawed. If you spoil their game, thwart them at every turn, you can beat 'em. On your day, you can beat anyone. Any team in the land, even the lowliest, on it's day can beat any other team, however high 'n mighty! Has anybody got anything to say?"

"Yesh bosh."

"What is it Splutter?"

"Will we 'ave sh-shorts thish time? One'sh what fit?"

"I have arranged for everyone to have not one, not two, but three..." loud cheer "... extra pairs of shorts so if there are any mishaps in the shorts department, we have contingency measures in place."

"And 'opefully shorts in place too boss. Ha ha!"

"Yes, that's right Korma. Hopefully your shorts will remain in place. We don't want anything brown and wriggly hanging out on the Jammy Trafford pitch, however small."

The others all laughed at poor Korma.

"That's no fair boss! I told you… I'm *The Brown Stallion*!"

"Yes, you told us. Is that what the girls in the *Late-Tackle Club* call you?"

"Well boss." He looked sheepish. "Not exactly…"

"No 'kin right they don't," hollered Dorksy. "They call him *Squishy-Boy*, boss! F'kin' *Squishy-Boy*! An' guess what they call Tubsy? They call 'im *Big-Fat-Squishy-Boy*! What a reet laugh that is!"

"Very informative Dorksy," said Ron. "So what do they call you?"

"They call 'im a f'kin' DORK o' course," chortled Sean, looking at the bear-like figure of the big centre-half, "Same as the rest of us do!"

"Very informative. Right, it's time we all got on the team coach and headed off to Jammy Trafford, so get your gear and don't forget nothing – OK lads? And don't worry – I'll be in charge of all the extra pairs of shorts."

"Yes boss!" they all chorused.

"So – what are we gonna do?"

"WIIIIIIIIIIIIIIINNNNNNNNNNNNNN boss!"

Eleven in the morning, Wednesday – the day of the replay, tomorrow is polling day

Tammy drove Dovehawk, Fiona and Angela round to Carefree Caravans for yet another interesting meeting with Jack Dugdale. Jack was outside wandering around his yard when they arrived. He immediately noticed the lack of a van on the back of their Land Rover, and this fact raised doubts and worries in the poor old chap's mind, as if he didn't have enough to fret about with this being the day that his beloved team were to take on the giants of the English and European Leagues: Jam United.

The Land Rover crunched to a halt. Dovehawk stuck his head out of the window. Jack hurtled over to him.

"What the bloody 'ell 'ave you done wi' my caravan this time? My WindCheetah 9000. What 'ave you done wi' my lovely WindCheetah 9000? Please tell me it's still in one piece…"

"Jack!" Stan reassured him in a hearty voice. "Jack, it's fine, it's still in one piece I promise."

"Oh thank god. Well where is it then?"

"Here – read this."

Dovehawk handed him the official Council receipt that he'd been given by the man from the environment. Jack read. He got to the bit where it said *impounded.*

"Impounded! What do you mean it's bloody impounded. Well you'd better get it back then Mr Dove'awk – you're responsible for a very valuable piece of equipment there, a WindCheetah 9000, they don't come cheap y' know!"

"Read a little further Jack. Please…"

Jack read. He got to the bit where it said *£475*.

"Four 'undred 'n seventy five pounds! Four 'undred 'n seventy five pounds? a WindCheetah 9000's worth far more 'n that! Go an' get it back straight away."

"Ah good. That's what I was hoping you'd say. Hop in the Land Rover. And don't forget your cheque book."

Jack looked stunned. "Cheque book? What for?"

"Four hundred and seventy five squids, that's what for," said Dovehawk. "Now hop in and we'll get it straight away."

"Now 'ang on, 'ang on," said Jack between clenched teeth. "You got my caravan impounded. You'll 'ave to pay to get it back."

"Me? I haven't got that sort of money. I'm only a lowly backbench MP; well, *almost* a lowly backbench MP. Plus, it costs an extra fifty quid a day for every day it's not picked up… So if I take a week to raise the four-seven-five, it'll have gone up another three-fifty and we're still no nearer raising the necessary sum to get it back. Plus, as you very rightly say, it's *your* caravan, so if you want to recover your property, you'll have to pay to get it back."

Jack harrumphed, but realised he would have to give in if he ever wanted to see his beloved WindCheetah 9000 sailing along the highway again.

"Then what I'll do is this: when you're MP, if you're MP, and you start drawing all them MP's expenses, you can pay me back. Is it a deal?"

"OK it's a deal. I'll pay you back a fiver a week. That's the deal."

"That doesn't sound like much of a deal to me."

"It's the *only* deal. We're hard at bargaining us politicians."

"You're also bloody experts at destroying and losing caravans. You'd be no good in business."

"Of course that's true. That's why we mess the economy up. It's our job."

"The one thing you're good at?"

"Not the only one, but it is top of the list of achievements of every Government that's ever been formed. A 100% record you could say."

"Come on, let's go and retrieve my property."

Jack climbed in the back.

"Mind Prickface!" shrieked Tammy.

"Bloody cheek!" bellowed Jack. "Just because you're rich with a posh 'ouse you think you can call us salt-of-the-earth types names. We make nearly all the money what goes around in this country – and don't you forget that!"

He got out of the Land Rover, slammed the door and glared at her.

"I shall take my own Rover thank you. I'll meet you all at the pound.

"I was only trying to warn him," said Tammy huffily. "He'd have moaned more if he'd sat down on the beastly thing."

"Yes," said Dovchawk. "That he would. Now be a good girl and give it a stroke. It's had a nasty experience with an arse that size poised to sit on its face."

* * *

They arrived at the car pound.

"Car pound," said the little Hitler in the gatehouse.

"Good," said Dovehawk. "Here it is…" and gave the man a pound.

"Very funny," muttered the man from under his peaked cap. "If I 'ad a pound for every time I 'eard that I'd be a rich man."

"You should be rich already at £475 a go," spluttered Dovehawk. "That's robbery with menaces that is… When I'm MP I shall be shutting this little money-making racket down. Unless I get a cut of the takings that is…"

Dovehawk leaned towards the man in confidence.

"That was another joke by the way. Just in case you thought I meant it and you were off to tell the newspapers."

"Yes, OK. Well that will be £475 please. Plus VAT."

"Plus VAT! I didn't read that bit on your little leaflet!"

"It quite clearly states in paragraph 9 on the reverse in 6-point typing that the amount charged for vehicle recovery is liable for VAT at the standard rate."

"Is it on there in Braille too?"

"No but we have a tape for people who are visually impaired."

"Why the hell would you be recovering a car if you were visually impaired? You couldn't drive the bloody thing!"

"As a matter of fact, the tape isn't used very often."

"As a matter of fact, the gentleman who is just arriving in the posh Rover behind me is the one who will be paying your astronomical and extortionate £475 plus VAT. We meanwhile shall drive in and hook up the van while he sorts out the finances."

"Oh no no no no no. Can't do that. No no no no no. The barrier cannot be raised until the money is cleared and in our bank account – that can take three days!"

"But you charge an extra £50 for each day it's not collected."

"True. You have noticed the beauty of the system."

"Good god, you don't need Council Tax payers with this racket running do you. You can support the whole Council on the proceeds of just one car pound."

"Some people don't bother picking them up. Then we crush them."

"Oh yes! I can imagine the look on Jack Dugdale's face while he watches you crush his WindCheetah 9000. But I can't let that happen."

Dovehawk leaned out of the window and gave a shrill whistle. Next second, the baboon swung across the tops of all the impounded cars and vans, leaped through the opening in the kiosk where the officious operative sat and pressed one of the big green buttons on the panel. The barrier lifted. Tammy hit the throttle and they were in.

"I shan't let you out again!" shouted the jobsworth from his den. "You won't get away with interfering with Council property!" The baboon laughed and pressed all the buttons on the panel. Lights flashed all around the yard, hooters went off and various barriers went up and down like the gates on a busy level-crossing. Jack drove up and got out his cheque book.

"You know it takes three days to clear," the little man started explaining all over again.

Stan and Angela hitched up the caravan, Tammy drove towards the exit barrier and it lifted just as they reached it. The baboon screeched with glee, then legged it out of the gatehouse and into the Land Rover, proudly wearing the pound-keeper's cap. Jack groaned and added another £20 to the amount on the cheque.

The Dovehawk cavalcade roared off into the sunset… The press followed them, keen to see what the next adventure might be…

"Where do you want to go, Duvvy?" asked Tamara as they took the corner of the High Street with the caravan leaning over on its outside two wheels as she made sure of beating the red light.

"To Hetherington Sidney FC," chanted Dovehawk. "We shall put in a sending-off appearance for our team, to give them our best wishes and all the luck we can muster up for them!"

"God I hope that's the only sending-off they get today," said Fiona from the back.

"Oh Aye," said Angela, "I do 'ope that too."

"Grooooooorrrrrk!" said the baboon.

When they got to the ground, it was only in the nick of time because the team were about to climb on their coach for the trip to Jammy Trafford. Dovehawk *harrumphed* as he looked at the proceedings through the window of his Land Rover, because he realised he had been gazumped. There, in an orderly queue, waiting to shake hands with the departing players was not only Adelina dressed in a bright red skirt and top, but the Conservative, the Liberal Democrat, and the Monster Raving Loony. The press too were attending in their usual force.

Jack's Rover purred into the car park and took up its customary position in the space reserved for "Chairman". Jack got out and Dovehawk hurried over to him. Meanwhile, the press stopped filming the players and candidates as soon as they found out that Fiona and Tamara were now available for an impromptu modelling session.

"Jack," effused Dovehawk warmly, "Any chance you could line the players up in front of my caravan… I mean *your* caravan for a photo opportunity? It'll be great publicity for Carefree Caravans."

"Aye, that it will!" said Jack, "But I suspect you'd be more interested in the twelve inch high letters spellin' out *REAL PEOPLE VOTE REAL LABOUR* – am I right Stan?"

"That would be a happy coincidence, I agree."

"The problem is, the Club can't be seen to be taking sides in the election. I mean, we'll 'ave to live with 'ooever gets voted in, so we mustn't create any unwârranted animosity on the day before the poll."

"What do you mean, whoever gets elected? It's obviously going to be me – I have a ten point lead in the opinion polls."

"So you don't need a photo of your… I mean *my*… caravan then, do you?"

"But it's a WindCheetah 9000! How can you deny it its moment of glory?"

"Oh god you 'ad to say that didn't you! You're tearin' at me 'eart-strings… That was below the belt Mr Dove'awk… But no. I still

’ave to refuse your request. We must be seen to be impartial – I mean apart from the loan of the caravan that is.”

“Yes, see – you’re already implicated... Go on Jack – just one photo.” Dovehawk looked around at Mission Control and saw that all the newspaper and TV cameras were already trained on it. The Hetherington Sidney players looked on, standing there, shivering in the freezing weather, waiting for someone to take some notice of them. All excep Sean who was between the two girls standing on the top step of the WindCheetah 9000. “Forget it!” Dovehawk announced triumphantly. “I don’t need your help after all – it seems my election team has it all under control!”

Jack groaned as he saw a posse of disgruntled politicians making their way towards him.

“I say old chap!” It was Sir Roger St John Buttplug, the Conservative candidate.

“Sir Roger!” Jack took his hand and shook it enthusiastically. “How very nice to see you ’ere at our little football club...”

“Yes, it is rather, very nice. But I really must raise a complaint – the press are taking photographs of your player in front of a rival candidate’s caravan! That is very shabby I must say!”

Jack’s face turned purple. “Shabby? Shabby!... My caravan is *not* shabby – it’s a WindCheetah 9000 I’ll ’ave you know. Royalty ’ave holidayed in such luxurious conveyances as those!”

“Oh? Oh yes, I’m sure, God bless Her... But that’s not what I meant. It is not acceptable that the press have all Mr Dovehawk’s nauseating slogans in their sights when we are supposed to be attending a footballing occasion of such importance for the town of Hetherington. I ask that you remove you player and his concubines immediately to another location.”

Before Jack had time to reply, Dovehawk exploded with loud mirth. “You’ve only got six percent in the opinion polls! What the hell difference will it make where you get photographed... You’ve already lost your deposit! Go back to flogging dead horses... Or whatever else it is you flog for fun...” Dovehawk lowered his voice and spoke in confidence. “I hear you feature on a few websites. You know – *dodgy* websites – my researchers have been busy – they’re very thorough.”

"I am not talking to Mr Dovehawk." Sir Roger turned his back on Stan and spoke directly to Jack. "He has run this campaign most sordidly and negatively. All I ask is a fair crack of the whip…"

"There! I told you!" shouted Dovehawk.

There was a roar and whoops of delight from behind them and they all spun round to see what was happening. Fiona was now topless. She covered her breasts with her hands, but not with any strict intention of keeping them hidden. "Com on love!" shouted the photographers. "Give us a wave! Go on Fiona love!"

The baboon, shrieking like a monkey, trotted over to Dovehawk and presented him with Fiona's T-shirt. It was emblazoned across the front in large lettering, *SEAN SHAGDME.*

"Very tasteful," muttered Jack, who then shouted across the car park. "Right – time to get on the coach everyone! Come on! Look lively!"

The players started to trudge towards the luxury vehicle; well, it had a toilet. The politicians suddenly realised they were going to miss their chance at being seen glad-handing the Hetherington team and ran across the icy mud to head them off. Sean blew kisses at the cameras and sauntered over to join his fellows, a girl on each arm. Dovehawk grabbed up Angela, who had been left behind at the caravan, and escorted her, following in the tracks of the three stars of the show.

The candidates formed a little line, shaking the hand of each player as they climbed onto the bus, wishing them the best of luck against the mighty Jam United.

"Jolly good luck," said Sir Roger.

"All the best for tonight," said Brian Boring, the Liberal Democrat.

"I'll see you in the bar at half-time," said Sir Giant Jugs, the Loony.

"Give us a kiss," said Adelina, "I 'ope you do your best an' your best is good enough… mwah."

"Grooooooorrrrkk!" squawked the baboon.

"Get off me!" grumbled Piccalilli, "I don't want green, red, blue monkey disease! *Gerrroffffffff*!"

Gerrroffffffff is *Give us a snog* in baboon language. Piccalilli eventually broke free and ran onto the coach and straight to the toilet, but Tubsy was already in there and three other players were trying to pull him out as he was wedged against the sides.

"Water, soap, disinfectant, bleach!" shouted Piccalilli to anyone who would listen.

"Shut the fuck up, you sound like a girl!" said Dorksy and slapped him round the head.

Dovehawk missed arriving in time for the handshakes, but was standing next to Sean and the girls by the time they took their final salute to the cameras. They all waved. It was incredibly cold and Fiona's nipples stood out like strawberry fruit pastilles. Only certain front pages would be able to feature this picture; while some could put it on page three. The others cursed their luck. The photographers all zoomed in, hoping a quick email to *The Fun* or the *Daily Smut* would make up their wages for the next month.

7.42 on Wednesday evening – this is the replay! – 3 minutes to kickoff

The Jam U private satellite orbiting Jammy Trafford beamed a live feed from the ground to the whole world, and while an English FA Cup third round replay wasn't exactly the final of the UEFA Champions League, the importance of the event and its poignancy in respect of the sudden demise of the Jam United manager in the previous fixture between these two sides meant that the match was attended by important football nonentities from around the globe, including no less a personage than the FIFA President, who had booked himself out of the clap clinic especially for the occasion.

Ron Conference was by now completely recovered, his head having a normal temperature and a delicate greyey-pink hue. Ron Accrington who was co-commentating on the match was happily and warmly ensconced in the superior facilities provided for the purpose with on-line bar; on-line meaning that there were several lines connected to multiple alcoholic beverages which could be ordered and consumed at the press of a button on the special Jam U remote control.

In the away dugout, sponge man Phil was poised, eager, like a praying mantis, ready to pounce on any injured player should the circumstance arise when his almost mythical skills would be required. Ron was sitting next to him, waiting for the whistle to signal the start of the game, chewing gum like he meant it.

Up in the Directors' box, Jack was trying to make sense of Jam United Chairman Miser Hilton Tightfist's New York accent. The American also had the same trouble understanding Jack, but that was only when Jack could get a word in – he concluded that Tightfists obviously weren't so tight when it came to things which were free, such as speech.

Tammy and Fiona sat in the WAGs reserved area. Dovehawk had decided that a bit of "help in the community" wouldn't go amiss on the day before polling, so he and Angela had prime position, on the touchline, just behind the goal – they had signed up to be St John's Ambulance helpers for the day and the lovely ladies in the St John's Quartermasters Stores had managed to find a uniform big enough to cover the copious politician, while Angela looked simply adorable and waif-like in her white shirt, black drill skirt and black nylons. The other candidates in the by-election were all hobnobbing it in the various boxes with their various backers and hangers-on.

An announcement came over the tannoy: *Please can everyone stand for a minute's silence in respect and remembrance of our esteemed manager who sadly passed away at Sidney Park the week before last. I am sure you would all like to remember him with due dignity so no calling out or whistling during the silence please – thank you.*

Scrape scrape scrape went the people getting to their feet, then nothing… After a minute, the referee blew his whistle and the Jam U team, all wearing black armbands, clapped while the whole ground joined in.

And now, I'd like you all to welcome our new manager who has kindly taken over at short notice, even though he already had jobs with two lower league clubs and a national side, Mr Sven Svensson Svengali! Let's hear it for the new manager! Thank you!

The crowd cheered. The referee planted the ball on the centre circle and looked at his watch.

7.45 on Wednesday evening – kickoff!

Pheeeeeeeeep!

"Now their only chance here is to survive the first half without going a goal down," said Ron Accrington in the commentary box. "If they can survive the first half, then they're in with a squeak – only a little squeak, but still a squeak.

Pheeeeeeeeep!

The referee blew his whistle and pointed to the centre circle. The Jam U goal had been scored with exactly sixteen seconds on the clock.

"They've scored!" screamed the commentator. "What were you saying, Ron? They haven't managed to survive half a minute, let alone half time. What do *you* think Ron?"

"They're fucked," said Ron. "Oh fuck! Sorry everyone – didn't meant to say fuck on the telly. Sorry Gary back in the studio – you'll have to bleep that one out... Mind you, compared with what Gary called me last night in training, my language just now was kiddies' TV stuff... He's a right c..."

"Yes, quite Ron, quite..." the commentator quickly interjected... "I've heard a lot worse – I think you'll just about get away with that one, which is more than Hetherington Sidney have managed... What do *you* think Ron?"

"I think my bet on Jam U winning four-nil is still on track, that's what I think."

The other Ron was on his feet on the touchline, shouting and screaming at his dejected players who looked like they had lost a winning lottery ticket.

"Let me at 'em wi' me sponge!" shouted Phil, rushing from the dugout carrying his bucket. "Just let me get this cold wet sponge round Shagsy's knackers an' 'e'll score for sure!"

"Come on lads!" implored Ron. "Don't let your 'eads go down! Keep at 'em! Close 'em down! em down! You can do it!"

Pheeeeeeeeep!

Sean tapped the ball forward and Billy Bell passed it back to Stainsy on the right wing. Stainsy just hoofed it up in the general direction of the Jam U penalty area.

"Not like that!" screamed Ron from the touchline. "You've got to keep the ball not give it away!"

But Sean had made a run forward as soon as he had kicked off, and was now hurtling towards the edge of the opposition box. All the Jam U defenders were looking up in the air at the ball to see where it would land. Sean couldn't believe his luck. One of the defenders bumped into another one, who stuck his leg out to stop himself falling. His leg went right across the front of Sean just as he arrived. He made sure he touched it then sprawled in the muddy grass, sliding five yards on his stomach from his pace into the box.

Pheeeeeeeeep!

The referee pointed to the penalty spot, then hid by the corner flag.

Pheeeeeeeeeep! Pheeeeeeeeeep! Pheeeeeeeeeep! Pheeeeeeeeeep!

He blew and blew while the Jam U players surrounded him.

Ron hugged Phil on the touchline and spun him round, so the contents of his bucket sprayed out like a fountain.

Sean took the ball, placed it on the edge of the spot nearer the goal, retired six paces and waited for the referee to emerge from the scrum of players by the corner flag. When they did depart, the referee clutched his chest and dropped to the ground. Dovehawk and Angela rushed onto the pitch and began giving cardiac massage to the deflated whistler, while the other St John's Ambulance personnel simultaneously leapt for their Zimmer frames and chased after them. Obviously Angela and the pompous politician had been recruited as a "rapid deployment force", and the crowd all cheered.

Dovehawk was pleased to see the referee splutter back to life. The referee came round looking up at Angela's caring eyes; he thought he'd died and gone to heaven. He smelt her perfume and admired her cute features. He then looked to the right and saw the jowly-faced Dovehawk.

Fuck, thought the referee, *God's had a shave! And he's much uglier than in the pictures…*

He got up, took note of his surroundings and tried to remember what he had been doing. Then he saw the football. He walked unsteadily over to it, picked it up and walked off towards the centre circle where he plonked it down for a kick off. Now he was surrounded by a different pack of players, while the fans in the stadium were cheering like mad at the thought they had got away without a spot-kick.

"You gave a penalty, ref!" shouted Dorksy, trying to stop himself from picking the official up by the ears and rubbing noses.

"Did I?" The poor confused soul didn't fancy another mauling.

"Yeah, you did honest," said Korma, more reasonably than his team-mate.

"Yeah, and you need to send off some o' them Jam U lot!" grumbled Gherkin. "They just beat you up!"

"Did they?"

"Yeah, they did honest," said Korma. "Go an' ask your linesman. He'll tell you."

The linesman was hopping up and down on the touchline, waving his flag, trying to attract the referee's attention, but not daring to go onto the pitch in case he bacame the first assistant referee to get sent off.

"Yeah, go on," said Shagsy. "Ask the linesman before 'e 'as a coronary an' all!"

The ref trundled off to consult the flagger, now surrounded by the Jam U players again. Sven Svensson Svengali also joined in, causing the referee to blow his whistle and point his finger towards the dugout, indicating that the Jam U manager's presence was unwelcome.

"What's the ref gonna do here!" shouted Ron Accrington into his microphone. "He's got to give the penalty, the assistant referee's got to tell 'im what happened!"

The Jam U players all suddenly looked despondent and turned their backs in disgust as the referee blew his whistle again and pointed back to the penalty spot.

"Quite right!" boomed Ron Accrington. "Good on you ref! They're lucky there's no sending off for that disgraceful display. If it hadn't been for the prompt reaction of the St John's Ambulance there could have been much more serious consequences. I just hope the ref's fit to continue..."

Sean picked up the ball and placed it on the spot once more.

Pheeeeeeeeep! went the referee's whistle.

Sean trotted up, went to kick with his right foot, feinted as the goalie dived, and side-footed the ball into the open net with his left.

"Yeeeeeeees!" screamed the commentator, "Hetherington are level. Well would you believe it?... What do *you* think Ron?"

"I think I've lost me bet on four-nil! But never mind – for the sake of the game it needed that. Funnily enough, I've got another little flutter on it going to penalties after extra time..."

"Oh, I think you're hoping a bit there, Ron. I'd like it to go to penalties, but I really can't see Jam U being held for the full hundred and twenty minutes. Or can they?"

"Yeeeeeeees!" screamed Ron Conference, and Phil and Tammy and Fiona and Angela and Jack and the five hundred or so travelling Hetherington Sidney fans.

Sven Svensson Svengali looked impassive. Miser Hilton Tightfist choked on his bagel.

Pheeeeeeeeep! went the referee's whistle and the Jam U centre-forward kicked off.

8.32 on Wednesday evening – one minute of added time to go in the first half

The ball went out for a corner to Hetherington Sidney. Dovehawk, who was at the end with the Jam U goal, threw it back in. Korma took it, placed it by the corner flag, looked up and whipped in a low fizzer across the face of goal. It hit the giant Tubsy on the head and rebounded at ninety miles per hour. In a split second, the Jam U goalkeeper got his hand up to palm it over, but it wasn't going in anyway. Instead, it hit the crossbar before launching itself out of play, splattering the poor bloke's fingers in his glove, crushed between ball and woodwork.

He dropped to the ground, clutching the broken phalanges with his remaining good hand, shrieking one of his famous curses along the lines of: "*voulez-vous mama-mía sacre fernando super-trouper name-of-the-game SOS chiquitita*" while writhing around in agony. Dovehawk and Angela were getting good at this, reaching the hapless goalie in less than seven seconds, armed with a bag of frozen peas for instant relief. Dovehawk hoped an amputation wouldn't be necessary. Angela applied the freezing vegetable balm, while the goalkeeper looked into her eyes and smiled. "Bella bella bella!" he expounded. Obviously the prompt and soothing treatment he was receiving was working. The Jam U sponge man arrived at this point with his dripping bucket.

"Right luv – I'll tek over now!" he ordered peremptorily and patronisingly.

His injured player looked at the physio, horrified. As the sponge man went to wrest the traumatised hand from Angela's tender care, the goalie exploded in latin wrath. "You for sure can fucky right off!" he blasted in his best Anglo Saxon slang, aimed at the gobsmacked quack-doctor. I have nursey!" and he looked back at the loving Angela, purring as she poured her healing powers into his ravaged digits.

"But I 'ave to tek over – or the manager'll be givin' me a right rollockin'!"

The goalkeeper spoke without turning his head away from Angela's eyes. "That your problem matey…"

"But I could get the sack!" the poor man was desperate. "Please let me just 'old yer 'and…" He went to take hold of the goalkeeper's glove containing his good hand."

"No no no no no NO!" trilled the goalie. "You go to manager and tell him I be better soon! I in good hands…" and he carried on looking at Angela's sweet face while she gently massaged his bruised fingers through the frozen peas.

"But, but… he'll be angry!"

"So jus ignore heem like I do… I canno understand a fucky word he say!"

The referee came along to inspect the damage. "Do we need a stretcher, nurse?" We've got to get the game re-started or the crowd will get restless."

Angela gazed at her bronzed muscled patient. "Have you got any pain?"

"No pain."

Angela removed the peas and massaged directly onto his fingers.

"Have you got any feeling? Can you grip my fingers?"

The Jam U player gave her hand a little squeeze.

"You have lovely small hands," said the goalie.

"My god, this is better than the telly!" said Dovehawk.

Just then, the stretcher arrived. The goalkeeper saw it and leapt to his feet. He put his arm round the tiny Angela who was at least a foot below him and cuddled her as she walked off the pitch, finally giving her a swift pinch on the bum to show his appreciation.

Pheeeeeeeeep! went the referee and the rehabilitated player launched the ball up to the other end of the pitch from his goal kick. There was one minute still to play, even though the time was now twenty to nine, a full ten minutes after the first half should have been completed. The Jam U forwards ran onto the bouncing ball, chasing it towards the Hetherington Sidney penalty area. The left winger trapped it, went wide to the bye-line and pinged in a looping cross back to the edge of the box where the centre-forward launched it first time along the ground towards the right corner of the goal. Piccalilli dived to his left and finger-tipped it round the post for a corner to Jam U. As he did so, he skidded across the frozen muddy surface and, unable to stop himself in time, banged his head on the upright. It hurt so much he couldn't yell.

"Now *their* goalie's injured!" shouted Ron Accrington, beside himself in the commentary box, leaping up and down so much he spilt his spiced rum.

Angela and Dovehawk were at the wrong end to attend this injury without running the full length of the pitch. By the time they got there, not only had Phil arrived with his bucket, but half the St John's at that end of the ground had fired up their Zimmer frames and were cruising to the scene of the action like a flotilla of ships, all arriving at the same time.

"He's not moving!" expounded Ron Accrington in enthusiastic tones, as if a death on the field would make up for the lack of excitement in the first half. "This could be the longest three minutes of injury time in history! Do you know what the record is?"

"I think the record's a week and two days, when Copa Plate Cabana played Los Strangulidos from Uruguay and one of the team took out a gun and shot someone on the other side in stoppage time."

"Really? Well let's hope it's a bit quicker than that here – I don't think we've reached an Undertaker Situation yet…"

Phil was busy with his sponge. Angela held Piccalilli's hand. The first drops of freezing water hit Piccalilli's brow and he groaned, showing there was still life existent.

"Oh please god, don't let him be concussed!" Ron Conference prayed to the heavens with his hands clasped. "We're playing Jam U – we *need* a goalie!"

Piccalilli opened his eyes and saw Angela, which soothed him so he went back to sleep again.

"We might need the stretcher this time," said the ref.

"I know 'ow to get 'im back on 'is feet!" shouted Sean. He ran off towards the fans and started asking questions. A murmur went round the ground, then a large female, grinning from face-piercing to tattoo, came down from her perch in the stand and joined Sean on the pitch.

He hugged her, took her hand and walked to the supine Piccalilli, while the crowd all cheered and wolf-whistled. "I've got a job for you love," said Sean. "What's yer name?"

"Sam" she said in husky tones.

"Right, Sam, when we splash some more water on our goalie, I want you to be the first thing he sees, so get in close right next to 'im, OK lass?

"Right OK Sean – whatever you say…"

She knelt over the snoring keeper, then Sean gave the signal to Phil to apply the fearsome cold liquid to the unsuspecting forehead, while everyone around looked on in interest, especially the referee who still had thirty seconds on his watch to play.

Splaaaaash went the shudderingly cold shower onto Piccalilli's face.

He opened one eye. His face contorted. He shut it quickly then opened both eyes. Immediately he sat upright as if someone had stuck a poker up his arse and screamed, "Rrraaaaaaaarrrrrrrrrrrrrrrrrr!!!"

He flailed his arms around for some grip, causing his erstwhile helpers to step back and, jumping to his feet, rushed off at lightining speed across the pitch still screaming "Rrraaaaaaaaarrrrrrrrrrrrrrrrr!!! Rrraaaaaaaaarrrrrrrrrrrrrrrrr!!! Rrraaaaaaaaarrrrrrrrrrrrrrrrr!!! It's a SCUNTLEPOOL GIRL !!! Rrraaaaaaaaarrrrrrrrrrrrrrrrr!!! Get me outa heeeeeeeere!"

The referee looked at his watch for the seventy third time. "He seems to be better now," he observed matter-of-factly. "Would you like to get him back so we can take the corner?"

"I'll try," said Nobsy. "Sean will have to tek this lass 'ere off t'field or e'll never come back though…"

"Come on lass," said Sean, taking the girl's arm."

"What was that all about?" she asked the famous centre-forward. "Is that what were sposed to 'appen?"

"You did perfect," said Shagsy reassuring her. "If we win the game, it'll be because o' you."

"Don't say that! I'm a United supporter – I'll get beat up by all me mates if you tell 'em I won you the game!"

"Don't worry… it'll be our secret…"

Sean popped her back over the barrier and took his place on the pitch.

Pheeeeeeeeeep! went the referee and the Jam U right full-back slid in the corner. It whacked Tubsy on the head, as most things did, and rebounded up to the halfway line where Sean was waiting to collect it. He saw the opposition goalkeeper off his line, hit it first time and chipped it towards the Jam U goals. Higher and higher it went. The goalkeeper looked up and saw that it might be close, too close to take the risk and leave it. The ball levelled out, then started its descent. The Jam U goalie started to shuffle backwards to his goal line. The ball headed down on top of him, getting bigger and bigger. He reached the face of the goal. The ball rushed towards him. He had to tip it over, just in case. The ball arrived and the goalkeeper stuck out his hand. Thwack went the ball onto his glove, smacking it into the crossbar again.

Dovehawk was knackered by the time he ran the full length of the pitch again – *if he kept this up*, he thought, *he would no longer be fat and ugly… He would be thin and ugly instead.*

Angela could run a lot faster than Dovehawk, even when she was wearing a skirt, but by the time she reached the victim, he was under the not-so-tender care of the Jam U physio who had out-sprinted her. The Jam U goalie stopped his writhing and moaning for a second, looked up and saw the bloke. Then he saw Angela appear, coming to him like his guardian angel, the Madonna of the North. The physio tried to fend her off, putting his bulky body between her and his patient. The goalkeeper, seeing this, stood straight up and smacked the physio in the gob with the fist of his good hand, a full clanger, teeth and blood flying everywhere. The trainer staggered out of the way, while the goalie awaited, arms outstretched, to embrace his Saviour.

"I think we're on course to break the all-time record you mentioned!" enthused Ron Accrington to his viewers and listeners. "We might be having a wedding before the second half kicks off!"

When Dovehawk finally arrived on the scene, he saw that the goalkeeper was being well tended and so thought he had better take charge of the Jam U sponge man. Seeing the mess his face was in, Dovehawk called for a stretcher, waving his arms wildly at the Zimmer frames crowding the touchline. Three minutes later the stretcher arrived, while the referee kept tutting and looking at his watch. At this rate, the by-election would be counted and the new MP sworn in before anyone would know which team was in the fourth round. The St John's ambulance itself revved up and drove onto the pitch to carry out the rescue. The referee thought this most improper and tried to send it off by brandishing his red card.

"He's showing the red card to someone!" roared Ron Accrington so loudly that five thousand TV sets woke their owners up. "I can't see who he's sending off, but it's definitely a red!"

The passenger door of the ambulance swung open and a very short figure dressed in a St John's Ambulance uniform hopped lithely onto the pitch, ran round the back of the vehicle and undid the double doors at the rear. The Jam U physio lay on the stretcher, looking at the dark night above him and the fifty trillion candle-power floodlights which were illuminating his predicament. He felt himself being lifted, then bumped along, then slid into the ambulance.

"Groooooooork," said the baboon, his face peering out from under his St John's Ambulance cap.

“Fuck!” said the Jam U sponge man, “I want the pretty nurse like the one my goalkeeper got!”

The baboon ignored him while it busily prepared the rectal thermometer.

The ambulance finally chugged off the pitch. The Jam U goalkeeper kissed Angela and bid her farewell with promises of undying love and a request to meet her after the game.

The referee picked up the ball, handed it to the goalkeeper and went *Pheeeeeeeeep!* to restart the game with a goal kick.

“It can’t be a goal kick,” said Sean to the ruffled whistler, “It hit his hand! It must be a corner…”

“Oh, right, yes!” said the ref.

Pheeeeeeeeep! he went again and pointed to the corner flag.

“How long ’ave we got left?” he asked the ref urgently.

“The ref looked at his watch. “Ten seconds.”

Sean grabbed the ball from the goalie and ran to the corner, plonked it down and booted it without even looking up. It started out towards the near post, then swerved with the spin on the ball so it was five yards out by the time it reached the area. Dorksy nudged it on with his head, then Korma, following up, rose at the far post and *Pheeeeeeeeep!* in it went.

There was a groan round the ground. The Hetherington players all celebrated. The referee picked up the ball and walked off. The Jam U players asked him if it was a goal.

“No goal,” said the ref, “I blew for half time just before it went in…”

The home side all cheered and, as the word went round, so did the crowd.

“Bollocks,” said Ron Conference. “I thought we’d scored!”

“ I thought they’d scored,” said Ron Accrington, “But it turns out the ref’s blown for the end of the first half before it crossed the line.”

“Well you couldn’t write the script for this one, could you Ron?” said the commentator, using one of his stock phrases.

"But I've got a feeling," continued Ron, "That actually they're better off being one-one at half time rather than two-one up. It's funny you know, but now they can still got out and win it, whereas if they had the lead, they'd have to defend for another forty five minutes – and they'll not do that against this Jam U side. Yep, I really think they're better off at one-one."

"It's an interesting thought Ron. Maybe you'll be proved right, you never know in this game..."

The first half had finally ended at eleven minutes to nine – that was nineteen minutes longer than it should have taken.

9.04 on Wednesday evening – start of the second half – it's still 1-1

"Well," said Ron Accrington, just as the referee blew his whistle to start the second half, "I can't see this match ending without a few more goals being scored – quite a few I should think!"

9.51 on Wednesday evening – end of the second half – it's still 1-1

"Well," said Ron Accrington, just as the referee blew his whistle for the end of normal time, "That was dire compared with the first half, but at least I'm still on for my bet – we could have penalties yet you know!"

10.26 on Wednesday evening – the last minute of extra time – it's still 1-1

Sean was tired, as were all his team-mates. Even the super-fit Jam U players were knackered. It looked like penalties would have to settle the outcome. Several players were down on the ground with cramp, so the referee had temporarily stopped play. Dovehawk thought it was time to act. Sean stood there, panting, his hands on his knees, head bowed. He noticed Dovehawk beckon him from the touchline.

"What's up?" said Sean.

"A word in confidence," said Dovehawk, drawing Sean's ear to his mouth. "I've been wrestling with my conscience, but I've decided you ought to know."

"Know what?" Sean was keen to find out the mystery.

"It's about last night – were you with Fiona?"

"No course not – we're not allowed to stay wi' our girlfriends night before a match."

"It was her then. Don't worry." Dovehawk patted Sean on the back. "That's all I needed to know."

"What do you mean? Why? Where was she then?"

"No. I'd better not tell you – you'll be angry."

"You've bloody got to tell me now! Where was she?"

Dovehawk saw his bait taken and gave himself a hearty internal grin.

"Well I may be mistaken, but I saw her getting into a car with one of the Jam U players."

"No… Which one?"

"I can't say."

"Why, didn't you see him?"

"Oh I saw him all right."

"Which one then? You've got to tell me!"

"Wreckham."

"That fuckin' creep – I knew he was after 'er. I'm going to smack 'is 'ead! Where is 'ee?"

"No, don't do that," said Dovehawk in fatherly fashion, "You'll get sent off. Hurt him where it counts – score a *goal* instead…"

Sean ran back on the pitch, seething. He ran up to the Hetherington supporters end, held out his arms for their acclamation, then dropped his shorts, checking first that the referee wasn't looking.

"Eh oooоppp – I think something's up here!" chanted Ron Accrington.

"Really? Can you see that far?" queried his fellow commentator.

"The Hetherington number nine has just had a word on the touchline with one of the St John's Ambulance men, and now he's gone to the other end and dropped his kaks! I think the atmosphere of this game is about to change completely! Look at the expression on his face! He's as fired up as a phall curry!"

"Yeeeeeeeaaaaaaaaahhhhhhhh!" screamed Fiona and Tammy in the stand.

"Yeeeeeeeaaaaaaaaahhhhhhhh!" screamed all the other girls in the crowd.

"WHIPPET SHAGGERS!" shouted all the male Jam U supporters.

The referee went *Pheeeeeeeeep!* for a drop ball to restart the game. Sean thought he had better not take part in the ball dropping in case the ref noticed that it wasn't just one ball that had dropped. Korma did the honours, but the Jam U player won it and passed it back to a team-mate. The player looked up to see who was about. Sean saw his chance. He felt as if he was floating across the surface of the grass, unaware of his feet pounding the hard and frosty turf. He must have covered the twenty yards to make the tackle in less than two seconds.

"Watch out!" shouted a Jam U player to the man on the ball, but it was too late. Sean slid along on his bare arse, wrapped his leg around the ball and deftly flicked it out from under the other player's feet without even touching him. Sean then gracefully regained a standing position, not having come to rest, now in possession and now working out his best approach to the Jam United goal.

"Korma!" he yelled. "Up the wing!"

Korma hurtled off on the left wing while Sean ran diagonally to the right, with Billy and Freddy just behind him so they couldn't be offside. Sean went to kick with his right foot, as if to pass to Korma who had taken a couple of defenders with him, but instead of connecting with the ball, Sean shimmied, feinted and flicked a short one to Freddy Bell on his right, who then bombed forward. Freddy squirted it back to Sean just as they were approaching the penalty area. Sean didn't look up; he knew where the goal was. He just hit it first time as hard as he could. If it was on-target, someone would have to get in the way of it to stop it. If it was off-target, someone might accidentally deflect it in. You win both ways. He had never hit a first-time shot harder. He hardly felt it come of his boot, such was the timing and balance – it just pinged like a tennis-ball off the middle of a racquet, or a golf-ball off the sweet-spot on a driver.

Mama fernando fucky-bollocks! thought the Jam U goalie as the ball whizzed past his flailing fingertips – luckily for him he didn't manage to reach it! At one hundred miles an hour it hit the post. Rebounding at a mere ninety, it hit Wreckham in the nuts, doubling him up like a deckchair. The prize testicles had removed a lot of kinetic energy from the shiny white football, but it still had some left. It looped up towards the opposite top corner of the goal and, highlighted by the floodlights like a shooting star, lazily lobbed into the net.

"Groooooooaaaaaaaaaaaaaaannnnnn!" went most of the crowd.

"Yeeeeeeeaaaaaaaaahhhhhhhh!" went the small band of travelling supporters.

Pheeeeeeeeep! went the referee and pointed to the centre circle.

And the scorer was – was – was – was – WRECKHAM! announced the announcer over the loudspeakers in a shocked voice.

"They've gone and done it!" chortled Ron Accrington from his commentary position. "They've bloody gone and done it!"

The camera followed the Hetherington celebrations for a while, then homed in on Wreckham who was lying flat on the ground. The Jam U sponge man was indisposed in the treatment centre, so there wasn't even anyone around to hose down the ravaged celebrity-testicles. Dovehawk and Angela headed to the scene. Sean gave him another stamp in the groin area, just to make sure. The referee went *Pheeeeeeeeep!* again and waved his red card. Just as Angela arrived, Sean winked at her, then turned and headed for the tunnel, waving to the crowd who booed him all the way off the pitch. Angela knelt down, produced a fresh pack of frozen peas from her black bag and spread them gently into the shorts area of the superstar player.

"I'm not sure he'll be able to continue," said Ron Accrington. "He looks wrecked to me... ha ha... I like that one... wrecked eh? He's wrecked-'em!"

"Yes very good Ron; I can sense the people at home will be liking that one too... What do you think of the frozen peas then Ron?"

"I think I probably don't want to eat them now I know where they've been... ha ha ha!"

"Very good Ron. Do you think they get a fresh pack out each time? Or do they just re-freeze them?"

"Well I'm hoping it's a fresh pack, but you never know with these old fashioned organisations like the St John's Ambulance – they don't like waste..."

The referee hovered over Angela, looking at his watch every ten seconds. It was now after half past ten in the evening and his wife was going to be mad that he was late for his night-time cocoa.

"Do we need a stretcher nurse?" the referee asked Angela.

"More like we need a splint," said Dovehawk jovially. "Have you got a small one? A lolly stick should do it…"

"It's not in the manual, Mr Dove'awk!" said Angela, still cooling the bruised bollocks. "I wouldn't know how to fit it."

"I know where I'd bloody fit it!" Dovehawk was enjoying himself, but the referee gave him a hard stare. "I shall have to send you off if you keep on with the wise-cracks Mr Dovehawk."

The politician looked at the frustrated whistler in disbelief. "Send me off? Send off a member of the St John's Ambulance? You're 'avin a laugh! Now that really would make history that would! You'd go down as the biggest c… in refereeing history – and believe me there have been a few of *them*!"

"Right! That's it!" *Pheeeeeeeeep!* went the referee, while he reached for his pocket, brandished the red card and pointed to the tunnel.

The press photographers all homed in with their zoom lenses – they couldn't believe what they were seeing – the referee was sending off a St John's Ambulanceman… but not only that… a St John's Ambulanceman who also just happened to be the Real Labour candidate in tomorrow's by-election! Dovehawk turned and slowly ambled away, while the refereee, truly impatient of ever finishing this game, called for a stretcher. The stretcher-bearers rushed on the field and placed it down on the pitch. Dovehawk saw his chance: he collapsed down on it with the full force of his great weight, clutching his heart. Angela deserted the superstar knackers and ran over to her boss.

"Mr Dove'awk! Mr Dove'awk! What's the matter? Can you 'ear me? Say sommat… please Mr Dove'awk!"

The stretcher-bearers tried to lift the corpulent politician on his canvas framework, but his volume was too much for them and they gesticulated to the touchline to bring on reinforcements. The referee looked at his watch. Ron Accrington was incandescent with derision:

"This referee's a c…"

"Yes, quite Ron, quite..." the commentator quickly interjected...

"No, he *is*," said Ron, "He really *is*..."

"Ron... ssssshhhhh" You'll lose your job again!

"But I've never seen anything like it! The St John's Ambulanceman being sent off! And now if the poor old sod's had a heart attack – well – this referee – he'll have to live with his conscience... And the scorn of every newspaper in the country!"

Dovehawk winked at Angela, then groaned and clutched his chest even harder. By now, two more burly chaps had arrived as backup. Everyone was huddled around the cortege as he was conveyed off the field; Wreckham sat up, looked all about him, and saw he was totally alone; everyone was ignoring him. Wet green juice dribbled down the inside of his thigh. He had been enjoying a pretty girl tenderising his garden peas; but now she had buggered off and left him. There was nothing to do but carry on with the game. In a crocked fashion, he creaked up and onto his feet.

"Well, looks like Wreckham's ready to get back in the action," chirped Ron Accrington. "It's not the sort of injury you can run off though! He may be hobbling for the rest of this match!"

"As we've only got a minute left on the clock, I think you can safely say that, Ron. What do *you* think Ron?"

"Oh! Hang on a minute! We've got another stretcher being brought onto the pitch!"

While the referee was busy watching the swift expedition of Dovehawk from the field of play, two more stretcher-bearers sneaked on without being noticed by the match official. These were Tubsy and Splutter. They walked straight up to the sore and hobbling Wreckham and placed their portable couch on the ground. Tubsy used his huge bulk to shield his team-mate from the ref, while Splutter kicked the unsuspecting Wreckham in the bollocks, felling him like a young sapling with a chain-saw. The two of them rolled him onto the stretcher, then carried him quickly off the pitch to the opposite side, so the referee was none the wiser. They quickly delivered him to the St John's Ambulance, where the baboon swiftly undid the doors while they loaded Wreckham and his stretcher into the back. The smartly dressed animal then slammed the doors shut again while Tubsy and Splutter ran back to rejoin the match.

Pheeeeeeeeep! went the referee, thankful that at twenty five minutes to eleven he could at last get the game underway, hopefully to its conclusion with just one minute remaining on his watch. But immediately he blew for the restart he was surrounded by a load of Jam U players.

"We're a man down, ref… you can't start the game – we've only got ten players on the pitch!"

"Who's missing?" enquired the referee.

"Wreckham's missing…"

"Didn't he go off injured? Maybe he left the field of his own accord."

"Well we didn't see him…"

Splutter joined in. "He'sh gone for a pish," he said, helpfully. "He shaid would you mind waiting for him?"

"Mind waiting for him? Mind waiting for him!" exploded the referee. "We've been here all bloody night, there's one minute to play of extra time, and he wants us to wait for him while he goes to the toilet?"

"Yesh."

"Thish ish ridiculoush!"

"Are you taking the pish, ref?" asked Splutter, his feelings hurt.

"Oooooh sorry Splutter. It was an accident – I copied you by mishtake – I mean mistake. Sorry old son."

"That'sh OK."

"Right, we're playing the last minute of extra time, like it or not."

"Can we get a substitute on, ref?"

"Oh very well – hurry up then…"

Another minute passed as the players went and told the manager that they were a man short, and another was hastily despatched into the fray.

Pheeeeeeeeep! went the referee; it was now twenty three minutes to eleven and the night air was freezing up fast.

Jam U got the ball straight away and piled up the Hetherington Sidney end. So did all the Hetherington Sidney players.

"Pack the goal-mouth!" shouted Ron Conference from the side of the pitch, barely able to contain his fear and trepidation of letting in a 121st minute goal. He needn't have bothered telling them: all the Hetherington forwards and midfielders stood on the goal line, ready to block any shot, while the four big defenders guarded the edge of the six-yard box like a line of giant sentries, ready to head away the crosses that would be coming at them from all angles. The ground was alive with sound, choruses of cheers and shrieks coming from the Jam U faithful, while the few Hetherington supporters whistled as loudly as they could for the full time whistle. No-one heard the banging coming from inside of the St John's Ambulance which was parked in its specially reserved place in the corner between the stand and the end terraces.

The Jam U players had possession to themselves, so they relentlessly flung balls into the area while Splutter, Dorksy, Tubsy and Gherkin hoofed them back up the field or headed them into the distant areas of the touchline. With twenty seconds left on the watch, the ball was clanging around in the area, the forest of feet and legs making it difficult for the crowd or the referee, or even the players, to see where it was. The passenger door of the ambulance flung open and the crowd gasped as the dishevelled figure of Wreckham, who had finally managed to escape from captivity, launched himself from the white vehicle and back onto the pitch. A Jam U player shot from just outside the area: the ball ballooned up off Tubsy's head and over to the touchline. Wreckham controlled it, then curled in a beautiful ball which deceived all the players in the box. The defenders on the goal line watched it streak towards the top corner. They all jumped in unison to keep it out, but with six inches to spare above their heads it found the angle of the woodwork and ricocheted into the net. The crowd went wild. The poor Hetherington players collapsed in a heap in the penalty area – they had been so close to the fourth round. Ron Conference buried his face in his hands. Sven Svensson Svengali stopped dreaming about all the porn films he had starred in and acknowledged the cheers of the supporters with a courteous wave.

Pheeeeeeeeep! went the referee and pointed at the centre circle to award the equaliser. Now he was never going to get his cocoa – it would be penalties.

"It's penalties!" screamed Ron Accrington at the top of his voice. "I've got a tenner at fifty to one on it being penalties! Oh yes – come on you little beauties!"

"Steady on Ron," said his co-commentator, "That'll only buy you a couple of cigars."

"Yes, but bloody big cigars," huffed Ron happily.

The referee looked at his watch. He only had a couple of seconds remaining so there wasn't going to be time for the kick-off. Then he heard the announcement over the ground's PA system.

And Jam United's goal, in the one hundred and twentieth minute, was scored by… WRECKHAM!"

The referee came to his senses. *Wreckham?* he thought. *Wreckham? He's off the pitch!*

He looked at all the red and white players on the field and counted them. Eleven. Then he looked in the Jam U goal. Plus the goalie. Eleven plus the goalie.

"No goal!" he shouted as loudly as he could. He blew his whistle two long hard blasts to end the match. Everyone thought it was penalties. The referee grabbed the ball and ran over to the two team benches where they were expecting to have to nominate penalty-takers. He started by talking to the Jam U manager.

"Your goal-scorer was substituted!" he announced to Sven Svensson Svengali. "You had twelve men on the pitch!" Some of the players overheard and starting squabbling. "You've won two-one!" he shouted to Ron Conference. Their final goal is disallowed – the scorer was not supposed to be on the field of play!"

"Yeeeeeeeeeessssssssssss!" screeched Ron Conference, hugging his sponge man.

When the referee turned round from delivering his verdict on the outcome, the whole of the two sets of players were involved in a gigantic punch-up, including all the unused substitutes who had jumped up off the bench and joined in.

"This is chaos!" bemoaned Ron Accrington, "I've lost five hundred quid!"

"Oh dear. The police are getting involved now. There are about fifteen of them in a maul – it's like Rugby Union – what do *you* think Ron?"

"What do I think? I think I'm gonna wring your bloody neck you bloody little twerp! Why do you keep asking me what I think? I've lost five hundred quid because of this stupid referee! He's a c…!"

"Sssssshhhhhh, Ron! You'll lose your job again."

Slap – "Waaaaaaahhhhhhhh! Sob, and now it's over to Gary in the studio, sob, sob…"

"Well thank you there, Ron and the other bloke – we apologise for the slight technical hitch with the commentary there ladies and gentlemen – terrible scenes these at Jammy Trafford – as you can see, all the players are still on the pitch – we don't really know yet what's happening – if Jam United's equaliser was given as a goal then it's now going to be decided on penalties – that is if the players stop fighting long enough to take them. On the other hand, the referee has departed the field under police escort, which would indicate that the game is over – what do you think Hamish?"

"As far as I seeeee it, there's nay doot aboot it – Wreckham was off the pitch injured – we saw him carried off on the stretcher by the two very helpful Hetherington Sidney players – the substitute was brought on – here he is looook, you can see him coming on in the replay. The ball is played into the box, bounces off the defender, and loooooook! Here comes Wreckham loooooook! Wreckham jumps ooota the ambulance, straight onnny the pitch – the referee doesny seeeeee him – the ball goes straight to Wreckham and he hits a marvellous first time shot – it woulda bin a contender for goal o' the season if it had bin aloood to stand – but it canny be a goal because he shouldny be on the pitch. So it's still two-one to Hetherington Sidney – game ooover – they're in the fourth rooond! An' looook here – now we see the referee blows for a goal – he hasny realised that it was scored by a player who shouldny be on the pitch. All the Hetherington players, they're all lying on the ground crying – they don't know either. So what happens now? The referee goes to the centre circle to restart the game, and just as he's abooot to blow for the kick off, he hears the name of the goalscorer on the tannoy. He waves his arms, and – loook at his lips – you can see him saying 'No goal' to the players – but the Jam U players, they don't want to believe it. He blows for full time – there's less than ten seconds left on the clock so there's no time to restart – and then we've got the scenes we see on our screens now – a great big punchup between all the players…"

"Yes. Or maybe the referee just wanted to get off home for his cocoa."

"Well, you never know, Gary."

Ten in the morning, Thursday – polling day

"Right. Gather round you lot." Ron surveyed the sorry state of his team. Swollen lips, black eyes, puffy cheeks and bent noses abounded. Piccalilli even had his head bandaged up. "My god – you lot must have had a good time yesterday! What time did the police let you go?"

"Two in't mornin' boss," said Dorksy sheepishly.

"Two in the morning, eh? What a place to choose to celebrate – in the clink."

"Are you upset with us boss?" asked Korma, his normally fine features displaying distinct signs of a battering.

"Upset?" Ron put on his serious voice. "Upset? With you lot?" He paused for dramatic effect. "I bloody love you all!" he cheered, and went into the middle of them and hugged them all in turn. "We're in the bloody fourth round of the cup! We *BEAT* Jam United!!! And I thought you lot were losers! But you're not – you're bloody winners!"

"Hooray!" they all cheered.

"One thing though," said Ron more cautiously, "Being serious, how many of you lot are going to be fit for our league game on Saturday?"

"We'll all be fit boss," said Stainsy. "Those Jam U players are just girls when it comes t' fighting… You should see what a mess they were in when we'd finished wi' 'em!"

"Yeah, proper smashed up! Ha ha!" said Nobsy.

"So you're all fit enough to play, then?"

"Aye course we are – well all except Shagsy, cos 'ee got sent off so 'ee's suspended."

"Ah yes," Ron frowned. "So why did you get yourself sent off then Shagsy?"

"Weren't my fault boss, honest… I just tripped…"

"You tripped?"

"That's right boss. Wreckham was lyin' there, moanin' an' I tripped over 'im. Accidentally caught 'im in the nuts!"

"Well it was a good shot for an accident I must say. Never mind. You need a rest I suppose, what with scoring the winning goal."

"He did NOT score the winnin' goal boss," said Gherkin. "That were Wreckham's nuts what scored the winnin' goal! When Shagsy tripped over 'em, 'ee were just congratulatin' them!"

"OK OK, that's enough," said Ron as they all started laughing and mucking about. "I suppose you lot have earned a day off – so I'll see you here tomorrow morning at the usual time. And well done lads! Up the Whippets!"

"UP THE WHIPPETS !!!" they chorused.

Ten in the morning, Thursday – polling day

Dovehawk was in the polling station, being filmed casting his vote.

"Are you feeling OK today, Mr Dovehawk?" asked one of the journalists. "Any ill effects from being sent off at Jammy Trafford?"

Dovehawk smiled and held up the front page of *The Fun* which had a giant picture of the referee showing his red card to the gobsmacked politician, with a smaller picture inset of him being carried off on his stretcher while theatrically clutching his heart.

"Mr Dovehawk," gushed one of the Hetherington ladies who too was there to make her choice at the ballot box. "Mr Dovehawk, I think it's a shame… a terrible shame… sending off a member of the St John's Ambulance Service like that – I have so many of my friends who raise money for them as well – a fantastic job they do. That referee should be struck off! That's what *I* think!"

"Groooooooorrrrrk!" said the baboon – and handed the lady her blank ballot paper.

"Oh, thank you," she said, looking at the fluffy specimen warmly. "What a cute fellow *you* are…" Then she turned back to Dovehawk. "I shall definitely be voting for you, anyway Mr Dovehawk. This town needs a *real* person to represent it in parliament, and who could be more *real* than yourself, someone who has been sent off at Jammy Trafford?"

"Yes, indeed… Thank you madam you are most kind," gushed the flattered politician. "Would you mind joining me by my side in a few pictures for the press? I'd like to be photographed with a *real* person from the *real* voting public such as yourself."

"Oh really Mr Dovehawk? Well if you would like me to, then yes I will. Is my hair all right?"

"It's lovely Mrs, Mrs er?"

"Smoggrate…"

"Smoggrate? Blimey!"

"What do you mean, Mr Dovehawk?"

"No, no offence Mrs Smoggrate, it's just that…" Dovehawk bent down and whispered in her ear. "I know your husband – we'll not tell the press about that or they'll think it's a set-up."

"Very well," whispered Mrs Smoggrate back to the politician, "We'll keep quiet about it."

The two of them smiled for the cameras and waved, then Dovehawk bade her and the rest of the room farewell and made his way outside to his waiting Angela in Mission Control. The Traffic Attendant was just issuing a parking ticket.

That's OK, thought Dovehawk, *old Squiffy Spankbottom can afford to pay a few of those*!

"Good Day" said Dovehawk brightly to the Attendant and nimbly hopped through the doorway and into his office. "What's the plan for the rest of today then Angela?"

"Look at all the flags and bunting everywhere Mr Dove'awk! In't it grand? It's like Christmas 'as come t' 'Etherington all over again!"

"Yes Angela, it's quite beautiful – all the town's colours on display. A pity the flags aren't for me, but I suppose reaching the fourth round of the FA Cup is more important than electing some pompous old fart as the next MP."

"Oh yes Mr Dove'awk, certainly it is..."

"Well thank you for your vot of confidence – I thought you were my campaign manager? You're supposed to encourage me."

"Oh don't worry Mr Dove'awk, you do come second in my affections. There's only the team, and its players, what come first before you."

"Well that's a relief to know. Let's just hope I don't come second with the voting public. There's no prizes for coming second in this politics game."

"Nor in football either Mr Dove'awk."

"Really? I'm not so sure. I think that if Hetherington were to get to the Cup Final and lose at Wembley, that could be considered a great success, equivalent to a win in my book."

"Maybe, but we'd still be gutted if it 'appened! Come on Mr Dove'awk – the whole town's in a party mood – let's go an' knock on some more doors – get those last minute votes in."

"Party mood? Yes indeed. Let's hope it's the Real Labour Party mood that they're in. Come on girl – I'll follow you! Let's promise the voters whatever they want – even a trip to the Cup Final!"

Two in the afternoon, Thursday – polling day

"Heh, Smoothass, how's it goin' man?"

"Shagsy man – you're my maaaan! I saw that winnin' goal maaaan! Straight outta tha trainin' manual'! BANG-SLAP-YEAAAAAHH!"

"Yeaahhhh – we're in the fourth round now. That's why I'm ringin' – have you sorted me out a juicy transfer yet? I reckon Jam United'll want me after that display..."

"I'm lookin' in all de right areas, man. But I don't think Jam U gonna wanna talk right now – them still smartin' bad..."

"Any other top clubs interested? – what about Cheesily or Anusoil?"

"I haint heard nothin' from dem two, man, but I think Snotterham Tosspurt are in the market for a striker."

"Course they are, man – Snotterham Tosspurt are always in the market for a striker cos they can't never score any goals! Surely I can get a bigger club than them?"

"Man – what are you sayin? I only live down the road from them and I'm on the pulse, man. Plus, you may notta noticed, but you just got sent off! That doesn't make you worth any more money, man – you know what I'm sayin'?"

"So you haven't got me a transfer – that's what you're sayin' then Smoothass?"

"Like I said, I'm workin' the *areas*, man. I'm jus checkin' out the best deal for you."

"Yeah, I know – Snotterham Tosspurt… Some deal… So how much d'you reckon we're on for now then? Six and a half? Seven million?"

"At least, Shagsy my man, at least. Aim high is my goal – you know that, man."

"OK Smoothass. I believe you… I think… Keep me up to date, man…"

"You know I always do Shagsy – as soon as one o' dem big clubs comes in, all the others will follow. Later my man…"

"Later…"

Sean hung up.

"So. Has your wonderful agent got you a transfer to Jam United then sugar-cakes?" said Fiona, rubbing her hand up and down Sean's chest beneath his shirt.

"Er… not quite yet… But he's workin' on it…"

"Baby, he's been working on something – but I don't think you're it. Smoothass Blackcurrant, the slimiest agent in the country – couldn't you get someone nice?"

"Nice?" Sean looked at Fiona incredulously. "You don't get football agents who are *nice*! They're a bunch of c…"

"Yes angel – you've told me. Well how about one we can trust, then?"

"TRUST? That's even more stupid. First you want NICE and now you want TRUST as well! Fifi, baby, you just don't understand football at all, do you?"

She giggled and undid his trousers.

"Smoothass Blackcurrant can only dream of this!" she said, sliding her hand down inside Sean's jeans.

Ten in the evening, Thursday – polls close

Dovehawk and Adelina were both present at the same polling station when the time came to seal the ballot boxes and load them up for their journey to join all the others from all the polling stations across the constituency.

They watched as the formalities were carried out, then Adelina turned to the raddled old politician and smiled at him.

"Well now it's all done, Stanley. Nothin' can change what 'appen now. Shall we still be friends when dis is all over?"

"Of course, Adelina. I have never had anything other than the utmost respect for the way you have run your campaign, and your demeanour during the course of our rivalry has been nothing but exemplary."

"Well thank you! You are so kind… Will you be stayin' up for de count?"

"What, you mean the count with a silent 'o'?" Dovehawk made a show of looking all around him. "I can't see her anywhere… Maybe she's swallowed some of her own saliva and died of bitch-venom. I thought she followed you around everywhere?"

"Stanley, you are very unforgivin' about de Ms Puckerin'… I tink, deep down, she loves you – what wid de baby on de way an everytin'…"

"She hates me. In fact, she hates me even more now… She has something growing inside her which is half *me*! And she can't bear it, if you'll pardon the pun…"

"Dat jus' natural. She will soon get used to de idea – an' den she will love it…"

"You think so?"

"Yes. Come on Stanley." She took Dovehawk's arm. "Let's go for a drink – then we'll stay up all night an' see who's won!"

"May the best Labour candidate win!"

"Indeed, Stanley, indeed!"

Seven in the morning, Friday – the day after polling day

Hetherington Community College's main hall was the venue for the count. Tables were set up all around the room, and each one was covered in ballot papers, arranged into smaller and larger piles, while twenty people sifted through them, some checking which belonged to whom, others counting the numbers in each pile and tallying them on a bit of paper, probably a supermarket till receipt or a bus ticket, as was traditional.

By-elections are all about tradition, thought Dovehawk as he watched the numbers of votes in his piles build up higher than all the others. *This same scene has been enacted up and down the country for the last couple of hundred years – it is democracy in action; real democracy; Real people voting Real Labour for Real change…*

The counting was nearing its end. The other candidates, most of whom didn't have a hope, chatted to one another excitedly, pleased to be involved in the process and having enjoyed their campaigns. Brian Boring however was slightly edgy as he thought the Labour vote, being split between Dovehawk's Real Labour and Adelina's old fashioned Labour, might let him slip through the middle to deliver a really boring result for the ultra-boring Liberal Democrats. Adelina and Pree were also nervous – it looked like it would be a close-run fight between the three of them, although Dovehawk's piles were mounting up nicely.

Finally, after much fluttering of paper and scratching of calculators and tapping of heads, a buzz of expectation went around the room.

Councillor Balderson mounted the rostrum and called the candidates to join him. Dovehawk started to make his way to the podium. As he passed through the tightly-packed crowd, suddenly he was face to face with Pree Puckering. Pree took one look at him, then a sombre pallidness swept over her features; she clutched her mouth with her hand and fled, parting people from her rapid path as she went. Dovehawk wondered on the effect he had had, then continued on his way to join all the other candidates. They jockeyed around on stage, trying to get the best places where the cameras could see them, although this was difficult as the Loony candidate wore the biggest felt hat covered in giant rosettes and badges. When all were settled, or mostly settled, Councillor Balderson looked around to make sure everyone was paying attention and then proceeded to give his address:

"I, being the Returning Officer for the Hetherington constituency, do hereby announce that the votes cast for each candidate in the by-election were as follows:

"Alan Dean Harwich, British Naughty Party, five hundred and seventy three.

"Ronald O, Chinese Football Party, twelve.

"Helen Back, Divorce Party, thirty seven.

"Neil Oliver Brakes, Campaign For Real Asbestos, eleven.

"Peggy Enid Nelly Iris Smith, Real Pensions For Real Pensioners' Party, two hundred and six.

"Sir Roger St John Buttplug, Conservative Party, three thousand eight hundred and ninety eight.

"Adelina Jasmina Omov, Labour Party, eight thousand one hundred and ninety seven."

A large cheer rang around the auditorium.

"Brian Lawrence Alexander Boring, Liberal Democrat, eight thousand and forty two."

Cheers again from the Labour supporters.

"Stanley Vincent Dovehawk, Real Labour, eight thousand seven hundred and sixteen."

Yeeeeeeesssssssssss! came the shouts of triumph from Dovehawk's cohorts and supporters as they all hugged each other.

"Quite please," requested Councillor Balderson, "And finally, Sir Giant Jugs, Loony Party, nine thousand three hundred and seventy."

"What?" shouted Dovehawk.

"And I hereby declare that the said Sir Giant Jugs is duly elected member for this constituency."

The baboon, not wishing to be associated with a loser, leapt from Dovehawk's shoulder and onto the Loony candidate's giant party-breasts which he was wearing and stuck his shiny purple arse in the new MP's face. The Loonies in the hall all went wild, even wilder in fact, but up on stage one of the tellers was having a quiet word in the Returning Officer's ear, while the other candidates stood around in a perplexed huddle.

"Attention!" cried Councillor Balderson. "I have just been informed by the head teller that we have a slight decimal point problem on my little bit of paper here – or a comma in the wrong place – at any rate it looked like a comma to me – it must be an ink smudge. The number of votes cast for Sir Giant Jugs, Loony Party, was nine hundred and thirty seven. I am very sorry about that. I therefore hereby declare that the aforementioned Stanley Vincent Dovehawk is duly elected member for the Hetherington constituency. Mr Dovehawk, you may now address the hall…"

"Thank you Councillor."

Dovehawk surveyed his audience.

"I have just one thing to say:"

He paused again to prolong the moment. The crowd waited, the odd cat-call ringing out around the room.

"*Real* people vote *Real* Labour!!"

He raised his arms aloft, took the plaudits from the hall, then stepped down.

Walking through the gathering of press, supporters and enemies, he met enemy number one, once again, one to one again, face to face again.

"Ah, you're back," he said to Pree, trying not to sound too smug. "Are you here to congratulate me?"

She sneered at him.

"You make me sick!"

"I do my best."

"No, you really do make me sick. In the mornings."

"What?"

"It's half past seven in the morning. That's when I feel sickest."

"Aaaaaah, I see, yes. Well I'm sorry about that. That it's only in the mornings I mean. I'd like you to feel sick all of the time."

"I shall, now that you are MP."

"Excellent. I shall cherish the thought."

Pree's phone went off and she turned away from Dovehawk to take the call. Dovehawk wandered off to have a word with Angela and Fiona. Tammy of course was in bed – it was far too early in the morning for her to put in an appearance.

Pree suddenly reappeared, making her presence known by tapping him on the shoulder.

"I've got the Prime Minister on the phone," she said in a bubbly voice that didn't sound like the voice of someone with morning sickness.

"Does he want to talk to me?"

"No, no – he said I could just pass on a message."

"Oh yes? What's that?"

"He's calling a general election."

"What?"

He's been to the Queen and asked her to dissolve parliament."

"What?!"

Pree's eyes were filled with joy; a smile widened her immaculately painted lips.

"You're no longer the MP for Hetherington, Stan. You'll have to stand again for re-election!" She thrilled at the sight of the realisation spreading throughout his face. "You didn't last five minutes as an MP, Stan! That must be a record!"

Dovehawk puffed out his ample cheeks and blustered…

"The C✻✻T !"

Another great book from Luvbutton Press

'Nickers Off Ready When I Come Home

by *Jon Mountfort*
ISBN 978-0-9557635-0-2

If **NORWICH** stands for 'Nickers **O**ff **R**eady **W**hen **I** **C**ome **H**ome, then what would **BLACKPOOL** stand for?

> How about: **B**ums **L**egs and **C**olossal **K**nockers, **P**ostcards **O**f **O**verlarge **L**adies

or **INVERNESS** :

> **I**s **N**essie **V**anished **E**vermore? **R**emember **N**ot **E**veryone's **S**o **S**ure !

or **EDINBURGH** :

> **E**at, **D**rink, **I**mbibe **N**ine **B**eers, **U**rinate, **R**ant, **G**et **H**ammered

The author has compiled over 150 of these sayings for towns and places in Great Britain to produce this most original and funny book. With a commentary linking each place to the next, we embark on the Cheekiest Tour of Britain - EVER

This book also includes horse-racing themes such as Epsom, Ascot and the Grand National and football clubs too such as Chelsea, Liverpool, Arsenal, Tottenham and West Ham, even Wembley:

Where **E**ngland **M**ostly **B**loody **L**ose **E**very **Y**ear !

Forthcoming title from Luvbutton Press

The Spanking Good Diet

by *Jasmine Cliff*

ISBN 978-0-9557635-2-6

Learn how to lose weight by eating slap-up meals, like:

strapping sausages…
tanned baked beans…
thrashed potato…
whipped custard…
belting good banoffee pie…
walloping waffles…
beaten egg caramels…
celery and carrot canes…

And if you put on a pound?

Gently rub some delicious ice-cold raspberry coulis onto that sore sore spanked bottom…

Contains the most outstanding recipes to revolutionise your relationship between you, your partner and your weight.

So exciting you won't be able to put it down, or sit down, for a week!